Focus on the Wind

An Anisian Convergence Novel

Mike Wyant Jr.

Copyright

Also by Mike Wyant Jr.

ANISIAN CONVERGENCE TRILOGY

Fallen Hunter

The Futility of Intent

Into the Æther

ANISIAN COLLECTION

A Courier's Delivery

ANISIAN CONVERGENCE NOVELS

Last Bid for a Dying Earth (Prequel)

Focus on the Wind

ECHOES OF A FORGOTTEN WORLD

Soundless

Lavender Footsteps

THIRTEEN FATES

Chronicles of a Mad God

Dedication

Something something dark side

Chapter 1
CERIAT

Ceriat hated FTL.

It had this humming sound that, if you listened hard enough, developed into a high-pitched screeching, like a cracked vacuum line.

Or the souls of people lost in this fracture in spacetime. The FTL lane.

Maybe the carbon-fiber plate in the right side of his skull—and the embedded transmitter beneath—made it worse, maybe not. Did it matter?

Eyes squeezed shut, Ceriat plucked at the small, circular disk attached to the necklace he wore. He rubbed at it as if the repetition of polishing could drag the anxiety from his veins, the tension from his shoulders.

And it did. It always did, even though each time it rubbed away the letters stamped into it. Even though each trip meant sacrificing a bit of an old friend.

If Gerry were here, he'd have told Ceriat to open his eyes, to watch the ripple of reality in ambers and gray beyond the viewscreen. To focus on the wind roaring past.

But it wasn't wind. Ceriat had always pointed that out to Gerry. Wind didn't screech like that, didn't rend your mind.

Ceriat was a terraforming specialist nowadays. He should know.

Gerry would laugh as he stared at the twisting lights and hummed along with a melody only he could hear.

Gerald Harris. His best friend. Dead nearly two years now when his ship exploded in the FTL lane outside Terrera-2.

It was one of Gerry's dog tags Ceriat had between his fingers, the erstwhile military data storage chip wiped and repurposed to hold terraforming instructions for Teegarden c, a project ten years in the making.

He and Gerry had traded their tags years ago.

That meant one of Ceriat's tags was somewhere in this void, maybe still clutched in Gerry's frozen fist... if the lane hadn't atomized him.

A welcome tone issued from the speakers of the cockpit. "Ceriat, we are approaching Teegarden."

Ceriat choked on spit when he tried to reply, breaking into a coughing fit made more awkward by the five-point harness holding him in place. The old war wound in his left hip complained at the sudden movement.

"Are you well, Ceriat?" a cheery, feminine voice asked from the speakers in the dash before him. "Do you require a lozenge?"

"No, Izzy," he replied to the ship's AI. Ceriat cleared his throat and shifted in his seat to relieve the tension in his hip. "Just surprised."

Now his eyes were open, he couldn't help but stare at the writhing, twisting mass of *wrong* displayed on the viewscreen. Where others saw beauty, he saw the tearing flesh of the universe as he shot through it like a bullet.

Against that backdrop, the dashboard of the *Sparrow* looked decidedly out of place. The *Sparrow* was a single-person transport he'd purchased in the months after Gerry's disappearance. He'd read an article that said smaller vessels were less likely to tear holes in FTL lanes.

It didn't really matter if it was true.

"Dropping out of Sol-Teegarden FTL Lane in ten seconds," Izzy said.

Ceriat squeezed the disk between his fingers. "Acknowledged."

"Exiting in three," Izzy said, "two... one."

Ceriat dropped out of FTL.

And into a warzone.

"Izzy! What's going on?" Ceriat cried out as the comm station flashed to life. Proximity alarms went off, red light rippling through the tiny cabin.

The deep void of space served as a backdrop to dozens of small ships spinning amongst themselves, hulls flashing crimson in the dim light of the red dwarf in the distance. Artificial amber lines spread from each on the window display, flickering and changing as Izzy tried and failed to apply flight path tracking to them. Luckily, he didn't need her assessment to know their focus wasn't on him.

Farther off, Ceriat made out Gatewood, the only populated planet in the system, a blue-green marble partially lit in the ruddy light of the solar system's star. Beyond it, Teegarden c floated, white and pristine—a planet-sized snowball waiting for purpose. For development.

Which made it all the more confusing why there were ships visibly exiting its atmosphere to join the fight between the two worlds.

"Multiple incoming transmissions," Izzy said.

"From who?"

Whatever Izzy said in response was lost in the static shock-wave that followed. Three small fighters exploded less than a kilometer from him, brief flashes followed by scattered diamonds of shrapnel fanning away from the point of impact, and toward the *Sparrow*.

Ceriat cursed and kicked a pedal near his left foot.

A flight stick extended from the dashboard. He grabbed it and yanked.

The dual engines a dozen feet behind him roared, rattling the interior bolts of the ship. On the dash, the inertial suppressor lights flashed from green to yellow as Ceriat spun the *Sparrow* around to avoid debris hurtling toward him at several hundred kilometers an hour.

He pulled the *Sparrow* to what he considered up as the cloud of daggers expanded into a massive arc of death. Even with the inertial suppressors, it felt like a tank pressed into his chest. Each breath became a struggle.

But breathing was going to get a lot harder if that shrapnel perforated the hull.

"Inertial suppressors require venting," Izzy said as the dash light went red. "You have ten seconds until—"

"Shut up," Ceriat hissed, counting down the ten seconds before he ended up splattered against the seat from the g-forces when the suppressors gave out.

At times like this, he wished he had his F-268 fighter back. Those had a good sixty seconds of high-g before they needed venting, not like the ones in the *Sparrow*. These were consumer grade, meant only for coming in and out of FTL lanes. They didn't have longevity. Hell, they were meant to be vented in atmosphere, for Christ's sake. He'd have to dump the emergency plasma-dampeners just to keep the ship from cooking him alive.

Sweat streaked across his forehead and down his cheeks from the pressure leaking around the suppressors.

He counted to nine and leveled out the ship, decelerating as quickly as he could.

The suppressors gave out with a harsh whine, his body whipping toward the dash as the *Sparrow* slowed to a steady acceleration. Carbon-fiber skull notwithstanding, if he hadn't been wearing his harness, it likely would've killed him.

As it was, his head swam from the change. He felt like he'd been hit by a truck.

"That has to be enough." Ceriat tapped the digital display beneath the inertial suppressor indicator so it could vent the excess energy, now converted to superheated plasma, into the void.

It wasn't.

Alarms screeched.

The popcorn popping sound of shrapnel ripping through steel.

A second, louder tearing sound rattled through the *Sparrow*; the engine hum spiked, going from a dull vibration to a high-pitched screech before shutting down with a low, fizzling echo.

The lights on the dash winked out. The viewscreen powered off with a flash, leaving him encased in a tiny, silent tomb. Everything went black besides a few small lights scattered around the cockpit.

Ceriat cursed and rubbed Gerry's dog tag to keep his heart steady, but in the now-blank glass before him, someone he didn't recognize stared back. Someone with haunted eyes set deep in a pale, thin face with more forehead than hair.

An ache filled his veins.

The expression in those eyes made him search the console for some signs of life. If there was power, the auxiliary would kick on shortly. If the engines were blown, he'd have to rely on the mechanical oxygen tank under his seat.

Should've worn a helmet. The thought rose to the surface just in time for him to crush it beneath his heel.

Never again.

"Izzy? Are you there?"

Nothing. That wasn't good. Izzy was tied into emergency systems. If she was offline, all power was down. Auxiliary wasn't going to kick in, then.

The *Sparrow* was dead in the water.

In the middle of a battlefield.

Cursing with every ounce of his being, Ceriat popped open a panel on the right side of the cabin and kicked on his emergency distress signal.

There was nothing to do now but wait and hope no one was

trigger happy enough to take out an immobilized ship broadcasting an Earth Terraforming League—ETL—distress signal.

With a deep sigh, Ceriat plopped his head against the hard headrest behind him.

"I hate space travel."

Chapter 2
ELENI

Eleni Mallias savored the pain screaming through her body.

Her joints rebelled at the gravity hauling her to a distant place beneath her feet. Reinforced veins ached as her newly enhanced heart slammed in her chest, shooting blood through her limbs at a pressure they'd never experienced before. The freezing chill carried on the wind set the exposed skin at her neck afire. That alone made the animal part of her brain panic. Air on skin meant death in a skirmish... but not here. Here, it meant she lived.

So, she smiled. Cherished the way her arms fell straight when she relaxed. At how, when she breathed, there was a pressure there, like each breath was an act of defiance to the gravity holding her in place.

Or maybe it wasn't defiance. But in that moment, as the daytime sky, a brilliant blue brushed lightly with wispy white clouds, sparkled with the explosions of missiles intercepted by Shiva's aerial defenses, defiance *felt* like the right word.

Her destination stood a good three hundred meters ahead, a tall, resin-printed guard tower with artificial heat and snacks to keep her strength up while the battle raged in the stars above.

Running late, she knew she should hurry... but how many chances did a Spacer get to breathe real, pristine mountain air? Check-in could wait a few more minutes. After all, the evacuation was still going smoothly. A third of Arctic had already made it to the new base camp several kilometers outside the settlement limits. Eleni flexed her hands in and out of fists, the tension building in the joints relieved by the movement.

To her, this all seemed premature anyway. Her brother, Victor, had left a month ago to disable the fusion missiles Gatewood was sure to have on their flagship. It'd felt premature then, but now reality had caught up, Eleni was proud of him for the forethought. Victor was a lot of things, but a failure didn't happen to be one of them.

Still, her brother was on a hostile warship...

A flutter of anxiety tickled her stomach like an annoying bug. She crushed it beneath her heel.

Victor never failed. He'd get the job done.

"Trust me," he'd said.

Once again, Eleni turned off the filters on her *manju*, the helmet she'd kept from her Erias Mining Security armor, and sucked in another frigid breath. A crispness there, tinged with hints of oil and machinery from the wagon train a half kilometer distant, made some deep part of her light up in satisfaction. The hair in her nose froze. Her lungs ached.

She smiled. Despite the war being fought above against invading Gatewood, this moment was hers.

And this planet, if they won, too. Not just for her, but everyone who'd joined them in their search for a place free from corporations, from the greed that wrote off lost life as a tax deduction.

A real home.

She turned to look behind her. There, beyond six square kilometers of squatter hovels, makeshift survival systems, and anti-aircraft weaponry, sat the ETL installation. A single ebony spire rose into the atmosphere, thousands of spiky protrusions dotting every side of the structure. Those spikes, once activated, should begin the rapid process of terraforming the planet. It would raise the ambient temperature from -12^C to somewhere near 15^C, and then, as the ice melted, they'd have a chance to make a place for themselves, something better than strapped-together tin and printed honeycomb habs—a real settlement.

This wasn't about mining rights or getting rich. This was about creating a haven for her people.

That was worth fighting for.

The radio interrupted her thoughts. "Mallias!" Static riddled the transmission, obscuring the voice behind it, but the frenzied panic came across as clear as quartz.

Using the built-in optical scanners in her *manju*, Eleni kicked her filters back on to prevent interference in the transmission. "Mallias here."

It didn't help much. "Get to the sentry tower! You need to—"

She saw it a split second before the air exploded with sound. A fireball speared through the sky despite the burst of materiel spattering around it. With the haze of reentry obscuring it, she couldn't make out details... but she didn't have to. She already knew.

The missile never should've launched. The governor, Sariah Kelly, had had a plan. Victor should have stopped it.

But he hadn't, which meant he must be dead.

She had no time to process that. A moment later, the air shuddered at the sound of the missile breaking the sound barrier. Eleni's helmet adjusted for the worst. Still, she clapped hands over her ears.

But she didn't look away; she couldn't. She'd been in situations back at Erias, specifically in crowd control, when everything slowed down, when you could think your way through a problem before action.

Not this time.

The spear of fire traced amber arcs through the sky, sliding and skimming back and forth, but despite its many twists and turns, it always turned its trajectory back to the surface.

Toward the settlement. Toward Arctic, where hundreds of people still waited for evac.

She only had time for one word, and it slipped out, filled with the cold panic splashing across her body, with the anxiety rattling her reinforced heart. "No!"

That fiery streak, somehow snaking between anti-missile battery fire, appeared, flashed, then buried itself in the settlement between herself and the ETL installation. A brilliant white dome sprang into being alongside a deep roar that rattled her bones and set her teeth chattering.

It expanded, consuming and destroying as it spread. Debris cascaded away in all directions, the shockwave preceding the explosion.

Her *manju* predicted the explosive radius. Alarms sprang to life before the data displayed.

Too close.

She was too fucking close.

Cursing, Eleni turned and, on instinct, jumped, expecting a long leap to carry her toward the guard tower and the safety her *manju* claimed lay there. Instead, she came down after a meter and hit the ground in a painful roll.

Gravity.

Her heart slammed in her chest as she scrambled to her feet, rough rocks chewing at the thick gloves covering her hands. She'd only just gotten up when the ground bucked beneath her feet. Maybe if she'd had more time on planet, she'd have caught herself, but instead it sent her back down, *manju* slamming into the rough tundra soil. The display glitched and went dark, leaving her with the muted colors of reality.

Below her, the ground rattled and rumbled.

Eleni managed to spin onto her back in time to see a shimmering wall of force pushing scattered tin and concrete forward. She managed to get her arms up just as it swept over her, sending her tumbling, tumbling until she struck something hard.

Then, a bright flash of azure light... and everything disappeared into darkness.

Chapter 3
CERIAT

After six hours of silence and pure, terrifying luck, Ceriat had a front-row seat to the bombing of Teegarden c.

Through the frosted glass of his cockpit and the mist of his breath, he watched a missile launch from the single, massive warship orbiting Gatewood and run a broken zigzag through the fighters and freighters littering orbit around Teegarden c. Planetary defenses lit the clouds of the icy planet as the bomb dropped into the atmosphere, where it transformed into a terrible fireball from the heavens.

Clouds disintegrated as it blew through them, followed swiftly by rapid-fire explosions tearing holes around it as ground-air batteries desperately tried to detonate the payload. Then, barely longer than it took him to suck in a teeth-chattering breath of canned O2, the flaming munition disappeared.

And the fighting stopped.

In his mind's eye, white domes of destruction dotted a verdant landscape, leaving nothing but char and horror in its wake. Memories of ash and smoke filled his nose despite the years since he'd last smelled the combination.

His hip roared in phantom pain. He blinked away the memory, swallowed spit down a dry throat, and tried to breathe.

Gatewood fighters rolled back toward the planet and their warships. The mismatched ships and converted freighters from the Teegarden c side did the same, rallying into a protective shield around the planet.

What the hell just happened? He knew, though, didn't he? Hell, he'd seen it dozens of times before, but a part of him rejected the reality of a fusion detonation on a planet that clearly had settlers, even if it was supposed to be empty.

He knew a new crater dotted Teegarden c's landscape. And people had died.

Ceriat sat, gut twisting and bile rising in his throat, as the armies arrayed themselves around their planets, leaving him floating, alone and almost out of emergency O2 somewhere in the middle.

"I-Izzy?" Ceriat asked, a shiver interrupting him.

He slapped the emergency comm panel with little effect. He rubbed at his chest through his jacket to keep his blood flowing and the worst of the chill at bay.

For now.

The tube running from his oxygen mask to the tank below his seat kept getting in the way. More than anything, he wanted the damned thing off. A helmet would be more practical, but since Shaal Tu, he just... couldn't. The idea of having anything wrapped around his head again...

Bile rose in his throat. With scrabbling fingers, he snagged the toilet module adapter from beneath his seat and, pushing away the realization that he regularly stuck his dick in this thing to relieve himself, let alone what he did to shit, proceeded to empty the remnants of his lunch into the tube. He hacked, forcing the material up and out of his throat, careful not to inhale any globules floating inside the container.

Eventually, Ceriat covered the opening and returned the hose to its place beneath his seat. Acid and bile coated his tongue with filth, vision swimming with tears he had to wipe away in zero-g. With trembling fingers, he gave the vent button a tap. It should've dumped both the vomit and his dehydrated waste.

It didn't work.

Of course it didn't work. "Nothing fucking works anymore."

Ceriat choked down panic as it threatened to roil his stomach again and switched his focus to the emergency beacon. He'd kicked it on hours ago without any ping or response. Or rather, no one had come to pick him up yet. If someone had radioed him, he couldn't do anything about that right now. Still, the skirmish appeared to be over, and he was somehow in one piece. This should be the time for a rescue.

Shit. The beacon was off. Ceriat tapped the beacon switch again. The indicator light kicked on with a harsh flick. Any relief he felt disappeared as the light quietly turned off after a long second.

Anxiety crawled in his chest, and an awkward laugh escaped Ceriat's throat. "Eh, heh..."

No. He gave the button another tap, and watched it kick on, transmit for a second, then turn off. Ceriat's mind raced. Why wasn't it working? The emergency distress system not only had its own power system but was connected to every other power source as well. As long as the *Sparrow* had electricity of any sort, the distress beacon should work.

Of course, *should* was the operative word here.

Movement from beyond the cockpit caught Ceriat's eye. He turned away from the beacon in time to see a small fighter floating by. Eerily similar to the *Sparrow*, the ship rotated end over end in a delicate backflip. The red light from the system's sun caught the silver paint uncharred by plasma blasts and sent it sparkling like a jeweled necklace tumbling down a shallow stream.

He stared in morbid curiosity as it spun along his viewing angle. Just before it disappeared, Ceriat learned the fate of the pilot. Just a quick flash, but as it swung out of view, there it was: a single, fist-sized hole in the cockpit.

There was so much debris out here, going every which way.

Eventually, his luck would run out, and some fragment of metal would shatter the cockpit. He didn't have the benefit of an exosuit to pretend at a chance of survival if that happened. As if on cue, something smacked hard into the glass, making the *Sparrow* ring like a bell. Luckily, the window held up.

For now.

The chill air misted his breath and sent a shiver down his spine. Hell, too much longer, and he'd be dead from exposure.

"Space popsicles," Gerry had called them. Pilots left in the void for too long, frozen in their seats, tears and spittle iced on their faces. The image stuck in his head and, for a moment, Ceriat almost surrendered to his fate.

I'm not going to end up as a goddamned space popsicle. The thought slammed into him, sent his heart racing. *Not today.*

With a shuddering breath, he took in the darkened instrument panel. One more time, he ran through the process of restoring main power, then auxiliary. Again, nothing happened. Staring, breath coming quicker than he knew he should allow, Ceriat hammered a fist on the panel.

Nothing changed.

He screamed at the futility of it all, slammed gloved fists into the useless electronics before him.

After several long minutes, Ceriat bounced his head off the headrest of his seat. Unless someone looked his way and realized he wasn't part of the debris, he'd be dead in a few hours. Idly, he turned his gaze back to the distress beacon. He tapped it back on. It clicked. A moment later, the light went off.

Wait. Ceriat held his breath. He did it again, but this time he gave the button another tap before the light shut off on its own. It turned off at his touch.

Which might mean it's transmitting during that second...

He wracked his brain for the old Morse code lessons from bootcamp. It'd been nearly two decades since he'd shown up as an awkward teenager on Luna Base, fresh from high school, and full of hopes and dreams of flying amongst the stars, but they'd hammered that old SOS into them even when he and Gerry had asked why.

"Three short, three long, three short," Sergeant Henderson had said in response right before making the entire unit drop and do pushups for the interruption.

"Three short, three long, three short," Ceriat muttered.

Now, if anyone else had been forced to learn archaic communication lessons, he had a chance. If not, well, at least he'd keep himself busy until he went hypothermic and died.

Sighing in resignation, he started tapping.

Chapter 4
ELENI

"Mallias?"

Too much pain. If she kept her eyes closed, maybe they'd hit her again with the morphine, let her fade back into that cloudy space where nothing hurt and no one mattered. From somewhere distant, a pained scream echoed, and in its wake came low moaning.

"Eleni? I need you on your feet."

Sariah. She groaned. Why would the governor come see her?

Despite every part of her body screaming to stop, Eleni forced her eyes open.

And immediately shut them.

"I knew you were there. Sleeping on the job?" the governor asked, a smile plain in her rough voice.

Eleni tried to respond, but failed. Dirt and dust filled her mouth and swelled her tongue.

"Oh, here."

A moment later, blissfully chill water touched her lips through a sponge and trickled into her mouth. With that came the iron stink of spilled blood buried beneath layers of harsh antiseptics, and... something else. As the fog lifted from her mind, the realization set in.

Carefully this time, Eleni opened her eyes. As they adjusted she found herself exactly where she'd expected. Above her, an emergency structure, all brown resin walls and hanging lamps, sprang to life. Moans and crying filled the air alongside the smell of blood from earlier, but now she could make out that other scent—burnt flesh.

Eleni's new heart slammed as memory flooded over her.

Of the missile.

The detonation.

The shockwave rolling over her.

Somewhere nearby a machine began beeping.

And then Governor Sariah Kelly filled her vision. Sariah had short, dirty-blond hair streaked with gray that framed a narrow face. Unnaturally golden eyes stared at Eleni, but the dark circles around them held more baggage than Eleni remembered. Somehow, she'd aged since Eleni had last seen her.

"Take a breath, Mallias," the governor said, smiling a flat-lipped smile. Her eyes flicked to somewhere out of Eleni's line of sight. "Breathe."

"What...?" Eleni had meant to ask what happened, but her body screamed for more air, making her gasp, and sending her heart racing.

She tried to grab Sariah's shoulder but couldn't. Was she restrained? *Why?* The beeping grew louder.

"Get your heart-rate under control, and I'll tell you," Sariah said.

Eleni did. Deep, steady breaths became the job until the beeping behind her finally tailed off and stopped. Her body relaxed, heart settled.

"Good," Sariah said, still staring over Eleni's head. She turned her attention back to Eleni. "Those Gatewood bastards got the bomb off."

Eleni closed her eyes. The explosion... the facility.

Her stomach dropped through the floor. The ache in her

chest expanded into her arms, ran through her reinforced veins, and into her toes.

Victor.

Sariah must've realized what she was thinking, because the governor's face twisted. Her eyes shimmered in the false light as she turned away. "The strike team was intercepted. I'm sorry about your brother."

Everything disappeared beneath the grief spreading through her like a bonfire.

Victor and his stupid grin. Victor and the pranks he'd play when he thought she worked too hard.

The two of them, standing on that hill overlooking the ETL installation, talking about the future. Building something better than the nothing they'd had in the Erias Mining Belt habs on Hobelt.

"I'll be fine, Els," he'd said as he'd boarded the stolen Gatewood Conglomerate freighter. "Nothing's killed me yet."

A joke they told each other. Always... *Yet.*

They'd had plans. Find spouses, have stupid kids who grew up with cousins, amongst family. Victor would manage tech expansion in the colony. Eleni would watch over it all. Together, they'd grow old, feeble, and make their respective grandchildren take care of the crotchety brother and sister duo who just wouldn't die because nothing had found a way... yet.

Yet.

A machine behind her screeched to life.

Sariah muttered wordless platitudes, held her hand, and told her to breathe.

The ache in Eleni's chest exploded into a grief worse than the pain of gravity, than the torn and broken skin covering her body. It speared her soul to the wall, left it dangling in a chill wind that swung through the building.

Someone screamed alongside the cold. People shouted, though not in panic. Doctors trying to keep order, to save yet another body.

Then the breeze disappeared... and with its disappearance went her grief.

But it left scars. Embers of fury, stirring in the ragged waving of her tattered soul, burned bright as she squeezed away the last of her tears. The machine slowed and stopped.

This time, when she opened her eyes—when she finally caught the governor's gaze—Eleni didn't flinch or wonder.

Instead, she said one thing. "We're gonna make 'em pay."

"Yes," Sariah replied, a sad smile framed by wrinkles joining the word. "Yes, we are."

Chapter 5
CERIAT

FUBAR didn't come close to describing how far sideways this mission had gone.

Crushed against the steel wall of a room about the size of the broom closet in his apartment back on Earth, Ceriat closed his eyes and tried to pretend the shuddering banging rattling this damned ship as it descended into the frigid nightmare of Teegarden c's atmosphere wasn't happening. A harness attached to the wall held him firmly in place. His hands slammed into his stomach by the force of reentry.

He'd tried using his emergency comm system, the one buried behind the plate in his head, to contact Izzy, but that'd only resulted in silence. She must still be powered down. At least he hoped that was all that had happened.

On the plus side, he could stretch his hip now.

Still, four minutes of terror as his chest was crushed and light-bulbs screwed into his eye sockets. Even with the inertial suppressors, reentry in a freighter this size *sucked*.

Then it stopped. Weight pulled him toward the floor, putting the pressure firmly on his chest and shoulders. Still, some heaviness leveled onto his booted feet for the first time in a day—a small thing to be grateful for, but grateful he was, nonetheless.

Standing did wonders for his hip and his head.

Beyond the walls, the wind—real atmosphere—wailed against the hull. He cracked his eyes open to confirm that, despite the screeching, no, nothing else had changed. Illuminated by a single emergency light, the small cargo hold he'd been dumped into was still a tiny closet, useful only for storing dehydrated feces or an ETL representative who'd run into some crazy squatters.

Finding out your saviors had a predilection for pointing plasma weapons at your face hadn't been a pleasant surprise. Knowing they had a cell set up for just such a captive hadn't helped, either.

Luckily, the closet wasn't doing double duty today, or the smell would be unbearable. As it was, the stink from sitting in a cramped cockpit for eight hours without moving still tickled his nostrils with the sweet stench of his own body odor. A sonic shower would be *great* right about now.

A man's voice crackled over an aged speaker. "Reentry complete." He sounded suspiciously like a rough-and-tumble cowboy from some of the ancient Earth vids, all chew and growl. "Welcome to Shiva."

He rubbed his eyes in a vain hope of relieving the pressure building there. The pilot must be equalizing with the atmosphere as they dropped. "You renamed the planet?" Ceriat asked, not expecting an answer, not from a closet.

"No. We named it."

Apparently there were microphones everywhere. Good to know.

Still, with the sounds of a living world and the tug of gravity, Ceriat's mood had already begun to improve, even if he was locked up in a closet. "Named, renamed," Ceriat replied to the empty room. "Potato, tomato."

A pause. "Not to us." Any pretense at friendliness disappeared, not that there'd been much in that vein since the freighter had swung out and yanked the *Sparrow* aboard.

"Okay, then." Ceriat wanted to ask why they'd chosen something so unoriginal but held his tongue. Maybe they wanted their planet to share a name with a hundred and thirty other icy planets? Didn't mean anything to him if they wanted to be blissfully derivative. "Happy to be on Shiva."

"We'll set down outside what's left of Arctic," the pilot replied, his grimace coming through in the change in tone. "Then you can talk to the governor."

What's left of Arctic? "What does that mean?" Ceriat asked, a worm of worry working its way up his spine.

As far as he knew, there was only one installation on Teegarden c—Shiva, he reminded himself—and it was the terraforming tower. If that was damaged, then all of this, the decade of work by the ETL that had led to this moment, was for nothing.

"You'll see."

"See what?" Ceriat asked again. When no response came, he asked again. Nothing.

Several minutes passed with the screaming wind and rattle of the transport in eddying gusts. Each jostle knocked Ceriat's teeth together while the ship chattered like a sack of broken glass.

The wind disappeared in a roar of jets; the world shifted position. Ceriat's vision swam for a moment before a deep, sinking sensation swept over him. The transport shuddered suddenly as the jets roared one more time, then cut off, leaving a hissing whine in their wake.

They'd landed.

Groaning, Ceriat tried to stretch a bit in the new gravity. It was one thing to read the numbers on the mission brief, and another to actually experience the gravity of a new planet. Technically speaking, Shiva should have less intense gravity than it did, given its diameter, half that of the Earth. However, its core consisted of some alloy that dragged the gravitational needle just over a standard G. Ceriat felt like he'd thrown on a backpack full of rice cakes. As such, while it didn't cause too much strain initially, he knew the next week or so was going to hurt as he adjusted.

A series of sharp snapping sounds pulled his attention to the door just in time to see it swing open. A stoic woman stood there, head shaved and tattooed in concentric circles. Ceriat had seen the design on Spacers the galaxy over, though this one decorated a visage made to frown despite the rose-colored lipstick on her lips. An aged exosuit wrapped her from the neck down, the insignia that'd once been over her left breast scraped off. Her height made Ceriat wonder, however. Spacers tended toward tall and lanky, while she stood only a little taller than the average Earther.

The man behind her made up for that. Well over two meters tall, and already bending at the middle from the gravity, his wrinkled, balding pate carried faded versions of similar tattoos. Unlike the woman, there were several Christian crosses amidst his head tattoos, and the hint of a crucifix at the visible bit of his neck. He, too, wore the same vintage of exosuit with the logo scrubbed away. Normally, that'd catch Ceriat's attention and bring questions up, but the plasma rifle in his hands was far too attention grabbing.

"Don't move," the woman said, stepping close to disengage the harness holding Ceriat in place. She smelled of rose water, of all things. "Jeret'll pop your head like a water satchel if you try anything."

In response, Ceriat smiled disarmingly. He hoped.

As the last restraint disconnected, Ceriat finally felt the full force of Shiva's gravity. He slumped forward, right into the woman.

"Ai!" She gave him a hard shove, sending him slamming back into the wall and driving the air from his lungs. "Watch it, Earther."

Strong for a Spacer. She'd spent her formative years someplace with gravity, that was for sure.

While he gasped, she took the opportunity to snap plastic restraints around his wrists, then gave it a tug. "Come on."

If he'd had breath, Ceriat would've started asking questions, but, well, that wasn't in the cards. Instead, this tattooed woman dragged him along like a misbehaving dog. The man with the plasma rifle, Jeret, followed behind, the odor of overworn clothes and sweat preceding him. Periodically, he'd push the barrel of the rifle into Ceriat's back, as if he could move any faster.

When Ceriat had been brought aboard, three fully suited and helmeted soldiers—or so he thought—had ushered him through the cargo hold and along several barely lit hallways before depositing him in the closet he'd just left. This time, the woman and silent Jeret dragged him back through a single, well-lit corridor lined with access panels showing enough wear and tear along the edges for a lifetime.

How old is *this freighter?*

Despite the periodic echoes of detached voices, they didn't encounter anyone else until the lady stopped at a closed door. She tapped in an access code with a quickness Ceriat found interesting. Gravity always threw off Spacers, but she barely acknowledged it. Definitely grew up on a planet.

A glance over his shoulder showed Jeret, despite the obvious discomfort he felt, handling his weapon and footing with as much ease.

Maybe not, then.

Which meant... *How long have they been here?* When he'd dropped into the Sol FTL lane this morning, there'd been no talk of squatters or settlers, no indication there'd be a goddamned war when he popped out of the lane.

Yet here they were. Despite every part of him begging for answers, he kept the questions to himself. The way Jeret kept glaring at him didn't hint toward any positive outcome there, anyway.

The door opened with a hiss, and with it came a blast of freezing air. The chill swept over Ceriat, sending a shiver through him. Still, the crispness made him smile...

Until he smelled the old, familiar stink of death on the air.

The woman sucked in a shuddering breath and stepped outside. The hollow thudding of magboots on metal stairs echoed back through the opening. Ceriat turned back to Jeret. "What happened—?"

"Move," the tall man said without emotion, giving him another shove ahead.

"Fine!" Ceriat snapped and made his way through the door. Acrid smoke tainted the sharp scent of arctic tundra. Twisting amongst it all lay something deeper, darker. "Oh. God."

A breeze flitted by... and the gentle touch of something soft stroked his cheek. Ceriat lifted a hand to his face. When he pulled it away, his gloves were gray with ash.

All the imagery he'd seen before leaving Earth had showcased breathtaking wintry vistas, violet sunrises, and pristine, rocky plains, untouched by sentient minds. In those videos, the ETL Spire had gone up in carefully choreographed time-lapse. A single unit installed at the equator, ready and able to transform this dead, yet beautiful world into another new frontier for humanity.

Just like all the others, it'd filled him with hope. With meaning and purpose. But instead of that glorious sight, Ceriat stood at the edge of a crater the likes of which he'd seen before, many times, though only once from a vantage like this.

Blackened, turned earth spread before him as far as he could see. Ash floated on the wind in visible eddies, voiceless songbirds dancing and spinning. The breeze disappeared into the distance, and with its departure, a ragged roar broke through to him from the lopsided resin domes dotting the edge of the crater. As he watched, a group of people, coated gray and ebony with soot, scrambled out of that blasted place carrying a gurney.

Ceriat's breath caught.

A tiny form lay strapped atop it, though from this distance he couldn't make it out.

Don't be a kid, don't be a kid...

"Move."

Ceriat turned back to Jeret one more time to ask... something, but the question disappeared at the stricken look on the tall man's face, at the anger boiling its way up his pale neck.

So Ceriat turned back. This time when he looked, he caught sight of something else. Something familiar.

A towering structure covered in spines like a hundred-story tall cactus snapped in two stood across the crater. Blackened smears dotted the entire side facing him, spreading halfway up to where the spire suddenly ended in broken shards of steel and concrete. As he watched, some of those smears began disappearing from the bottom up as the automated service nanobots struggled to work through a scenario they weren't developed for.

It'd recover... eventually. But for now, and the foreseeable future, the ETL tower was shot. That opened a pit in his gut. Ten years down the drain.

Why would the Gatewood Conglomerate do that? They'd spent so many credits on getting Teegarden c terraformed, why destroy the ETL tower? Was this dispute worth it?

Ceriat's gaze was dragged back to the crater, to the fragments of structures poking from the dirt like burned toothpicks.

War. Always fucking war. *Why do humans keep murdering each other like this?*

"Move." This time the word came with a painful jab of the rifle barrel. It sent Ceriat stumbling toward the metal emergency stairs leading from the freighter to the landing strip below.

To where a group of settlers, all in thick, brown jackets and thermal gear, waited for him, plasma rifles held in front of them like they wanted a reason to use them.

He'd seen that look before. They needed someone to hate for this, and he made a great scapegoat.

None of *this* was on him, but still... they didn't know how right they were.

With his own shuddering breath, Ceriat descended the steps into a nightmare.

Chapter 6
ELENI

Eleni sat on a stool outside the emergency tent. She'd needed the air after half a day in a bed, infused with pain relievers and anger.

There'd been too much emotion, too much chaos in her soul to stay inside the tent any longer. At the time, she'd thought maybe if she could just get a breath of Shiva's frigid wind, catch the slightest bit of the peace she'd felt before the bomb had gone off, this hate brewing in her stomach would disperse. Maybe she'd find that calm again, sitting outside wrapped in thermal blankets.

It hadn't worked. The air carried burnt flesh on its gusts, danced with the ash of incinerated friends. The emergency encampment roared with shouted orders and panicked people, of parents crying over still forms, of children wailing for missing mothers, fathers.

At first, she'd tried to identify them, to catalog the faces and names as they walked by, shouting for their loved ones. But the ash and soot smeared their features, turned them into nameless spirits wandering this muddied tundra. Maybe if she still had her *manju*... but she didn't have any idea where it'd ended up. That pained her more than she'd expected. It'd been a part of her for the better part of a decade. With it, she was Director of Security Eleni Mallias. Confident. Proven.

Capable.

Outside it... well, who was she without it? Just Eleni. Eleni the orphan. A sister without a brother. A girl without a home.

No one.

Still, she stayed out here now because, even with all the chaos of the camp and the horror on the wind, it still smelled better than the surgical tent. She didn't need the bed anymore, not really. The governor had prioritized her spot on the nanobot surgery list, so as of an hour ago, the hundreds of exterior wounds covering her body had disappeared in a buzzing, writhing mass of tiny ants screaming across her body. She'd heard some newer 'bots managed a pain response during surgery.

No such luck here on Shiva.

This is gonna suck. Slowly, she took in a shuddering breath.

Pain rattled across her chest and down her spine. Copper flecked her tongue.

Now to deal with the internal damage. The broken ribs, bruised liver, etcetera, etcetera. She'd tuned out when Doctor Jeffries had told her the extent of her injuries. It hadn't been on purpose, obviously. Jeffries was doing his best in a horrible situation, but at some point, it'd stopped mattering.

If nanobots couldn't fix you in a time like this, you died. Simple as that.

With a sigh, she stared at the mug of dark liquid cradled between her hands. Her breath misted the space between, diffusing over the heat radiating from the cup. Maybe if she squinted, she'd be able to see the millions of little robots in the morass, waiting for a chance to get to work.

Above and to her right, the roar of jets caught her attention. Turning, she watched the *Lucille* swing in and drop smoothly to their makeshift landing pad. The sight of the old girl made her smile. She'd arrived in the Teegarden system on the *Lucille* and had spent a good year and a half aboard, undergoing the extensive cardiovascular and muscular treatments necessary for her to survive on Shiva. Now that Arctic was a gaping crater, only *Lucille* still felt like yesterday.

A shadow fell across Eleni's feet, and with it came a familiar voice. "You gonna drink it or stare at it?"

She turned back, smile disappearing as she took in Doctor Jeffries. A small man amongst Spacers, Doctor Jeffries was head and shoulders shorter than she. He liked to joke that even back on Earth, his ancestors had been small, so why would the galaxy do him the favor of making him taller?

Dark-skinned with black hair and narrow features, he looked like the sort of handsome that'd end up on the Feeds hawking pet food or delivering news to the galaxy. Unfortunately for the galaxy, he'd decided he wanted to become a doctor after an attempt at intergalactic comedy hadn't panned out, or at least that was what he told people.

Usually, he made her laugh. But not now.

Not today.

With a sigh, she tipped the mug back and drained the contents in one long, gritty gulp. "Ugh," Eleni muttered, smacking her lips together. Just like a warm protein shake. "Can't ya add flavor to it?"

Jeffries pulled the stool out next to her and took a seat. "And ruin the gentle bouquet of pine tar? Disrupt my balanced textures of gravel and mud?" He grinned at her, though she noticed it didn't make it to his eyes. "Never."

Eleni didn't reply, just stared at the dregs left at the bottom of the plastic mug as she waited for it to happen.

"What are you thinking about?" Jeffries asked.

Eleni knew what he was doing; she wasn't stupid. She went with it. Still staring at the mug in her hands, she said, "Thinkin' about rage."

"What do you mean?"

"I mean..." Eleni said, rolling the cup around in hands lined with soot stuck in the grooves of her skin. Whose skin lay buried in her fingerprints? Which friend coated the creases across her body? God, why hadn't she washed her hands better? "When is it... justified?"

Her stomach twisted on itself. Something inside her throbbed. *There it is.* Eleni ground her teeth.

"Waxing poetic?" Jeffries said, scooting forward and obviously trying to get her to look at him. "Eleni?"

"I hear you!" Eleni snapped. The throbbing transitioned into a sharp, hot, burning sensation. "Little bastards just popping out my guts."

Jeffries nodded and held his hand out to her. She did the same, keeping her own a few inches from his. His gesture hadn't been an invitation to touch, after all. Spacers didn't do stupid shit like that. But proximity helped.

"It'll only last ten seconds while the nanobots—"

"I know what they're doing, Tim," Eleni said, using Jeffries' given name for the first time since they'd come off the *Lucille* together, "but it still fucking hurts." The last words came out as a harsh whisper between gritted teeth.

She knew what the nanobots did, why they did it, but as the stream of microscopic robots cut themselves free from her upper stomach to spread through her body and repair the internal damage, it didn't change the fact it felt like fire in her gut.

Man, the next 24 standard hours were going to be a bit of a mindfuck. All that activity tended to mess with the chemicals in your head for some reason.

She just had to hope things would calm down for a minute.

Jeffries grunted and leaned back. They'd met on Hobelt, been friends for years; he knew when she needed space and time. Unfortunately, he'd never been great at providing enough of either.

"Chucklenuts." The word slipped between clenched teeth as a wave of agony swept over her.

Jeffries laughed.

Eleni grimaced at him. "What?"

"Never heard 'chucklenuts' before," Jeffries said, shrugging. "Might adopt it."

"Can't," Eleni said, lips twisting into a smile. "It's mine."

Another flood of agony, this time just beneath her lungs, stopped any further conversation. Eleni wasn't sure how much time passed while she huddled over in pain, but thankfully, it finished just as it started.

Quickly.

That throbbing feeling reentered her stomach, one more sharp pain, and then a lump hit her gut like she'd just binged seven meal rations. With a groan, she leaned against the resin wall behind her and let out a painless sigh.

"Better?" Jeffries asked, grinning his lopsided grin.

Eleni gave him a smile full of teeth, but before snapping back a retort, she caught a bit of movement at the *Lucille* out of the corner of her eye.

A man, clearly an Earther from his height and lack of tattoos, stomped his way down the mobile steps from the ship. That alone wasn't too strange, but the fact old, grumpy Jeret prodded him along with a plasma rifle and into the waiting arms of a group of her security troops made it different. Especially since no one had told her about it.

"Who's that?" Eleni asked, unable to keep the venom from her voice.

"Him?" Jeffries asked, pointing. "That's the ETL guy."

Eleni frowned. "ETL guy?"

"The guy sent to turn on the tower," Jeffries said. "I think."

"Looks Gatewood to me." Eleni narrowed her eyes in his direction.

Jeffries shrugged. "Like I said, I don't know." He grinned at her, crooked teeth just hidden behind his lips. "If only we knew the Director of Security, maybe we could find out."

Eleni gave him a look and rolled her eyes. "Ha. Ha."

From within the building, someone called for Jeffries. "Duty calls," he sighed dramatically, getting to his feet.

She waved at him as he left.

However, he stopped and turned back, face serious. "Eleni?"

She didn't tear her eyes away from the man as Jeret joined the rest of the security forces. Too bad she couldn't tell who led the group from here. God, she missed her *manju* already. "Yeah?"

"On the rage thing." Jeffries cleared his throat. "Rage blinds people, makes them do stupid shit. We both know that."

Eleni didn't respond. Didn't need to.

"Just... remember to think before acting, all right?"

"Yeah," Eleni said, voice little more than a whisper as she tracked this new Earther's movements.

Her guards were taking him to the governor's structure. She knew because the flag they'd created flew over the top of the building a hundred meters distant—ice blue with a symmetrical, ebony asteroid smack dab in the middle.

Could he have something to do with the missile? The anger boiled to the surface again. Without the mug in her hands, she knew they'd be shaking.

"Eleni?"

Her guards took him in to see the governor. Without her.

Fuck. That.

Eleni swept to her feet and handed Jeffries the mug. He took it, but the look on his face showed he clearly wasn't thrilled by what was coming. "I hear you, but I got someplace to be."

"You're not even in uniform!" Jeffries said, eyes darting back to the sound of someone still calling his name.

An urgency tinted the tone now.

"This'll do," Eleni said, pulling the thermal blankets over her shoulders. The light boots they'd given her would keep her feet warm for now. "Good enough."

"Jeffries! Where the fuck is Doctor Jeffries!" This time the call came clear as day.

Groaning, Jeffries gave her a pleading look one more time. "Don't do anything rash. Please?"

Eleni smiled but didn't respond. Instead, she stalked toward where the stranger now spoke with the governor.

She needed answers, and she'd bet a thousand credits that son of a bitch had them.

Chapter 7
CERIAT

A dull drone filled Ceriat's ears. Screaming faces stained his vision, their crimson-streaked bodies covered in ash. Sobbing children huddled around makeshift tents, clouds of mist mixing with ashen snowfall against a blue sky.

Still, despite the devastation, Ceriat's mind was plagued by ghosts.

Phantom plasma bolts rang through the noise.

Muffled, dead voices screamed over long-disconnected comms.

The hiss of oxygen and the chill of the void seeping through a crack.

Unmoored, he cast about, confused, for the familiarity of his bomber cockpit. But instead of blasted earth filled with blood, he found sooty slush and filth.

He smelled the fear and anguish above the heady stink of bodies and death. One child hugged something to their chest, but whatever it was blended with their clothes in an clouded film.

It melded with old memories and dragged him, screaming, back there on the cliffside with Gerry. To the desolation the bombers had left behind.

"How can you stand to be on planet," Gerry had said, stricken as he'd cast about at the destruction they'd caused, "when this is what's here?"

Ceriat had never had a good answer for that, just a flashing light in his mind telling him his oxygen was nearly depleted.

But this wasn't a memory. This, right now, was reality. Still, he didn't raise his eyes from the ground again for fear of what he'd see above. The rational part of his mind told him there'd be nothing there besides that blue sky and falling ash.

The rest of his brain told him he'd see Shaal-Tu's burning clouds.

The sharp pain of a rifle between his shoulders snapped Ceriat out of the moment. "Move."

Ceriat raised his hands and began walking again. He hadn't even realized he'd stopped. "Sorry, just having a moment."

"Have it somewhere else."

"Gladly," Ceriat said, finally breaking his gaze away from the children. A larger resin structure resolved amidst scrambling people ahead of him. "Where are we going?"

He turned to get a look at his escort. Most of the group had dispersed during the walk, it appeared, leaving only two armed guards with him. Jeret still followed, but his plasma rifle had been tossed over his shoulder, not that he was doing any sort of guarding. The lanky man just walked along, a haunted look in his eyes Ceriat found awfully familiar.

The man behind him, however, had no such expression. Instead, barely contained rage rattled the skin around his eyes and sent the muscles in his jaw a-bouncing. "Governor wants to see you."

They have a governor? How long had the settlement been here before the missile dropped?

And what would they want with him? "Any idea why?" Ceriat asked.

"Nope," he snapped, jamming the tip of his rifle into Ceriat's spine. "You can ask her yourself. We're here." Then, to someone beyond Ceriat, "He's all yours."

Ceriat swung back in time for another armed guard—a woman, tall like Jeret, but all blond hair and blue eyes—to grab him by the shoulder with a mitt the size of his head. "Through here, Earther."

Just before he was shoved through the open doorway into the freshly printed resin building—the distinctly sharp scent of acetone gave it away—Ceriat caught sight of a flag on top of the building. A flash of blue with a black oval of some sort in the center.

They had a flag. That stuck in Ceriat's gullet like he'd swallowed a bone. If they had a flag, they hadn't just shown up this morning. And if the settlement was as large as the crater he'd seen —and they had the materials on hand to create an emergency compound of this size—that meant these people had been here for a while.

This was no group of squatters, but a settlement. A real one.

Which begged the question: why the fuck hadn't he been briefed before he left?

With a final shove, the big Viking woman pushed him into the dark room, leaving him blind as his eyes adjusted. Smells hit first. Beneath the harshness of acetone, oil, and steel lay the sweet stink of unwashed clothes and clustered bodies. Low cursing hit next, followed by the sound of someone spitting.

Then his eyes adjusted. Shadows drew dark lines around the curved outer walls. A dozen or more people huddled around tables on that edge, small lamps lighting the source of their studies. Still, with his entrance, their attention was dragged from whatever projects they were working on to the stranger entering this inner sanctum.

Ceriat turned to the brightest light in the building. The single hanging globe was centered over a familiar sight—a Battle Tableau, generally referred to as a BT. It'd been years since he'd seen one last, especially once military grade HUD implants and contacts had become the standard rather than the exception. That was after his time, though.

This BT presented the status of the space battle. On one side, an icy globe, Shiva, stood as a three-dimensional hologram; on the other, the verdant wonderland of Gatewood. Arrayed around each were hundreds of ships with ordnance and status layouts indicated in tiny letters around them. The settlers seemed to have numbers, while Gatewood had a single massive warship. A quick glance was all Ceriat needed to know about how well the war was going.

The settlers were in deep shit with that Gatewood monster in place.

The display dissolved into a hiss of pixels, revealing two figures beyond.

The woman grabbed his attention. The way she stood reminded him of commanders he'd seen in mission briefings—solid and stoic. Firm. The uniform helped with that impression, all grays and blacks, the jacket high-necked in a way reminiscent of Protectorate captains. Holstered at her hip was an ancient pistol. He could only see the grip from here, brown on black steel, but any sort of combustion projectile weapon sent a shiver of anxiety through him. In space, they were horrible weapons.

Luckily, on planet, they only ended up being bad for the person at the other end of the barrel.

Usually.

With a dismissive wave of a hand, she sent the shorter man next to her away. He swept by Ceriat, taking time to grimace in annoyance, a long scar dragging his upper lip and setting his pale face into a sneer, on his way out. That in and of itself was strange. He'd only have a scar like that if he'd been injured someplace without modern medical equipment handy for years. Once scar tissue built up enough, well, that's when you transitioned into reconstructive surgery and that cost a pretty penny.

"I know you're ETL," the woman behind the table began, demanding his attention, "but I don't know who you are." Her voice carried the confidence of a woman used to issuing commands and having them followed. With a deep breath, she ran a hand roughly through her styled salt-and-pepper hair, then dropped into something resembling parade rest. "So?"

For a moment, he considered lying, but then realized, despite the way everyone kept looking at him, he didn't have anything to hide. "Ceriat Parker," he said, "and yes, I'm ETL, so I'm not entirely sure why I'm being treated like a criminal."

"No?" she asked, coming around the table. When the globe of light hit her straight on, Ceriat reassessed his first impressions. Wrinkles surrounded her golden eyes; eyes weighed down from having seen too much. She knew how much trouble they were in; the panic sat clear as day behind her harsh exterior. "And the rocket launch on your arrival, that's just a coincidence?"

"Hey, my ship was disabled when that happened—"

She cut him off with a scoff, brow furrowing in clear anger. "You expect me to believe that you showing up just as our settlement was destroyed is a coincidence?"

"Can I at least get your name?" Ceriat asked. Maybe if he humanized the conversation...

"Governor," she snapped. "You can call me Governor."

This wasn't going well. Ceriat sucked in a breath and let it out, scanning the room. The ache in his back from the constant rifle prods, the shuddering reentry, and the gravity change already weighed on him. He pointed at a couple folding chairs next to the BT. They looked ancient, but were still better than standing, especially if this went sideways.

"Can we at least sit if you're going to grill me?"

With a dramatic bow, she gestured to the chairs. "Oh, by your leave, sir."

Grimacing, Ceriat ignored the sarcasm and took a seat in one of the chairs. It creaked beneath his weight but held. The governor grabbed the opposite chair and pulled it several feet away, then plopped down. She crossed her legs, then leaned forward. "Why are you here, Earther?"

"I'm here—was coming here," he amended, the memory of

the shattered ETL tower fresh in his mind, "to start the terraforming process."

Governor made a noise in her throat. It took him a moment to recognize it as a snide chuckle.

"What?" Ceriat asked, neck getting hot. "I'm telling the truth, goddammit!"

The rattle of weapons brought Ceriat around until he stared down Jeret and the nameless guard pointing plasma rifles at him.

"It's fine," Governor said, waving her hand at them like they were misbehaving dogs. Then, eyes locked on Ceriat's own, she continued. "Tell me what the brief said."

"The brief?" Ceriat only pulled his gaze away from the guards after they turned the rifles away—not that he'd be able to do anything about it if they decided to shoot. It wasn't like he had a combat exosuit anymore. "It said—" he closed his eyes, remembering the verbiage "—'Teegarden c is ready for terraforming procedures. Depart at 0600, land at the tower coordinates, and begin processes.'" He opened his eyes and noted nothing had changed. "That's it. Honestly, I thought I might be home to feed Gerodin."

Confusion clouded Governor's face alongside something else. Concern, maybe? "Gerodin?"

"Ginny for short. My chihuahua," Ceriat said, a smile breaking across his face despite himself. The tiny little fucker had more personality in her two-kilo body than the entire Protectorate. "No rush, though. I got a sitter."

"Hope you paid them well," Governor said, leaning back. The barest flicker of a grin tickled her lips.

Ceriat followed suit, matching her relaxing body language. Talking about pets always made people open up. He didn't really know why, but at least this time he didn't need to lie about it to keep from getting gutted. Ginny really was a tiny little treasure.

"As long as I'm back by Wednesday, shouldn't be any problems."

Governor frowned. "It might be."

Shit. "Hey," Ceriat said, keeping his tone as calm and even as he could, "I don't know what's going on here—" She opened her mouth to speak, but he continued on in a rush, "—but I didn't know about you, this settlement." He gestured around. "My reports mentioned no one. This was a solo operation."

"You didn't find that strange?" Governor asked, putting her hands in her lap. "Doesn't the ETL usually send people in groups of four?"

"I like the solitude." How the hell would she know that? First the brief, now this. It dawned on him then that he might not be able to talk his way out of this. "Regardless, with the tower down, I have no purpose here and, honestly, I just want to go home."

"To see your little dog?" Governor said, pouting her lips, eyes narrowing.

She's mocking me. "That's most of it, yes."

She sighed and looked around the room. Then she stretched like a tiger about to pounce. "If I believed you, your precious pup could have her Earther back—"

"I don't know anything about this! I didn't even know anyone was settled here!" Ceriat yelled, voice cracking at the end. How had this swung so wildly out of control?

"Bullshit," Governor said, acid in her words. "We've been here for years, Earther, and you know it."

Ceriat searched the room, hoping to find some sign of compassion, something that told him this hadn't just twisted exactly the way it seemed. Instead, he found himself staring at the doorway, or more specifically, at the tall figure framed by light standing there. At first, with the backlight of a bright sky, he couldn't make out features, but then the aquiline nose came into view, the dark skin and scarred hands clutching a blanket around wide shoulders. Her eyes, still dark in the contrast, glittered like sable in starlight, but with anger or compassion, he couldn't tell.

The certainty of it all hit him then, and with it came the most flaccid words he'd ever spoken. "I'm just the guy who activates the towers. That's my job."

Governor climbed to her feet, dusted her hands of imaginary grit on her pants. "Well, you'll find that job is much harder in a cell."

Ceriat watched her stand and gesture to the guards, but though he didn't fight, he also didn't move. Why make it easier for them? Hands grabbed him under the arms, eyes downcast as they hauled him up and dragged him from the room, and back into the frigid wind of Shiva.

As he passed the woman in the doorway, their eyes caught for the briefest of moments. Sure, it might have been wishful thinking, but Ceriat thought he saw compassion. Understanding.

Then she was gone.

And Ceriat was alone.

Chapter 8
ELENI

Eleni watched as the Earther was dragged into the distance. They'd most likely take him back to the *Lucille*. It wasn't like there was anywhere else to keep him.

He'd seemed truthful to her. None of his words rang false, though it was clear he'd had some training in de-escalation procedures at some point. If she could see that, Sariah certainly had.

"Get in here before you catch a chill."

Speak of the devil. Eleni turned away from the man disappearing into the distance and stepped into what she assumed was the new governor's mansion. The old one had been a two-story structure of mined granite and concrete. This one... well, to say it was a step down would be an understatement.

At her entrance, a chorus of muttered whispers filled the room.

"She's alive!"

"I thought they said she'd lost a leg?"

"You sure that's her? Where's her *manju*?"

The last one snagged on something inside her. She hugged the blanket tighter around her shoulders and neck. Sariah closed the distance, the smell of burnt flesh and ash blown away in the fresh scent of the governor's shampoo. Lilac, Eleni thought it was called, though it might've been another 'L' word. Whatever it happened to be, the smell fell firmly in the category she'd come to call 'flowery,' though she had yet to see, let alone smell, a real flower.

"How'd surgery go?" Sariah asked, searching Eleni's eyes for... something.

That was strange. "Just right," Eleni said, turning away to scan the room for familiar faces.

Instead, she only found other members of Sariah's Cabinet there, including Gareth Brightman, director of the Military. Tall and fit, with a distinctly military look about him—short-shorn salt-and-pepper hair and a severe look—his appointment made visual sense at least. In reality, he always seemed too quick to fight, though if it looked like he could gain Sariah's favor by avoiding a battle, he'd back down. Like Sariah, he carried an ancient combustion weapon: an ivory-handled, silver revolver he kept polished to a blinding sheen. Anyone who asked about it would get a fifteen-standard-minute presentation on its history.

Eleni had never probed him on it. She didn't care for those weapons. Still, he gave her a neutral nod, then turned back to whatever he was working on. Technically speaking, his duties overlapped hers... or had. Eleni's responsibility was for the safety of Arctic. That sent a spear of guilt into her stomach, even though she knew there'd been nothing she could've done about what happened.

Still... what was she supposed to do now? One person would have an answer for that. Eleni took one more look around the room.

"Where's Duncan?" she asked.

Duncan was her second-in-command, predecessor, and the man who kept the general guard forces in order. When she'd arrived, he'd happily handed over the authorization codes and, with a rare smile creasing his much-wrinkled mug, had announced he'd never go to another Cabinet meeting as long as he lived.

Sariah let out a breath. Was that a shudder? "He didn't make it."

A pall fell over Eleni, sending a shiver through her that wasn't from the cold. "Oh." There were no more tears left in her, but still, her face and chest ached with the loss. "Anyone else vac'd?" she asked.

"A lot of people died, Mallias," Sariah said, reaching out until she almost touched Eleni's shoulder. After a second, she pulled her hand away. "But let's not focus on that right now. Now that you're on your feet, I need you back to work."

Despite herself, Eleni let out a snort.

Sariah crossed her arms, eyebrow shooting straight up. "Something funny, Director Mallias?"

Old habits kicked in. Eleni straightened, chin going up. "No, ma'am." Then reality killed the reaction. Sighing, Eleni shriveled under the weight of everything. "But..."

"But what?"

Eleni stepped to the side and gestured out the now-closed door. "What'm I supposed to guard? It's over." That same ache filled her voice, lending it a waver at the end that made her want to scream.

Sariah's cheeks flexed for a moment, then she let out a sigh and came in close enough Eleni could pick up the acrid stink of coffee on her breath and something else she couldn't identify.

Something... chemical? No. Had to be her imagination.

"I need you to get over this self-pitying shit," Sariah whispered, eyes flashing. The grip on Eleni's shoulder was a surprise, but the ache as Sariah squeezed came from far more than physical pain. "People are counting on me. On us," she added quickly, voice little more than a hiss. "If we don't show a united front, we don't have a chance to win this war."

Win this war.

Eleni stood straight and shrugged her shoulder out of Sariah's grip. For a moment, she was overwhelmingly aware of how much taller she was than the governor, than nearly anyone in the room.

Every other Cabinet member had come on planet in the first wave because they'd grown up in some semblance of gravity. Eleni's appointment had been a source of pride, the first Spacer to take a leadership role on Shiva.

"But not the last," Victor had said with his stupid grin.

And now... now they sat in a warzone on an inhospitable planet with their resources destroyed—their agriculture and water treatment facilities pounded to dust—and Sariah spoke of war?

"War?" Eleni asked, stepping back. "This ain't war," she hissed, then at the sight of the others turning her direction, she finished in a low voice. "That out there? That's slaughter."

"Shut your fucking mouth," Sariah hissed, scanning the room like she expected everyone to defect right then. "This needs to be a unified front, Mallias. If you can't do that—"

It felt like someone had punched her in the gut. "Are you cutting me?" Everything went numb, disconnected. Like a dream.

Sariah stared back at her, face hard as iron, and for a moment, Eleni thought she knew the answer.

But then Sariah softened and let out a sigh. "No, Eleni. I'm not firing you."

"Good," Eleni replied, not quite sure if that was true. "Cuz it sounded like—"

"No," Sariah said, stepping back to the BT. She shook her head in the negative like she was trying to convince herself of the answer.

Eleni sucked in a breath and let it out. Empty excuses filled her mind. *Sariah is under a lot of stress... she's trying her best... this is trying for everyone.*

It worked, but not as well as usual, so Eleni changed the subject. "Who was the Earther?"

"Parker?" Sariah asked as the BT spun back up, holograms flickering to life.

"Sure."

"Terrorist."

Eleni raised an eyebrow. "Saw that *interrogation*."

If Sariah noticed the tone or the eyebrow, she gave no indication. Instead, she zoomed in on orbiting troop readouts, brow furrowing as she did. "And?"

"And," Eleni said, stepping closer, "he wasn't lying."

Sariah let out a light laugh. "About the dog? No, I believed that."

"No. About us," Eleni said.

Sariah shook her head and cursed under her breath at some reading on the BT before turning back to Eleni. "Of course he was. They always do."

Eleni gave Sariah a look in response.

"You'd take the word of an Earther over me?" Sariah asked, crossing her arms again.

It took everything in her power not to roll her eyes. "Come on. This ain't a 'you versus him' thing. This is my job. I trained for this."

"And I didn't?"

"Fuck, Sariah, this ain't about you!"

The silence that filled the room as her voice rebounded off the resin walls was deafening. Every eye turned Eleni's direction, looks smearing from disapproving to outright anger.

All except Sariah. Her face had gone stony again, flat. And that meant she was *furious*.

"Sorry. The 'bots are fishing in my head and—"

Sariah held up a hand, cutting her off. "Listen," Sariah started, voice even as she enunciated every syllable as if she were addressing the colony, "you've been through a lot. It's understandable. So, if this bothers you so much, go interview him."

Relief flooded through Eleni. She'd thought it was going to be much worse. "Thanks—"

Again, Sariah held up a hand. "And after you speak with this terrorist, report to Doctor Jeffries for a psychological workup."

And there it was. "Sariah..."

"That's all, Director Mallias," Sariah said before turning back to the BT.

The dismissal hit her like an asteroid, but still, old habits kicked in. The chin went up, shoulders back, a snapped salute.

And then back into the cold she went... though she couldn't shake the thought that it was warmer on the tundra than it'd been under Sariah's glare.

Eleni replayed the conversation in her head as she walked. How'd it go so poorly? And why? But over that, in the gray snow still falling over the encampment, loss weighed her down.

Duncan. Victor. God, how many people had died today?

And why? It was one thing to fight over settlement rights, but to openly bomb *innocents*? That was a war crime, plain and simple. Eleni cast her eyes to the blue sky above, but no Protectorate frigates dropped out of FTL to sort this out. Hell, the BT hadn't shown any outgoing transmissions, not that she'd seen anyway.

So what the hell was going on?

Something was wrong here, Eleni knew it, but she couldn't figure out what the hell it was...

But she did have one lead. This Parker.

With a deep breath of frigid, acrid air, Eleni centered herself. She'd go see him and find out what he actually knew.

But first, she needed her clothes, and that meant talking to Jeffries again.

With renewed focus, Eleni stalked back to the medical tent.

She hated unknowns, despised mysteries, especially ones that claimed the lives of friends and family. But she'd unravel this one just like she had all the others. Eleni hadn't gotten where she was by leaving threads unplucked or answers unmined.

She would figure this out, no matter the cost.

She'd done it before.

"And I'll do it again," Eleni promised the ash floating on the wind.

Chapter 9
CERIAT

"This is getting old," Ceriat said as Jeret locked him back in the closet on the dropship.

Jeret grunted in response but said nothing else. Instead, the Spacer secured the straps around Ceriat's wrists and left. The door slid shut behind him, dropping Ceriat, and everything else, into pitch black shadow.

Ceriat's heart skipped a beat in the dark. Straining, he listened for the telltale signs of life beyond the walls, the hiss of recycling atmosphere. Anything.

The only sound came in the form of his heartbeat in his ears, the throb of blood pulsing in his veins.

"Hey!" Ceriat shouted, straining against his restraints just to hear them creak. "Turn the fucking light on!" The echo rattled around, distorting his voice in the close confines until it turned into little more than a buzz.

Still, no response.

Ceriat sucked in a tight breath. A buzzing filled his ears. Shadows danced in formless swirls.

"Breathe," Ceriat whispered to himself. "Breathe, you fucking coward."

He'd been here before. He'd be here again. For now, he just needed to breathe. Stay calm.

God, it's so fucking hot in here. Why is it hot in here? Panic arced across his chest, sent his limbs twitching in their restraints. Body heat. The room had warmed because he was in here and it was tiny.

Which might mean the space was airtight.

Jesus, if it was airtight, how long did he have? It couldn't be more than thirty minutes in a room this size. Was that right? He couldn't remember the math, the dimensions of this fucking room.

But what if it was?

Maybe twenty minutes before he started to suffocate. Sweat stung his eyes at the thought, at the memory of the last time. Thirty minutes before, gasping through hallucinations, he'd succumbed. Until the void had finally caught up with him.

Hot sweat soaked his forehead.

Not like this! Not like this!

Terror wrapped him in its close embrace, whispered wordless nothings into his ear, stroked his chest... muscles clenched in its wake.

Ceriat screamed.

A *whoosh.*

Sudden light blinded him, cutting off his terrified yell.

Ceriat squeezed his eyes shut, the sudden flare as welcome as the chill breeze that came with it. *Breathe.* Slowly, he sucked in a slow, deep breath. The rushing of blood in his ears faded. His heart steadied.

He opened his eyes and found himself staring at a tall Outer Rim security soldier. The helmet sent a worm of worry up his spine, just as intended. An emotionless mask of bronzed titanium alloy, the facemask's only disruption the red optics beneath a crafted, furrowed brow.

As foolish anxiety ebbed away, Ceriat took in the rest of the security soldier and quickly reassessed. The uniform was all wrong. There was no armor plating to speak of, or corporate logos anywhere. In fact, this soldier happened to be less geared up than even Jeret, which meant they weren't active in the orbital war. The only sign they had authority to enter this space was a key fob, a small rectangle of programmable aluminum hanging from their belt.

Also, one of the optics kept flickering, like there was a short in the helmet's wiring. There was something about the way they stood, too, the arms across a chest which, Ceriat noticed, showed some definition he finally realized were breasts instead of bulky body armor. And the cock of her head tickled him with recollection.

"Do I know you?" Ceriat asked. He licked his lips and swallowed spit down a throat raw from screaming. *Idiot.*

The soldier straightened, arms falling to her sides. "Parker?" The helmet muddled her voice, lending it a digital rasp meant to disguise the wearer.

Couldn't have easily identifiable security forces beating protestors, now, could you? Her voice still came out with a slightly higher pitched lilt, but otherwise, Ceriat wasn't sure he'd be able to match it to a person without more clues.

"Yeah. Ceriat Parker." He made to lift a hand, but the restraints kept him tight to the wall. With the lights on and the fear of suffocation gone, so too went the claustrophobia that'd attacked him in the dark. The chill coming through the door relaxed him. Sure, the air smelled like death, but it was someone else's death. An ache of guilt hit him then, but he shoved it into the pit of his stomach with the rest of it. It made for cramped company. "And you are?"

"Asking questions," she said, stepping into the small room with him. The soldier leaned against the far wall and crossed her arms and ankles. The message was clear: you're no threat. "Why you here?"

Ceriat rolled his eyes, but deep down, he had the distinct feeling he might be fucked. She had an accent to match her helmet, a Spacer lilt that softened the trailing consonants of each word into a muddle. If she'd been in security forces... still, better to see where it went. "Do you all not communicate or something?"

She made a noise in her throat. A chuckle? "Want the door shut, Earther? No problem, *piendo*."

"No," Ceriat said quickly. Too quickly. *Shit*. He tried to change the subject. "I'm not familiar with *piendo*."

"Buddy," she said, shrugging. She twirled her hand in the air. "Something like that." He swore she smiled beneath that helmet as she switched back to her original question. "Then... why you here?"

Fine. "Like I told your governor, I came here to activate the ETL tower. That's it. End of story."

"You know about us?"

The question caught him off guard, but still, he shook his head. "No. My brief didn't mention any settlement on this planet."

One second, she stood against the far wall. The next she was right there before him, mask centimeters from his face. He pulled back, smacking his head into the wall behind him, sending sparks across his vision.

This close, the mask showed signs it'd seen better days. Gouges covered it all, tearing silver lines into the protective outer coating. A long gash raked across the optical that kept flickering, tiny bits of the crystal there cracked from whatever had happened.

He expected her to do something. Hit him, throttle him, maybe growl in his face.

But she didn't. Instead, she stood there, chest rising and falling slowly, breath hissing inside the mask.

"Do you know Victor Mallias?" she asked after a lifetime.

Ceriat shook his head no.

"Say it."

"No," Ceriat said, voice barely more than a whisper. "I don't know him."

"Bullshit," she snapped back at him. "Should vac you now and save the trouble."

Fine. Time to control the narrative. Ceriat gritted his teeth and leaned closer to the emotionless mask until his nose nearly touched it. "Tough. It's the truth." He stayed there, desperately trying to see the woman beneath the mask, but it didn't work. "Who was he to you?" No movement, barely a whisper of breath. "Husband? Boyfriend?"

A wry chuckle. "Cute, Earther."

"Family then. Father?" No response, so he went closer. "A brother?" Ceriat said, smiling as she took a half step back. "That's it. You lost family, and you need someone to blame."

"Shut yer mouth, Parker." The synthesized voice couldn't hide the acid in her words.

He knew he was pushing it, but a flicker of light caught the key fob, and the seed of a plan stuck in his brain. "He probably deserved it."

Stars flashed. Copper filled his mouth.

Something tightened around his throat as the room spun, sparking red lights spinning, twirling alongside. A carbon-fiber plate in your head didn't do much against a concussion, despite what the Feeds liked to show; he just didn't have to worry about a skull fracture.

"You don't know me," she hissed, emphasizing each word. His vision filled with two red lights and brass. The cold, hard surface of the mask pressed into his face, squishing his nose to the side. "If ya did, you'd know to stop now afore you get hurt."

Ceriat squeezed his eyes closed, gathered his thoughts...

And laughed in her face.

She pulled him forward by the neck, then slammed him against the wall. Pain lashed up his back, but still he forced a persistent chuckle.

"Somethin' funny?" she asked.

Ceriat smiled at her, sure blood trickled along his teeth. "You're easy to rattle, Ms. Mallias."

Her face didn't change, but the shape of her shoulders did. They slumped despite the force of her hand around his throat intensifying. For the briefest of moments, he thought maybe he'd gone too far. After all, she wasn't wrong: he didn't know her, but he did know the Outer Rim security forces. Violent, yes. Murderers, usually not.

Usually.

They stood like that until, without another word, she released him, turned, and left, little more than an eddy of sweat-stained wind in her wake.

But she left the door open, and through it came light and air.

Ceriat's exhale came out as a harsh whine. That'd been quite the gamble.

Then he smiled and turned the key fob over in his right hand.

There wouldn't be much time before she realized what he'd done. Hell, even getting off this ship would be a challenge, but if he could do it—if he could get to the transmission station inside the ETL tower—perhaps he could get a message to the ETL. Get a rescue. Shit, maybe even get the Protectorate out here to straighten out this mess.

If it's still intact, anyway. He shook away the thought. One thing at a time.

First, he had a job to do. With that thought, Ceriat began cutting into the restraint with the sharp edge of the key fob. He might only have a few minutes.

Time to make every one of them count.

Chapter 10
ELENI

Despite everything, the people left in Arctic parted around Eleni. In her *manju*, they knew her. With her mask, she became someone else. Something else.

Then why'd she let Parker control her like that?

Vac-sealed idiot! Eleni cursed herself as she stormed through the encampment. That hadn't happened since training, since she was a goddamned kid. Fucking nanobots.

She sucked in a breath of warm, filtered air, the world dissolving around her in a haze of flickering digital vision. The beginnings of a headache flittered through her skull. Of course the broken optical was going to be a problem. Jeffries had said as much when she'd picked it up. Eleni had just been so happy to see it in one piece, malfunctioning or not.

But with it broken, that meant she hadn't been able to scan Parker properly. The heartbeat detector had kept flickering, pulse kept spiking. Just on visuals, he'd seemed earnest, but the *manju* said otherwise.

Or it'd fucked up.

She shook her head, booted feet pounding into the slush at her feet. No, she had. Naming Victor was a mistake, but she'd needed to know.

And look what good it'd done. Instead of answers, she'd let some self-righteous Earther dig into her mind, pluck at the strings of her weakness like a dissonant orchestra. All because she'd gotten impatient.

She wasn't ready to be back. Snow crunched beneath her feet, a chill wind dragged through her borrowed thermal uniform, pulling a shudder from her. Sariah had had it right. Her mind... it wasn't stable. Too much death. Death too close... it made her unreliable. Weak. And the nanobots didn't help.

A shadow fell long and cold over her. Eleni drew to a stop, just realizing the snow had come up past her calves. For the first time since she'd stormed out of the *Lucille*, she looked around her. Undisturbed tundra swept past, purpling as the red sun disappeared behind the eastern mountains. She spun to see how far she'd gone in her rage. To the south lay the encampment, to the west, the crater that'd once been Arctic. And beyond that, the crumbling ETL tower.

The temperature plummeted with the darkness. With a curse, she retraced her steps back to camp.

"Diagnostics," Eleni muttered. Her *manju* should've warned her about oncoming nightfall. Nights on Shiva were dangerous. Properly outfitted, you could survive, but dressed like her? She'd turn into a space popsicle before long.

Her *manju* flickered as if it was going to start diagnostics, but instead of alternating prompts, the system rebooted. The digital enhancements that'd layered over her normal vision disappeared. The shadows grew deeper, the trail before her disappearing in drifting snow and natural light.

Shit. Groaning, she picked up the pace, breaking into as fast a jog as the snow would allow. Out of instinct, her hand went to where her security key fob—recovered from Jeffries with her *manju*—swung. She'd had it pop off while chasing a thief once, and the chief had had her ass.

It wasn't there.

Eleni stopped, then scanned the ground for any sign of it. She hadn't been running before, so it must've disconnected in the last few steps. Cursing audibly, Eleni retraced her footprints in the snow while waiting for her *manju* to finish rebooting.

If she didn't find it, Sariah wouldn't just chastise her. Eleni would lose her position. God, she was already EVAing without a tether here; if she lost her security fob, too?

"Fuck!" Eleni shouted into another snow drift as she dug around with gloved hands.

By the time her vision lightened as the *manju* turned back on, she still hadn't found anything. An ache built in her stomach. She'd lost it. Lost it somewhere between the *Lucille* and here. That was too much distance to scan, too far to retrace without anyone figuring out what she was doing.

Groaning, Eleni grabbed the sides of her *manju* as she pivoted, ordering the system to scan her tracks for indications of divots or fallen objects. Besides a few chunks of ice, nothing popped up. She'd lost it. Lost it in the encampment. Lost it on the *Lucille*. Lost it—

She froze, hands still on her head.

Parker.

He'd pushed her during the interrogation. Why? There'd been no reason. He wouldn't get anything out of angering her. There'd been no strategy to it, but she'd just thought he'd been trying to get under her skin. To piss her off.

But why?

Eleni grabbed at the place where her fob should be, then ground her teeth. "Son of a bitch."

He'd stolen it. Since she hadn't heard an alarm, that meant he'd probably escaped already, and it was her fault.

Eleni screamed again, then took off for the encampment at a run.

The right thing to do was report this to Gareth, let him know Parker was free.

But if she did that, she'd lose her position for sure. And if she wasn't Director Mallias, who was she?

No, she'd fix this herself. She'd find him, get her key fob back, break his goddamned legs, then report to Jeffries.

In that order.

Focused for the first time since the missile fell, Eleni ran.

She had a terrorist to catch.

Chapter 11
CERIAT

Ceriat huddled beneath the heavy thermal jacket he'd taken on his way out of the dropship. Sure, it happened to be a bit too big in the arms, but it'd still been a blessing, one he intended to take advantage of. God knew he couldn't be caught walking around this place in an ETL flight suit. For the first time since the *Sparrow* lost power, Ceriat was thankful he'd decided against a full exosuit. No jacket would've been able to hide the forest green of those ETL monstrosities. As it was, covering the ETL logo—a towering green tree with roots that spread across the bottom and writhed up around a white, circular symbol—was hard enough.

He made his way toward where the shattered terraforming tower still sparkled in the last vestiges of daylight, eyes down and shoulders slumped. No sense drawing more attention to himself than necessary. After all, he hadn't found any replacement gear for his lower body, nothing that could keep him warm in this climate anyway. Instead, he'd smeared ash along his legs to cover the distinctive green slashes around the thighs.

He hoped that'd be enough.

As it was, he still hadn't lit on a single plan for actually getting to the tower to access the ETL dedicated comms there. He'd taken a risk on that damned prison ship and tried accessing their communication system using the key fob he'd taken, but all he'd gotten was strange hissing static. ETL comms should still work, since they had dedicated FTL hubs, but the static meant Gatewood must be signal jamming the settlement, if not the entire planet. That, of course, was a bad sign.

If Gatewood thought these people were gone, they wouldn't be jamming anything. It also begged the question: it'd been hours since the bomb dropped; what were they waiting for? Ceriat shook that thought away as he walked. Not his problem. He had a job to do, and right now that meant calling ETL command and reporting... this. *That's all I can do*, he told himself, whether it was true or not.

To keep his mind off the choice, Ceriat took in his surroundings. Around him, the shouting and crying had mostly died down as night fell over the encampment, as if silence paired well with the frigid darkness. The roar of portable furnaces was few and far between, though smaller traditional fires dotted either side of the makeshift trail he wound his way through.

Greasy black smoke spiraled away from the flames, carrying an acrid, poison bouquet of chemicals and carbon. He'd been caught unaware at the sight at first, but that surprise only lasted as long as it took him to see forms huddled around those flames, coughing into the oncoming night. Better to risk choking than die frozen. He could get behind that.

Despite a few welcoming calls as he walked, Ceriat didn't stop to warm himself at a fire, even though the chill had begun working its way through the jacket.

"Least my legs are warm," Ceriat muttered, casting a quick glance over his shoulder to see if anyone was following him yet.

In the flickering light of a fire barrel, the freighter that'd picked him up sat several hundred meters behind him. A wave of relief flooded over him. No one had come out yet, or at least no one had started screaming about his departure yet. That meant he had time and a chance. Now he just—

"Well, shit."

Just as he turned back around, a familiar form stormed her way up the stairs to the dropship. Mallias did not look pleased.

That meant she knew about the key fob.

Despite the panic attempting to writhe its way out of his stomach, a tiny bit of amusement threaded through him at the realization. *Wait until she realizes I took this jacket, too.* A small grin pulled at his lips as he turned away from Ms. Mallias.

She'd be furious.

Best be getting out of here, then.

With that thought driving him forward at a more aggressive pace, Ceriat resumed his trek out of the encampment. He neared the edge of the temporary hovels thrown up in the wake of the destruction of their settlement and set about searching for transportation of some sort.

There. Set deep in frigid shadows stood a snowtracker buried under a drift of its namesake. Grinning, Ceriat took a quick look around to make sure no one was watching him and, when it appeared clear, jogged over to the machine.

He'd never used one before, but the snowtracker—essentially a tank tread with a seat and steering column attached to it— looked easy enough to use. With a few awkward swipes, Ceriat wiped most of the snow off the seat and around the vehicle. Carefully, he mounted it and grabbed the handles he assumed steered it.

Nothing happened. "Um..." Ceriat squinted in the darkness, looking for something resembling an activation switch or the like, but nothing jumped out at him. There wasn't even a standard touch panel interface. Maybe voice commands? "Start." Nothing. "Ignition?"

Footsteps sloshed in slush behind him. Ceriat jumped off the snowtracker in one hop, then fell into the snow like an idiot. When he pulled himself to his feet, another man stood a few meters away, carrying a heavy pipe like he knew how to use it.

Firelight behind him made it impossible to make out much besides the heavy, mundane weapon he brandished.

Still, Ceriat put his hands up. Mundane didn't mean non-lethal.

"Need something, *piendo*?" the man asked, taking a step closer to Ceriat.

Mind spinning, Ceriat let out a grunt. "Yeah, just need to head out to the blast zone."

The pipe hit the man's gloved palm with a heavy thwack. "Now? At night?" Now that he was closer, and Ceriat's vision had adjusted a bit, the man's face had more definition, enough to see bushy eyebrows arc with a furrowed brow. A heavily bearded face twitched as a single word formed on his lips. "Why?"

Good fucking question. A dozen ideas flashed through his mind. Reconnaissance! No. They wouldn't, not yet. Salvage? At night? No. Then it hit him. Grief. He pictured Gerry, remembered the way it had felt when the news came in that he'd died in FTL. Ceriat thought back to the night in Basic when Sergeant Henderson had pulled him from his bunk to tell Ceriat his mother had died suddenly from a brain aneurysm. If he'd been there, she'd have made it. Aneurysms didn't kill anyone anymore. They weren't supposed to, anyway, not with immediate medical care, but she'd been alone in the house with him gone to training. No one had found her for a week.

It was a closed casket funeral.

"Asked you a question."

"Family," Ceriat whispered, vision blurring as he pulled every bit of emotion from those moments to here. Now. "I'm going to look for my family."

For a moment, Ceriat thought the man was going to start hammering away with the pipe anyway. But then he sighed, the weapon falling to his side. "Can't wait until morning?"

Ceriat met the man's eyes, searched for them in the darkness. He couldn't see shit. "No. If they're still alive, I can't wait."

They stood there for a long while and, moment by moment, Ceriat felt the façade slipping. *I'm fucked. He knows. If I charge—*

"Henry," the man said suddenly, stepping forward.

"Ceriat," Ceriat replied, then immediately cursed himself for using his real name.

Henry gave him a nod, then jerked a thumb behind him. "Let me suit up, and we'll go."

Relief hit first, followed swiftly by uncertainty. "That's not necessary, I can go it alone—"

"Nonsense," Henry said, setting his pipe down next to the lean-to. "We all lost *famding* today. Least I can do is help close on yours."

Ceriat stopped short of asking Henry to explain what that meant. With the clipped way these people talked, he was having a hard time keeping up. Luckily, he got the gist. "Really, you don't need to help," Ceriat said, damned near begging. *Please don't fucking help me.* "I'd like to do this alone."

Henry turned back to him, a big eyebrow shooting up. "And let you take Bertha into that slurry? Not happening." The big man gave a smile that was more a movement of facial hair than anything else. "Be right back. Need the key."

Ceriat tried to say something else, but then Henry was gone around the corner, leaving him alone. He turned back to the snowtracker—Bertha, he guessed. Henry had said something about a key. A quick glance beneath the handlebars revealed the archaic ignition mechanism. What kind of person used a key nowadays?

A smart one, he guessed. Even if Ceriat had had time, he didn't know the first thing about hacking those, or whatever the proper terminology was. Did they still call it hacking?

As it was, he didn't have time to process the thought. Henry came back around, wearing a heavy thermal suit, and carrying two helmets. He handed one to Ceriat and proceeded to somehow shove all his own hair inside it without obstructing the faceplate.

Ceriat, however, just held his and stared at the waving flames in the glass.

"Helmet up," Henry said as he straddled Bertha.

"Is there a mask or something I can wear?" Ceriat asked, licking his lips. His heart thudded in his ears at the thought of shoving his head inside this tiny space.

"What? No," Henry responded, voice muffled as he fiddled with the ignition. "Mask don't protect your ears."

"But—" Ceriat was interrupted by a grinding sound coming from Bertha, followed by a low wail as she stuttered to life. A moment later, the arrhythmic roar steadied into a steady rumble. It was a sound Ceriat hadn't heard in years. "Is this carbon fueled?"

Henry nodded, but if he responded, it was lost in the roar of the engine. The big man tapped his head again and gestured to Ceriat.

Again, Ceriat stared at the helmet. It wasn't airtight, and this wasn't space. "It's just a stupid helmet," he said, trying to psyche himself up. "Just put it on."

Still, despite Henry's confused stare, his hands didn't lift the black helmet with the visor. Couldn't. It was like his arms belonged to someone else, and that person would rather freeze to death on the tundra than enclose his head in one of these again.

He couldn't do this.

And he was just about to tell Henry as much when a sound caught his ear. Shouting.

He tore his gaze away from the helmet and took a step out from behind the lean-to so he could see back toward the dropship.

There, stalking through the crowd, were two ruby eyes.

Staring right at him.

Mallias. Her arm swept up to point and she dropped into a run.

Fear swept through him, and before he realized it, his hearing went dull, vision blurred as the helmet became snug around his head. Then without another thought, Ceriat hopped onto the back of Bertha.

Henry gave him a thumbs up, a puzzled look still in his eyes. Ceriat smiled and returned the gesture.

With that, Henry hauled on the throttle and Bertha roared forward over a hump of snow before angling westward toward the crater and Ceriat's true goal, the ETL tower. With sudden panic, Ceriat wrapped his arms around Henry's thick waist for dear life. He swore the big man chuckled. Strange for a Spacer.

As the wind roared in his ears, Ceriat risked a look back toward the encampment.

There, sparkling in the dark, two crimson flames followed them until Henry took them down a hill, and Mallias disappeared from view.

For now.

Chapter 12
ELENI

"Henry, ya stupid son of a bitch," Eleni muttered as the fat, old bastard cranked his ancient snowtracker out toward the blast zone.

Big heart in that guy. Too big. Always helping idiots do idiotic things. He and Jeret were a match made in heaven.

Back on Hobelt, when she'd first started working as an enforcer, Eleni would look the other way at a missing SourcePak, because she knew Henry had stolen it to feed some kids. But this time? He'd taken a damned thief—a terrorist—on a joyride into the tundra.

With *her* key fob. Her future. Worry and rage warred in her chest as she watched the spiraling snow from Bertha disappear from view in the last vestiges of dusk's purple haze.

How had everything gone so wrong so quickly? Eleni sucked in a breath of recycled air and let it out in an attempt to steady her heartbeat, to gather her wits about her before she did something just as stupid as Henry. Still, she stared into the darkening distance, to the blackened smear that'd once been Arctic. Already, lighter streaks muddied the blast zone as Shiva reached out snowy fingers to reclaim her land. If it snowed soon, all the debris, the proof they'd once had a colony, would disappear beneath drifting powder.

And with it, her home would truly be gone, the grand Spacer experiment lost in careless snow, trapped out of view by the icy tundra. An ache accompanied the thought. It very nearly dragged Eleni to her knees, but somehow she remained upright, staring westward.

"Get out your head." A simple memory in Victor's voice. "You can't fix anything if you don't get out your own way."

Eleni's face warmed, vision blurred. She sucked in another breath, then another, until each intake of air became smooth and steady, the shudder lacing everything moments before disappearing with the sun.

The chill of a Shiva night did its best to encroach on her thermal suit, but the unit kicked on internal heaters, easily keeping the ambient temperature in the suit a toasty 13^C. Another breath in, another out.

She needed a plan. Contact Henry? Probably not. The old bastard kept his tech simple and only turned on his radio in an emergency—if he'd even remembered to bring one.

Then what? Chase them? To where? Eleni pulled up the lowlight rendering on her *manju* and stared into the west. What in the void could Parker be looking for out there? She scanned the horizon, taking in a dozen clumps of unrecognizable debris in the shadow of the ETL tower.

She kicked herself when she saw it. Of course, he was going for the tower. Even collapsing, it still stood, which was a far cry from every other building out there.

Worry filled her chest at the realization. Henry wouldn't have taken Parker out to the tower. That meant Parker had lied about his destination.

Henry was in danger.

"Idiot," Eleni muttered, watching as the snowtracker tracks disappeared beneath a drift of snow from a sudden gust of wind.

Now, she wasn't just trying to save her own ass, she had to save Henry's.

When it was just her career on the line, running solo had made a lot of sense. But now? With Henry in the crosshairs? She should report back, tell Sariah about the missing key fob, about the interrogation and how she'd lost control of it.

That Parker was on his way to the tower, with oblivious Henry in tow, because of her failures. She didn't know she was grinding her teeth until the sound ached its way into her ears, echoed through her head. The right thing to do was radio Sariah.

And lose her appointment. She hesitated... but her pride wasn't worth a man's life.

Cursing, Eleni brought up the Security comm channel. "Mallias calling for the governor."

The only answer she received came in the form of hissing static. Eleni swallowed a ball of anxiety and repeated the call. "Mallias calling for the governor's mansion. Is anyone there?"

Still nothing. That was strange.

With increasing confusion, Eleni tried several other channels, only to find the same wordless static coating them all. That didn't make any sense...

Eleni turned back to the encampment, jogged her way to the first group of survivors she found. Despite thinking she had a near encyclopedic knowledge of all the settlers in Arctic, she didn't know these.

Two men and a younger teenage child surrounded a short metal fire pit. Blackened masses melted and bubbled inside the fire, the acrid stink of burning plastics filling the air. One of them, clearly a Spacer, given his height, which was visible even hunched over the fire, turned as she approached.

His look took in her thermal suit and *manju*, face transitioning from welcoming to distrust as quickly as a slap, and just as effective. "What do you want?"

Eleni held her tongue, but just barely. Since landing on Shiva, she'd been treated with respect befitting her office. This? This behavior hadn't existed this morning. But maybe she deserved it? After all, it'd been on her watch the settlement was destroyed.

Thoughts for another time. Eleni cleared her throat and stepped closer to the fire, holding her hands out as if she could feel the heat through her gloves.

The other man, smaller in stature, but still taller than the average Earther, frowned as she closed the distance.

"Farouk asked you a question."

"Be polite," the teen said, brown eyes taking Eleni in quickly before looking away. "This is a director."

The first man, Farouk, grunted. In the flicker of flames, the distrust in his eyes stood out like crystals buried in shadowy pools. "Question stands."

Eleni pulled her hands away from the flame. This was going well. "I'm trying to connect to the comm network, but all I'm getting is—"

"Static?" Farouk interrupted before barking a humorless laugh. "No shit. Comms are down. How the fuck do you not know that?"

The teen squirmed, "Dad, stop."

"Why?" Farouk demanded, face twisting as he stared down his child. "They were supposed to protect us!" A finger jabbed in Eleni's direction, the harsh firelight highlighting the crisscrossing crimson lines of cracked skin there. "*She* was supposed to protect us." Farouk spat and turned to Eleni, words stuck behind his teeth as the other man grabbed his hand and stroked it as if trying to soothe a wounded animal. Still, he wasn't done. "You all can step out an airlock for all I care. Every last one of ya." Farouk spit at her feet despite the soothing murmurs coming from the other man and the quiet fury emanating from the kid.

Eleni swallowed a rock, waited for it to hit her stomach, and sent it writhing in discomfort. She wanted to howl back at him that she'd lost people in this, too, that she'd almost died in the explosion, but instead, and for the first time in her life, words stuck in her throat.

"Sorry to bother you." They weren't the right words, not even close, but they came out, and with that, she stepped away from the fire.

Eleni ground her teeth, hands balling in and out of fists. With comms down, she'd have to head back to Sariah on foot. It was the right move, officially, but even running, she wouldn't get back to the governor until Parker was long gone, and Henry's life likely forfeit.

Turning back to Farouk and his family, Eleni let out a sigh. She'd let them down. Let everyone down. She wouldn't let Henry down, too.

Goal clear in her mind, Eleni got back to work. After all, she didn't know how much time Henry had left, not with a terrorist ready to kill him at a moment's notice.

No, she'd have to do this herself. Alone.

First, she needed a ride.

She realized with a smile, since her position was forfeit anyway, she had just the thing.

Chapter 13
CERIAT

Ceriat's teeth chattered inside the helmet, though with the slashing sleet and snow cascading against its visor, he couldn't tell. Not with the constant assault on his visor and the titter-tat of ice filling his ears. The biting cold of Shiva's night alongside whipping winds as Henry guided Bertha through the deepening crater that'd once been a settlement left Ceriat numb from the neck down. Even his thermal pants struggled to keep him warm in this bitter cold. Then again, some of that numbness likely came from the decisions he had to make soon. Because at some point, Henry would stop driving blindly for Ceriat and demand a location.

He'd bought himself some time early on when they'd stopped at the edge of the crater before diving into it.

"Whereabouts d'you live?" Henry had asked, voice muted and muffled behind the helmet.

The kindness and empathy in his eyes belied the tough exterior established by the heavy beard and thick arms. Even in the dark, Ceriat had seen it in the shrug of Henry's shoulders, the way his voice rose and fell.

It'd made the guilt gnawing at Ceriat's stomach howl in glee. "The western edge, nearest the tower," Ceriat had lied, pointing in the distance and happy the darkness helped blend away the doubt twisting his words.

Henry had simply nodded and taken off, cutting through the center of the crater as if it weren't littered with the ashes of the dead. Why Henry hadn't taken the lip of the crater instead, Ceriat didn't know, and certainly wasn't able to ask. The trip had been fraught with quick turns and sudden stops. Broken frames of hardier buildings that'd somehow remained in the wake of the detonation sometimes exploded from the shadows, but Henry's quick thinking and familiarity with Bertha saved them each time.

Intellectually, Ceriat had known what the payload on that missile had been. He'd seen the flash, after all. Only one payload did that—a fusion bomb. Centuries ago, they'd been outlawed for use in any sort of combat, but with the advent of minimalized detonation radii, the ban had been partially lifted.

Ceriat had plenty of experience with this tech from his time in the Protectorate. Too much. With down-to-the-meter detonations, an army could take out something as small as a convoy or, according to regulations, as large as a small town. He'd used one on Shaal-Tu. That was when he'd found out the Protectorate had a different definition of "small town" than he.

And just like then, now, driving through this mess, steel skeletons shining in Bertha's headlights, Ceriat couldn't understand why the ordnance existed. These people hadn't had a chance. Once the missile had entered the atmosphere, it'd been over, like ancient Pompeii watching as ash and stone dropped from fiery Vesuvius.

Honestly, how so many of the settlers had survived was a mystery unto itself.

Ceriat's thoughts were interrupted as the ground angled upward beneath Bertha. Her engines roared as the edge of the crater steepened. Ceriat squeezed tighter to Henry, lest he get tossed off the back by the periodic bit of debris crushed beneath Bertha's treads.

With a heavy throttle, Bertha shot into the air, then slammed back onto the icy stone of the tundra above the crater, leaving Ceriat's heart somewhere amongst the bones of the settlement behind.

But he was already searching ahead for his destination. Somewhere beyond the reach of Bertha's headlights lay the remnants of the ETL tower and, he hoped, a way to get help. With Shiva's sun long ago set behind the eastern mountains, the tower blended into a black, moonless sky.

Henry let off the throttle and came around, putting the tower behind them. At least, Ceriat thought it was behind. Carefully, Henry angled the snowtracker until the headlights shot out over the edge of the crater, then cut the engine.

The sudden silence left Ceriat deaf as he released Henry and staggered to his feet on numbed legs. After a short adjustment period, the wind whipping at his borrowed jacket resumed its low howl, and with it came Henry's voice.

"We're here," Henry said as he lifted the visor of his helmet. In the sterile glow of the headlights, ice crystals shone on his mustache and beard around his mouth. "I'm sorry, friend."

Ceriat nodded, stepping closer to the ledge, as if truly searching for a home in the mess below. He gave the facemask a thankful flip. With the sting of cold, the anxiety working away in his belly retreated a step. The freezing chill wasn't welcome at all, but the sight below him sent any discomfort howling away.

"Jesus, it's all gone," he muttered, real awe lacing each word.

There were several hundred survivors back at the camp, at least in his rushed estimation. At first, Ceriat had assumed that'd been everyone, that they'd been evacuated or the like. But either the payload on the fusion bomb had been overbuilt—which was unlikely—or there'd been closer to a thousand people in this settlement.

Why wasn't I notified of this? Ceriat thought again, staring at it all with morbid fascination. Everything he'd found out about this settlement was in stark contrast to what he'd expected. Something this large on a terraforming target should've had a detailed write-up alongside the planet breakdown, regardless of its proximity to the ETL tower. But to put one this close and leave that out of his notes?

He couldn't begin to fathom how this oversight had happened, though that word stuck in his head. *Oversight.* He sighed.

"You seen enough?"

Henry shocked Ceriat out of his reverie. He turned to where the big man sat comfortably atop Bertha, gaze locked on the crater below. Ceriat balled his hands into fists. This man didn't deserve what he was about to do to him. Henry had done nothing but offer a helping hand, and Ceriat was going to repay that by knocking him out? Leaving him for dead out here?

But what choice did he have? "Almost," Ceriat said, closing the distance between himself and Henry slowly, dreading what was coming. He looked past the big man. "ETL tower is that way?" he asked, pointing into the solid black.

"Eh?" Henry turned to look behind him. "Somewhere abouts."

This was it. Henry distracted, Ceriat with the leverage to knock him over Bertha.

All he had to do was charge.

But he didn't.

"Why?" Henry finished, turning back, breath misting in Bertha's lights.

Ceriat sighed and took off the helmet. The chill sent needles across his skin, but the relief outweighed the cold. Quickly, he closed the distance and handed the helmet back to Henry, who refused it with a furrowed brow.

Grimacing, Ceriat held onto it, then made his way in the direction Henry had indicated. The time had passed. and with it, any chance of motorized transportation to the tower. Maybe a younger version of himself could have done it. Maybe that faithful soldier back on Shaal-Tu would've taken out the man who'd helped him selflessly, only to leave him for dead.

But that wasn't him. Not anymore.

"Hey, brother, where you going?" Henry's voice followed Ceriat into the shadows. The pounding of feet alerted him to the big man's proximity, so Ceriat turned, planting his own in a tuft of snow. Henry skidded to a stop at the sudden change in posture. The big man's hands went up, face twisting in suspicion. "What's your damage, man?"

For a moment, he considered lying. It'd be easier, that was for sure. But... fuck. "I'm heading to the tower," Ceriat said, cursing himself all the while. "Gonna call for help."

Henry let out a quick snort. "You can't call from there. Even if it wasn't snapped in half, I thought you needed ETL credentials to get in..."

Ceriat shrugged the admission.

Henry's face changed, shoulders squared up. "You lied to me?"

"Listen—"

"No!" Henry barked, his kind voice morphing into something deep, threatening. "You don't have family here? Do you?"

"No."

"None?" Henry asked, voice cracking, changing pitch. Begging.

"None."

Henry shook his head but didn't otherwise move. "Then who are you?"

"I'm an ETL tech," Ceriat said, despite the doubt gnawing at his gut. If this went sideways, Henry wouldn't be left out here to die. One of them would just be dead. "I dropped out of FTL into that shitshow off-planet. Some of your people found my disabled ship and—"

"ETL tech?" Henry asked, one gloved mitt rubbing the top of his helmet. "You're the terrorist they snagged?"

Ceriat raised his chin at the word, heat flooding his face despite the chill. "I'm no terrorist."

But the large man wasn't listening. Instead, a string of

muttered curses filled the void between them. "I'm so fucking stupid."

"Henry—"

"No!" Henry snapped, jabbing a finger in Ceriat's direction. He paced as if amping himself up. It was a sight Ceriat had seen many times over the years, usually in the mirror. "You shut yer mouth."

Ceriat did, for a moment. Since entering this damned system, everything had gone wrong. Why'd he think this would go any differently?

Grimacing, Ceriat played the only card he had left. "I'm going to the tower."

"I said shut up."

Ceriat ignored him. "I'm going to radio for *help*, both for me and for your settlement."

At that Henry stopped cursing, though the tenseness in his shoulders still reeked of aggression. "How?"

"I'll call for the Protectorate," Ceriat said, hoping it was enough, "report on what Gatewood did here."

For a moment, it looked like Henry might still attack him, but then the fight went out of the big man, and he deflated like a balloon.

Old instincts screamed at Ceriat. *Attack!* they yelled as Henry let down his guard. *Take the snowtracker, complete the mission.*

But he didn't.

"Fine," Henry said, voice heavy. The wind picked up, plucking at his next words. "Good luck. Bastard." And with that, the big man turned away. He mounted Bertha and, without looking behind, the snowtracker roared away.

Ceriat watched the pools of light from Bertha's headlamps follow the long path along the upper rim of the crater. It wouldn't take long for him to get back to camp, maybe thirty minutes.

Should be enough time to access the tower at least.

So much for not freezing his balls off.

With a sigh, Ceriat faced the darkness to the west. Now that the lights were gone, the broken spear that'd once been this planet's hope was rendered stark against the navy blue of the night sky, the lack of strange stars lending it more form than anything else. It couldn't be more than a klick away. Easy. With that thought came a gust of wind that broke his balance, made him brace against it or risk being tumbled across the tundra.

Right, easy.

He'd need to wear the helmet, he realized. Without it, or some other head covering, there was no way he'd make it without risking frostbite. As it was, the chill in the air made icicles in his nostrils if he breathed too quickly. So despite himself, Ceriat put the helmet back on, visor cracked, but down, and started walking. His attention was focused on closing the distance between himself and the tower. With the chill wind wrapping up and around the covering, his anxiety eased.

This wasn't a sealed exosuit helm. Just a fancy hat.

At least, that's what he told himself.

It mostly worked.

Wind whipped and whirled as he went, constantly threatening to trip him as he stepped blindly into short drifts of snow. Without any light, the world was cast in grayscale, each long finger of grainy white stretching infinitely into nothingness. Between each stack of snow, long stretches of rocky tundra tricked him into thinking the way would be easy, that each step on those rocks would have grip.

Turned out he was wrong. The rocky sections, especially at night, hid a thin layer of ice that stretched across everything. After his second unceremonious fall, Ceriat began a longer zig-zag pattern, stalking through the drifts to keep his balance.

That extended his travel time, however, and by the time he stalked up to the base of the tower, his flight suit could no longer keep the chill at bay. The jacket, lacking a power supply, sat heavy on numb shoulders.

Still, teeth chattering, Ceriat smiled. A sharp flare of pain lit his upper lip at the motion, leaving a trickle of copper in his mouth. He doubted the heating system inside the tower was still intact, otherwise settlers would've figured out how to take refuge there, but just getting out of the damned wind would be a godsend.

The base of the tower was easily forty meters in diameter. Like most ETL towers, it had once had somewhere between thirty and fifty stories, with spines along the exterior, depending on the habitability of the planet. The less habitable, the more gear was needed to terraform the planet. This one appeared to have been on the shorter side, no doubt due to the abundance of frozen water, breathable atmosphere, and the comparatively warm temperature. Still, there was a drastic difference between seeing a thirty-story building snapped in half from a distance, and getting a nice, up close and personal view.

The structure had been massive, but with the explosion, it rose only ten or fifteen meters above him before disappearing into inky darkness. Before the sun had fallen, he'd gotten a good look, though. It'd broken off a few stories from the base, then collapsed to the west, in the direction of the shockwave from the fusion bomb.

Just then, a whip of wind whistled through the debris, sending something creaking like a blast door about to give. Ceriat turned his gaze skyward, trying desperately to identify the source of the sound. After a moment, he had to admit it'd be easier to figure out what *didn't* look like it was about to collapse on him.

Luckily for him, the comm panel should be on the second floor. The big question was, did it still work? Ceriat didn't know anything about the engineering that went into these things, just the floorplan and how to make said tech work after it was already built. Did the comm center need special power? Did it use the tower as an antenna? Fuck if he knew.

Rubbing his arms against a perpetual shiver that'd set in over the past thirty minutes, Ceriat stalked up to where the main access door should be. He cursed. Scattered around the base of the tower were twisted pylons and shattered polycarbonate shielding.

In the darkness, finding his way through that mess would be damned near impossible. Still, Ceriat stepped up to the wreckage. He didn't dare tug on anything yet, but he scanned the lighter areas, hoping for some indication the door was still intact, or at the very least, accessible.

It was lucky he'd been looking, because if he hadn't, he'd have missed the flash of light. Spinning, Ceriat had just enough time to jump off the wreckage before a plasma bolt disintegrated the pylon he'd been perched upon a moment earlier.

He slammed into the hard, icy rock of the tundra and slid a meter, rough edges shattering like broken glass as he skidded across. Not for the first time, Ceriat was thankful for the heavy gloves and flight suit.

That hopefulness didn't last.

Scanning behind him, he caught sight of two flames a dozen meters away, and beyond that, some darkened machine outlined by the reddish hue coming off the encampment beyond. He didn't have time to figure out what the machine was or how it'd gotten here without him knowing.

What he knew was, Mallias had found him, and she had a gun.

A hissing whine filled the air a split second before the night blossomed into silver light, blinding him. Still, Ceriat rolled, hoping and praying he'd gone in a direction the enforcer hadn't anticipated. A flash of warmth off to his left gave him the good news just before heat ripped into his left arm.

Cursing, Ceriat rolled again, coming to his knees as Mallias reloaded the plasma rifle. A quick glance showed she'd nicked him, carving a hole through the thermal jacket he'd stolen back at the encampment. It burned like hell, but whether that was from the plasma or the freezing air attacking his skin, he didn't know.

Mallias snapped the plasma rifle up, the same hiss filling the air again as she pointed it at his chest.

"Wait!" Ceriat shouted, snapping his visor open. He raised his arms above his head. His shoulder complained at the motion alongside his always angry hip, but better pain than dead. "I'm just trying to help!"

For a long moment, he was sure she'd pull the trigger... but despite the barrel never wavering, she didn't.

"By breaking out? Stealing?" she asked, her voice somehow even more artificial than usual amongst the hiss of the wind.

"No one believed me," Ceriat shouted back, hoping his words made it to her over the howling. "Your governor would've strung me up first chance she got. Anything to keep you all tame and quiet." He didn't know if the last part was true, but damn if it hadn't felt like the governor was looking for a scapegoat during his interrogation.

The pause before Mallias responded told him he might be right. "Maybe," she said, getting closer, the barrel unwavering. "And my key fob? That one not you, either?"

Ceriat flashed a smile that probably wasn't visible outside this damned helmet. "That one I am sorry about—" Mallias lifted the pulse rifle, finger wrapping around the trigger, "—but I needed to get out so I can get help."

"Help yourself, you mean," Mallias snapped, digitized voice a deep growl that sent a shiver down his spine.

"Help everyone," Ceriat replied. He gestured at the remnants of the tower behind him. "Second floor, there's a comm station. I can call for help, get the Protectorate involved."

Mallias didn't move, though the nervous energy twitching in her shoulders made Ceriat wonder why she hadn't already shot him. "Comms are down. Jammed."

"Not this," Ceriat said quickly. "ETL towers use their own FTL comm buoys. Different signals, different jamming tech." He hoped.

"And what ya know about jamming tech?" Mallias asked. She came closer, barely more than two meters away.

Ceriat smelled the ozone coming off the plasma rifle. He didn't like it. "I don't know much about the tech," he admitted, swallowing a ball of anxiety he hoped didn't choke him to death, "but I know ETL is a neutral party here." When she didn't respond, he lowered his arms. "Let me *try* at least."

Mallias closed the distance, but stopped well enough away that even if he'd been at peak physical shape still—which he wasn't—there was no way in hell he'd have a chance of disarming her. "What's to stop ya from holoing Gatewood like a good li'l slave and marking us for another drop?"

Ceriat stared at the emotionless mask, at the steady pulse rifle for a moment. *Fuck it.* Heart in his throat, he crawled to his feet, plasma burn complaining the entire way. "I don't know," Ceriat said. The mist of his breath rimmed Mallias in an otherworldly halo. "Nothing?" The plasma rifle shifted. Hummed. "But I'm not going to. What happened here—" Ceriat looked past her, to the dark smear that'd once been a settlement, "—it's a war crime. I should know."

"How's that?"

Ceriat shrugged. *I made a career out of it*, he almost said, but he didn't. "I've seen it before."

Mallias stared hard at him for a long moment. He really wished he could see through her mask, get an idea of what was going on beneath the titanium alloy.

Time stretched long enough, Ceriat opened his mouth to say something just as Mallias dropped the rifle barrel so it no longer pointed at him.

Relief flooded through his veins. "Thanks."

"Don't thank me yet," Mallias said, gesturing with the rifle for him to move toward the tower. "Ya might still get shot."

Ceriat shrugged and made his way back to the tower. "Fair. But once we get this debris moved, it should only take a few—" The laugh surprised him. He spun, head cocked to the side, only to find the stoic enforcer staring once again at him. "What's funny?"

"'We.'"

Brow furrowed, Ceriat looked between her and the pile of

debris several times before it dawned on him. "Wait, you're not going to help?"

In response, Mallias shrugged, then sat cross-legged on a stony section of the ground. She laid her plasma rifle across her knees. "Nah."

"Really?"

"Mhm."

"Well, that's just fucking great," Ceriat muttered, shuddering as another chill wind streaked across the flat tundra. "This jacket doesn't have a power supply, you know."

"Should've stolen better, then," Mallias replied. Was that a smile in her voice? "Best get to work. It's void cold out here."

"Really?" Ceriat asked one more time, reality settling on his shoulders like buckets of shit. "You're serious?"

"Chop, chop." Mallias waved him forward with a gloved hand.

Ceriat turned back to the tower, to the mass of destruction between himself and the doorway. He'd freeze to death before clearing this. Right? Already, a deep chill had taken root in his chest, in his fingers. Needles coated his cheeks, the skin around the bit of burnt flesh still exposed to the air. This was madness. Insanity.

"It's gonna get a lot colder tonight, man. It ain't gonna clear itself."

Grimacing, Ceriat approached the tower. She was right. He hated it, but even if she weren't here, he'd be doing it anyway.

Time to stop bitching and get down to business.

He made his way to the first section of twisted metal he *might* be able to move on his own. As he stepped up to the bent steel, a patch of ice sent him flying, weightless, before hammering into the earth with a thud.

Stars danced in his vision; pain flared throughout his limbs.

Just above the rush of wind and blood in his ears, a robotic laugh filled the night.

In response, a single word slipped from his lips. "Fuck."

Chapter 14
ELENI

Eleni hadn't actually planned on watching Parker move the mass of metal alone. It'd been a power play, something to set the terms of their limited partnership.

But goddamn if it wasn't funny to watch. It'd kept her here, seated on the ground like a child, instead of in the artificial warmth provided by the *Lucille*'s dropship, which she'd commandeered to chase Parker.

For the last thirty minutes or so, Ceriat had successfully moved three or four chunks of debris and, in the process, fallen a half-dozen times. Every time Eleni started to feel sorry for him, he lost his footing or slipped and careened into the darkness, arms flailing like a kitten learning to move in zero-g. Unfortunately for him, gravity always dragged him back to the ground in a cursing heap. Or she assumed he was cursing. The wind had picked up into a howling buffet that drowned out most sound.

Quite the boon for her. Each time she'd laugh again, and her moral timer would reset as he resumed work, grumbling the entire way.

In the time between his falls, before sudden joviality she hadn't experienced since the bomb dropped surged back, Eleni worked through a different kind of puzzle. Something she'd said earlier with Parker had stuck in her mind.

Why *hadn't* Gatewood swept in to finish them off?

Sure, the BT in Sariah's tent had shown a decent chunk of their orbiting forces still intact, but with the surface-to-air batteries destroyed in the attack, all Gatewood needed to finish this, to wipe them off the planet, was one more assault. It didn't even need to be a fusion bomb. Any orbital bombardment would be enough. Hell, even a frigate firing on them in atmosphere for a few minutes would be enough to make sure Arctic disappeared from the galaxy and erased them from history.

So why let them recover? And if Gatewood had stepped back, then why jam signals to and from the planet?

Wait. The BT had had live updates on the ships in space, which meant Sariah had contact off-planet. Forget how she had that signal, if the governor had contact, that meant Sariah should've sent a distress signal hours ago.

FTL comms between Luna and Teegarden took four standard hours at the most. The Protectorate should've been here as soon as Sariah reported a fusion bomb had been detonated over a legal settlement. Eleni checked the clock and had her *manju* run a worst-case scenario on Protectorate response.

They should've been here seven hours ago.

Fury lit inside Eleni at the realization. The Protectorate was part of this. Those bastards must be egging Gatewood on, pushing them to wipe out Arctic, to take Shiva. It'd make sense. It certainly gave fuel to her anger, purpose to her actions.

But a thought kept cycling in her head.

Sariah had signal off-planet. How?

As Parker crawled and cursed his way through debris removal, Eleni kicked on her local channel. Once again, harsh static filled her ears, so she worked her way through the network, stopping at each only to verify the signal jammer was still in place. After several long minutes, Eleni hadn't found any clear options, and certainly no answers.

Maybe if she went back to the dropship, she could amplify the signal strength somehow? If it worked, what good would it do? And if the Protectorate was involved, why let Parker keep doing what he was doing?

Doubt filled her stomach, giving voice to a thought that begged to be said aloud.

Eleni shoved it away unspoken.

Parker's gasping voice rose over the roar of the wind, dragging her attention away from the radio and her own turbulence. "This is bullshit," he said, stomping his way to her.

If she hadn't seen him slowly devolve into fatigue, Eleni might've felt threatened. As it was, she noticed the slump in his shoulders, the dragging left leg as he tried to come off as intimidating. Still warm inside her thermal suit, Eleni got to her feet in one swift motion, plasma rifle across herself like armor.

"What's that?" she asked.

The sight of the rifle halted him in his tracks. His eyes didn't come off it. "You could liquify half this shit in seconds if you wanted."

Rippling thudding filled the air as gusts pummeled the barren landscape, flurries obstructing her view for a brief moment. "Maybe," *but I don't have enough ammo for that*, "but I'm not gonna."

"Why?" he asked, damn near whining.

"'Cuz—" Eleni started. She didn't get to finish.

A bright spotlight flashed over the tower. The howling wind transformed then, from an innocuous winter gale to the thudding of helicopter blades.

If she'd been facing the other direction, even with her *manju*, she'd have been blinded. As it was, Ceriat reeled from the blinding light, arm going up too slowly to protect him. He stumbled backward, tripping on something and falling, still trying to protect his eyes.

Eleni spun, plasma rifle held to the side. Her *manju* automatically adjusted for the spotlight, saving her from temporary blindness.

Before her, a half dozen meters above the dropship, hovered a recon helicopter—a RecHop. The blades snapped hard against the air, snowflakes eddying around it like orbiting debris. She'd seen them used several times, but had never been this close to one, as they were under Gareth's purview in the settlement. How this one had survived the bombing, Eleni wasn't sure, but there wasn't time to debate that.

Next to the bright spotlight, and currently spinning up, sat the RecHop's plasma cannon.

Eleni cranked the speaker volume of her *manju* to maximum, then waved her arms in surrender. "Wait! I'm Director Mallias! This man is my prisoner!"

Behind her, Parker's cursing grew loud enough she heard it over the slapping wind.

If the pilot heard her, they gave no indication. Instead, the RecHop's cannon angled past her.

At Parker.

"No!" Eleni screamed as the tip of the cannon flashed bright blue, searing a slashing afterimage onto her retinas.

Parker cried out, though in pain or fear, she didn't know.

What happened next came as a blur. All instinct.

Up came her plasma rifle, the weapon already buzzing with energy. The cannon turned to her. A hissing filled the air. A flash.

The spotlight went out.

The RecHop reeled backward, sending a blizzard at Eleni. She dodged to her left, rolling with her plasma rifle, which prepped its final slug. Through the sleet and snow, the RecHop was a shifting shadow, flickering flame barely making it through to her.

A sound rang through the distance between her and the RecHop. Panic ran down her spine. A solid *thunk*, as if a piece of steel had dropped to the floor.

Or a magnetic payload connected to a target.

"Down!" Eleni shouted, though she didn't even know if

Parker was still alive, or if he mattered. She crashed to the ground, plasma rifle held out before her as a shield.

Which she only had a moment to realize was a stupid plan. The damned thing was armed.

A moment later, the world erupted in heat, fire, and shrapnel as her dropship detonated. Pain erupted along her outstretched arms and legs. Jagged shrapnel gouged down her back, sending a brief suit alarm through her *manju*.

Eleni put her head down as her HUD caught dozens of incoming projectiles.

That simple action saved her life.

Something hard slammed into the top of her head, at the thickest part of the *manju*.

The world exploded in pain and sparks. Her teeth snapped together, copper on her tongue. Then... nothing for a short while.

Groaning, Eleni opened her eyes, and saw nothing. With growing panic, she reached for her *manju*, but collapsed before getting her arm more than a few centimeters off the ground. Her spine felt like it'd been pulled between two starships, then dropped into a black hole. The rest of her wasn't any better, from her nose to the tips of her toes. Pain filled every inch of her skin, and the chill working its way alongside it told her the suit was offline.

Good news and bad.

Good: she wasn't paralyzed. Bad: her suit, and therefore her *manju*, was offline.

Fuck. Gritting her teeth, Eleni tried again, succeeding this time at getting one hand behind her head. She plucked away at the seam there, unease growing. She did so in the dark, the muted sounds of howling wind and roaring flames taunting her, until her glove finally caught on the latch.

Freezing air flooded into the helmet. The stink of burning plastic and blasted steel filled her nose. Crackling flames battled rushing wind. And beneath it all, that same repeated thudding from the RecHop as it disappeared in the distance.

With one final yank, Eleni pulled her *manju* free.

Smoke swirled, vibrant and bright against the stark black of the night sky. The crackle of flame filled her ears, punctuated by a periodic *pop* as another circuit board or partially combustible material disintegrated in the heat. The burning stench turned her stomach, but a quick shift in the breeze pulled it away, leaving her encased in the pristine, frozen chill of the tundra.

Eleni sucked in a slow breath, the hair in her nose freezing as she did so. Her lungs ached with it, but still, she held it before letting it escape into the world. With that breath, focus on the present sprang back to the fore.

What the fuck just happened?

Crunching footsteps interrupted her thoughts. Moving as fast as she could, Eleni scrambled to her knees, body protesting the entire way.

She found herself staring at Parker, plasma rifle held in his arms like an old friend. Shock rang through her. How had he survived the cannon blast? The exploding dropship?

Then she saw the streaks of blood, the crimson tint to the belly of his jacket.

Maybe he hadn't.

Still, now he had the plasma rifle, which changed things. Carefully, Eleni got to her feet, joints and tendons screaming at her to sit the fuck back down. Still, she managed to stretch upward, a low groan escaping her lips despite herself.

Parker, for his part, didn't react either way.

The far-off look in his eyes as he took her in, detached and distant, edged panic into her voice as she spoke. "You made it."

Whatever had plagued him disappeared at her call. He shook his head slightly, then met her eyes. A smile embedded itself in a face covered in stubble. "I did."

With that he raised the rifle.

"No!" Eleni screamed, eyes closing and holding her arms out, like that'd do anything against a plasma blast.

A click. The plasma rifle hissed and spit. A moment later, there was a small detonation.

Eleni spun around and caught sight of the debris blocking the door to the ETL tower cooling rapidly into slag and revealing a clear way to the door beyond. Cracking ice drew her back toward Parker. He stepped forward and clearly sized her up.

Then he held out the rifle. "Thanks for saving my life."

Not knowing what to say, Eleni took the weapon from him despite the fact that it was useless now. That was the last of the ammunition she'd had on her. Still, it'd make a decent club until she ran across some plasma cartridges. "You're welcome," Eleni said.

He didn't move, instead staring at her with intense brown eyes. Instinctually, she touched her face. Her *skin*.

My manju.

Eleni turned away, then put her back to Parker despite everything. She searched the ground for the mask. *There.* A crawling desperation worked its way through her stomach as she fell back to the ground hard enough to shock her knees. Her teeth chattered as she set the rifle down and picked up the broken helmet. Two dead sockets, both crystals shattered, the furrowed brow ravaged by shrapnel and there, at the crown, a divot nearly three centimeters deep. The mask stared back at her, twisted into a parody of the authority it'd once had.

"No," she whispered, flipping it open so she could see inside.

There, tiny tendrils of smoke writhed away, circuitry buried inside the helmet proper still shorting out as the damage from whatever had crushed into the top spread its way throughout the system. There was no coming back from this.

It was destroyed.

"You okay?" Parker asked, stepping up next to her.

From the corner of her eye, she saw his hand come up, and watched it come close to her shoulder.

Eleni recoiled and hopped to her feet, *manju* still cradled in her hands, leaving the rifle next to Parker.

He glanced to the weapon, then back at her again. For a moment, it appeared he was going to say something, though what, she couldn't say. Some empty platitudes, no doubt, as if he could ever understand what this meant to her.

But instead, he simply cleared his throat and picked up the rifle. "I'll, uh, hold onto this for you."

Eleni didn't respond, didn't match his gaze. Instead, she stared at her broken identity, lost and wandering in her own mind.

The sound of thudding RecHop blades pulled her eyes to the horizon.

There, illuminated for a moment by the lights of the encampment, two RecHops beelined for the ETL tower.

No, for us, she realized.

Parker saw it as well. "Get inside," he said, all empathy disappearing from his voice as he hefted the empty plasma rifle, as if it could do a goddamned thing. "Now."

"They're my people," Eleni whispered, watching the two helicopters close the distance.

"Yeah, well," Parker said, turning to jog the distance to the ETL tower, "your people fired on me and blew up your ship, so maybe they've got a problem with you, too."

"That don't make sense," Eleni said. Still, she followed after him as he stepped over rapidly cooling slag to get to the sliding door at the base of the tower. In the flickering firelight, it appeared twisted. "They have no reason."

"Besides you shooting down their RecHop?" Parker asked. He pulled something from beneath his shirt and placed it next to the door. A panel sprang to life, outlining his fingers in blue light before disappearing again.

"I didn't shoot it down," Eleni said, turning back to stare at the settlement and the dark space between where the RecHops currently flew.

They blended into the night sky, their blade strokes dissolving nearly perfectly into the whistling wind. Behind her, a metal-on-metal screech set her teeth on edge. She turned back to see Parker stepping into the tower. He turned back to her and waved at her to follow.

"I... can't," she said, looking between the encampment and the tower.

Parker shrugged. "Fine. Get shot," he said, but the flex of his jaw in the darkening firelight stood in stark contrast to the cavalier attitude.

With that, he disappeared into the tower. But the door stayed open.

A demon crawled in Eleni's stomach and clawed its way up her throat. Her new heart slammed in her chest with a fierceness she'd never experienced. Veins throbbed painfully at its urgency.

The RecHop had fired on Parker. Not her. Sure, he'd been close, but it hadn't been meant to take them both out.

Right?

She'd fired back for a reason, but whatever it was had disappeared in the adrenaline of the moment. Surely they'd forgive that, a quick reaction by a seasoned enforcer.

Eleni pictured Sariah hearing the news of her perceived betrayal, watched the gears in her head connecting it to her insubordination earlier, to Eleni's desire—no, *need*—to interview Parker.

To Parker's escape.

A cold certainty fell over her. Eleni looked then, not at the horizon or the tower, but the mask in her hands, at its familiar curves and texture. At the destruction it'd kept her safe from.

And at a life she might have just lost.

Kneeling, Eleni set her *manju* in a pile of snow and covered it as the cold numbed her fingers and caused her cheeks to ache from the chill. Maybe she'd made a mistake here. Maybe this was her downfall.

But if it was, maybe she could recover.

If she could get a call out to the galaxy, get someone, anyone, to come and protect them, Sariah would have to forgive her.

Right?

With one last glance at the mound of snow covering her old identity, the sound of RecHop blades growing more defined by the moment, Eleni stood, turned, and entered the tower.

The door screeched shut behind her, thudding closed with a finality she felt in her bones.

Chapter 15
CERIAT

Ceriat couldn't find the lights, and he made sure everyone inside the tower knew it.

"Where are the goddamned lights!" He flailed in the inky dark that'd filled the entry chamber as soon as Mallias had followed him inside, door had groaning shut behind her.

Beneath his feet, shards of something flexed and cracked as he walked the perimeter. At least it was warm(er) in here. Some part of the life support system must still be active.

He'd only gotten a brief look at the face of the woman who'd threatened him twice and laughed at his misfortune most recently, but she hadn't been what he'd expected. The digitized version of her voice had painted a picture of a scowling monster, all furrowed brows and gritted teeth.

Instead, he'd seen a darker-skinned woman in her late twenties with a shaved head, blue whirls tattooed upon it in the Spacer style. She seemed confused by the world. Lost.

That look was what had stopped him from pummeling her with the plasma rifle and fleeing inside alone. That was what had pushed him to take a chance on her, like she'd taken a chance on him.

"Why are you asking me?" came the response in a much more feminine voice than he was used to. "Thought this was your tower?"

Sarcasm. Great. Maybe letting her come had been a mistake, though a part of him livened at the banter. It'd been a long time since his old squadmate, Ouroboros, would ridicule every decision he made. Pre-flight, of course. Ouroboros was all business once in the air.

She'd died back on Shaal-Tu.

With that, a fist grabbed his heart and squeezed. He let it. The ache reminded him of the loss. Grimacing, Ceriat followed the curve of the wall, hands scanning along the edges for any indication of a control panel or the like.

"The lights should've come on when the door opened." He rammed into something hard and only just stopped from dropping an expletive-laden rant in response.

Between his old hip wound, what he was absolutely positive was frostbite on his shoulder, and the damned plasma burn, it was turning into an absolute fucking *joy* of a day.

A moment later, the room flooded with light, blinding him for the seven thousandth time. "Goddammit!"

"Sorry."

After blinking away the shock, Ceriat looked around, catching sight of Mallias standing at the far side of the room next to a touch panel. At least this time she had the good grace to appear blind as well.

"Jesus." The main foyer was a disaster.

The thin glass that'd coated the ceiling to protect the lights had shattered during the bombing, leaving jagged shards hanging haphazardly above them. The remaining bits had turned into diamond landmines covering the floor. The interior walls, typically a chic brushed aluminum look for some damned reason—which he didn't understand, as roughly six people ever saw them—showed signs of the explosion. Long strips of metal sheeting hung, bent at the middle, from where they'd disconnected from wall anchors. Behind those disconnected sheets lay a more familiar bulkhead style of framework. He'd seen something similar on a few frigates he'd served on. That alone explained why the building still stood, even if it'd broken in half farther up. These things needed to be strong if they were going to trigger volcanic activity in the planet's core.

At the far side of the room, where they'd entered, the large sliding door that'd given them access revealed a deep gouge across the side facing him. As he watched, it kicked and shuddered in place, like it'd failed to latch properly. Directly across from it, and right behind him, sat the pressurized lift that'd take them up to the comm level. Thankfully, it appeared to be in working order, though they'd have to try it to be sure.

The rest of the room was noticeably empty, though that wasn't out of the ordinary. If things had been normal, it would serve as a staging area for him. He'd have parked the *Sparrow* outside the doors and loaded in his things, including the matter replicator and SourcePaks that would provide his food and water for the duration. On other, less hospitable planets, the space doubled as an airlock, keeping the upper levels, where all the magic happened, safe while the tower operator inspected the planet's progress over the first few months. Or in his case, weekly shifts until he could bring Ginny with him.

Ceriat kicked at the broken glass and sent it tinkling toward the elevator doors. "No magic now."

"What's that?" Mallias asked, rubbing her eyes, then blinking rapidly and squinting while trying to take in the room. "They all busted like this?"

"No. The walls usually aren't unrolled like loose toilet paper." He rolled his eyes, then swept a path to the elevator through the broken glass with his boots. "This way, and watch your step."

"Don't wanna break more glass, am I right?"

"Are you going to be like this the entire time?" Ceriat asked, closing the distance to the elevator.

"Probably."

He heard the shrug in her voice.

Ceriat fished in his shirt and pulled out Gerry's dog tag. He pressed it against the space where the authorization panel should be. "Should've left you outside, then."

Crackling glass told him Mallias had gotten close, so he turned to keep her in sight.

That allowed him to catch sight of the first flicker of human emotion he'd gotten from her.

A grin. "Yeah, probably." A quizzical look hit her face when she saw what he was doing. "That's a messed up key fob. Speaking of..." Mallias held out a gloved hand.

"Yeah, one second," Ceriat said.

The authorization panel flashed then, a cerulean square embedded in the brushed aluminum walls, and the doors screeched open to reveal... an empty shaft. The elevator itself was missing, though somehow the tube appeared capped and closed— otherwise there'd be a drift of snow in there. The emergency lock-down procedures must've worked. Still... "What the fuck?"

Mallias' hand extended before him. "Key fob. Now."

Distracted by the lack of elevator, Ceriat first slung the dog tags back around his neck, then reached for where he'd had the key fob clipped to his belt—and again, found nothing. Grimacing, he turned away from the shaft and scanned his belt. Patted his pockets.

"What's the holdup?"

"Er," Ceriat mumbled, pulling his stolen jacket from his shoulders to check the interior pockets. Still no key fob.

"Parker."

He looked toward the door leading outside. "I might've left it out there."

"What?" Mallias' face went hard, hand snapping back to her side. She followed his gaze. "You better be joking."

Ceriat patted himself down again. "Unfortunately, I'm not."

For a moment, Ceriat thought she'd come at him out of sheer

frustration. Instead, she groaned loudly and stomped to the exit doors. All the way, she muttered wordlessly, though the rare word would jump out at him. Words like "legs," and "break," and "burn alive."

"Are you going back out?" Ceriat asked, watching her stalk and slide through the room.

"Yes," she said, voice flat as she reached the door.

"You can't," Ceriat said. Leaving the missing elevator behind, he joined her at the far wall.

She grunted at his response. "I can, and I will."

Standing in front of the door, it made the same sucking crunch noise from earlier. The tiniest breeze swept through with it, dragging a miniscule trail of snow that already had formed a small puddle on this side.

Ceriat stepped up next to her. "If you do, they're going to find you."

"I'll be quick," she said, scanning the wall. Her eyes held an intensity as she did, frustration clearly growing as she did so. "Open the fucking door."

"Mallias—"

"Stop," she snapped, sucking in a harsh breath before turning to him. "If they find my key fob, it's over."

That struck him. "What is?"

"The... void blasted..." Her voice trailed off, face flushing red. She slammed a palm against the malfunctioning door, making it ring with the impact. "Just open it."

"If I open that, I risk everything. Everyone," Ceriat said, trying to pull her attention away from whatever point beyond the wall she currently stared at. "You see that, right?"

When she turned to him, Ceriat took a step back. The mask had been intimidating, but this look... maybe she hadn't needed it after all. "Open the door, Parker." Her eyes flicked to the chain beneath the collar of his jacket. "Or I'll open it myself."

The wind went out of him then. "Didn't I just save your life?"

Her gaze flickered. "You don't know that."

"I don't?" Ceriat asked.

A dull, repeating *thrum* radiated through the floor then, tickling his toes. The RecHops were here.

"Shit," Mallias whispered, the intensity in her eyes disappearing. Still, she stared at the door as if she could phase through it. "I needed that."

Ceriat let out a long sigh. "I'd have given it to you."

"If I don't have it, I'm..." She trailed off, sputtering and shaking her head.

For the life of him, he couldn't figure out what she was worried about. The key fob was a white sliver of plastic somewhere on an ice planet in the middle of the night. The likelihood of anyone finding it was damn near nil. He said as much.

"That don't matter," Mallias snapped.

"Then what is it?"

She turned to him. The flush in her cheeks from earlier disappeared into the high neck of her jacket. Anger flashed in her eyes. "It's *my* responsibility." She jammed a finger hard into his sternum, forcing him a step back. The glass cracked beneath his retreating feet. "And you fucked that up."

"Whoa, now," Ceriat said, putting his hands up and dancing backward as she approached. "I'm sorry I lost it—"

"Sorry?" Mallias snarled, face twisting as she stalked toward him. She stood seven or eight centimeters taller than him and made use of every last one as she squared off. "This is yer fucking fault. None of this woulda happened if you hadn't dropped on planet, showed up here." She gestured at the general direction of the encampment.

Ceriat stopped retreating at those words. A fire lit in his belly, and he straightened, staring back at her as she approached. "I had *nothing* to do with this!" he shouted, waving his arms around them. "The fact I got us in here should prove that."

"It don't prove shit," she said, voice low, barely more than a growl. "Only that you're a devious, backbiting son of a bitch."

Again, she got close, though this time he wasn't bound. Mallias glared at him, begging, daring him to do something. To lash out and make it his fault.

Oh, he wanted to oblige. From the moment he'd dropped out of FTL, everything had gone wrong. Every conversation had ended with him somehow guilty for something he had no hand in.

But something gave him pause. A smell.

Her breath filled the space between them, stale and acidic. He pulled back, brow furrowing. Old memories flooded back with it. The nanobot sludge he'd had to drink after they'd found his fighter, wrecked, a month before his discharge. Too much time had passed for his hip to heal properly with the nanobots, they'd said, but at least he hadn't lost the leg.

Still, his head had been all over the place in the day after he'd taken it, and shit, he'd been angrier than a stowaway cat on a vegan long-haul freighter.

So instead of doing exactly what they both wanted, Ceriat sucked in a deep breath and softened his stance. "Listen—"

He didn't get to finish.

Mallias swung around, dropping as if expecting someone to tackle her. "Do you hear that?" she hissed.

"No?" Ceriat replied. But then he realized he was both right and wrong.

He didn't hear anything.

Not even... "The RecHops—"

"Shh!"

Then, as they stood there quietly, they heard a dull, now-familiar *thud*. They had but a moment to exchange a look, recognition passing unspoken between them.

"Run!" Ceriat shouted. He grabbed Mallias by the arm and pulled her after him. They only had one place to go.

Together, they leapt into the empty elevator shaft. Panicking, Ceriat ripped his necklace off. The dog tag caught the light as he swiped it on the panel outside the door. He yanked his arm back inside just before the elevator door slid shut and dropped them into utter darkness. A heavy sound Ceriat hoped was the pressurization locks rattled his teeth.

A suffocating silence filled the dead space.

Ceriat's heartbeat hammered in his ears. His breathing mingled with Mallias', echoing in the tight space like whispering wind. They stood there, silent, for a long moment.

Then, in a whisper as loud as a shout in this tomblike silence, Mallias asked, "Maybe it wasn't a bomb?"

Her answer came a moment later.

The silence disappeared in an eardrum-shattering *thud*. Screeching metal topped out Ceriat's eardrums; the ground rocked beneath their feet, sending them heavily into the wall of the shaft. Ceriat covered his head as dust and bits of debris fell, slamming into the earth around them. Something hard crashed into his right arm, dropping him to the ground wrapped in seething pain.

I'm gonna die.

I'm gonna die.

The thought rattled around his head alongside falling steel and concrete outside. Somewhere beyond the shaft, something heavy screeched, then snapped, grinding its way down the exterior wall behind them. A sudden angry slash appeared high on the wall. Bright, artificial light filled the shaft.

Then it stopped. The earth rested. Debris swung and dropped one more time.

Ceriat uncovered his head and inspected his right arm in the new light. A long, crimson gash made its way through the thermal jacket and laid open his skin from elbow to palm. A quick prod revealed nothing broken, but goddamn, it throbbed. Carefully, he pulled the jacket together and put pressure on the wound to slow the bleeding.

To his left, Mallias was in the process of getting to her feet and dusting off her own clothes. He didn't see anything physically wrong with her, but the look on her face, even behind the caked dust, was stricken. Shock, he assumed.

Shock passed, though, so he called it a win.

They lived.

For now.

Chapter 16
ELENI

They know I'm in here, but they did it anyway.

Through the explosion, the collapsing tunnel, that thought ran on a loop. Now, ears ringing, Eleni dusted herself off, as if the sheer act of wiping away the debris could somehow change what had happened. Flickering light from whatever spotlights were in use outside filled the shaft, giving Eleni a good look at the destruction. Around her, twisted scraps of black girders littered the area, alongside clumps of concrete pierced with exposed rebar. The heavy door that'd shut just before the explosion went off had buckled under the shockwave and now looked like a giant had pressed their palm into it, bowing it inside and securing it shut.

Until they set another explosive, anyway.

They know I'm in here, but they did it anyway.

On its left, and previously covered by a brushed aluminum panel, sat a bright red manual door lever that was likely useless now. To the right of the door, handholds were embedded into the steel and concrete. She followed them upward to what appeared to be another of these portals, complete with another manual door lever just off the ladder. If they didn't want to die, that ladder needed climbing.

They know I'm in here, but they did it anyway.

Parker's groan caught her attention. Eleni turned to him and saw the crimson slash along his forearm. It didn't look horrific, but this trauma was something she could deal with right now.

After stepping over several fallen clumps of stone, Eleni knelt next to Parker as he tried to squeeze the remnants of his jacket around the open wound.

"Stop that," Eleni ordered, fishing at her waist for the emergency pack she always carried with her on patrol, then cursed herself.

Of course she hadn't brought it. *This fucking day...*

Parker turned a sardonic look on her, lips twisting into a grin. "Stop? You trying to kill me in the most ineffectual way ever?"

Grimacing, Eleni knelt before him, then grabbed the fabric around his jacket and yanked it apart.

"Ow!" Parker hissed.

Eleni *tsk*ed as she tore the jacket the rest of the way around, then snagged the interior layer and pulled it free. "Stop being a baby."

"I'm not—Jesus!" Parker cried as she wrapped it around the wound and squeezed it tight. "I still need blood in my hand."

"You need your blood inside your body," Eleni replied, forcing down a grin that threatened to spread to her face. She held out a hand to him. "We need to climb."

Parker appeared confused, but then he saw the ladder next to the door. He sighed. "Of course we do." He accepted her help with his left.

Eleni hauled him to his feet and proceeded to the ladder. "Since you're injured, I'll go first—"

"No way," Parker snapped, stepping up next to her like he intended to push her out of the way. "I go first."

Any amusement she might've felt on a different day disappeared as the refrain played again in her mind. *They know I'm in here, but they did it anyway.* "Once you get your broken ass up to the top, how do you intend to open the door?"

"I'll use the fob," Parker said, gesturing to the broken end of the necklace hanging from his pocket. "Just like before."

"Oh? And where would you put that trinket?" Eleni asked, pointing to the blank wall on this side of the door. She pointed to the door above, which similarly lacked an access panel. "You need to haul on the emergency lever to open it—"

"Then I'll do that—"

"You'll just bleed on it and make it harder for me when I need to save your ass," Eleni snapped, elbowing him out of the way. "Now sit back and follow me up once the door is open."

She didn't wait for his answer. Instead, she hauled her way up the handholds, rung by rung. Each pull made her head pound. Maybe she had a concussion? Maybe not. It really didn't matter, so she focused on the job at hand. Hand up, foot up, pull.

Each foot between herself and the ground made her chest hurt. It had nothing to do with exertion.

They know I'm in here, but they did it anyway.

Despite the battering she'd taken yesterday, the climb was easy enough, thanks in large part to the nanobot treatments she'd received. Treatments Sariah had authorized because she'd trusted her. Eleni ground her teeth at the image of Sariah's face. What would she say during their next meeting? Would it be anything, or would Sariah's greeting end with a plasma blast to Eleni's temple?

Eleni hauled her way up until she was even with the long, red lever next to the door. If she opened this, there was no going back. If Eleni brought Parker up here with settlement forces outside actively hunting them, what could she say when they met again? Could she rewind this? Pretend it never happened?

With a cautious glance, Eleni looked down at Parker. There he sat, expectant, yet worried, and nursing that arm. Heavy crashing sounds made their way through the walls. Settlement forces had entered the tower. They'd be at the elevator soon, and if their actions so far were any indication, another explosion was in their future.

Eleni cursed herself for an idiot. But still, idiot or not, she'd committed to this as soon as she'd blown out the plasma cannon on the RecHop.

Time to follow through. Hand shaking, she grabbed the lever with a gloved hand and gave it a shove. It didn't move.

"'Course," Eleni grunted, bracing herself inside the ladder grooves as best she could so she could gain some leverage on the handle. "Nothing is fucking easy, is it?"

"Everything okay?" Parker called up.

Eleni didn't respond. Stupid questions didn't need stupid answers. Instead, she gripped the lever, then pushed hard with her legs, straining at the effort. This time the lever ratcheted forward, the door to her left squealing open as it did so. And stopped.

She turned to survey the progress from the movement and cursed. "Ya got to be kidding me."

"What?"

"Only opened a few centimeters!" Eleni snapped, staring at the darkened room beyond the crack she'd opened. "Who makes void-blasted shit like this? This is gonna take forever."

From below came more crashing.

"I don't think we have forever."

Eleni swallowed an insult, and instead focused on the lever again. Once again, she pushed against it. Once again, it ratcheted open. After several minutes, she'd only succeeded in opening it up ten or fifteen centimeters, maybe enough for her to stick a leg through, but not much else.

"Sounds like they're moving something in there," Parker said, voice rising at the end. "I'm coming up."

"Whatever," Eleni snapped, breathless.

The effort of holding herself upright on the ladder, let alone messing with the stupid manual system—a system clearly intended only for use when the operator stood on a level with it, which made no damned sense—strained even her nanobot-recovered body. Muscles she hadn't known she possessed screamed at her to stop, begged her to relent, just for a moment.

But she didn't. As Parker closed the distance between the

ground floor and her, she kept pushing, resetting, and pushing again. Her life turned into a repetitive cycle, one hand constantly scrabbling for purchase on the damned handle for a modicum of progress.

"How's it going?" Parker asked, suddenly close. His words carried a strained edge she didn't have time to ask about.

"Just—" she reset again, sweat stinging her eyes, "—fucking —" with everything she had, Eleni pushed on the red lever one more time. It clicked, and the door squeaked behind her, "—dandy."

Before she had a chance to brace herself, Parker's voice stopped her.

"I think I can fit through there. Can you go up a little bit?" he asked.

"What?" Eleni hissed. She turned a bit until the door came into view. Indeed, it appeared wide enough now. The room was still nondescript in shadow, however.

"Oh, thank God." She considered going in before him, but honestly, her muscles would never accommodate the twisting necessary. Not until she let them rest for a moment. "Sure."

With that, Eleni pulled herself up on the ladder leading to a splotch of darkness a couple meters above her. The light from the slash in the wall didn't penetrate deeply here, but every now and then, shards of wicked, twisted metal sparkled. It must be where the tower had snapped, though maybe the tiny flashes of light were from exertion. Regardless, it didn't matter much. She needed the rest, so she took the opportunity to press her face to the cool wall and catch her breath.

Below her, Parker grunted his way up the ladder. A moment later, a scrambling sound followed by a sigh of relief told her he'd made it inside. Not ready to move, Eleni looked toward the door to see Parker covered in dust, sweat streaks running tired trails down his face, staring up at her. Was he paler, or was it just concrete dust?

"All right," Parker said, awkwardly gesturing to her with his left hand. "Your turn."

Nodding, Eleni lowered herself, body screaming at her to stop, until she was level with him. Parker filled the small doorway. Open less than a meter, it'd take something of a leap of faith for her to reach the ledge without falling. She looked to him, incredulity no doubt clear on her face. "How the fuck you make that?"

Parker shrugged and grinned. "Pure dumb luck."

She stretched out her left leg until it caught the edge of the lip, but as soon as she put weight on it, her boot slipped, and she damn near fell the two stories to the debris-filled pit below.

Her heart filled her throat as she swung backward wildly, gripping the handholds for dear life.

"Whoa!" Parker shouted, leaning out to watch her grab onto the ladder. "Are you okay?"

"No, I'm not fucking okay!" Eleni screamed, pressing her face into the wall. "I need a second!"

"I—"

"One goddamned second!"

"Okay," came the quiet response.

She spent several moments taking deep, steadying breaths with her eyes closed before reassessing. Something had made her slip. That could be remedied. Heart steadied, Eleni opened her eyes and turned to the doorway. Something wet covered the edge of the doorway. In the dimmer light up here, it barely shone, but if she squinted, it had a darker color. Almost red.

Realization dawned on her, and she met Parker's concerned gaze. "You bled all over it."

He blinked. "Excuse me?"

She nodded toward the ledge. "You bled on the doorway and almost killed me."

"Oh," Parker said as he finally saw the smear from his wound. Using the back of his bandaged forearm, he wiped up the slick smear, then gave her a thumbs up. "Sorry about that."

Eleni rolled her eyes, then extended a leg to the lip again. This time, she found some purchase. "Just be ready to catch me if I need it."

"Got it."

Something about the way he said that made her pause. "You do, right?"

"Do what?"

"Got it?" she said, eyes narrowing.

He cocked his head to the side. "Yes?" Then a shadow passed over his face. "What are we talking about?"

"Me!" Eleni shouted, nodding vigorously toward her foot. "You got *me*! I'm the 'it!'"

"Oh, yeah," Parker said, squaring off with the door. "Of course."

Eleni cursed under her breath. Carefully, she put more weight on her toes, then removed her left hand from the rung to reach for the edge of the doorway.

She wrapped her fingers around the frame, a grin splitting her face as she transferred her weight to her left side.

The world shook as another explosion rocked the tower. Eleni's eyes went wide as her foot slipped, her hand sliding down the doorframe, unable to find a handhold. Below her, a shockwave rattled the air, blowing dirt and grit up around her.

They know I'm in here, but they did it anyway.

And down she went, metal and stone skittering along beneath her left hand.

Then, pressure around her wrist. Her shoulder went painfully taut, and she careened into the wall, slamming hard. Lights erupted in her vision at the impact, followed swiftly by numbness that soon blossomed into agony. Squinting, she turned her eyes skyward to find Parker there, both hands wrapped around her wrist, his feet pressed tight against the unopened door and the frame. Even from here, she saw the blood seeping from his bandage, making its way down his hand, and onto her gloves, but she noticed it as if it was happening to someone else.

As if the blood of an Earther wasn't dripping its way down to her.

"Grab on!" he shouted, strain and pain warring in his voice. "I'm losing you!"

The words fell over her without meaning as a high-pitched hiss unleashed itself on her eardrums. Why was he doing this? He didn't need to. Hell, if he let her go, that'd only help Gatewood and the Protectorate.

"Mallias!" he said, voice high and weakening. "Let me help you."

Unless he cares. The thought came unbidden, like a docking ghost ship. And if he cared... then the rest of what he said might be true.

With a sudden burst of energy, Eleni reached with her right hand and grabbed his wrist. Now she was secure, Parker pulled her up the rest of the way, dragging her painfully over the ledge.

Then it was over, and they lay next to each other on a flat surface, the stink of detonated explosives tickling their nostrils.

Eleni laughed. The loss of the last day. The ridiculousness of... everything. She turned to look at Parker, who looked back at her with a confused stare until he joined her. She patted his chest as if he were her brother, let out another chuckle, and got to her feet. Despite some dizziness from the blast and, well, nearly dying, she stayed upright. She helped Parker to his feet. He swayed as well, but also managed not to drop.

Together, they stared at a darkened room, only the slightest sliver of light revealing its contents. As she stared, the outline of a machine stood out at the far side of the room, next to a bank of what might've been monitors. Still, just like downstairs, the room lacked power. At least the floor seemed clear here, leaving the room blissfully intact.

"Can you get us some lights?" Eleni asked Parker as she made her way farther into the room.

"Yep," Parker said. Then, "Um."

Eleni turned back at the noise. "What?"

There Parker stood, outlined by a shaft of light, his snapped necklace held by one end, and noticeably bare. His face twisted as he stared at the bare chain. "I..."

The dog tag was gone.

Chapter 17
CERIAT

Mallias closed the distance between them in a flash.

"How's it gone?" She snatched the chain from his numb hand and stared at it, jaw flexing in obvious frustration.

"I don't know," Ceriat said, scanning the floor, then fishing inside his pockets fruitlessly. He only succeeded in bleeding all over his pants. He'd lost Gerry's tag. "It's just... gone."

She stared down at him, brown eyes searching his for something he couldn't give her. The muscles in her cheeks hopped. A vein bulged just over her right eye. Then she spun away.

"Fuck!" she shouted, stomping farther into the room.

She grabbed a chair from near the bank of monitors at the far end of the room and launched it into the wall with another curse. It hammered home with a sharp *crack*, then fell to the floor, clearly broken. She stalked to it, picked it up, and proceeded to slam it against the ground until the wheels snapped and the frame twisted.

Normally, Ceriat would've joined her. Maybe it was the blood loss, but he didn't. Even the grief he knew would overwhelm him later—if he had a later—sat muted in the corner of his mind, a dull ache against the dim shock settling over him. Instead, he stood there, numb from the neck down and staring at empty, blood-stained gloves. Carefully, he peeled them off, revealing skin creased with dirt and grime despite the covering. A smear of blood had pooled around the cuff of his right hand, running a dried line of browning crimson along his palm.

A tiny voice in his mind whispered at him to move, to try to power up the station anyway. That this wasn't the end. Not yet. And it wasn't wrong. He could try. After all, he did have familiarity with this equipment, and could probably rig something up.

But a louder voice said one thing, and it nailed his feet to the floor. *You lost Gerry's tag.*

He probably would have stayed there until the people chasing them crawled up behind him and brained him if it weren't for Mallias.

After the chair snapped in half, she dropped the pieces, chest heaving from exertion. She turned to him and said something, the sound of her voice barely piercing the buzzing veil of disbelief.

Then she stood before him, catching his eyes with her own. Ceriat followed her gaze, lifting his chin until they stared at each other. He cleared his throat, suddenly aware of her closeness, of the hand hovering over his shoulder.

And of the scuffle of feet and scraping metal from below.

"What?" Ceriat managed, blinking through a thickening haze in his mind.

"How do we turn this on?" she asked, staring intently at him. "How do we get the message out?"

Ceriat closed his eyes, cleared his mind the best he could. "We need to turn on emergency power."

"Good," Mallias replied, stepping away. "Tell me what to do."

"Give me a second, my brain is..." Ceriat grabbed the bridge of his nose and squeezed.

The pressure barely registered, though the smell of iron and a hot wetness remained. He held out his right arm to find his hand covered in blood. New blood. He'd made his wound worse. The bandage wasn't working anymore.

"Parker." Mallias' voice snapped him back to the present.

"Under the left panel," Ceriat said, blinking as sudden dizziness swept over him. He took a hesitant step forward, the room spinning. "Might be an emergency circuit there."

"Got it." A moment later, the room filled with light. "Now what?"

Ceriat reeled at the sudden brightness. He hit the wall, then careened to the side and lost his balance. A moment later, the floor rushed up to meet him, driving the air from his lungs. A dull roar filled his ears, backed by the slowing hammer of his heartbeat.

His body moved on its own, someone else's arms shifting him onto his back. Mallias filled his view as she fussed over him, checking the bandage. Her eyebrows furrowed; a muttered curse left her lips but missed his ears.

"Ey, stay here," she said, only just audible over the droning filling everything. "We can do this."

Then her gaze snapped up. Ceriat's followed.

The governor stood at the ledge in full battle gear, including a half-helmet with clear target identifiers drawn on the HUD shield covering her face. The edge of a ladder was visible behind her. Instead of the antique pistol she had holstered at her hip, the governor hefted a plasma rifle much like the one Mallias had carried. Pointed at them.

As a wave of darkness swept over him, Ceriat had time for one thought.

Shit.

Chapter 18

ELENI

Eleni weighed her options, and found that, for the first time in her life, she had none.

"Sariah—"

"Shut up," the governor snapped, plasma rifle still trained on Eleni's chest. You didn't need a headshot with these weapons to be fatal, after all. Sariah's face twitched, eye kicking up and down. "You don't get to talk."

You don't get to lie. Eleni ground her teeth, biting back the retort. Still, she didn't flinch beneath the stare of the barrel. Instead, Eleni stood, bringing herself to her full height so she looked down on the other woman. If she died today, she'd do it on her feet.

But no light flashed from the end of the plasma rifle. Instead, Sariah continued staring, head shaking back and forth almost imperceptibly. "What the hell are you doing here?"

That took Eleni aback. "What?"

"With him?" Sariah said, gesturing to Parker, who was still in the process of slowly bleeding out.

His wound must've opened up during the climb. Or when he'd caught her. The damned fool was going to die because of her.

Eleni chewed her cheek at the realization but didn't turn her gaze away from Sariah.

"Why ain't you called for help?" Eleni asked, pulling attention away from Parker.

Sariah blinked, mouth working wordlessly before snapping shut. "Signal jammers—"

"Bullshit!" Eleni interrupted. "Liar."

"It's the truth!" Sariah yelled. From below, concerned shouts echoed up the shaft.

Eleni shook her head. "I saw the BT. Signal's good off planet."

Sariah's face went flat. "It isn't."

"You have live ship feeds," Eleni said. "Fuel. Ammo."

"That doesn't mean anything."

Eleni barked out a humorless laugh. "It means you have off-planet signal. Gatewood coulda jammed a planet, but they can't squash the system, Sariah. Don't treat me like a fucking Earther."

The governor stared at her for a long moment, stoic and emotionless before nodding to herself. The plasma rifle went over her shoulder to latch onto the metallic backplate of her battle armor. Still staring at Eleni, she popped open a secure pouch at her belt and fished inside for something.

"What're you doing?" Eleni asked. The change in demeanor and sudden intensity set her back on her heels. Maybe she'd pushed too far?

"This," Sariah said, pulling out a flat disc from the pocket. With the same hand, she planted the device against a spot next to the half-opened door that appeared to be an access panel.

Behind her, electronics buzzed to life, followed swiftly by the *swish* of recycled air as filtration systems kicked on with a rattling *clank* that soon evened into a light hum. Smoke trickled around Sariah's legs and into invisible vents embedded in the walls.

"You've got the tags?" Eleni asked, gaze flicking between the booting system behind her—all black screens and scrolling text—and Sariah. "Why?"

Sariah's eyebrow shot up at that. "Because he dropped it."

"You know what I mean."

"Because I should've just shown you before this got out of hand," Sariah said. She let out a breath and shook her head. "Because I'm not the villain here." She sighed. "I need you to trust me, Eleni." When Eleni didn't move, Sariah gestured at her to move. "Go on. Try calling for help."

This must be a trap. But if it was, why would Sariah give her access to the communication array? Licking her lips, and not taking her gaze entirely away from Sariah, Eleni made her way to the main operations station. A quick glance revealed the system was still in lockdown for some reason, though at a glance she couldn't figure out why.

"Can I have that?" Eleni asked, nodding in the direction of where Sariah had once again pocketed the key fob.

Sariah stepped over where Parker lay, his breath getting shallower by the second. Her gaze swept down as she passed. "Lot of blood."

Then she held out the key fob between two fingers.

Eleni snatched it away. "Yeah. If you'd wrap him while I do this, that'd be great."

Sariah snorted.

"Want my trust?" Eleni snarled. "Wrap him."

"Really?" Sariah asked. "You want me to save a terrorist—" She stopped at Eleni's glare, then knelt, pulling an emergency pack from her belt. "Ridiculous," she muttered, the rest of the sentence disappearing as her voice lowered. But still, she started the process of properly bandaging Parker's wound.

At least he had a chance now.

With that handled, Eleni turned back to the machine. She placed the fob on the authentication panel next to a digital keyboard. A pleasant *ding* chimed in the room, and the login window that'd been plastered over the central monitor transitioned into one of the most complex system management tools Eleni had ever seen.

Half of it was pure gibberish, though periodic life support

phrasing popped out at her. Ambient temperature, oxygen satura-
tion, etc. However, the vast majority consisted of words she'd
thought she knew until just now.

"The hell is 'tectonic plate disruption?'" Eleni muttered. She
reached out and scrolled down the screen until finally coming
across what she wanted. *ETL Comms.*

Eleni gave it a tap, opening up the module. The central screen
lit with an image of herself, and Sariah behind her bandaging
Parker's arm. Eleni flinched at her own face and the streaked
blood and grime covering it and her skull. With gentle fingers, she
touched the worst of it just over her left eye and probed for a
wound. She found nothing but the perpetual acne from where
her *manju* sat against her skin.

It's not my blood. Again, she looked at Parker, stomach
writhing with the realization that someone else's blood covered
her skin.

She shoved that away. He'd risked his life for her. The least she
could do was return the favor, even if it backfired spectacularly.
With a quick tap of the central screen, she began recording.

Eleni straightened, clearing her throat, and put on her best
politician voice, careful to lose as much of her accent—and
profanity—as she could. "This is Eleni Mallias, director of Security—" Sariah snorted at that, but she ignored it, "—for the settlement of Arctic on Shiva, formerly known as Teegarden-c.
Targeted fusion ordnance has been dropped on the settlement by
the Gatewood Conglomerate. We're requesting immediate
Protectorate assistance." Eleni stopped, sucked in a breath, then
added, "Your technician," Eleni closed her eyes, forcing herself to
remember his first name, "Ceriat Parker led us to this tower, but
was wounded." She licked her lips, trying to think of the right
words to use to urge the ETL to contact the Protectorate, but
only one thing came to mind. "Please help us."

Eleni stood there for a long moment, watching herself shiver
in encroaching panic, heart in her throat, her own face staring
back, bloody and scared. *Coward.* Then, before she could delete

it, she snapped out a hand and hit send. The video disappeared in a flash, leaving her staring at the comm panel.

And waiting. In a few hours, they'd have their answer.

"Happy?" Sariah asked, dragging Eleni's attention away from the terminal. The governor stood over Parker, arms crossed, disgust clear in the curl of her lip.

Parker's forearm shone bright white from the emergency wrappings. With the medication embedded in the bandages, the wound should close up shortly. Good.

But still, Eleni didn't answer. Instead, she turned back to the machine, waiting for a response. Or confirmation. Anything.

Logically, she knew it could take eight-ish hours for a response if the system was slow, but she waited anyway. Sometimes it was immediate, after all. Sometimes.

She didn't know how long she stood there, but it couldn't have been long. Others joined them via the ladder. Men Eleni knew arranged themselves around the room, plasma rifles in hand, betrayal and anger warring on their faces. The stink of smoke and spent explosives covering them dragged a quiet cough from her lungs. Jeret was the last to arrive, his long visage drawn and thinner than she remembered.

Instead of taking position next to Sariah or the others, Jeret stepped up next to Eleni, rifle still attached to his back. "Did it work?" he asked.

She looked at him, at the hope that dawned and died in his eyes as their gazes met. "I don't know."

"Did you know about this?" Sariah asked him, voice angry.

Jeret shook his head in the negative, though he didn't turn around. "No. You were both loud enough, they probably heard it back at the encampment."

"Oh."

"But," Jeret added, a weak smile breaking his face in two, "some hope is better than none."

At that, the screen flickered. The room filled with audible gasps. A response had just come in.

That was quick.

Before Sariah or anyone else could do anything to stop her, she tapped the ETL Comms module again. A smile forced itself onto her face as she opened the reply. Then her stomach fell through the floor.

No video, and barely any text, displayed in a short message.

"What's it say?" one of the guards echoed, the same expectant lilt that'd filled Jeret's voice a moment earlier tinging his.

Eleni tried to read the words aloud and failed, as if her mouth was filled with sand, lips sewn shut.

Jeret sighed. "Let's go."

Silence filled the room. Eleni stared at the screen, unable to attach meaning to the words displayed there in their stark, emotionless form.

People spoke behind her, voices melding together into a hissing susurrus. She didn't hear them. Scraping and scuffling as guards moved and people left. A big hand gripped her shoulder and pulled her away from the screen, where those words danced, as her heart slammed and her eyes ached.

As Jeret pulled her to the ladder, Parker already gone somehow, Sariah stepped forward and whispered in her ear, "I fucking told you."

Then Jeret pushed her to go down the ladder, and she did, like she was on puppet strings.

She paused only to squint one more time to make out the five words on the display before dropping away.

Your request has been denied.

Chapter 19
CERIAT

Ceriat woke with a start to find himself lying flat on his back. He stared at a temporary hab ceiling a short space above his head. Pain in his forearm pulsed in time with his heartbeat, throbbing faster as he tried to move, only to realize he'd been restrained. Again.

Beyond his arm, a deep, abiding chill had taken root in his back and legs. He wiggled his fingers and found them nestled back inside his gloves. At least he shouldn't have to worry about more frostbite. Small victories. Still, every movement felt as if he was scraping a piece of sandpaper through a tub of stasis gel. Even a good flex of his toes revealed a numbness that set his teeth on edge.

It felt too much like atmo-loss for his taste.

As alarms squealed in his mind, Ceriat squeezed his eyes shut, sucked in a breath, counted to four, let it out, then repeated the process. Each breath forced the memories away, each shuddering intake of air centered him, reminded him he wasn't flying through the void. That the wind whipping outside wasn't a broken vacuum seal.

"There's O2 here," a familiar voice said, an edge there he couldn't place. "No need to freak out."

Ceriat lifted his head as far as he could while restrained. The hab was tiny, even for an emergency unit. Cramped didn't begin to describe it—roughly three meters in diameter, with a caramel-colored, domed roof that resembled a honeycomb through which sunlight currently leaked. It was more jail cell than home. *Great.*

The gentle hum of a heater crackled to life. It filled the room with a sound that made the room vibrate and tickle his quickly waking limbs. Sitting upright to his left sat Mallias, head resting on her fists as she took him in. Her face—what he could see from this angle, anyway—appeared drawn and thin. The blue swirls on her head stood out stark against her skin, though he couldn't make them out in detail from here.

He assumed he shared that likeness, minus any new tattoos.

Unlike him, they'd taken her gear, leaving her in a thin, stained, white shirt, and loose-fitting black pants. At first, he didn't notice why she hadn't moved, but then the plastic straps around booted feet and hands purple with cold explained it away. She must be frozen to the bone, but the blasé way she lounged certainly didn't showcase that.

Still, she looked like shit, and he told her so.

That drew a snort from Mallias. "I'm not the one who almost bled out for nothing."

Panic drew a cold finger up his spine. The statement caught him off guard, and he forced himself into a position where he could see her better.

Straps pulled painfully on his right arm and wrist, but he didn't care. "What do you mean?"

Mallias met his gaze, brown eyes flashing, before shaking her head and looking back down at her hands.

"Hey," Ceriat said, straining at his bonds, "what happened?" He scoured his memory, then froze. "I lost Gerry's dog tag."

"Almost there."

"The governor," Ceriat whispered. He squeezed his eyes shut and cursed everything. "She stopped us."

"Nope, she didn't," Mallias snapped, brows furrowing as she took him in. "She made me try, actually."

"Wait, what?"

Mallias shook her head; let out a humorless laugh. "I sent the message requesting help."

"But the tag—"

"She brought it up," Mallias said, then reached out with a restrained hand as if trying to pass along a secret. "Gave it to me." The hand pulled back to her chest, held there for a moment before dropping.

Ceriat wrinkled his brow in confusion. "Then, what did you mean—?"

"I mean," Mallias said, voice little more than a whisper, "the Protectorate abandoned us."

"They wouldn't do that." The phrase came out on its own, slipping through Ceriat's lips with an immediacy that only comes from training. Still, he didn't question the words as they poured from his mouth. "The Protectorate wouldn't let this stand. The Protectorate—"

Mallias' dead laugh cut him off. "The Protectorate is thick in it. All of it, Parker."

"No."

"Shit," Mallias said, another humorless laugh accompanying the curse. "You said you saw Shaal-Tu. You know what they do."

Ceriat gritted his teeth at that. Smoke burned his nostrils as memory sparked to life. *No*, he told himself. *This isn't the same. Right?*

Burning brush, blasted sands. Screaming. So much screaming.

Ceriat squeezed his eyes shut, flexed his fingers, and pulled against the restraints, to no avail. Images flashed behind his eyelids. *A valley littered with black craters, each still smoking as tiny fires consumed what remained. Ash on warm wind, touching and sticking to everything.*

Gerry, dazed, staring at the destruction they'd wrought.

"No snappy Protectorate propaganda to spit back?" Mallias

asked, voice rising at the end in condescension. "No cheerleading?" She waited a moment before snorting and spitting something on the ground. "That's what I thought."

Ceriat barely heard her. Instead, he opened his eyes and strained as his vision narrowed to a point somewhere beyond the recessed ceiling above.

Panic screaming at him, Ceriat jumps free from the SB-13 and falls the two meters to the ground, his shattered hip buckling in agony beneath him, but blissful, beautiful oxygen fills his lungs. Sure, it might be riddled with pathogens, but the Protectorate will take care of that. For now, he needs the air and freedom from that damned helmet. From a system that nearly killed him.

"What did we do?"

Those are the first words Ceriat hears from his place on the ground. Then he smells the wind, picks up the scent of char from the zephyrs whipping through this wild wood where they landed. Ceriat pulls himself up and looks to the source of the voice.

He finds Gerry on his knees at the edge of the ridge. His flight suit, disconnected in his haste to activate the emergency hatch on Ceriat's bomber, is a tangled mess about his limbs, but he doesn't notice. Instead, he stares into the distance.

Ceriat wants to join him, but he can't move, only stare at the destruction beyond.

In the valley below is nothing, just blasted black craters where a city should stand. Shaal-Tu is gone. They destroyed it.

Except that wasn't exactly how it happened, was it? Time had a way of twisting memory, of softening or intensifying the events.

Gerry never stayed. He was a better man than that.

No, the truth hurt more. Much more.

"You really gonna stay quiet?" Mallias said, voice breaking through the memory.

Ceriat hauled in a heavy, shuddering breath, counted, then released. Still he smelled burning wood, charred flesh on the wind. It took him a moment to realize why, but when reality settled back on his shoulders like a hair coat, Ceriat shuddered beneath the weight of it.

"What's there to say?" Ceriat managed finally, a waver in his voice he couldn't control. "I was wrong."

Mallias made a noise in her throat, but didn't have time to respond. A moment later, a door somewhere behind Ceriat's head sucked open, a blast of cold air coming along with it.

"Let her go," Ceriat said quickly, straining to face the newcomer. Instead, he caught sight of Mallias, one eyebrow raised at his outburst. "She didn't do anything."

"Shut up," a grizzled voice said in response, then, "On your feet, Eleni. Governor wants to talk to you."

"Happy to, but yer gonna have to cut the restraints first," Mallias said, jutting her legs out before her. "Can't walk all trussed up."

A quick flash in the light caught Ceriat's eye, then Mallias stood, leaving behind a scrap of plastic on the ground.

"All right, Gareth," she said and stepped out of Ceriat's line of sight.

Then, with the hiss of the door swishing shut, Ceriat lay there in silence, alone with memories that dug their way free from the box he'd so desperately tried to force them into.

Chapter 20
Ten Years Earlier

"These bastards aren't going down easy, boys," Major Henderson said, long, thin Spacer face stoic and fierce over the communications panel. "So we're taking the fight to them before they can hurt any more of our own." The faintest impression of a smile appeared on his perpetually down-turned 'U' of a mouth. "You know the drill."

The hum of the *Goliath* softened Henderson's harsh voice, lending it a compassionate lilt Ceriat knew from experience didn't exist. That same vibration filled the cockpit of his SB-13 bomber —more affectionately known as a Floating Bomb—rattling the hull itself with a life he felt beneath the touch-sensitive fingertips of his flight suit.

"We're taking them out, boys," Henderson said. He always used the male noun, despite nearly half the flight crew identifying otherwise. Might as well move a star than get Henderson to change. "The six of you are about to stop a war. This is going to save a lot of lives, boys. Time to teach these fuckers what it means to attack the Protectorate."

Fire shot up Ceriat's spine at the words, but he kept his face flat. There were scores to settle with these Shaal-Tu monsters—

Elise, Dareth, Wolfgang, Archita, all dead at their hands—and today... today they'd be repaid in blood.

The rumor going through the ranks was that the Righteous had set up base in Shaal-Tu.

He salivated at the chance to repay those bastards for the destruction they'd brought on his home of New Eden. A million dead, and hundreds of thousands poisoned by radiation from their dirty bomb. His aunt and cousins—Jane, Siri, and David— murdered by religious extremists. It was time for payback, and goddammit, he was ready to get it.

He'd be doing them a service here, really. Better a quick death than the lingering mess otherwise. They should be thanking him for wiping them out of the galaxy.

"Vulture is on point for delivery," Henderson said, using Ceriat's codename. With the words, Ceriat's bomber flight controls unlocked, the ship thrumming to life. "Harris on wing. Ouroboros, you keep them safe for the payload..." the rest of the flight assignments faded as a *hum* filled Ceriat's ears.

The giddy grin he'd kept at bay since being woken an hour earlier with the news of the mission finally broke through.

They'd finally pay, and he'd be the one to deliver that justice. No one could pinpoint a target like him, not even Ouroboros. Everyone in the galaxy knew it, and if these Shaal-Tu fuckers knew he was coming, they'd flee the system.

Intel said they had no idea the Vulture was coming.

Ceriat was so caught up in the moment, he nearly missed the incoming transmission notification on the HUD of his helmet. Sometimes he wished they could wear the experimental, contact-based tech, but high-Gs did a number on your eyes, and the last thing you needed was your HUD slipping out of position and blinding you in the middle of a firefight.

With a quick tug, Ceriat pulled the helmet on and flicked open the private channel.

"*You ready to take out some of these bastards?*" Gerry's voice filtered over the comms, though he was in the process of doing a damn near spot on impression of Henderson. "*Oo-rah!*"

"That's pretty good." Ceriat snickered.

"*I've been practicing.*"

"Obviously," Ceriat said. The main mission screen turned off then, and a launch timer kicked on in its place. "But they deserve it after everything they've done."

Gerry didn't respond right away; he must've been running through his flight checklist, so Ceriat did the same. A moment later, his launch order activated.

"See you out there, Harris," Ceriat said to Gerry as he started the autopilot undocking procedure.

"*Yeah.*" Gerry's response was uninspired.

The Floating Bomb maneuvered its way on autopilot over a dozen rows of smaller fighter craft on its way to the far end of the flight bay. There, he waited for the rest of the squadron to join. When they did, the end of the bay sealed off and depressurized in a harsh cacophony of extracting atmosphere.

As the last of the air hissed away into nothingness, Ceriat's heart steadied. There was just something soothing about the silence of space, the lack of input besides your own breath and the beat of your heart.

It calmed him in a way nothing else could.

Gerry hated it.

The diagnostic light to the right of the bay doors switched from a bright red to green, and they opened without sound to reveal the deep emptiness of space.

Henderson's voice filled his helmet. "*Launch.*"

"On me," Ceriat said over the squad channel. He grabbed the flight stick and sped into nothingness.

A chorus of '*aye-ayes*' came back to him as he throttled the Flying Bomb below the *Goliath* and around. The scale of the massive warship always boggled his mind. As it sped by beneath him, the engine of the Flying Bomb rising in pitch as he neared max acceleration, Ceriat marveled. The ship was crewed by nearly a thousand soldiers and staff, and carried enough ordnance to wipe out a small planet.

Which, Ceriat assumed, was the point.

"Prepare for exposure," Ceriat said as the lower edge of the *Goliath* came up fast ahead of him.

Ceriat swung the nose of the Bomb upward as it passed beneath, then spun the ship so the verdant planet rising before him took center stage on his display.

Shaal-Nar, a planet of rivers and jungles, of multitudinous species native to the planet. Additionally, it was home to an over-whelming number of non-native creatures introduced from Earth, despite the Protectorate's explicit prohibition on seeding planets with Earth-native fauna. From here, he couldn't see the genetically-engineered boa constrictors slithering alongside the living vines of the towering Medusa trees that dominated the equator. Couldn't see stalking tigers, cloned and returned from extinction to thrive on this planet, devouring passive creatures who only knew to avoid trees—the planet's only native carnivore—not each other.

Shaal-Nar showcased a planet without rules, without order. A planet that violated everything the Protectorate held dear. All tainted by the Edenites and their attempts to play God on a new garden world.

And the Righteous. Those bastards were a waste of oxygen.

As Ceriat beelined to the dark side of the planet, clouds and unseen zephyrs swirling storm clouds in the atmosphere below, he focused his attention on the source of all this chaos. Shaal-Tu, the capital city of the Edenites. There, the entire known population lived in a city of stone, surrounded by the perverted imitation of nature they'd created.

Still, despite reconnaissance revealing imagery that resembled paintings of Ancient Greece, replete with robes and other tech-avoidance silliness, the anti-assault turrets sprinkled throughout the forests were no joke. If they caught sight of the squadron, it would be over before it began.

"Going silent," Ceriat called over the squad channel. "See you all on the other side."

Another chorus of '*aye-ayes*' came over the radio, then nothing. They knew the mission; once they went into the atmosphere, there was no turning back.

Good.

Which was why, as the darkened plane of the planet grew before him, Ceriat pulled his bomber down into the atmosphere, then engaged aggressive reentry protocols. Heat shields slammed shut around the cockpit as the first bit of turbulence rattled the ship. The five-point harness keeping him seated tightened, his helmet snapping back to the headrest to keep him from flailing about inside the cockpit.

A roaring filled his ears as they dropped through the ionosphere. Sweat beaded his forehead while the temperature spiked, despite the insulation and heat dispersers built into the bomber. Everything rattled, as if a giant had grabbed the ship and shook it like a child's toy. Still, Ceriat grinned. His heart slammed in his chest, eagerness begging him to grab the flight stick, to take control and rain Hell on those bastards below.

Training stayed his hand. If he took control now, the chance of their success dropped precipitously. Their only chance to enter the atmosphere unseen was by using the interference from the rising sun, and the resulting electrical storm, to obfuscate their entrance. Changing the pre-programmed flight path was sure to trigger the anti-air turrets.

After several long minutes of howling wind, the shaking mostly stopped, though a dull roar still filled the cabin. Blast shields slid away, revealing dazzling twilight on the planet for the briefest moment before torrential rain slammed into the glass, obscuring everything.

Lightning flashed. Ceriat reeled, blindly reaching for the flight stick.

They had all of sixty seconds to drop to an altitude of one

hundred meters, or all this would be useless. And he was fucking blind.

Still, instincts kicked in. The flight stick filled his hand. He kicked it straight forward and sent his stomach into his mouth.

Wind and rain roared beyond the walls of the cockpit, sending the Flying Bomb jumping back and forth. Ceriat blinked repeatedly, the purple afterimage of lightning finally fading—just in time for a new lightning flash to illuminate a downright massive Medusa tree directly ahead. Its long, vine-like branches extended toward him, reaching as if he were one of the monstrously-sized birds that covered this hemisphere.

Ceriat cursed and yanked back on the flight stick, trying to level out the bomber. Below him, maneuvering thrusters roared. Little-used wing flaps rattled under the effort.

"Come on," he begged.

The horizon pitched. Ceriat's stomach heaved, vision blurring for a moment despite the inertial dampeners taking the brunt of the G-forces. Then his head equalized, attitude leveled, and Ceriat let out a breath. That was close—

The Flying Bomb stopped, ripped to the side, then spun. His ship had been caught by the Medusa Tree.

The world went into a pirouette. Inertial dampeners flashed G-force warnings. They hadn't had a chance to vent yet, which meant he had bare seconds left before the pressure knocked him out, or worse, he stroked out.

The cabin flashed red with warning lights. Alerts blurted in his ears. Ceriat ignored them. Instead, he grabbed the flight stick and pulled against the spin. In the darkness, the flash of lightning over the tops of this forest they'd come down on became a slow-motion descent to death. Every splash of light revealed him getting closer to the maw at the center of the tree.

Closer.

He pulled back on the stick, then rolled to the left, hoping the action would counter the spin.

Alarms screeched. Ceriat screamed. The Flying Bomb leveled.

Behind him, the inertial dampeners shuddered, then vented the stored kinetic energy in a blast of heat behind him.

Ceriat let out a quiet breath. His heart hammered. Everything came alive. His fingers around the flight stick. The certainty that, if he'd been a second slower, he'd have been smeared across the ground of this foreign planet. All of it came together in one joyous chuckle.

It quickly caught in his throat. Scrambling, Ceriat turned off the alerts—he'd have to deal with them later—and pulled up the short-range signal ID system. They were only meant to be used in tight proximity, specifically on stealth missions like these.

The screen came up... and Ceriat let out a long breath. Everyone had made it. A quick glance out the window to his right displayed a rendered overlay of Gerry's fighter in the black of night.

Grinning, Ceriat dove to the tree line, though high enough to avoid any other unpleasantness from the carnivorous trees. He hammered on the throttle.

In a little over six minutes, they'd reach Shaal-Tu. He'd drop the payload, and they'd exit the atmosphere before the sonic boom reached the bastards.

The fusion bomb would hit a moment later.

Shaal-Tu deserved it, and he couldn't wait to be the one to deliver the message.

Chapter 21

ELENI

Jeret brought Eleni to the governor, as promised. The trip through the settlement had left her numb. It had nothing to do with the cold. Word of her betrayal had clearly spread throughout, furrowed brows and muttered curses left in the wake of her escort. Despite a brilliant blue sky free of clouds, Eleni had never felt more unwelcome.

At one point, as she closed in on the governor's dwelling, Jeret near behind, she caught sight of Jeffries. He stared at her from a transparent strip of plastic set in the side of the medical tent. Eleni had turned and nodded.

In response, he'd shaken his head and disappeared.

"Almost there," Jeret had whispered, nudging her lightly with his plasma rifle. "Let's get you out of sight."

She hadn't realized she'd stopped walking. In response, Eleni had nodded and resumed walking, closing the last dozen yards in a dazed trance interrupted only by the sour ache in her stomach and the vise on her heart.

Then the doors to Sariah's command center stood before her. Jeret snuck around her, swiped his key fob to the right of the door, and it slid open, revealing a room encased in a darkness her eyes worked to adjust to.

I never found my fob, Eleni realized as warm air cascaded over her. Guilt rose alongside the ache in her stomach.

Some Director of Security.

"Take a seat," Sariah said from somewhere within.

As Eleni squinted, Sariah resolved from the shadows, seated at a small table. Her unnatural eyes shimmered amber despite the darkness.

She gestured to a collapsible chair across the table from her. "Let's talk."

Jeret turned Eleni around and snipped off her hand restraints. He caught her eye, lips flattening into a line, before turning and leaving. There'd been something in his eyes, something she'd never thought she'd see in Jeret.

Hopelessness.

Eleni rubbed her wrists until she regained the feeling in her fingers. Eyes adjusting to the darker atmosphere within, Eleni took in the space that, yesterday, had bustled with the other directors as they'd tried to reconcile the settlement's situation with reality. Today, however, it sat noticeably empty. Quiet.

Even the BT was unlit, just a makeshift digital display in the center of the room, no more interesting than a coffee table in a settler's home. Sariah, for her part, appeared serious. Still dressed in combat gear, she'd remained seated when Eleni arrived, digging at her nails with a small, copper-handled knife. Her telltale pistol was nowhere to be seen, however.

"What's going on?" Eleni asked, still rubbing her hands together.

Sariah pointed again at the chair across from her, this time with the knife, the copper glinting in the light. "Take a seat, and we'll talk it out."

For a moment, Eleni considered declining. Standing had already helped bring sensation back into her limbs, and she was finally on her way to warming back up—not that she'd admit to something like cold. Even on Shiva, the chill was nothing compared to a newly pressurized cargo hold.

Still, Sariah had trusted her back at the Tower, and in the aftermath, hadn't shot her as a traitor. There wasn't anything to gain in declining the offer.

So Eleni sat. The chair, some light metal—aluminum probably—chilled her behind some, which made her grimace.

Sariah saw that. "Problem?"

Eleni ground her teeth, then lay her hands out on the plastic table before her, palms flat on the cool surface. "No."

"Okay, then," Sariah said with a twist to her lips.

Is that a smirk? That confused her. Sariah wasn't known for her humor, even of the dark variety. So why the levity?

"Why'm I here?" Eleni asked, leaning back in her chair with a creak. She crossed her arms over her chest and tried to pretend it wasn't to warm herself. "Way I see it, I broke rank, disobeyed orders—"

"Helped a suspected terrorist," Sariah interrupted.

"He's not a terrorist."

Sariah leaned forward, face flat and emotionless. "And how do you know that?"

Eleni gritted her teeth again. "Because he wanted to help."

"He wanted your help to get off this rock, not to help us."

"No," Eleni said. She ground her teeth before responding. "He wanted to protect us. Him jetting was just a bonus."

Sariah stared at her for a long time, face empty of any indication of what she was thinking. Then... "Okay."

"Okay?"

"Sure," Sariah said, allowing a small, humorless smile. "I'll accept that. For now."

Eleni raised an eyebrow at the governor but didn't say anything.

After nearly a minute of silence, Sariah's smile disappeared. "What?"

"This is weird," Eleni said. "Right?"

"Which part?" Sariah asked, leaning forward. She set the tip of the knife against the plastic tabletop, then spun it slowly with her right hand. "The part where you betrayed your people?"

"Sariah—"

Sariah's face twisted at the interruption, but she continued as if Eleni hadn't spoken. "Or the part where you let a man detained on suspicion of conspiracy free? Oh!" Sariah snapped her fingers and leaned back again, gesturing in the air with the knife. "Was it when you fired on one of our RecHops? That's the one, isn't it?"

"It fired on me," Eleni snapped, shaking her head as heat flooded up her neck, "and I could've taken it out, but I didn't, did I?"

"No," Sariah acknowledged with a nod, "you didn't."

"Goddamn right I didn't," Eleni said, the words tumbling from her as anger fed on the frustration and doubts of the night before, on the pain of the bombing. In another time and place, she'd have kept her head, but whether from the nanobots or the insanity of the last day, she didn't. "If you hadn't been so fucking shifty, there would've been no doubt in me at all."

Sariah narrowed her eyes. "Careful."

"Careful?" Eleni barked out a laugh. She held up her wrists, showing purple bruises from where the restraints had been all night. "You locked me up without food or water and threatened to vent me; what's next?" Eleni asked. She didn't give Sariah a chance to respond, though. "I mean, despite everything, it made sense at the time. I mean, I thought..." She tailed off, the fire that'd sustained her a moment earlier disappearing into a formless mass between them, like a star dragging them into orbit.

Sariah must have felt it, too. "You thought what?"

I thought maybe you did it, Eleni admitted to herself. *That you bombed the town.*

She didn't say that aloud. "It don't matter what I thought."

"No?"

"No," Eleni said, "because I was wrong. The Protectorate ain't coming to save us, and if the ETL bounced over the message, they ain't, either."

"Does this include your precious Parker?" Sariah asked, sneering.

Eleni shook her head. "No. He got duped with us." At Sariah's rolling eyes, Eleni gritted her teeth. "I scanned him with my *manju* before it went tits up. He didn't know about it." Not quite a lie. Not quite the truth, though, either.

Sariah held up a hand in defeat. "Fine."

"Good."

"Okay, then."

They sat there quietly, Sariah staring at Eleni, who tried her best to look anywhere but at the woman she'd have died for if asked only a dozen hours earlier. The moment stretched into a minute, that minute into ten, and still neither spoke.

Somewhere around the fifteen-minute mark, Eleni met Sariah's flat stare. "Now what?"

Sariah stood, stretching out her lower back with a creak of battle armor. "Now, we put this behind us," she said, then turned back to Eleni. The governor extended a hand. Eleni noticed the small knife had disappeared in the movement. "And we balance the scales."

Eleni stared at the gloved hand for a moment before turning to match Sariah's look. "Just like that? All's forgiven?"

Sariah smiled. "No, but you'll make it up to us," she said. "You and Parker will even the odds."

"How?" Eleni asked, struggling to keep the flicker of hope in her stomach from overwhelming her senses.

"By taking their warship," Sariah said, eyes flashing, "and giving the assholes who killed your brother and *our* people an ultimatum. Leave the system. Or die." The governor held out a gloved hand. Eleni realized she'd have to take hold of it to accept.

And she did. That spark of hope blossomed into flame as if an O2 line had snapped above it. It flashed to life, filled her veins, sent her heart slamming away. Fury connected with it. Faces, vaporized in nuclear murder, sped through her mind, ending with one she knew better than any.

Victor.

The glove was warm beneath the bare skin of her hand as she accepted. Sariah hauled Eleni to her feet.

Eleni sucked in a breath and let it out. She met Sariah's eyes. "When do we start?"

Sariah pressed her lips into a flat smile. "As soon as you convince Parker to help. I have a plan that'll work, but it needs him." Sariah stared into Eleni's soul. "Can you do that?"

Eleni straightened and saluted. "Yes, sir."

Chapter 22

CERIAT

"Why not?"

Ceriat squeezed his eyes shut to keep from seeing the impassioned look on Mallias' face. "Because I don't do shit like this anymore. I made a promise."

Even if it didn't include nuking a settlement, he couldn't go back to war. Not again.

"What's that mean?" Mallias asked, annoyance clear in the timbre of her voice. "ETL techs do a lot of covert ops, do they?"

Haven't always been a tech. Ceriat opened his eyes, met Mallias' gaze, and saw a fevered intensity he was far too familiar with. "Listen, you've lost a lot of people, I get it—"

Her eyes sparked at that. "Oh, you get it? Had a lot of fusion bombs dropped on your home?"

Yes. "You know what I mean—"

"I don't, actually." She crossed arms now wrapped in a dark gray jacket that made him realize just how cold he was. "Why don't you explain?"

Could he trust her? The number of people in the galaxy who'd gut him as soon as they found out who he was outnumbered those who'd clap him on the back, that was for sure. He stared at her for a long moment before letting out a humorless laugh and turning away.

"Is that a 'no?'"

"Yeah," Ceriat said. He ground his teeth as burning and screaming filled his mind. "I can't do this for you."

Eleni made a noise he couldn't identify, then sighed. "Listen, the governor's plan needs you. Anything else gets more of my people killed," she said, footsteps growing closer as her voice got quieter. "If you help, we'll keep a lot of folks safe *and* finish this thing."

Save a lot of lives. Ceriat squeezed his eyes shut again. His heart slammed in his chest.

Something settled over his body then, and he opened his eyes to see Mallias laying a blanket across him. She met his confused stare and smiled. "Think on it. Help me help them, Ceriat."

He swallowed but didn't say anything else as she disappeared in a *whoosh* of freezing wind, leaving him alone with memories.

Chapter 23
Ten Years Earlier

The thick, black canopy of the alien rain forest transformed from a formless mass into a shimmering emerald plain in the light of the rising sun. After dropping into atmo, they'd slashed across half the planet under cover of darkness without issue.

Two hours of silence. Two hours for Ceriat to work himself up. Nervous sweat trickled down his spine as the horizon came at him at six thousand two hundred kilometers per standard hour.

Still, the edge of the forest came too quickly.

Beyond lay a bustling city. Hundreds of skyscrapers pierced the morning sky, that bright sun catching the out of place structures like shattered glass caught in a web. Surprise tickled his brain, but he shoved it away.

Ceriat flicked off the safety on his bomb release lever. He sucked in a breath full of anxiety and let it out until he sat pleasantly empty, ready to do his duty, despite the rising feeling that something was off.

The city radiated away from a central structure, a single tower rising higher than all the others. Beyond that, concentric circles laid out a place that housed people. Hundreds, Ceriat had thought, but now?

Thousands. Hundreds of thousands, maybe more, and not a Grecian temple or statue in sight.

A flicker of anxiety, of doubt, came and went in a moment. There was no changing things now. Ceriat had a job to do.

The Flying Bomb sped over the edge of the city. With their low altitude, he caught sight of faces turning skyward, of a park filled with joggers coming to a halt. Ahead of him, the central spire rose.

He pulled on the release arm. The bomber shuddered. "Payload away," Ceriat said, even though the radio wasn't active. Six seconds until detonation.

Six.

With that, Ceriat jerked the flight stick to the left and up, sending the inertial dampeners screaming as he cut to the south toward the planned exit trajectory. The air exploded with ordnance. His blast shields slammed shut, and the internal display jumped into action, rendering the exterior view in near-perfect detail.

Five.

The sky transformed into a horror show. Scraps of metal and debris rattled around the exterior of Ceriat's bomber like hail slamming into a tin roof. Without the blast shield, he'd be dead already.

Four.

The radio shouted to life, despite the blackout.

Ouroboros. "Mayday! I'm hit! Repeat—"

Her screams cut off in a haze of static, short-range ID disappearing from sensors. All that energy, all the presence Ouroboros had bottled up in her tiny, genetically-modified frame, gone in the blink of an eye.

Three.

"Break, break, break!" Gerry's voice filled Ceriat's helmet as he, too, broke radio silence. "Scatter!"

Two.

Ceriat gritted his teeth and pulled the bomber into a tight

spin to the south as flak filled the air. Alerts screamed to life as multiple incoming surface-to-air missiles launched. He didn't have time to check his position, let alone that of his squadron.

One.

This was life or death. He spun, the missiles gaining.

Ceriat kicked his countermeasures, a series of mindless drones that mimicked his flight signature, and shot straight up.

Ceriat felt the explosion before he saw it. A deep, solid *thud* rattled through the bomber and set him gasping as air drove from his lungs. The bomber squealed alerts.

He had to be far enough away. With a quick flick, he pulled up his map. Ceriat's stomach dropped. He'd flown back over Shaal-Tu.

The bomb exploded beneath him.

A single, panicked idea gripped him. Ceriat cranked the throttle to maximum. He shot straight into space.

Go go go go go go!

The inertial dampeners flashed alerts as his speed increased. The ship rattled and bucked beneath him. If this were an ancient jet, he'd already be dead. Even with all his tech, the exit angle was all wrong. If he outran the shockwave from the blast, he'd still slam into the upper atmosphere and probably explode.

Probably was better odds than dead, but at least this gave him a chance.

"Come on," Ceriat whispered, the image of a growing mushroom cloud beneath him driving him forward despite not knowing what was actually happening down there.

Ceriat scanned the sky, though for what, he didn't know.

Around him, the blue darkened, stars poked through as he pierced the exosphere. He was going to make it! The inertial dampeners flashed on the display. One word blinked in a deep crimson. Full.

With that, the emergency systems throttled down. Flaps reduced his speed. Panic flared in his veins. He slammed back into his chair as whatever G-forces were left after the deceleration hammered his body. His vision swam, chest compressed.

Something hit the ship. The bomber spun, and with the inertial dampeners still at capacity, Ceriat found himself pressed into his seat, hand grasping in futility for a flight stick mere centimeters beyond his fingertips. Blinding pain filled his left hip.

Ceriat screamed.

Then it slowed, and he could breathe. Move. His vision cleared, though it felt like someone had tried to touch his brain through his eye sockets. Everything moved slowly, as if God had set the world to half time. He turned to see what'd happened to his hip.

The bomber had collapsed on that side, pinning his leg in place. A quick probe with a gloved hand sent sharp pain lancing through him, dragging a muffled cry from his throat.

Ceriat tapped at the control console, a harsh hissing he couldn't process filling his ears. Something was wrong with his fingers. A numbness filled them, sending a warning rush through him that his addled mind couldn't quite translate.

That sound...? His vision shifted. Alertness returned.

The O2 light flashed.

20% and dropping.

Cursing, Ceriat shook his head clear, and saw the mist shooting from his visor. A crack, just visible out of the corner of his eye, vented his precious O2 into the cockpit. A cockpit, he realized, that had been destabilized in the explosion, or the Medusa Tree attack.

Did it matter?

His only chance was to get back into the atmosphere. Scrambling, mouth dry as panic tried to set his heart racing, Ceriat pulled up engine controls.

Offline.

He ran through emergency restart procedures. Nothing.

Ceriat pressed his gloved hand against the crack in his helmet, driving it to a low hum, and searched the cabin for the first aid kit that should be beneath the seat. Inside should be some emergency sealant.

It wasn't there.

"Okay," Ceriat whispered, teeth chattering as a deep cold caused his breath to mist inside the helmet. Behind his head, his flight suit's heater struggled to keep up with the dropping temp. "Am I going to die?"

The question hung there for a long moment as he stared, head cocked to the side, at the rendered image of Shaal-Nar before him. The curvature of the planet split across the displays from the top left to bottom right, all greenery and untouched rivers and lakes.

Then it hit him: he'd cocked his head to set with perceived gravity, which meant he wasn't in free fall orbit. Nature would drag him back into the atmosphere.

Any hope that came with that disappeared as quickly as it came. If he reentered the atmosphere like this, he'd burn up and die.

So he sat there, O2 slowly escaping as the Flying Bomb turned to face the planet. There, the nose facing directly down toward the surface, it stopped, as if tidally locked.

In that moment, Ceriat faced, first-hand and for the first time in nearly a decade of fusion payload missions, the destruction he'd wrought.

The mushroom cloud split the atmosphere with its white mass. Diaphanous remnants of clouds scattered around it in a twisted corona. The surrounding forest had been knocked flat from the shockwave.

The sheer enormity of it hit him. The city in the forest, gone.

The people, the ones jogging in the park, vaporized.

How many people had he killed?

And for what? Revenge? He'd lost six friends in this war.

How many did I kill today? Ceriat wondered as his oxygen escaped, as the forests surrounding Shaal-Tu burned.

As his arc made its way back into the upper atmosphere of Shaal-Nar, her sucked in one more heavy breath full of the stink of an empty tank.

Ceriat closed his eyes and waited to die.

Chapter 24
ELENI

Eleni paced in her new quarters, next door to the governor's residence.

Sunlight transformed into muddled orange as it passed through the opaque exterior of the honeycombed emergency hab. The color set her teeth on edge. Back on Erias, amber served as the color associated with a hull breach, a fact parents drilled into children from birth. If a Spacer saw amber, they ran. Simple as that.

But Eleni was done running. Done hoping for some external savior to come and protect her or her people. It was up to her now. Somehow.

Still stalking through the small, single-room residence, Eleni pulled off her gloves and Security jacket and dropped them on the cot in the corner. She felt slightly chilled at the removal, but it wasn't unpleasant. The same light that set a piece of her mind on edge heated the room to a pleasant 16^C. She might as well enjoy it.

Cracking her neck, Eleni closed her eyes to block the light, forced a steadying breath, and got back on mission.

Parker. Without him, the plan was dead in the water. God knew these Gatewood bastards weren't going to welcome a random Spacer aboard, not after they'd murdered so many others. She needed him to pull off Sariah's plan.

Eleni hated that, but more importantly, she hated his defiance. She'd seen the sorrow in his eyes back at the ETL tower. He knew what had been done here was wrong. Why couldn't he see this was right? Just?

If the Protectorate wouldn't do its job, then it was up to her to do it for them. If only he would listen.

Cursing, Eleni dropped to the cot. It creaked beneath her weight. Another inhale and exhale. She dropped her face into her hands and flinched at the skin-on-skin contact.

The world was strange without her *manju*. With the mask on, everything made so much more sense. People, landscapes, all of it just fell into place with a steady data feed. Without it, she just felt so... ordinary.

With trembling fingertips, Eleni pushed at the sensitive skin around her eyes, and felt extra skin at the corners she didn't remember. The past day had been strange, both invigorating and terrible.

Without the *manju*, Shiva had transformed. Before the bomb dropped, she'd started breathing the planet's sterile air without filtration, thinking that somehow adventurous. But when her helmet had broken, when she'd left it behind, the air had taken on a body of its own, a fragrance buried inside that sterility.

Visually, the high-definition feed, so perfect a recreation, had stolen something from this place as well. Her *manju* had hidden its beauty, blocked it from her, leaving her separate. Alone.

She hadn't known because she hadn't—wouldn't—remove the mask.

Eleni dropped her hands into her lap and stared at them. Perpetual dirt and grime was worked into the dry lines on her palms and coated the wrinkles on her knuckles.

Back on the mining colony, there'd been several brothels. Video feeds showed these flawless men, women, and everything in between, wrinkle-free, and smiling dead smiles as they danced or seduced the desperate and lonely for a few moments of bliss.

She'd felt the desire to disappear into some stranger's arms, sure, but had never acted on those fleeting thoughts. Instead, she'd opted for the longer, more destructive route. Nothing hurt quite as badly as falling in love, only to have your heart shattered by someone you trusted.

Names flitted and fluttered in her mind, old lovers she wished she could forget.

William. Blond hair flipping over ice blue eyes filled with a perpetual smile. He'd left her for a holo actress.

Aaron. They'd seemed like they cared. Really cared. Begged Eleni to remove the helmet at home... and a week after she started to do it, they'd left her for greed in the Horsehead Nebula.

Hira. A flash of brown eyes and a hint of lavender on soft, olive skin.

Eleni grimaced. That'd been the worst, mostly because it hadn't even seemed like Hira had cared when she'd left. Yes, Hira had begged Eleni to join her on her freighter, but that had been unfair. She'd had Victor to look after, a life on Erias, her career—and it'd only been a couple nights.

Still, they'd meant something to her. It always meant something.

"Just not to everyone else," Eleni said to no one. She flexed her hands into fists and stood, then gritted her teeth and purged her mind of old loss.

She cast about then, searching for her *manju* on instinct before remembering. That sent a shiver down her spine, but still, she wouldn't let it stop her. Maybe others had issues with commitment, with dedication, but not her. Not Eleni Mallias.

This settlement, these people, they were her responsibility. She'd failed them once already, then had tried to make up for that, and failed again. But not again. *Never* again.

She'd get Ceriat to come around, even if she had to force him to do it.

Deep breaths to center herself, then she turned to leave. A knock came at the door, stopping her in her tracks. Brow furrowing in confusion, Eleni closed the distance. She opened the door, letting in a blast of frigid air.

There stood Jen, a young Spacer who'd come on planet around the same time as Eleni. According to Sariah, she'd found Jen on Hobelt a few years back, the tattoos already marking her as a Sco-Tak mercenary, despite her claims of being Martian. Eleni had always found it interesting that the younger woman had departed the organization, yet kept the markings. Most who left either ended up dead or had the marks removed. Or both.

Besides a shitty attitude, Eleni had had few issues with her in the past, which made her presence even more confusing.

"Need me?" Eleni asked through the open door.

Jen's face twisted into a more severe version of her perpetual bitch face. "Parker is asking for you."

"Really?"

"Yeah," Jen said, turning away. "Best go talk to your ETL lapdog before something happens to him."

Eleni had a hand on the woman's shoulder before she realized it. The touch surprised them both.

Jen twisted and stepped away, moving like a snake. There was a reason Sariah had recruited her. "The fuck do you think you're doing?" Anger clouded her face.

Eleni pulled her hand back, confused at the movement herself. Still, she ignored Jen's question. "What'd you mean by that?"

"By what?"

"'Before something happens to him,'" Eleni said.

At that, Jen smiled. "I mean, he's not real welcome around here, *Director*. Getting him off planet might be a good idea. You read me?"

"Don't fucking touch him."

"Or what?" Jen asked, head swaying back and forth as she

stepped forward, begging for a fight. "You going to turncoat your way into another promotion?"

Eleni reeled back as if struck. "What?"

"Sariah might've forgiven you," Jen said, nearly spitting, "but I haven't, and there's a lot like me here."

"I didn't—"

"You had *one job*!" Jen screamed, voice going feral. "Keep. Us. Safe."

Eleni ground her teeth and set her jaw to keep the guilt from sending it shaking. "That wasn't my fault."

"No?" Jen said, stepping close enough Eleni smelled lingering traces of the rosewater perfume she wore. The other woman's eyes searched Eleni's face, a tic pulling at her eye.

"No." Eleni didn't even believe herself.

Jen nodded then, sucked at her teeth, then spit at the entrance to Eleni's hab. "Parker is waiting." She clapped her hands. "Best get moving, *Director*."

With that, Jen left, leaving Eleni shaking in the doorway, fists balled at her sides, and filled with a sick guilt that twisted her gut into knots.

Chapter 25

CERIAT

The *swish* of the door and a burst of cold told Ceriat someone had arrived. A moment later, Eleni stepped into view, towering over where he still lay, strapped to the cot.

His arms and legs ached from remaining stationary for so long. Attempts to wriggle his way out of the restraints had only led to some pretty intense pinching about an hour ago, so now, despite his new guest, Ceriat didn't turn toward her. No sense in hurting himself when release was here.

"Heard you called," Mallias said, crossing her arms. "You in?"

Ceriat didn't look at her, didn't want to let her see the lie in his eyes. "I am."

"Good." Eleni let out a heavy breath, like she'd been holding it in for a long time. "I need your help."

"Well, as a sign of good faith, maybe you can unstrap me now?" Ceriat asked, finally turning to look at Mallias. "I can't feel my toes."

"Oh, yeah," she said, hopping into action. The straps loosened around his legs and chest, then the wrist straps came off. "Better?"

Ceriat pulled himself into a sitting position, though he held onto the blanket Mallias had given him earlier. He stretched luxuriously, every muscle and tendon in his body thanking him for the movement. Everything except his hip. That complained like it had every intention of popping out the moment he put pressure on it. He knew from experience it wasn't a light threat.

"Much better," Ceriat said, kicking his left leg out at the angle his physical therapy nurse had taught him. His hip immediately eased up.

Eleni noticed the movement. "Something wrong there?"

"War wound." Ceriat froze, jaw working as he realized his mistake.

Eleni crossed her arms, eyes narrowing. "Which side?"

Not 'which war' or 'what sector,' Ceriat noticed. *Which side.* "It doesn't matter."

"Oh, it does—"

A knock at the door to the prison hab saved him from answering the question. "You going to get that?"

Eleni glared at him, clearly unwilling to let it go. "Which side?"

Another series of knocks came, this time with more urgency. A muffled voice on the other side of the door came through as a series of muted grunts.

They stared at each other.

Then the door opened, revealing the tattooed woman from the ship that'd brought him in. A flush had set in her face, that perpetual sneer pulled back into something somehow angrier. "What the shit is going on in here?"

"Coordinating," Eleni said, not taking her eyes off him. "Wait outside, Jen."

"Your name is Jen?" Ceriat asked, disbelief pulling a grin onto his face. "You look more like a Clarisse to me."

"Vent yourself," the poorly named Jen said, still grimacing before turning back to Eleni. "Governor wants you both at the BT now."

"Be right there," Eleni said.

Jen clicked her tongue. "What part of 'now' are you not getting, Eleni?"

Ceriat turned a raised eyebrow on Mallias. "And your name is Eleni?" This time he did let out a little laugh. "You Spacers really don't name your kids well."

"Fuck off," Mallias—Eleni—snapped. She gestured for him to follow Jen out of the hab unit. "And go."

"Fine," Ceriat said, happy to let the conversation dissipate, "Eleni."

The Spacer frowned at his use of her first name but didn't correct him.

Thankfully, his hip settled into a muted rage instead of dislocation. His first step outside since being locked down on that cot was a brutal surprise. Freezing cold wind chilled him to the bone, immediately setting his teeth to chattering. "Am I going to get a coat at some point?" he asked Jen, trying to get her attention with a wave. "Not sure you've noticed, but it's fucking cold here."

Jen grunted in response. Whether that meant 'yes' or 'no' was anyone's guess.

Luckily, they'd let him keep his own clothes, so at least he wasn't slogging through slush and drifting snow in bare feet. It was bad enough he had a scabbed over slash down his arm and the lingering burn of frost bite on his shoulder. Losing toes on this planet certainly wasn't on his to do list.

What was, however, had everything to do with escape.

Eleni might be thirsting for revenge, filled with that desire, but Ceriat had already gone down that road. Nothing lay there but more death... and ash you couldn't get out of your skin or your mind. He stared at the ground, at the gray-brown muck layering everything in this blasted place. His stomach, empty and complaining, filled with a different sort of ache.

"Yer gonna tell me." Eleni's voice came clear from just behind him. "I promise you."

Ceriat only nodded in response. Maybe he should. Maybe then this weight would lift, and he'd finally be free of this guilt.

"But probably not," Ceriat whispered into the air.

Chapter 26
Ten Years Earlier

One sip.

Despite the fire in his chest, the dull roar of insanity and death dancing on his doorstep... only one.

With numb fingers, Ceriat smacked at the console before him. That had worked better a few minutes earlier. Hell, he'd had a plan when he started tapping away at the comm panel, but whatever that had been had disappeared alongside vented oxygen.

At least I'll have a view on my way down.

Rendered in excruciating detail before him sat Shaal-Nar in all its viridescent glory, thanks in large part to his new angle of reentry. He no longer had to stare at the mushroom cloud or the devastation directly beneath him. No, now he watched as vast swaths of thick forests transformed from a textured green smear to something real. He couldn't take his eyes off it.

An alert chimed someplace. Another sip of stale air alongside a pounding heart. He didn't look for the source of the alert. What was the point?

The Flying Bomb rattled with the first indications of reentry. Displays flickered and flashed as streams of crimson flame licked the hull. With a strange peace, Ceriat gripped the armrests of the cockpit. He sucked in one long breath and tasted the end of the reserve coated in oil and steel.

The Bomb jumped and threw him side to side. His vision tinted red. Everything grew fuzzy. Displays powered off, then, casting him into darkness as screaming air tore at the exterior.

One of the blast panels disappeared in a flash. The temperature spiked in the cockpit. Cool air washed across the back of his neck as his suit tried to equalize the heat.

Ceriat sucked in a breath, and panic arced through his chest as his lungs struggled to use what little oxygen he found there.

I'm going to suffocate. The certainty broke him, sent his fingers clawing at the helmet release, despite the knowledge that if he took it off, he'd still suffocate in the blistering heat.

I can't breathe!

Clouds scattered as his ship plummeted to the forests below. Air, so close, but so far. Ceriat tried breathing, pulled at the collar securing the helmet. He needed it off.

Now.

He tried to scream, but the world faded, limned with dark shadows.

His heart hammered.

The ship rocked.

And then... nothing. For a while.

The world slammed into him. Gravity pulled him forward in the seat. Ceriat gasped. Not enough air, but still, some.

With a clarity he'd lost, Ceriat finally caught the helmet release and ripped it off. Huge, sucking gulps of oxygen filled aching lungs. Foreign fragrances and alien particulates saturated every breath. His sinuses immediately complained.

Somehow, he'd landed in one piece.

Groaning, Ceriat pulled the emergency canopy release lever. It shot off the ship with a thudding explosion, leaving his ears hissing from the blast. Adrenaline and instinct screamed at him to stand, to get out of the ship. After all, he shouldn't have landed at all. The Bomb, with him inside, should've been little more than a smear of flesh and metal in the middle of the forest.

He tried to gain his feet, but a sharp pain shot through his side. Glancing down, he took in the crumpled steel around his leg. Panic overwhelmed his logical mind.

Ceriat pulled. His leg popped out in more than one way.

Pain screamed through him as a shard of steel slashed open his upper thigh, but his focus lay with the joint, at the space where it should've joined at his hip, but where only squishy muscle and flesh filled the gap. Agony flared, then disappeared in a numbing haze as it shifted freely inside his flesh.

Panicked, Ceriat grabbed his upper thigh, gloved hands slipping on hot, wet blood, and pushed the upper bone back against his pelvis. It thudded into place, grinding all the way. He cried out. A pain unlike anything he'd ever felt tore through him.

Tears clouded his vision, but survival still drove him. Ceriat pulled himself up and over the edge of the cockpit. He swung his legs over the side, then dropped, hoping he'd land on his good leg. He did, but the leg buckled beneath his weight in gravity, and he hit hard, his other hip sending pulsating anguish through him. Time passed and was lost as Ceriat struggled to his feet amongst the thick, penetrating grasses that littered the clearing he'd somehow landed in.

Using the Bomb, he managed to get on his feet, though putting pressure on his left leg sent him reeling. Still, now standing, he could take stock of the situation.

He'd landed in a clearing in the midst of massive, ancient trees that smothered the areas beneath their canopies in shadow. The brown and yellow grasses that'd cut at his flight suit and hands came up to his waist, all sharp edges. Around him, the ground rippled beneath the waving layer above in a shape he realized must've been trees that'd fallen ages ago.

Grimacing, Ceriat turned his gaze to the graying sky far above in time to catch a swirling black cloud dancing over the clearing.

The cloud spread above him, pirouetting on unseen gusts until it surrounded him in warm, unnatural snow.

Ceriat rubbed his fingers through the darkness, only to leave a greasy trail behind on his gray flight suit.

"What...?" he muttered.

Then he smelled it. Ash. Flame.

Terror filled his belly and sent him swatting at the mess as it settled across everything, despite his efforts.

"That's not going to help."

Ceriat turned toward the source of the voice. Relief flooded through him at the sight. "Thank God. Gerry, you made it."

Gerry stalked out of the shadows. Like Ceriat, he lacked a helmet, but if there was more damage, he couldn't make it out beneath the dark gray smears coating him head to toe. "Not sure He has anything to do with it," Gerry said, turning halfway back the direction he'd come from before catching Ceriat's eyes. "You good to walk?"

Something had changed in Gerry's gaze. Ceriat could feel it despite the new gulf between them. "Yeah," Ceriat said, confused. He cast about on the ground and came up with a long branch he could use as a crutch. "Have you radioed in? Mine is shot."

"Good," Gerry said, ignoring his question. Then he turned and walked back into the woods.

"Wait up!" Ceriat called out. It didn't help.

After a frustrating, hobbling walk through untouched forest, Gerry always a dozen meters ahead, Ceriat stopped, gasping for air.

"Where are we going?" he called out, ready to throw the crutch at Gerry's head.

His hip wasn't getting better, and he couldn't shake the idea that every step he took like this only served to injure him more.

"Almost there," came the response.

After letting out a string of curses and hobbling as fast as he could, Ceriat finally caught up with Gerry just as the tree line thinned and disappeared at the edge of a canyon.

"What the hell, man? I'm injured, can't you—oh." Any further complaints Ceriat had disappeared at the rough precipice.

Gerry only nodded as he stared out over the cliff, at the blackened mass in the distance, and the slowly dissipating mushroom cloud above it. At the flattened forest between them and the remains of Shaal-Tu a dozen kilometers distant.

As he watched, the valley below writhed. At first, he thought it was the wind, but then hundreds—thousands—of creatures took shape in that mass exodus. Familiar Earth creatures that'd been illegally transferred here—tigers, gorillas—ran alongside massive, fur-encased, lumbering mounds. At first, it was breathtaking. A mass of life rushing through an alien wilderness. But something was wrong.

Squinting, he made out the charred fur, the exposed, burned flesh in the dimming light. Ceriat's soul cracked farther at the sight of the wounded creatures. These beasts had had nothing to do with this. With any of it... and still, they suffered.

"We did this," Gerry said, gesturing at the scene before them, though whether he meant the creatures or the city in the distance... "All of it."

"We had a mission," Ceriat said. The words rang hollow and trite in his ears. "We followed orders."

Gerry turned on him then, brow furrowed as the lanky Earthling closed the distance between them. Instinctively, Ceriat scanned the area for observers, though there was no chance of that. Not here. Squads weren't allowed to fraternize. Not like this.

When Gerry's warm hands—he'd taken his gloves off at some point—grabbed hold of Ceriat's own, the old heat filled him, but only for a moment.

Gerry's brown eyes dug into Ceriat's, searching for something there only he knew. "We could've said no."

"We didn't," Ceriat said, squeezing Gerry's hands back like the gesture could bridge the chasm widening between them. "We didn't."

They stood there for a long moment, tears slowly filling

Gerry's eyes as he kept searching, searching, searching for something in Ceriat's own. Something he didn't find.

Gerry's hands disappeared in a rush of skin on fabric. He turned away to resume his vigil at the edge of the canyon. "I can't do this anymore."

That hit like a punch to the gut. Despite the pain in his hip, Ceriat lurched forward. "Do what?"

Gerry lowered his head but didn't turn around.

"The fighting?" Ceriat asked, an ache digging into his chest as he closed the distance. "Fine, we'll leave. I promise. I'll never hurt anyone else. I swear to God. We'll start that freighter company you want," Ceriat pleaded as the pain found purchase in his heart. He held out a hand to Gerry, wishing—hoping—he felt Ceriat's need, his love, across the distance.

In response, Gerry only shook his head. He reached up and pulled something from his neck with a sharp snap. When he turned around, tears had worn a groove through the soot on his cheeks, but his eyes were dry. He stepped up to Ceriat and held out a hand.

"Please." Ceriat didn't add anything. He knew it wouldn't matter.

Gerry's jaw worked for a moment, then he sucked in a breath and held out his hand again. Vision blurring, Ceriat held out his own. Gerry released his dog tags, nodded, then walked past him.

It didn't feel real in the glove, the cool metal of the data tracking chip spreading through the tactile sensors and onto his skin, telling him he held Gerry's tag. That their time, this thing they had—friendship, lovers, whatever the fuck you wanted to call it—was over. Over because they'd followed orders.

Ceriat pulled his gaze from the tag to the horizon. The cloud expanded, ash carried on its spiraling form. *I did that.* The realization slammed into him again. An entire city, gone in the blink of an eye, because he'd dropped a single bomb. Because he'd followed orders. A rock formed in his stomach, a barbed vine sprouting from it to connect to the pressure in his chest.

Could he blame Gerry for leaving?

I'm a monster.

Gerry's footsteps faded into the background, branches crunching as he made his way.

"Wait!" Ceriat cried. He grabbed beneath the edge of his flight suit jacket, found the chain holding his own tags, and pulled them over his head. He turned then, hoping Gerry had stopped, but half expecting him to have continued on despite everything.

There Gerry stood, face full of emotion, jaw working wordlessly.

Ceriat thumped along after him, ignoring the pain in his hip the best he could, until he stood within arm's reach of his old friend.

He held out one of his own tags. "Something to remember me by. The SOS beacon is busted, but..." Whatever else he'd been about to add disappeared into the lump in his throat.

Gerry looked at the tag glinting dully in the weakening light for a long moment before taking it from him. "I won't be able to forget you, Ceriat," he said, voice thick. "You can count on that." He hesitated for a moment as if considering one final embrace, then shook his head, turned, and stalked away.

As Gerry disappeared into the forest, Ceriat called out one more time. "What happened to everyone else?"

Gerry stopped, turned, face dark... or was that just the lighting? "They're all dead, man. We're all that's left." He shook his head and turned away. He paused, then added, "My tag's beacon still works. You should use it."

"What about you?"

Gerry gave him one last small smile. "My fighter flies. It's the stars for me, man. I'm done." With that, Gerry disappeared.

A few minutes later, Gerry's fighter shot into the sky, leaving Ceriat behind.

Ceriat stood there until darkness settled across the canyon, until the forest screeched around him like a wounded creature. Which, Ceriat realized, it was.

He stayed there, huddling in pain—paying penance—until the night grew black. Until the soot coated him, and everything tasted of burned flesh and charred plastic.

Then, despite his soul calling on him to stay—to let the planet devour him—Ceriat activated the SOS beacon in Gerry's tags.

Then he waited.

Chapter 27
CERIAT

The governor's mansion, or whatever they called it, was just as welcoming as the last time Ceriat had been "invited." Ash-covered strangers glared at him as he entered, the sounds of spit hitting slush following him inside. A glance skyward revealed a gray sky, but no indication of the raining embers that'd fallen on his arrival. Why they remained filthy was a mystery to him. With all the snow and ice around, water should be handy.

Then again, maybe they just didn't see it beneath the weight of everything else.

Eleni led the way into the building, her square-shouldered strut filled with confidence and drive. Jen trailed after him, no doubt to keep him from running again.

A warm breeze tinged with a sharp sweetness he couldn't identify struck him in the face as he reached the doorway, drawing a smile despite himself. He shivered pleasantly as the heat made its way through his body. Sariah stood near the center of the room in front of the BT, though it seemed to be powered off. Atop it sat what appeared to be three covered plates.

The smell on the air took a on a different texture then. His stomach rumbled.

"Welcome," Sariah said, turning around in time for Eleni to join her at the table. "I've prepared a lunch for this planning session."

Saliva flooded Ceriat's mouth, and his stomach twisted in anticipation. How long had it been since he'd last eaten?

Eleni stepped up to the BT and pulled a lid off one of the plates to reveal a steaming dish of... something that resembled a slimy pile of wet rice. Three large glasses of clear water sat next to each tray, no doubt made from the pristine ice and snow surrounding the camp. Eleni's face lit up at the sight. "I love Miner Slaw."

"It's all yours, then," Sariah said, stepping to the other side of the table. She took a seat in a chair Ceriat couldn't quite make out and gestured for them to sit. "Dig in."

Eleni did so and immediately devolved into an eager child.

Ceriat, however, closed the distance slowly, looking between the last two plates suspiciously.

"Your choice," Sariah said, a small smile working its way onto her face.

He made a noise, then lifted the lid of the dish closest to him. More of the slurry Eleni was in the midst of devouring presented itself, though from this distance, the acrid stink of fermented food wafted harshly into his nose. *Not that one.*

Groaning, he reached for the last tray. Sariah slid it over to herself before he got there, grinning. "Sorry, Earther. It's all Miner Slaw."

"Oh." Ceriat choked down the revulsion climbing his throat and pulled up a chair and the plate. He was starving and, gross or not, this food was going in his belly. "Thanks for the illusion of choice."

"It's my specialty," Sariah said. She spooned a heavy helping of the slaw into her mouth and closed her eyes, a smile tickling her lips. "It aged well."

Eleni made an affirming noise barely audible over the sound of her shoveling more of the mush into her mouth.

Ceriat stared at the pile of fragrant, rotten food on the plate before him. Rice mixed in a pale white gravy that seeped out the edges, like some sort of twisted oatmeal. The smell coming off it confused him, though. Sweet, yet layered with a heady aroma he swore reminded him of baking bread, the scent belied the reality of the meal's origins.

"What's wrong?" Eleni asked, dragging his attention away from the plate. She cocked an eyebrow and licked her lips. "Eat," she said, gesturing at him with a spoon, then tapped the edge of her plate with the spoon. "It's delicious."

"What is it?" he asked, turning back to the plate.

"Never had Miner Slaw?" Sariah asked. She took a heaping bite of the stuff. "Shame. Guess Earthers have more refined tastes, Eleni." The governor looked him in the eye, then took another bite. "Strange, that."

Oh, you like driving that wedge, don't you? Well, he wasn't about to let that happen. Without Eleni's trust, he had no chance of getting off this rock. Grimacing, Ceriat grabbed a spoon, heaped the strange, pudding-like material on it, and shoved it into his mouth. He swallowed immediately, hoping it'd bypass his tastebuds. It didn't work.

Yet instead of revulsion, his tongue rejoiced in the lingering sweetness, the slight alcoholic sting on his tongue that disappeared into a pleasant tartness.

"It's good," Ceriat said, not trying to hide his surprise. He took another bite and savored it for a long moment as his gut danced a happy jig. "Better than it looks."

"Number one rule back on Erias," Eleni said, flashing him a smile. "Everything tastes better than it looks."

Ceriat let out a chuckle and dug back into his plate of Miner Slaw. Together, they ate in silence for several minutes until, almost as one, they leaned back into their chairs with a chorus of groans.

"Filling," Ceriat muttered, putting a hand on his stomach.

Sariah grunted in response. "Shouldn't do anything on an empty stomach."

"Especially a suicide mission," Eleni added, face going dark.

The atmosphere changed with those words, the ache in Ceri-at's stomach transforming into something twisted and wrong.

"Move the plates," Sariah said, putting her own plate on a table behind her.

Ceriat and Eleni followed suit, each taking a moment to finish their water. Sariah kicked on the BT, and it hummed to life. It filled the air before them with holographic images of Shiva opposite Gatewood in the distance. At a quick glance, it didn't appear anything had changed since Ceriat had first seen a glimpse of the map, though now that he had time to look, he was surprised at the numbers involved. Gatewood was an established colony, having been terraformed and populated nearly a century earlier, yet the number of ships in orbit were substantially lower than those in a defensive posture around Shiva. That said, Gatewood had the warship in orbit, which pretty much evened everything out.

Sariah confirmed his read. "We've been at a stalemate since Gatewood bombed the settlement," she said, the blue and green lights from the holo lending her face a strange cast. "They can't get to us, but we can't get out."

"What does that mean?" Eleni asked, putting her elbows on the BT. "You can't block an FTL jump."

Ceriat nodded along with Eleni, turning a look on Sariah.

"Well, they are," the governor responded, pulling up the system log of one of the smaller ships in the armada surrounding Shiva. It showed a dozen failed attempts to access the FTL lane in the same number of hours.

Ceriat shook his head. "That's not possible. FTL isn't something you can jam. It just—" he struggled to find the word, then gave up with a shrug, "—is."

"Regardless," Sariah said, turning a raised eyebrow on Ceriat, "it is right now, though we did get one ship out of the system before they managed to jam everything."

"Which one?" Eleni asked.

"The *Nautilus*," Sariah responded, pulling up the manifest for a small freighter. "Haven't heard from them since departure."

Eleni nodded.

"Everyone fine if I keep moving?" Sariah asked, an edge creeping into her voice. She didn't wait for a response. Instead, she zoomed out, and then selected the largest ship in orbit around Gatewood. The nameplate identified it as the *Jocasta*. "This right here is the only ship in their fleet worth a damn. The *Jocasta*."

"Where Victor went," Eleni said, cheeks jumping as she ground her teeth.

Sariah nodded, her face clouding over for a moment before the same sterile look returned. "Best we know, Victor was caught trying to disable the fusion missile system. If he'd had any success, Arctic would still—" Sariah stopped, voice thick. She sucked in a shuddering breath.

Ceriat noted Eleni placed a hand within a few inches of the governor's own. The governor smiled in return, eyes wrinkling in appreciation. "I should be consoling you, Eleni."

"We're your people," Eleni said with a smile.

Ceriat watched the moment with more than a little confusion. He'd heard Spacers didn't touch each other, had seen fights occur over it on stations across the years—fists apparently didn't count—but whatever had happened here, this closeness over a distance was new to him. He couldn't help but feel like he was witnessing something personal.

He cleared his throat. "The plan is to take the ship?"

Eleni pulled her hand back, though not as if caught doing something untoward, Ceriat noted. *What's their relationship?* he wondered.

Gerry's face flashed in his mind, and his heart jumped. *Does it matter?*

Sariah, however, transformed in the wake of the words. "No," Sariah said, straightening. "Almost. You're to disable the *Jocasta*, and then I'm going to demand Gatewood's surrender."

"You're mad," Ceriat said, the words he'd been thinking since

Eleni had pitched the idea tumbling from him. She'd been distinctly lacking in detail; he now knew why. "That's crazy. There's bound to be hundreds if not thousands of soldiers on that ship."

Sariah nodded. "Correct."

Eleni made a noise, then sat there, mouth open and brow furrowed as if she hadn't considered armed resistance. "Then... what's the plan?"

Sariah smiled then, a disarming thing full of venom and deceit. Her unnaturally gold eyes glowed in the low light. She turned to Eleni. "You're going to be captured."

"What?" Eleni snapped, fury transforming her hands to fists.

"And you, my dear Parker," Sariah said, turning and holding out Gerry's dog tag to Ceriat, "are her captor."

Chapter 28
ELENI

"This plan is shit," Eleni grumbled as she settled into what couldn't be more than a twenty-centimeter-wide space behind the pilot seat of Ceriat's little transport, "and this ain't a goddamned chair. Too fucking small."

"Better than a closet," Ceriat said from above her, watching as she wriggled her way into what he'd assured her was a passenger seat.

Sariah had given him back all his equipment, so he now wore the forest green uniform of an ETL surveyor, the logo clear over his left breast.

The only thing she'd given Eleni was a sentence, one she'd heard before. *Do it for your brother.*

Eleni cursed as something pinched her inner thigh, then, as if her flinch away from the pain had suddenly opened up more room, she dropped onto a hard cushion, legs squeezed up against the pilot seat. "Hard disagree."

This ship of his was tiny even by Spacer standards, but it had to be if it had fit inside the cargo bay of the *Lucille*. Chuckling, Ceriat handed her a well-worn exosuit helmet, along with a black plastic tie to hold onto, then launched himself into the front with a familiarity she wished she had. A moment later, the seat shifted forward, clearing a few centimeters for her legs to extend a bit.

"You could do that the whole time?"

Ceriat made a noise in his throat. "Maybe, but there's no fun in that."

She growled quietly.

"Seriously, though," Ceriat said as the sound of flight prep made its way back to her. "I didn't know the seat moved. You're the *Sparrow's* first passenger."

"Never flown with anyone?" she asked.

Ceriat paused before answering, "Been a long time."

Eleni nodded, though she wondered at the delay. Something had happened in Ceriat's past, something dark that had resulted in him losing someone. She'd seen it in his eyes, in the way he'd flinched away when she'd probed, yet still he kept his distance.

It was a mystery—and Eleni hated mysteries. But for now, they had a mission.

Eleni set the helmet beneath her elbow and turned the plastic bindings over in her now-gloved hands. She disconnected the gloves at the wrist and stared at the bruises on her skin. They'd started going green at the edges over the last few hours, probably another benefit of the surgery she'd had. However, the nanobots were out of her system now. The epic, nanobot-filled shit she'd taken just before getting into the *Sparrow* had proved that. Any healing going forward would be hers alone.

"This is going to be hellish, isn't it?"

"Probably." Ceriat sighed. "Prob-a-bly."

He reached to a spot on his left and pulled on a lever near her leg. The motion caused his gloved fingers to brush along her knee. A thrill buzzed up her thigh, settling into her abdomen.

Ceriat flinched away at the contact. "Shit, sorry about that."

"It's fine," Eleni replied hurriedly, grimacing.

"I know y'all don't do the touching—"

"I said it's fine." Heat flooded Eleni's cheeks.

Ceriat craned around in his seat, his face a mask of concern. "I really didn't mean..." His eyebrow shot up as he got a good look at her. "Are you blushing?"

"Fuck off, Ceriat."

"Okey-dokey," he said, a stupid grin splitting his face as he twisted back around.

Eleni cupped her face in her hands and shook her head. The damned warmth was already dissipating, but, fuck, what a mess. Not for the first time, she cursed her body and its desires. Life would be so much easier without all of... this.

In the front seat, Ceriat tapped around for a bit, the silence between them full of awkward intensity.

"So—"

"Listen—"

They both stopped. Eleni smiled despite herself.

"You go first," Ceriat said, shoulders settling back against the seat.

Eleni cleared her throat and straightened her neck as that same warmth flooded into her. She caught the curve of his stubble-covered cheek in the light cascading through the cockpit, the slight turn of his grin. She'd been alone a long time now, easily three years since Hira came and went, taking Eleni's heart with her, maybe more.

This... whatever it was, felt much the same, a sudden infatuation due to extreme circumstances. *Story of my fucking life.* It'd never worked in the past; why would this be any different?

"Nerves." The lie appeared on her lips with an ease that bothered her.

"Nerves?"

"Right," Eleni said, raising her chin. "Nerves."

Ceriat was quiet for a moment before nodding. "Understood."

A moment later, the canopy pulled shut, half coming up over the left, the other over the right. A series of buzzing sounds followed by the hissing of oxygen and pressure in her ears told her it'd pressurized properly. Behind her, engines thudded to life, going from a guttural roar to a dull hum that tickled her skin in a matter of moments. The light at the far end of the cargo hold suddenly seemed very far away.

"Welcome back, Ceriat," an artificial voice chimed suddenly.

Eleni jumped, then immediately chastised herself. Of course this ship would have an AI. Had she thought he just traveled the galaxy alone?

Yes, a small voice chided her, and she felt very stupid. For a moment, she'd considered that, maybe, she'd run into someone as lonely as her. But that was never gonna happen.

"Happy to be back, Izzy," Ceriat said, a smile clear in his words. "How you holding up?"

"Can't complain," the feminine voice replied, though without the flat intonation Eleni was used to in AIs.

Eleni decided to ask about it. "Your AI sounds strange."

"Izzy is one of a kind," Ceriat replied. "Izzy, begin preflight system checks, if you please."

"Will do," the AI replied, then a moment later, "And you sound like a meatsack with vibrating cartilage, ma'am."

Ceriat barked out a laugh. "Be nice, Izzy."

"I will if she is," Izzy replied, an edge to the otherwise artificial voice.

The laughter at her expense did nothing for Eleni's mood. She already felt like an idiot for whatever the hell that whole touching thing had been. Now an AI was talking back to her?

Any remaining heat from the earlier moment disappeared beneath the familiar warmth of anger. "What the hell is this?"

"It's all good—"

"No, it's not—"

Ceriat sighed. "Izzy is just... protective of me."

"Someone needs to be," Izzy replied. "Flight calculations complete."

"Acknowledged," Ceriat said, then tapped out something Eleni couldn't see, "and what the hell is that supposed to mean?"

Izzy made a trilling sound. "It means you wear your heart on your sleeve and constantly get it hurt."

"Ouch, Izzy. Just... ouch."

"This is insanity," Eleni muttered. She shifted as best she could to ward off a cramp in her left leg. "You should reboot this AI. It's getting... excessive."

The AI trilled. "I will vent you into the void if you try."

"Whoa, Izzy," Ceriat said, his hands going up in the air as if placating a living, breathing creature. "Maybe introductions will help?"

"Probably not," Izzy and Eleni said together.

That made Eleni grin.

"We're doing it anyway," Ceriat snapped. "Eleni Mallias, meet Izzy, my ship AI."

"Charmed," Eleni said.

"I am sure," Izzy replied.

Ceriat sighed. "Izzy, meet Eleni. She's a... friend."

Izzy made a noise, but otherwise remained silent.

"Izzy," Ceriat said after a long moment, tone stern.

"Fine," Izzy replied. "Nice to meet you, Eleni."

"I'm sure," Eleni replied, though any anger that'd been there a moment earlier had dissipated as mirth worked itself onto her face.

Listening to Izzy and Ceriat argue was like observing an old married couple who'd stayed together for the kids, only to find out they were too old and stubborn for anyone else after they were left alone.

Still smiling, Eleni began the process of latching the five-point harness that'd keep her in place.

A radio chime interrupted the conversation. Ceriat tapped something out of sight up front. "*Sparrow*, here."

"*You're cleared for takeoff*, Sparrow," Sariah's voice came crisp and clear into the cabin. Why Ceriat didn't use a headset or a helmet left Eleni confused, but she was glad to hear unfiltered communications, so she kept the concern to herself. "*One adden-dum, however.*"

"What's that?" Ceriat asked, hand hovering over the launch controls.

"*Our records show you were a fighter pilot,*" Sariah said, voice unreadable. "*Is that true?*"

Ceriat hesitated before answering, and Eleni noticed he half-turned in his seat prior to answering. "That's true."

For which side? The question popped back into her head from earlier. He'd avoided answering then, and she'd let it slide in the middle of everything else, but that was when she'd thought he was some grunt. A foot soldier.

Now, she couldn't wait to find out the truth.

"*Fantastic,*" Sariah said. "*Hope you're not rusty.*"

"Why?" Eleni interrupted.

Ceriat answered before Sariah. "Because they're going to open fire on us."

"What?"

"Isn't that right, Governor?" Ceriat asked.

A chuckle came back over the radio. "*Got to make it look like a proper escape, don't we?*"

A bucket of ice water poured down Eleni's back. Most of the anti-aircraft turrets were still active, despite the bombing. They'd be shot out of the air in minutes, if not seconds. There was no way they'd get into the clouds, let alone escape the atmosphere.

"I'm out," Eleni said, disconnecting the belt she'd just finished latching. "Not doing this."

"*Sorry, Mallias,*" Sariah said, voice crisp and cold. "*Launch in three—*"

"No!" Eleni shouted, pulling harder at the harness, which only made it worse. "This is crazy!"

"*Two—*"

"Buckle back in," Ceriat said, all humor and amusement gone. "Looks like we're making a break for it."

"*One—*"

"Sariah!"

"*It'll be fine, Eleni,*" Sariah came back. "*Just don't die.*"

Eleni stared at the rear of Ceriat's seat, mouth agape at the words.

"*Launch.*"

The engines exploded into action behind her, sending Eleni's stomach crawling back along her spine. Roaring set her ears ringing. Ahead of her, that slash of light that'd seemed so far away such a short time ago expanded into a blinding flash. Her guts pulled into her back. Ceriat spoke, but whatever he said was lost amongst the ripping wind and screech of the engines.

And then they were outside, the engine sounds falling away.

"—met on now! Targeting is coming in—"

"Incoming artillery," the AI said with far too much poise.

The world spun, sending Eleni's vision swimming. Thuds erupted around them. The world beyond the windows disappeared into black splashes of debris and mess.

Ceriat spun the *Sparrow* off to the left of the explosion, then must've cranked hard on the stick, sending them into the sky again. Eleni's stomach protested mightily. The Miner Slaw still clung to her insides, though what dark magic made that possible evaded her.

The ship leveled out for a moment. Something hissed off to Eleni's sides. *Must be inertial dampeners.*

"Almost there," Ceriat said, voice strange.

Eleni cocked her head. Was he... smiling?

He's nuts.

"Fuck," Ceriat muttered then, and once again the ship pulled into a tight spiral.

Eleni stared at the seat back before her, trying desperately to avoid thinking about fermented rice or anything beyond keeping her stomach. The last thing they needed was for her food to come splattering into a flight cockpit.

Another jerk to the side sent her crashing against the side of the cockpit, helmet jamming hard into her ribs. With shaking fingers, Eleni pulled the helmet over her head and snapped it in place.

The sound equalized as soon as she did. Instead of the roar of wind or the thudding of engines, she now heard Ceriat's grunts and curses as he spun and twisted his ship out of range of the incoming materiel.

As the bursting splashes of color disappeared from the sky, the ship stopped rattling with the effort of avoiding destruction.

Finally, after what felt like an eternity, Ceriat let out a long breath. "Certainly didn't hold back, did they?"

"Sariah doesn't do half-assed," Eleni muttered, hands pressed into her stomach to try to ease its discomfort. "Thought maybe she'd change it up for once."

Ceriat laughed in response. "Yep." He cleared his throat. "Izzy, get us a vector out of here, please. Should be pretty easy since we're at the equator."

"No we're not," Eleni replied.

"What?" Ceriat said, turning in his seat again, even though he couldn't get an angle to see her.

"I said, we're not at the equator," Eleni repeated herself. "We're up at forty-ish degrees," she added, referring to Arctic's latitude.

"She is right, Captain," Izzy confirmed. "We are nearly two thousand kilometers off course."

Eleni stared long at the back of his head. Ceriat shook his head, and Eleni caught him drumming his fingers on the console.

"You okay?"

"Yeah," he replied, though the doubt layered in the word immediately struck a nerve. "Just... confused."

Eleni nodded, though he couldn't see it. "Then we have a mission... right?"

"Right, yeah," Ceriat replied, shaking his head and laughing off the delay. "Izzy, get us off this rock."

"Happily," Izzy replied.

The ship angled of its own accord, rocketing into the sky.

"You sure yer okay?" Eleni said as the sky darkened, and stars shone through the thinning atmosphere.

Ceriat let out a strange laugh. "Yeah. I'm good. You good?"

"Yeah," Eleni said, eyes narrowing on his right hand. It still tapped away on the console, the nervous tic betraying his concern.

"Best be tying yourself up," Ceriat said, stretching in the front seat as he assumed a cavalier attitude. "Could get picked up at any point now."

Eleni grimaced and wrapped the black plastic tie around her wrists, but didn't pull it tight. She hated the idea to begin with, but now? With the way Ceriat twitched and tapped, how he dodged questions, well, that made her nervous, too.

So, despite the plan, Eleni left the tie loose enough she could pull her hands free if needed.

She wasn't going to die today.

Chapter 29
CERIAT

*T*his can't be right. They have to be wrong.

Yet no matter how many times Ceriat ran through the conversation, double-checked the numbers, they were true. He hadn't been at the equator, but in the northern hemisphere of the planet, thousands of kilometers north of his destination.

That was a problem.

<Testing emergency comms,> Ceriat thought, hoping the private channel system hadn't been damaged in all the bullshit over the past days.

<Loud and clear, sir.>

<Perfect,> Ceriat replied, taking a moment to rub at the space on his chest where Gerry's dog tag sat again.

Around him, the atmosphere dissipated like so much mist, the last bits of turbulence shaking away with it. Comfort and panic came with the transition, the familiar edge that'd followed him from Shaal-Nar and had never truly let go of his soul, like a reminder of his sins.

<Yes, Captain?>

<Where is the ETL tower we were supposed to activate?>

Apparently, the sudden silence was enough to trigger Eleni's suspicions. "Everything all right?"

Ceriat cleared his throat, rattled his fingers across a part of the console that didn't respond to touch input. "Yeah, just trying to work through something," he said, hoping he was being vague enough.

It wasn't. "What's that, then?" Eleni asked, voice coming out of the cabin speakers, though a dull, barely audible mutter preceded it from behind him.

"Nothing important," Ceriat said.

Eleni snorted a laugh. "Bullshit, Parker."

"The ETL Tower," Izzy replied.

Ceriat smacked his head back into the headrest as stars filled the viewscreen. "Dammit, Izzy." <*That was supposed to be private,*> he added.

<*Apologies, sir.*>

"The tower? Just outside the settlement. We almost died there, yeah?"

"Not the one in our records," Izzy replied.

Ceriat cursed again. "Izzy, quiet."

"Would you like me to apply sensitivity filters?"

Eleni veritably screamed over him. "No—!"

"Yes—"

There was a long pause before Izzy replied. "I... am going to let you two figure this out. Good luck, Ceriat."

Ceriat grimaced. "Thanks, Izzy."

"Ow!" He wasn't expecting to get smacked in the head.

"Start talking."

Groaning, Ceriat turned on Izzy's autopilot. He'd preprogrammed a route around the planet that would avoid the Shiva forces just in case the governor decided to pull some garbage like they'd just experienced, so she should be good to go. He hoped.

Though maybe he should pretend he hadn't done that? Then he'd be able to avoid having this conversation.

"Parker."

Guess not. "The ETL tower I was sent here to activate is at the equator of the planet."

Eleni made a strange noise in her throat. "But it isn't. It's outside the settlement."

"There's definitely *an* ETL tower outside the settlement," Ceriat said, fingers itching to grab the flight stick, "but that's not the one I was sent to activate."

"You're saying there's more than one tower?" Eleni asked. "Is that normal?"

"No," Ceriat admitted, staring into space and trying to logic his way through the issue, "it's not."

So... why? Why install two towers on a barren planet? He'd never heard of anything like that before, not unless some natural disaster in the midst of the terraforming process took out the first. Hell, if ETL had dropped another tower *after* finding out about the bombing of Arctic, he'd understand it. But before?

Unless they knew. The thought knocked the wind out of him. It made sense for two towers to exist if ETL knew about the settlement, but still wanted to start the terraforming process. If that was the case, that violated all manner of settlement law, especially if, as it certainly seemed to Ceriat, they hadn't gotten approval from the settlers to start the process. And if they hadn't gotten approval, that meant the settlers wouldn't have had a chance to prepare for the resulting chaos that came with the activation of a tower.

Deadly wasn't the right word for it. An ETL tower did whatever was necessary to make a planet habitable for humanity. On barren worlds with solid or solidifying cores, that meant reactivating plate tectonics, flooding the atmosphere with greenhouse gases from the forced creation of volcanoes. Outside of an ETL tower, it generally wasn't even safe to be *on* a planet going through that process. People died when they tried, and they tried a lot, especially miners looking for a quick score.

Ceriat was so caught up in the realization, the sheer horror of what he'd been sent to do, he missed most of what Eleni was saying behind him.

"... another day. Mission comes first," she said. The sound of Eleni cracking her neck set Ceriat's teeth on edge. "Let's finish this."

"The mission," Ceriat said, turning to look out the starboard window at the snowball planet as the horizon rounded and transformed from tundra to the icy planetoid it actually was. "Right."

Several minutes later, that curved edge flattened again as the rocky, gray plains around the equator came into view. The tenuous grasp of gravity tickled his feet and dragged them back to the bottom of *Sparrow.*

"What's happening?" Eleni asked. "Why are we going back?"

Ceriat grimaced. He'd hoped she wouldn't notice until they'd dropped back into the atmosphere. "Scouting out the other ETL tower."

Ceriat's seat rocked forward; she must've hit it. It didn't worry him much; he'd heard her pull her seat bindings closed after takeoff.

"What? No," Eleni said. "Turn around."

"Reentering atmosphere for some reason," Izzy said, clearly confused. "Did we not already do this, Ceriat?"

"Yeah, we did," Eleni said. "So, turn around, man."

"Can't do that, Eleni," Ceriat replied. Then to Izzy, he added, "Prepare for reentry at a point nearest our original destination."

"Yes, sir," Izzy replied, leveling out the *Sparrow* and using their free fall momentum to carry them the thousand kilometers to the equator.

Ceriat's seat rocked forward again. "You fucking traitor!"

"Listen," Ceriat said, pinching the bridge of his nose, "I need to know what the plan was here—erk!"

The fishhook was unexpected. One moment Ceriat was in the process of explaining that he needed to make sure the ETL tower at the equator wouldn't wipe out the remaining settlers if activated, the next, a gloved finger had him by the cheek and pulled back against the seat.

Ceriat scrambled, grabbed for Eleni's hand with his left, but that was short lived.

Another gloved hand seized his left arm and yanked it back into the narrow space between the seat and the cockpit.

Clearly, she'd taken the restraints off somehow.

"Ferk!" Ceriat yelled as his cheek screamed and his shoulder complained. "Lemme shlow!"

"Turn around," Eleni said in a low, emotionless voice, "or I'll rip your fucking cheek open."

"S-fine!"

"What was that?"

"You have a shuckin' shiner in ma mouf—" Ceriat cut off as she pulled harder. Copper sprang to life on his tongue. "Yeth! Okay? Yeth!"

"Good."

Eleni's hands disappeared, leaving Ceriat aching and exceedingly emasculated in the aftermath. Groaning, he tongued his cheek. Sensitive, angry, but no lasting damage beyond that done to his pride.

"Izzy, take us—"

Alarms filled the dash with flashing red lights. A proximity alarm sounded.

Missiles incoming. Ceriat scanned the sky in a moment, noting several identified garbage satellites in orbit around the planet, but nothing like a missile.

Still in control, Izzy pulled the *Sparrow* out of orbit and sent them spiraling away on a tangent from the planet, engines roaring. Without the inertial dampeners, the g forces needed for the move would've turned both Ceriat and Eleni into a bone-filled puddle.

"What's happening?" Eleni asked, still somehow calm despite everything.

"Working on it," Ceriat said, voice cracking at the end. He

pulled up the action report and finally found the source of the alert. "Shit."

"What?"

At first, Ceriat had thought perhaps the missile had come from the surface, maybe some ETL defense battery, though he'd never heard of that before. But this hadn't come from Shiva. No, this attack had sprung into life from, according to the sensor array, a blob of debris that'd been following them since launch.

Ceriat pulled up the rear camera feed from a few minutes prior and cursed. Where the blob of debris had been listed sat a small fighter. He should've seen it, should've known Sariah would do something like this to keep them on mission.

"Info, Parker! Now!" Eleni shouted, pulling him away from his pity party.

"A fighter launched a missile."

The *Sparrow* lurched again, then sudden movements stopped. A hissing sound erupted from the rear of the ship as Izzy vented the inertial dampeners, dropping the kinetic-turned-thermal energy into the last remnants of atmosphere before entering the void of space.

Beyond the cockpit, an object rocketed past and into the darkness. Ceriat let out a low sigh.

"Fighter? You didn't see it?"

Ceriat frowned, a trickle of shame stoking the anger that'd been building since, well, he'd entered this damned system. "It jammed sensors, and I didn't see it on the camera, since you decided to attack me—"

"This shit show is all you, bud—"

He slammed a fist onto the display, making the output shimmer in its wake, but he didn't care for anything beyond the fire in his veins. "This is my ship; I'll blame whoever the fuck I want!"

"Children, we should go," Izzy interjected. "The missile is turning about."

A quick glance confirmed Izzy's statement. Far in the

distance, the object that'd blown by them had completed a tight turn. Now it blazed right toward them, the rear of the device flaring as its onboard rockets shot straight for them.

Anger made Ceriat grab the flight stick and disable Izzy's autopilot.

He flew straight at the rocket, ignoring Eleni's screaming and the slamming on the back of his seat.

A mad idea gave him purpose. He didn't have countermeasures anymore—he'd only had the one charge loaded, and that'd been spent in his first minute in the system—but there was one more thing to use.

It might be a little... unconventional.

The missile flashed. Proximity alarms screamed. So did Izzy.

Ceriat pulled back on the stick. Inertial dampeners hissed to life. The missile disappeared from view.

He slapped the toilet vent button.

An explosion hit them. The *Sparrow* careened away, pinning Ceriat to his seat as the g forces from the initial detonation overwhelmed dampeners, but it'd been enough to keep them from smearing the inside of the cockpit.

Eleni screamed behind him, though whether from fear or fury, he couldn't say.

The displays kicked off then, leaving them in spinning, twisting darkness as thick and empty as any nightmare.

Then, as one, the system booted back up, followed rapidly by a series of hissing sounds as Izzy stopped the spin. A low *hum* filled Ceriat's ears, while Izzy dispersed the dampeners into a controlled release onto the hull. They were going to need the plasma canister in the dampeners in case something else happened. The *Sparrow* slowed until she was facing the blue orb of Shiva in the distance, dozens of kilometers now between themselves and the planet.

Laughter surprised him. With a wry grin, the anxiety and panic that'd fueled him a moment earlier disappearing in a wave of relief. He turned around as best he could to find Eleni gripping the bridge of her nose, eyes squeezed shut... giggling.

"You okay?" he asked, smiling despite himself.

Eleni opened her eyes, met his, and broke out laughing in earnest.

Ceriat's grin became a chuckle. Then he turned, and a laugh tore from him.

Together, they sat like that, the humor of near death jumping in their veins like a Stardust-addled skipper until the chuckles tailed off into quick guffaws, followed by long sighs.

Eleni spoke first, voice thick from laughter. "Didn't know a jumper like this had flares."

"It doesn't. Well, I had the one drone system, but I used it when I arrived," Ceriat replied, grin spreading on his face again. "*Sparrow* is a lot of things; a fighter it is not."

"Then how did..." Eleni tailed off.

He laughed again. "My toilet vent."

A pause. "You vented your *toilet*?"

"Correct."

"At a missile?"

Ceriat's grin nearly broke his face. "Again, correct."

Eleni let out a long sigh that transformed into a whistle. "So... you blew a smart missile with piss and shit?"

"And vomit."

"Vomit?"

Ceriat cleared his throat. "Reentry was rough," he lied.

"That... was really stupid." Still, she made an appraising sound in her throat Ceriat took to mean she approved.

"Probably," he said, shaking away the giggles, "but it worked."

With a few strokes, he pulled up the view of the fighter that'd attacked them. With the distance between, the silver ship barely stood out against the white clouds covering a long mountain range on the planet beneath, but it was enough to see it wasn't chasing them. He told Eleni as much.

"Good. I'm assuming there's no more frozen sewage to vent if we need it?"

"Not unless you have to use the bathroom."

Eleni sucked her teeth. "Hard pass."

With a swipe, Ceriat shut down the video feed, instead staring out the glass at the ball of ice ahead of him. Somewhere on that planet was another ETL tower, one that was meant to transform Shiva into a garden world, and he couldn't get to it to find out what the hell was going on here, especially with the fighter shadowing their movements around the planet.

So it'd have to wait. Eleni would be happy, at least, even if leaving this thread unplucked left him with a rock in his stomach the size of a small moon.

With a sigh, Ceriat pulled *Sparrow* around and, putting Shiva behind, zipped off toward the second brightest star in the sky.

Gatewood.

They had a war to end.

Chapter 30
SARIAH

That was fun, Sariah thought as she settled her ship to the icy tundra between a small hillock and the ETL tower. It'd been a long while since Sariah had last flown a fighter, let alone fired on someone. Who knew she had yet another scratch that needed itching?

The wind down here hurt less, Sariah noted, as she left the tight confines of the fighter for the open tundra of equatorial Shiva. If her nasal passages weren't already charred, she imagined they'd burn from the chill. Adrenaline still pounded in her veins from the cat-and-mouse chase. While she hadn't actually been trying to blow Parker out of the sky, she had to admit he was a damn good pilot.

And with his and Eleni's "escape," the plan was in motion. Nothing could stop it now, not even Eleni's conscience.

Unlike her, Jen had no such qualms. As long as she'd lived, anyway. The *Sparrow's* cargo hold was tiny. An ache lit in Sariah's heart at the thought, but she shoved it away.

Above her, a cloudless blue sky spread from horizon to horizon, sending her stomach a-twitching at the vast open space, even after all these years. Far to the south, a mountain range jutted into the sky, snow-capped peaks purple in the distance. Sariah brought her gaze down to the surface, to the stretching tundra, dotted gray and black from long stretches of stone exposed and shining in the bright light of day.

The sun warmed her face, as if looking down at her in approval. Maybe it was. Maybe Teegarden agreed with her plans. After all, *two* garden worlds seemed greedy to her.

Sariah turned her attention to the black tower in the distance, glistening in that same beautiful light. Unlike the now destroyed building outside Arctic, it was imposing, towering into the sky like a God-driven spike into the stony ground.

Sariah's stomach flipped at the thought of the settlement, at the death and destruction that'd been so necessary. She sucked in a breath and let it out. When that didn't work, she fished in her upper jacket pocket for the small bag of Spacedust there. The old worry worked its way into her fingers as she unsealed the bag with clumsy, gloved hands.

Just a little while longer, she told herself as she tapped out a three-centimeter line of the silver substance on the back of her glove. *Almost done, then I'll stop.*

She needed the single-mindedness that came with the drug, the commitment. She'd handle her shredded conscience later. With a quick snort, Sariah sucked the dust from the back of her hand, filling her nostril with fire, but only for a moment.

Immediately, her worries disappeared in a haze of focus. The taste of arctic chill on her tongue diffused with copper, though perhaps it was from the air or the aftermath of the dust working its way through her sinuses, she didn't know.

A quick scan of the area revealed details she'd overlooked earlier. The edges of ancient hills on the horizon sharpened into peaks, as did each exposed stone covering the ground beneath her. Different textures of snow came into stark relief as it transformed from loose powder to ice and back again.

Those things didn't matter. There was just the Plan now. Only the Plan.

The distance between herself and the tower disappeared in a

blur, the Spacedust driving her forward with confident zeal. Righteousness flooded through her at the realization of impossibility come to life, of a world made for her, created for the sole purpose of providing for her and hers.

Soon, the ETL tower stood stark before her, a ring of wet earth surrounding it. The ground beneath her feet carried the lightest tremor, which should mean it was still active. The nanobot engineers still burrowed into the planet's crust in preparation for activation.

Fantastic. A smile made its way to her lips as she came near enough to touch the tower. Up close, the building held an otherworldliness. The black exterior sucked up sunlight, holding onto the energy there. Even her reflection in the shiny darkness appeared muddled and twisted.

It reminded her of the other tower, though in much better shape than it had been before the bomb. That one had lost this strange sheen, instead caked with dust and grit over the years, snow piled high around its exterior. She'd tried everything she had to get into it, short of blasting it with weapons from orbit. And once that had happened, it'd destroyed the tower, rendering it little more than a makeshift communications hub. She'd gone back to verify that after bringing Eleni and the terrorist back to the new settlement—and she had to make sure the key fob clone worked, obviously.

Those bastards had tried to keep it out of her hands, to stop her from bringing wealth and joy to her people. The Gatewood Conglomerate and the ETL's own greed couldn't be denied, could it? Not with such a tempting target as Shiva on the map. Otherwise, they wouldn't have sent this one, too.

Sariah reached out and touched the building, the tactile sensors in her gloves imprinting the warmth of the exterior onto her fingertips. The metal was smooth, flawless.

They'd thought she didn't know about this one. That she wouldn't find out.

"Idiots," Sariah said. A small part of her hoped the ETL still had contact with the tower, despite the FTL com buoy blackout she had yet to figure out. "I told you no, refused your plan, and yet you did it anyway."

Sariah pulled out the key fob she'd cloned from Parker's tag and held it up, picturing in her mind's eye the triumphant stance she must be presenting to whomever was watching—or would watch, once communications resumed. "This is *my* planet! Mine! You can't have it!"

The last words came out in a hail of spittle that floated on the air, shimmering in the noon light before drifting into nothingness. She licked her lips, mopped the worst of it from her chin before flipping off the building, then placed the key fob where the activation panel should be. The panel flashed to life as it was detected, then dimmed.

Eons passed as she waited, fob on the panel. Ages as the machine worked through its machinations to allow her access to the device, access to the most important part of the Plan.

"What's taking so fucking long?" Sariah spat just as the door slid open with a hiss, revealing a well-lit foyer beyond, replete with a lounging couch with side table.

Sariah blinked and turned to the sky to find the sun hadn't moved, that no time had passed at all. Panic arced through her chest, and in response, she stuffed the fob into her pocket as she entered the tower.

Carefully, she pulled the dust-filled baggie free. More Space-dust hit the back of her hand. Fire in her nose, euphoria sending pleasure writhing through her soul.

Beyond the door, Sariah collapsed onto a couch she barely saw as her limbs, tingling and wailing with joy, gave out. The bag fell from her hand. Across from her, the door hissed shut. She didn't notice.

For now, Sariah had all the time in the world.

Chapter 31
ELENI

The escort ships set Eleni's nerves on edge. To keep from screaming anytime some Gatewood bastard radioed in to speak with Ceriat during the process, she ground her teeth until her jaw hurt.

Now she had a splitting headache to go along with everything.

It hadn't taken long for Gatewood Conglomerate forces to locate them after the close call back on Shiva, especially not with Ceriat hamming it up with emergency calls. He'd made it sound like they'd beaten him near to death, and he'd only just escaped, albeit with a prisoner.

Now, as they floated toward the armada surrounding Gatewood, which itself was a rapidly growing green sphere, Eleni called him out on it. "We didn't treat you that poorly."

There was a pause before Ceriat replied, "You locked me, standing, in a closet."

"True, but there wasn't any torture," Eleni said.

"Standing upright for hours is a form of torture."

Eleni scoffed. "No, it isn't."

"In gravity, it is."

She made a sound in her throat. "Okay, maybe." She hadn't considered that, honestly. Standard security practice was to lock folks standing in low gravity, and since most all issues in Arctic hadn't required more than a few hours in lockup, it hadn't been an issue. "But still, you exaggerate the rest."

"Which part?" Ceriat asked, incredulity layering every word. "The part where you shot at me?"

Eleni scoffed. "I didn't hit you."

"Maybe the bit where your settlement's RecHop tried to vaporize both of us?"

"I'll give you that one."

"Oh! Or how about the time a fighter shot a missile at a transport vehicle, and the only reason we're both alive is because I vented my own shit?" Ceriat asked. "What about that one?"

"Okay, fine," Eleni admitted, "but—"

The radio buzzed then, and a different voice than the rest filled the cabin. "*This is the* Jocasta. *You're cleared to land in Dock 37A, Mister Parker. A security team will be at the ready for your prisoner.*"

Eleni snapped her mouth shut and ground her teeth again. *Prisoner.* She never thought she'd hear the word associated with herself. She'd always been on the right side of the law. Yes, Spacer law—Erias Mining law—but law, nonetheless.

Now here she was, getting dragged onto a warship like a common criminal.

Her stomach twisted at the thought. No, not a common criminal. After this was done, after she completed the mission, she'd be a pariah everywhere but Shiva.

A light vibration caressed her skin as the *Jocasta* filled the windows, stark and gray before the verdant wonderland of Gatewood. The ship was massive, the fore and aft unmoving, the engines and bridge likely sectioned off from the rest. However, the central third spun around an axis like a massive, spoked wheel. Altogether, the *Jocasta* was easily the size of some of the smaller colony ships she'd seen attached to asteroids and rocks around Hobelt. The difference was, this one buzzed with life. Ships encircled the entirety like bees protecting a hive. Automated drones attended to various tasks on the exterior. At least she thought they were drones.

How many people were aboard the ship? How many lives was she about to put in danger?

"Understood, *Jocasta*," Ceriat said, tapping away up front. *Tap, tap, tap-tap.* "Docking in 37A."

After the radio went silent, Ceriat kept tapping away, each thud of a finger against the display driving a new knife into her spine. What was he doing up there? She'd thought she could trust Ceriat, but really, what did she know about him? About his goals?

Eleni tried to look around the pilot's seat but failed to get a good view of the control panel again. She could just ask, weigh his words for lies, but she didn't have her *manju*, and without it, what was she? Who was she?

Eleni squeezed her eyes shut as a beast wriggled in her gut at the thought.

Tap tap.

This was a mistake. She'd given herself over to the enemy, trusted a traitor to help her get the justice her people needed to keep them safe, and now they'd die right alongside her.

Tap tap.

"Who you gabbing at up there?" Eleni asked, the words tumbling out all at once.

The tapping stopped. "Making notes for docking," Ceriat said, "that's all."

Had there been a wobble in his voice? A waver of some sort? Fuck, she couldn't tell without the waveform analysis. Why hadn't she spent more time without the mask? Maybe then she wouldn't be fucking useless.

"Bullshit," Eleni snapped, hoping she was right. "You been tip-tapping up there for a hot minute. Sounds like you're sending a message, like a goddamned traitor."

"Dial it back a bit," Ceriat said, craning around so their eyes met. He paused, then looked away for a moment. "I understand what you're trying to do. I don't agree, but I do get it."

"That's not an answer."

Ceriat flinched. "No, it's not."

They stared at each other, the *Jocasta* growing and spreading beyond Ceriat, but she wasn't looking at the ship. No, she stared Ceriat down, a dull, painful certainty filling her chest as he remained silent.

"Docking procedure initiated," Izzy said.

Ceriat glanced at her wrists and sighed. "You should put the restraints back on," Ceriat said finally, turning away. "They'll be waiting for you."

There it was. The truth. For a moment, she considered lashing out, trying to pop the hatch and vent Ceriat, since he wasn't wearing a helmet, or maybe hammer on him until his face disappeared behind bruises and broken bone.

But she didn't. Instead, she leaned back into the seat, the protestations of her cramped legs a dim pulse behind the overwhelming reality bearing down on her.

She remained silent, hands still loosely bound as the *Sparrow* matched the spin of the central hub. After several long moments, her feet pulled back toward the floor as they entered an open airlock.

The *Sparrow* rattled as it settled onto the docking bay and, behind her, a groaning *thud* indicated the outer doors had shut. A moment later, hissing surrounded them, followed swiftly by the reintroduction of ambient noise she hadn't heard in years. A deep, omnipresent *hum* filled every part of her body.

She was back on a space station.

Eleni's vision blurred. She'd promised herself she'd never leave Shiva, that never again would she live somewhere a small group could control the populace through basic essentials like water or oxygen.

Yet here she was. As the doors before them opened to reveal a docking bay filled with a dozen fighters and an approaching security force in Gatewood uniforms—a blinding array of lime and forest green—and full-face security helms not unlike her own *manju*, a certainty stuck in her mind.

Ceriat popped open the canopy. It unsealed with a *hiss* and screeched open like a bird flapping its wings at an enemy. He stood, pulled on some other lever, and another series of thunking sounds echoed alongside the general chatter of humans and the thudding of boots on a steel floor.

He stood, stretching, then looked back at her, sorrow writ large on his face.

"You're a bastard." Despite herself, Eleni's voice shook with the emotion threatening to send her screaming at him, fists flying.

His brow furrowed, confusion clearly etching itself on his face. "I'm—"

Whatever he'd been about to say was lost as something small slammed into his chest. Ceriat's body stiffened, arms shaking, rigid by his sides. The veins in his forehead stood out against his pale skin, then he collapsed backward, hitting the edge of the cockpit and falling over the edge. A *thud* came soon after, along-side a sickening *crack*.

Eleni stared at where Ceriat had stood, so proud and so sure of himself a moment earlier, in utter shock.

What the ever-loving fuck had happened?

Booted feet on the ladder outside dragged her attention back to a helmeted man, also all in greens, poking over the edge of the cockpit, shock rifle pointed at where she sat. She stared back, too stunned to move, too confused to let the anger sputtering in her chest free.

The rifle came away from her face, followed swiftly by the soldier jumping into the front seat. "Clear," a masculine voice shouted from the helmet. It was scrambled, but somehow familiar in a way that sent disbelief pounding away in the back of her mind like a low O2 headache. "Prisoner located."

The soldier stepped forward, offered her a hand. When she didn't take it, he glanced to his left, then touched a button at the bottom of his helmet. The voice that came out of the helmet was as familiar as her own.

"Els, come on. Only have a second here."

The disbelief disappeared like so much smoke, only to be replaced with a giddy happiness that dragged her to a standing position despite protesting legs. "Victor?"

"Told you they wouldn't kill me," Victor said, a smile clear in the tone of his voice. He reached up and turned the voice scrambler back on. "On your feet, traitor."

Those words spoken by anyone else at any other time would've sent a spear into her heart, but not right now. Not as she reached out and took Victor's hand in her own. Not as she descended the ladder to a dock, only to be surrounded by other soldiers who, she assumed, must be part of the group sent to stop the bombardment by Sariah.

She forced down a grin as Victor gave her a light shove. "Move, traitor."

It took everything she had not to turn around and hug him right there in front of everyone, but she didn't. Despite her assumption that the rest of this guard troop were part of the assault team, she didn't know that for sure, and she'd be goddamned if she got Victor killed after he'd survived everything he'd been through.

So she followed the instructions. She walked away from the *Sparrow*, risking only one glance back at the body lying next to the ship, one arm twisted unnaturally beneath his weight. As she watched, his chest rose and fell.

Better than he deserves.

With that, Eleni left Ceriat behind.

Chapter 32
CERIAT

At least the brig was nicer than the closet back on Shiva, though exactly how he'd arrived at this pleasant three-meter-by-three-meter cell was a mystery to him. That and the cast covering his left arm, veritably buzzing with nanobots as they worked to fix... something left an air of ambiguity to his present situation. These little magic demons had already patched up his wounds from the ETL tower, so he wasn't complaining.

Whatever had happened, his jacket was missing, and there wasn't any pain left in his arm by the time he'd woken in here on the bench along one side, opposite a door that likely served as an airlock in emergencies. In the corner atop a table bolted to the wall sat a plate heaped with rice and a package of water.

He had yet to touch the food, despite the pleasant aroma filling the space—not that he thought it was poisoned or the like. The Miner Slaw just hadn't progressed past forming a rock in his gut made of fermented slurry. Luckily, if it ever progressed past his intestines, a suction toilet sat opposite the table. Which, now that he'd stared back and forth between the two for roughly an hour, seemed pretty unhygienic, given the presence of atmosphere and artificial gravity.

He probably needed to start thinking about escape or

contacting someone, but thinking about the toilet and the rice, and the way the air smelled like a machine shop crossed with a functioning stir fry restaurant kept him from remembering the look on Eleni's face just before everything went blank.

Well, not everything. He remembered the prongs hitting him in the chest, the feel of them penetrating his flight jacket just over Gerry's tags, followed by an overwhelming pulsing sensation just before he lost consciousness.

With his good hand, Ceriat fished the tags from around his neck. Instead of the faded bits of metal he'd become so used to, cracks now ran the length, breaking up the aluminum façade that'd covered the embedded circuit board beneath. A breath hitched in his throat at the sight, and he tried running a thumb along the surface to calm himself.

Cursing, Ceriat dropped the tags. A sliver of metal had embedded itself into his thumb. Trying to keep the hitch from turning into a sob, he plucked the piece of metal out with a finger-nail and flicked it to the side before looking at the wound.

A deep red drop of blood welled out through the callus there. His first inclination was to suck away the seepage, but something stopped him. Instead, he stared as it grew like a brilliant crimson balloon before the surface tension let loose, sending his blood into a tiny stream that flew down the side of his finger. Cursing, he finally stuck his thumb into his mouth, but the drop escaped.

Following its path, he watched it splash atop the shattered dog tags on the ground and soak into the cracks. An ache joined the breath stuck in his throat. Before he realized it, the tags went back around his neck and beneath his shirt, where they laid, warm and out of sight, against his skin.

Ceriat leaned back until his head tapped against the wall behind him.

Eleni's voice filled his mind. "You've been tip-tapping up there for a while..."

With a quick nod, Ceriat cracked his head against the wall.

Stars exploded in his vision, but the pain from the impact made him feel better.

"It sounds like you're sending a message to someone..."

Another crack, but this one didn't ease his conscious as much.

She'd gotten that right. He had been communicating with someone.

Or rather, he'd tried.

As soon as the Gatewood fighters began their escort, Ceriat had attempted to access the FTL lane for a jump, with no success, then he'd tried to contact Earth, but every attempt to connect with the FTL buoy network resulted in a No Signal message. Still, he'd queued up messages requesting help from the ETL and the Protectorate, just in case the blockage expired while he was away from *Sparrow*. And, of course, he'd queued a message for Luce, the dog sitter, with an apology and credits attached for extending Ginny's stay with her.

He hoped it was enough. Ginny had made the last two years livable after he'd heard of Gerry's passing and dropped into a deep depression. That in turn had caused his most recent partner, Helen, to depart in a brilliantly excessive blowout fight that left him stunned, and her with most of his furniture.

"Helen, huh," Ceriat muttered, staring at the red smear on his thumb. "What. A. Bitch." He said the words even though they weren't true.

Jealous? Insensitive? Yes. A bitch... not really.

That moniker likely applied more to him than her. After all, he'd been the one still infatuated with his ex.

A sudden chime came from his left arm. He turned to it in time to see the cast disintegrate around the exposed limb, the space where his shirt sleeve suddenly ended right above where the cast had been. Beneath was pasty white skin that typically didn't see much UV light.

The bits that'd once made up the cast dropped to the floor and writhed their way to the door like a hive of angry ants.

Together, they stacked upon each other rapidly, until finally solidifying into a solid, white cube.

Ceriat had seen nanobots in action a few times, most notably in the failed surgery on his hip, but it still awed him that the little buggers existed. As a kid back on Earth, he'd heard of nanobots in manufacturing and such, of course, but medical uses had been outlawed, or so he'd thought. It wasn't until he'd joined the Protectorate that he'd found out the ban had been lifted decades earlier, though he wasn't that surprised. Earth wasn't the center of humanity anymore, not when humans stretched across the galaxy on innumerable garden worlds, most of their own custom creation. Hell, even he had called New Eden home instead of Earth until after Shaal-Tu.

Still, the little beasties seemed more like magic to him than science, these more so than any others he'd encountered.

A knock on the door pulled him out of his thoughts. Ceriat turned his attention on the door and waited. And waited.

After a long moment, brow raised in mingled amusement and confusion, Ceriat cleared his throat. "Come in?"

The door chimed and slid open, revealing a tall, helmeted spacer in full security gear, including what appeared to be a stun pistol in hand. *That explains that, at least.* "On your feet," a distorted voice crackled through the mask.

Ceriat did as requested, climbing to his feet with arms up. His left was stiff, and the action sent a strange pain rattling along his forearm. The guard swept in, pistol aimed at Ceriat's chest, and gave the block of nanobots a nudge that sent them into the hallway.

"Seems strange to knock if you're just going to threaten me," Ceriat said, still quizzical.

The guard responded by standing, sweeping the room, then stepping to the side of the door. "Clear."

From around the corner came a woman standing barely a meter-and-a-half tall. Dark brown hair that'd once been a brilliant, fake crimson sat in a tight bun atop her head. Brilliant blue eyes—artificially colored during a drunken weekend while on shore leave on New Eden—stared at him from deep brown skin. A bemused grin split her still pretty face, revealing sparkling white teeth.

Just like he remembered.

The gray uniform with silver captain's tags on the collar and the black cane, however... they were new.

Ceriat's arms fell in surprise, causing the guard to raise his weapon again, but he didn't care. "Ouroboros?"

Her grin broke into a full smile as his old squadmate stepped forward, still leaning heavily on the cane, the other arm going wide for a hug. "Parker."

He swept to her, vision blurring as he grabbed her tiny, still solid frame and squeezed. "You were dead. I heard it."

"Gonna die now if you don't calm down, Sergeant," Ouroboros squeaked, laughing at the end.

He stopped squeezing and released her, hands still on her small shoulders. A strange sensation after spending the last 24 hours with Spacer giants, for sure. "Sorry, it's just—"

"A bit much?" she answered, shifting her weight to her left leg and lifting the cane into the crook of her arm. "Same. Imagine my surprise at hearing we had Protectorate hero Ceriat Parker in the brig of all places."

At the word *hero*, his gut flipped, and Ceriat dropped his hands from her shoulders. Still, the smile stayed. "Ouroboros—"

"Linny," she said, holding up a hand, "or if you want to be formal, Captain Nova."

"'Captain Nova?'"

She shrugged. "Ouroboros sounded cool as a kid, but once people start saluting and can't pronounce your Ragnarok-inspired name, it gets old."

"Is that why I couldn't find you after...?" he tailed off.

A shadow passed over Linny's face, but disappeared as quickly as it came. "No. You couldn't find me because I didn't go back to the Protectorate." At the raise of his eyebrow, she continued, "I'd appreciate it if you kept this all between us, by the way. It's a good life here with these folks, and I'd rather not fuck it up."

"What about him?" Ceriat asked, nodding at the guard.

Linny turned to him, smile returning. "Victor? He's a good kid, aren't you, ensign?"

He snapped to attention. "Yes, ma'am."

"Picked him from an incoming freighter a couple months back," Linny said, then nodded back toward the hallway and started walking, cane snapping alongside her right leg. "He doesn't look like much, but he used to program, uh—" she paused as she reached the doorway, then turned back to him, free hand swirling in the air as she searched for the term, "—camera shit. He's a little rough, but without him, we wouldn't have eyes on the C at all." Linny stepped out into the hallway, then gave him a look he remembered from Basic. *You slowing me down already?*

Ceriat gave Victor a look, and at the guard's lack of response, joined Linny in the hallway. He followed his old comrade down a long, straight corridor that led to an elevator of some sort. A worry niggled at the back of his mind. *What about the missile? Who dropped the nuke?*

He asked as much.

Linny froze, then shook her head as he came up next to her. "Some Spacers made it onboard. Not sure if they missed or what, but they triggered a launch. Hit their own fucking planet." She resumed walking.

The realization slammed into him. Spacers had fired the fusion warhead? Why? It didn't make sense.

Then again, neither did Ouroboros—Linny—being here, alive.

One thing at a time.

"You're saying Spacers took the shot?"

Linny grunted an affirmative.

"But why?"

Linny cocked a perfectly carved eyebrow at him. "No fucking

clue, Parker. I'd say we could ask them, but they offed themselves after the launch."

A cold calm settled over his shoulders. It'd been a suicide mission? Again—why? What was the endgame here? And how did Sariah fit into this?

Now he had to choose which one to believe: the woman who'd captured him and blamed him for the bombing of her settlement, or the one who'd faked her own death, then flew around the galaxy without telling him she still lived.

If he believed Linny, he needed to tell her about Eleni—whom he assumed was locked up as well. If he didn't, then...

Shit, he didn't know. How was he supposed to decide these things? This wasn't his job. The truth was, Ceriat was only good at following orders. He went to planets and activated ETL towers, oblivious to the results, or if anyone inhabited those planets. Before that, the Protectorate had pointed him at cities and told him to lay waste to them.

He didn't know how to make choices, to define right and wrong, not on this scale. He'd always just relied on other people to tell him what he did was right. He'd thought he'd found a place with morals, with an altruistic goal in the ETL.

But now? Who could he trust?

With a deep breath, Ceriat cleared his throat and pushed all of it to the back of his mind. No time like the present.

"So... how?" he finally asked, gesturing at his old crewmate as he joined her.

"After... back then," Linny said as Ceriat came alongside her, "I got left behind."

"What? They couldn't—wouldn't—"

"Did," Linny said with a finality that shut Ceriat up. "Spent seven weeks dodging those fucking Medusa Trees and eating fuck all."

Ceriat gestured at the cane. "Is that how...?"

"This?" Linny asked, nodding at her reliance on the crutch.

"Fuck, Parker, you think a damned tree could catch me if I didn't want it to?"

"Almost got me."

Linny winked at him. "Yeah, but I'm better than you."

"Uh-huh," Ceriat said with a smile. The ease of an old friendship worked its way into his bones, only to be stopped by the anxiety rattling around in his head. "So, how'd it happen then?"

"You wouldn't believe me if I told you," Linny said as they made it to the elevator.

The thud of whirring machinery told him she must have some sort of access fob on her to automatically call the elevator. A quick look didn't reveal an access panel.

"Try me."

She eyed him and, as the doors opened to reveal a cylindrical space, she nodded and stepped inside. "All righty, Parker. I'll tell you."

He joined her, as did Victor, following close behind.

"Don't keep me in suspense now."

The elevator took off like a shot, sending his guts into his feet for a moment. Ceriat noticed Linny grimace at the pressure, but she kept it to herself. "Two years back, I was in the Horsehead Nebula, fighting for system control, when one of those space whales ran into my ship."

"Space whales?" Ceriat asked, forcing himself not to grin.

"Fucking real thing, Parker," Linny said, giving him one of those smiles that could still melt his heart. "Bastard took out my ship and sent me into the vac."

"That's how you hurt your leg?"

Linny snorted. "That wouldn't do it. No," she continued, "I managed to hook onto the beast and ride it back to civilization, but on the way, one of its babies ate my damned foot."

"Helluva way to lose a foot," Ceriat said, "but you're right; I don't believe it."

Linny eyed him, smiling. "Good. Because that's all bullshit."

"Figured."

"Not the whales, though." She paused, a small smile pulling at her lips. "They really are stunning."

After a long moment, Ceriat cleared his throat. "You ever even been to Horsehead?

Linny just grinned in response.

"So, how did it happen?"

At first it didn't seem like she'd answer, but then the words came out, tumbling after each other like she couldn't stop them. "A year ago, we were setting up orbital defenses, when this crazy squadron of mismatched fighters comes out of nowhere," Linny said, staring upward at a memory Ceriat couldn't see. "Hit the *Jocasta's* bridge, hard. We lost atmo almost immediately. Barely had time to make it into a pressurized space before—well, you know how that works," she added with a flip of her hand.

Ceriat turned away, guilt wriggling up his spine at the imagery. That was what he'd been sent here to do, in a way: take control of the ship. Could he still do it? Especially now that Linny had sprinkled in the doubt of who had, in fact, launched the missile that took out Arctic.

Linny smiled at the wall without mirth, clearly misunderstanding the look on his face. "Most of me made it into the cabin." She lifted the hem of her pant leg to reveal puckered, brown skin lined with black scars that ended at a prosthetic ankle seated inside her dress shoe. "Nanobots couldn't repair the nerve damage, so I'm stuck with this antiquated piece of shit."

"Oh, shit, Linny, I'm sorry."

"Don't be," she said, a forced smile on her face. At the same time, the distinctive feeling of gravity fading away plucked at Ceriat's stomach. "After all, most of the time it's a non-issue."

"Still, I'm sorry." The elevator slowed to a stop, only the faintest tug of attraction pulling him toward the floor now.

The door of the elevator slid open, and a roar of low murmurs and activity came flooding through as it did. Ceriat's gaze was pulled toward the massive viewscreen to his right. The digital display followed the slope of the ceiling as it extended from left to right. Where he stood, the resulting displayed image appeared warped and bent, but still... the sight of Gatewood glimmering in the void, the system's star shining red in the distance, was breathtaking.

Beyond that, the bridge bustled with activity. A dozen or more green-uniformed soldiers—scientists? Civilians? He didn't actually know—manned the same number of stations. One specific panel was surrounded by three of the people, one of which was gesticulating wildly.

"It's not us!" he said, pale face flushed. He hammered on his thigh. "I guarantee it."

The woman sitting at the station itself rubbed her temples. "Then what is it?"

"Maybe FTL is just down?"

The entire group snorted. A black-haired man to his left gave him a patronizing pat on the shoulder. "Right, and physics just stopped working."

"Well, it's not—" He looked up and blanched as he met Linny's stare. "Captain on the bridge!"

Everyone snapped to attention at the call with an efficiency Ceriat found admirable. Maybe they *were* military?

Linny waved them off and glided into the room on light steps, her cane under her arm like a riding crop. "At ease," she said, sliding into her chair and tapping the armrest. She lifted her eyes to stare at nothing, gaze moving and eyes flashing while she read something on her personal HUD. "Any updates, Garris?"

"FTL is..."

Linny swiped at the air. "Figure it out."

"Yessir," Garris said, shoulders slumping. The group around him huddled back together.

"What's going on with Teegarden c? Jenkins?" Linny asked. She gestured at Ceriat to join her, and he closed the distance, despite the many eyes watching him.

A tall woman to his left cleared her throat. Her gaze shifted between Ceriat and Linny. "Our sensors are still down, Captain—"

"Did we go blind while I went for a walk with an old friend?" Linny asked, the friendly tone from earlier disappearing as she turned to stare down Jenkins. "Optical scanners just gave up the ghost while I got a cup of tea?"

"No, sir," Jenkins said. Her cheeks flexed as she snapped to attention.

Bit of pride in that one, Ceriat thought.

"Then give me a visible spectrum scan in five. Victor fixed those, right?"

"Yessir."

"Then get on it."

Another "yessir" followed alongside a snapped salute.

Linny swiped quietly from her seat a few more times, before sweeping her hand down and bouncing to her feet with an annoyed grunt. "Contact me when you have those images, Jenkins."

"Yessir."

"And get me in touch with the Protectorate, Garris."

"I'm trying—"

Linny *tsk*ed. "Stop trying and fucking do it. Have I made myself clear?"

Garris looked like he was about to argue, but instead, he deflated and snapped a salute. "Yessir."

"Good." Linny jerked her head to the side, toward a door on the far side of the bridge. "I'll be in the Ready Room. Come on, Parker."

"Nice ship." Ceriat flashed a smile at the crew, but only suspicion and annoyance stared back.

They were right to be suspicious. What Linny was doing here, taking him through the ship, had all the hallmarks of a security breach. Yet still she led, and everyone kept quiet.

Either she ran the *Jocasta* with an iron fist, or the crew trusted her.

Ceriat was surprised to find he didn't know which could be more likely. After all, it'd been years since Shaal-Tu. A lifetime.

Still not long enough.

Eyes down, Ceriat followed Linny off the bridge with light steps in the low gravity.

A gentle breeze pushed at him as he entered, the lingering scent of citrus cleaner tickling his nose. The initial silence in the wake of the doors shushing shut was near deafening. A large, two-tone mahogany and silver table filled the majority of the otherwise windowless rectangular room. Ten executive chairs with the same color scheme surrounded its oblong shape. At the far end of the room was a blank wall that no doubt served as a display when needed.

True to form, Linny didn't waste time filling the silence. After gliding in and taking a seat at the far end of the table, she turned to him, a small grin tugging at her lips. "'Nice ship?'"

Ceriat shrugged. "I don't talk to people much anymore."

"Clearly." Linny gestured next to her. "Take a seat and bring me up to speed. Notably, how you ended up flying here from a planet filled with squatters intent on nuclear war."

"I'm not one of them," Ceriat said, pulling one of the chairs aside and gently lowering himself into it. Still, he managed to jam the armrest into his back the first time. Low grav was always worse than no grav in his opinion.

"Didn't say you were."

"You implied it," Ceriat said as he got comfortable. And until the words came out, hadn't he been? He placed his hands on the smooth, carbon-fiber tabletop, his choice made in the blink of an eye. "And I needed to say it."

Linny smiled, but just gestured at him to continue.

"Here's the deal," Ceriat said, staring at the table and wondering if the direct approach was the right one to take. But this was Linny. Beating around the bush would do nothing here. "They have settlement documents."

Linny furrowed her brow and leaned forward. "No, they don't."

"Yes, they do," Ceriat said. "I've seen them."

She bit her lip, then leaned back again with the well-practiced, cavalier attitude he remembered from Basic. "They must be falsified. Gatewood has terraforming rights to Teegarden c."

"That's what I said, but then they showed me the docs."

"They're lying, then," Linny snapped, hands white-knuckling on the armrest as her gaze darkened. "And why you?"

That question caught him off guard. "What?"

"Why you, Parker?" Linny asked, all mirth and humor disappearing. "Why are you here?"

"To activate the ETL tower," Ceriat said. He couldn't help the feeling he was being backed into a corner, and his body responded in kind. The next words tumbled free with nary a thought. "And, by the way, there are two towers on Shiva."

"Shiva?"

"Teegarden c," Ceriat corrected himself, cursing inwardly at the slipup. The last thing he needed was for Linny to think he was one of them, especially after getting here and seeing everything firsthand. "There are two towers."

"Why does that matter?" Linny asked. "And you still haven't answered my question."

Right. "I'm an ETL Activation Tech nowadays," Ceriat said, keeping his eyes on Linny. "Dropped into Teegarden to activate *a* tower on Teegarden c. So, 'why me?'" Ceriat shrugged. "Wrong place, wrong time."

"Story of your life, brother," Linny said, voice low and serious.

Ceriat didn't disagree. Instead, he stared at Linny, weighing the truth, and trying to find reality inside the twisting labyrinth he'd ended up inside, all to find the answer to one question: *who do I trust?*

Linny cleared her throat. Shook her head. "Still, why are you here, Parker? It's obvious you're not defecting like your message stated."

Ceriat cursed himself for that, but stayed silent. She'd caught him in a lie without even trying. God, he was bad at this. It didn't help that he didn't know what to believe anymore.

"Parker?"

"Hm?"

Linny leaned forward. "Do they know who you are?" she asked, eyes digging into his own. "What you—we've—done?"

Ceriat tried to respond, but the rock forming in his throat and the sudden stink of ash in his nostrils kept him from vocalizing. Instead, he shook his head in the negative.

Nodding, Linny let out a breath, then caught his eyes and held his gaze with her own. "Then why are you here?"

Heat flooded into his face, pressure building behind his eyes as he returned her look. "They don't know who I am, but they sent me for something—" he struggled to find the words, "—like that."

With those words, Ceriat chose his side. For good or ill, the die had been cast.

"Have you started the process?" Linny's eye twitched, but otherwise, she didn't move. Ceriat shook his head again, and Linny visibly relaxed. "Well, thanks for talking to me first before blowing up my people."

"I hadn't planned on that, Linny."

She shook her head, then turned away, a shadow passing over her face. "Who the fuck is this woman who can convince people to do shit like this?" Linny snapped her fingers as if trying to recall something important. "What's her name?"

"Sariah?"

"Yes!" Linny said, hammering her fist on the desk hard enough she bounced out of her seat a bit. "Hell, you've only been in system for what? Thirty-six hours?"

"Seems longer."

"I fucking bet," Linny snapped, grimacing. "Thirty-six hours and you've already been roped into a plan to destroy *my* ship by a sadistic bitch with a grudge a mile long." She paused, then stared Ceriat down. "Here's the real question, Parker. What're you going to do now?"

Ceriat barked out a mirthless laugh. "Obviously, I'm not going to blow the ship."

"You think?"

"To be fair, I never planned on it. I wanted to disable it." I *won't blow up the ship*. A chill shot down Ceriat's spine, and he looked hard at Linny, who recoiled at the intensity. Shit, what if Eleni had different orders? "Where's Eleni?"

Linny's brow furrowed and she cocked her head at him. "Who?"

"The woman who came in with me. We need to find her," Ceriat said, shooting to his feet with enough force he floated into the air. "Now."

"Wait, what?" Linny asked, remaining seated. "What's going on?"

"I wasn't alone on the ship," Ceriat said, pulling himself back down to the floor with help from the tabletop, "and if she doesn't know what happened, everyone here is in danger."

"You were the only one reported on the ship—" Linny grimaced and rolled her head back and forth, jaw flexing. "That motherfucker." She swiped at the air, eyes sparkling with her HUD. "Where's Ensign Mallias?" Whatever response came back made her curse, swipe in the air, and get to her feet. "Victor is missing."

"Wait. Mallias?" Ceriat asked. "His name is Victor Mallias?"

"Yeah," Linny replied, gesturing at him to continue.

The way Eleni had replied when he'd pushed her to reveal that she'd lost a brother back during their first meeting. What were the chances? "I think Victor is Eleni's brother."

"What?" Linny's face darkened. "God, I hate extremists, and now I have two of them on board." Her askance glance told him she wasn't sure if that number should be three.

"We need to find them before they blow the ship," Ceriat said. "I think I know where they're going."

Linny stood. "Where?" she asked.

Good old Linny. She didn't ask "why" or "how." That'd come later.

"The FTL drive."

"Of-fucking-course that's where you'd go," Linny snapped as she walked to the doorway.

Ceriat shrugged as the door to the Ready Room swished open, a strange pride filling him. "The plan was just to disable the ship, not destroy it, though I *was* good at blowing stuff up."

"Stop jerking yourself off and stay here," Linny replied back to him.

"Linny—" Ceriat cut off as she threw a withering stare in his direction.

Linny shook her head. "You've done enough, and we're going to have a *long* conversation about what the fuck you were thinking when I get back. Stay here."

Ceriat wanted to stand and scream he could help, but he'd seen that look many times over the years. Instead, he nodded.

"Good," Linny said as she stepped through the doorway, "and don't blow up my fucking ship while I'm gone," she added, her voice twisting into a light lilt that made him smile.

"Yes, ma'am," Ceriat replied with a smile and a salute. "Happy hunting."

Then Linny was gone, and Ceriat was alone.

Chapter 33

ELENI

"Trust me."

Victor's words echoed in Eleni's mind, his confident smile gone, replaced with nervous sweat and a flinch of the lips. Then he'd turned and left, alive and twitching with enough anxiety she didn't need her *manju* to verify it.

That'd been almost a standard hour ago.

Now she sat inside the mess hall where he'd asked her to wait for him. It had the perfumed scent of wealth and privilege, as spices mingled together into a heady mix of heat and sweet. The smells tickled Eleni's tongue. The conflicting tastes made her salivate and want to vomit at the same time, though the latter could be due to the crowded mess. All but the loudest of the soldiers dissolved into the dull roar cascading off the hard white walls of the room.

She'd adapted quickly to the idea of personal space while on Shiva. Suddenly being back in the crowded interior of a starship no longer felt comfortable, let alone calming. She tried to distract herself by scraping away at a matter replicator tray with a spork, separating risotto from the now-cold broccoli standing brown and wilted off to the side.

She kept her head down and waited. With the number of

people here—easily over a hundred at any one time; they shifted in and out like the tides—she doubted anyone would take too long looking at a lone soldier. Still, caution never hurt anyone.

After escorting her off Parker's shuttle, Victor had taken her to a small cabin, handed her a uniform, and given her directions to the mess for food. Then he'd disappeared out the door to of the cabin with those two words—*trust me*—and naught else.

She hadn't even had a chance to tell him the plan.

"Trust me," Eleni whispered, dragging the spork through the grease and mess on her plate until it held the barest resemblance to a blooming flower. Maybe. She couldn't recall what they looked like. With a snort, she scraped away the symbol. "How? Why?" she whispered to no one.

"'Why' what?"

Eleni jumped at the words, spork sending a piece of broccoli skittering onto the table. Across from her a short man in the same green uniform she wore set down his own plate. He flashed a grin as he did so, blue eyes flashing as they met hers as if he'd just received a message on his HUD. His badge read 'Psomas.'

Her heart slammed, a light tingling running through her chest at the sight of him, though whether from the worry that he'd somehow read her thoughts about Victor or something more feral, she couldn't tell in the moment.

What she did know was Psomas was beautiful.

"You dropped this," he said, grin pulling into a full smile, teeth just poking out behind perfect lips. He set her lost piece of broccoli on her tray with manicured hands. The barest whiff of musk tickled her nose as he pulled away. "Need to eat your veggies."

His smile fell back into a grin as she sat there. Staring.

Shit. Eleni cleared her throat and ran her fingers over the stubble above her ear as she turned her gaze away from him and to the table. She flinched at the old acne scars there, all callused and rough, before looking down at the plate again. God, she missed her *manju*. "Thanks."

"Not a problem," he said.

Only his hands were visible from where she stared, tanned and thin. He idly drummed his fingers across the tabletop as they sat there in silence. She found herself wondering if he played instruments with those fingers.

Go away, she prayed to whomever was listening, interrupting her own train of thought. She didn't need attention right now, especially not this kind.

Maybe if we were on Shiva, though...

Again, she ran her fingers over her ear. Again, she encountered stubble from her unshaved scalp and scars.

Probably not.

"So," Psomas said just before sticking his hand out to her, "I'm Shawn."

Eleni stared at it for a long moment, mind reeling at the contamination there. She didn't know where he'd been before walking over here, or what type of bacteria might be trafficking, unknown, on his skin.

Apparently, she waited too long, because he pulled his hand back suddenly, an awkward chuckle breaking free. "Ah, you grew up on a station, I assume?" His tone changed, the words lilting in embarrassment.

"I'm a Spacer, yes," Eleni said, a small smile cracking her own face despite herself. "Sorry."

"No need to apologize," Shawn said. "I should've known with the—" He cut off and made a swirling motion around his head.

Self-consciously, she covered the acne scars on her forehead and nose, but then it hit her. The tattoos on her head. She flushed despite herself. They were just a part of her, a piece of Spacer culture you didn't question, and she'd kept hers under her *manju* for so long, she'd forgotten what it was like when someone noticed. As she'd watched the soldiers milling about, their haircuts all close-cropped or grown out, Eleni had assumed they had markings under their hair.

Eleni's chest clenched. Had she been flagged by security

already? Was this a preliminary attempt to identify a threat? Or was he just... flirting with her?

No, it couldn't be that. Right?

Eleni's heart hammered; her vison narrowed. She had to get out of here, finish the mission, even if it cost her life; she could do it if it meant her people would have a home.

"Are you okay?"

The question stopped Eleni in her tracks. She raised her gaze and found Shawn staring back at her, blue eyes filled with what she thought might be concern.

Her worries dissolved under his gaze, and she found herself smiling and shaking her head. "Yeah, I'm just new." The ease with which the lie flowed from her lips surprised her. Still, Eleni gestured briefly at the mess and all the clearly planet-born soldiers filling the place, the kernel of a plan coming to bear. "Feeling a little..."

"Out of place?" Shawn asked, concern disappearing in the wake of a radiant smile. "Me, too."

"You?" Eleni couldn't help the grin now.

Shawn shrugged and made a face as if having just been dealt a great insult. "Yeah, me. You think it's easy being on a ship filled with people better than you at almost everything? It's difficult being the dunce."

Eleni laughed. Then snorted. Heat flooded her face at the sound, and she looked back down at her plate.

After a short silence, Shawn cleared his throat. "What's your name?"

"Eleni," she replied, then immediately cursed herself.

She should've lied. Then again, Eleni had spent her entire life enforcing the law; she'd never had reason to lie. Not really. The lies she'd already told in this conversation made a ball of anxiety grow in her stomach.

If Shawn was some security drone in disguise, he didn't give any signs. "Nice to meet you, Eleni."

"Likewise."

Another silence stretched out between them, only to end once again as he let out a low groan and got to his feet. "Well, it's been a pleasure, but I have to get back to engineering."

That caught her attention. "You work in engineering?"

Shawn flashed another smile, but this time it did nothing for her. "I do, down in the engine room. You?"

Eleni caught his eyes and smiled what she hoped was an enticing smile. "I think that's where I'm assigned, too. Care to show me the ropes?"

Before he spoke, Eleni knew his answer. His pupils dilated ever so slightly, tongue touching his lips in nervous anticipation. With one sweeping arm, he motioned her to her feet.

She didn't need Victor or Parker. Eleni would do this on her own and save her people.

The only thought slowing her down as she followed Shawn out of the mess hall was a bit of regret at his presence. But even pretty people die.

At least, that was what she told herself as she followed him to the lift, a nugget of guilt rolling in her stomach like a cancerous pearl.

Chapter 34
SARIAH

Sariah woke into darkness, a heavy throbbing behind her eyes.

The familiar stink of burnt electronics lingered in her nose and on her tongue, threaded through with rust and iron. Groaning, she sat up, swiping at her nose. The back of her hand came away with crusted blood, and she cursed herself. She'd done too much that time. If she wasn't careful, she'd end up like old Eustace, screaming in the dark as he died from the nosebleeds.

The ceiling, at first dark, brightened slowly as the tower detected motion. Still, as the lumens increased, so did the intensity and reach of the headache, as if a tiny demon had been gestating in her skull and finally reached maturity. Now, the little bastard ran rampant down her spine and into her arms and legs, dragging that deep, throbbing ache along with it.

Behind it, Jen's nervous face flickered in her mind.

Sariah leaned forward and pressed the heels of her hands into her eyes until starbursts shone and scattered. It did nothing to relieve the pressure, though it smeared away the guilt-fueled face that'd haunted her through her unplanned nap.

Nothing got rid of the pressure. Well, almost nothing.

"Just a little," she muttered. "Just enough to take the edge off."

With shaking hands, Sariah reached into her pocket for the packet of Spacedust there—and came up empty.

Everything became a blur. Each pocket in her jacket and pants turned out, fuzz and debris examined for traces of the precious dust. She found the key fob clone and tossed it away. It didn't matter. Nothing else mattered.

"No, no, no." She'd had it when she came in. Took a hit right after entering...

Sariah tried to stand, but the ache in her bones and joints, in her soul, sabotaged her. She spilled to the floor in a heap. Not that she cared. The floor was where she needed to be. She'd dropped the packet. It must be here.

She cast about, searching the ground with trembling fingers, while she ignored a tiny voice in the back of her mind whispering four words.

What are you doing?

"Just a little," she repeated, crawling along the polished floor.

A floor clearly maintained by some automated cleaning system. Fear grew into a stone in her throat. What if the system had engaged while she slept? What if the dust was gone, vacuumed and dumped into some incinerator?

"Nonono." The word turned into a rolling murmur, the rock in her throat pushing against the inside of her head, combining with the headache until her vision blurred.

Sariah blinked, sending hot tears streaming down wind-chapped cheeks.

Her fingers swept through something. Hope surged in her chest as she skittered forward on all fours, wiping the tears from her eyes with the back of her hand until she saw it.

A torn baggie, the snow-white dust spread out amongst the grit from the bottoms of her boots. A low, mournful wail escaped her throat at the sight. Ruined. It was all ruined.

She swept the pile of dirt and dust into a makeshift pile, the typically pure white powder an off-color tan from the contamination. Even then, there wasn't enough to get her through this. To finish the Plan.

Not that she was considering it. That'd be crazy. Too far, even for her.

Sariah licked cracked lips and stared at the small pile on the ground before her as if it were a mirage and she a wanderer in the desert.

"Sterile," Sariah muttered, still licking her lips as her body threatened to give out from the hopelessness wriggling its way alongside the building pain. "Soil is sterile."

They'd checked that when they'd arrived. Shiva had had to start a fertilization program to grow anything. Sterile. The dirt was sterile.

Sterile. Sterile. Sterile.

Her face scraped against the floor. Fire roared into her nostril, harsh and painful, like daggers in her sinuses. She jammed the heels of her palms against the pain and tried to force it away.

She collapsed against the floor, every part of her rebelling at the action, closed eyes leaking tears of shame as reality swept over her.

Eleni. Victor. Jen.

The people who'd trusted her. Everyone on Shiva who hadn't moved quickly enough...

Duncan, that old fucker. He'd been so surprised when she'd pulled the trigger, as if he couldn't reconcile reality with the way the world worked in his mind. But he'd figured everything out too soon.

The Plan couldn't stop. Not now. Not after everything she'd sacrificed.

Sariah collapsed in on herself like a dying star and listened to the voice as copper filled her mouth.

What are you doing?

This had to be rock bottom. She'd finally hit it. A drug addict snorting dirt from the ground, tricking herself into thinking she was part of some grand plan. She needed help. Needed to get clean. Again.

Her body eased. A small smile broke her lips as the pain faded away. The world slowed, and everything fell into place.

Sariah opened her eyes and raised her face into the sterile white light from above, as if God himself was shining his Glory upon her, urging her toward her goal.

She would find help, after. Once the job was done. Once the drilling started, and shipments left in exchange for credits untold. Riches for her people, enough to build a home on the other side of the planet, even if the worst came to pass, or an empire on Gatewood if everything worked as planned.

That'd be her penance. The payment for her sins. A future for her people, whatever the cost.

Then it'd be over. Then they would be free. Truly free. And she could rest... God, she was so tired.

But first, the Plan must be completed. She wiped a line of blood from her nose, dried it on her jumpsuit.

Sariah got to her feet, the room swimming around her. She turned to the elevator and stooped to pick up the key fob she'd thrown away in despair eons ago, purpose pumping away in her veins once again.

"Let's terraform this bitch," Sariah said with a grin.

Then she went upstairs.

Chapter 35
ELENI

The very air pulsed with vibration as the *Jocasta's* dual fusion engines sent atoms cascading in and out of bonds. The constant flux thrummed through Eleni's body as she descended, weightless in zero-g, through the tight, eggshell white maintenance tube running between the two systems. As she stared past Shawn floating ahead of her, his nervous yammering barely making it back to her over the roar surrounding them, Eleni found herself wondering if this is what dying would be like. An endless white tunnel leading to the afterlife.

Jeret would say so. He'd say at the end lay Christian Heaven, full of angels singing hymns amidst righteous humans from history. Then he'd get that dark look like he always did and follow up with, "... for some folks, anyway."

Eleni didn't think that was what happened. Not really. Even if it *was* an option, did she want to sit down with men from medieval times who thought women should be baby factories? What would those conversations even look like?

"Hi, I'm Eleni."

"Oh, good. The help is here."

It sounded horrible. An absolute nightmare.

It's lucky, then, there's no way I'm going to end up there, she thought, an ache crawling up her chest at the thought. No matter what took place after she shut down the engines, people would die.

And it'd be her fault.

"… through here… magic happens." Shawn's voice flitted over the engines and her own thoughts as he stopped and activated a previously unseen panel in the wall of the tube.

It opened toward her, blocking her view of the rest of the tunnel, as well as what lay beyond. The cacophony around them screamed to a fever pitch. A spike of tinnitus screeched in Eleni's left ear, then faded quickly.

With the same grin that'd been plastered on his face, she asked him to show her inside. He glanced at her, then made an awkward attempt at a bow and gestured for her to enter. A warm breeze wafted into the hallway from the doorway. It smelled of oil and steel.

Ignoring the waves of shame and self-loathing flooding over her at the manipulation, Eleni forced what she hoped was a flirty smile and did so. She still hadn't figured out how to handle Shawn without hurting him, and that was only if she could get the engines powered down without killing herself. Yes, Sariah had provided the schematics and told her where the shutdown controls were, but reading something on a diagram and actually doing it were two different things.

"Eleni? You okay?" Shawn's voice snapped her out of her own head.

"Oh, sorry." With that, she sidled around the door. The tight confines meant she brushed up against Shawn as she did so, her behind pressing into his chest.

God, he's short.

Still, the contact sent a tingle up her spine. The smile on her lips this time was very real.

"Right, um, through here," Shawn said, voice little more than a whisper as she contorted around.

Once past, she turned back to him, the smile transforming into a grin. "Such a *shenjin*." The word slipped out before she could take it back.

Hopefully, he only knew the word meant 'gentleman.' The last thing she needed was for him to know she'd just called him sexy.

Shawn let out a short laugh and rubbed his hand through his hair. "I try."

Eleni hesitated, eyes locked on his and the desire clearly written there. For that moment, she just wanted to exist, to feel the connection without the reality of what was to come spoiling it.

Let's be honest, if you weren't cracking the ship, it'd fail besides. You'd find a way to fuck it up. Always do.

With that thought, the moment dissolved into so much vapor. Of course she'd ruin things. Either she'd care too much or too little, or he'd leave her for a freighter captain and wanderlust.

Eleni spun away, hoping Shawn hadn't seen the emotion on her face.

She found herself staring at the antithesis of the maintenance hallway. The space was dark, illuminated only by track lights on the floor, barely visible against the flood of light invading the space from the hallway. Those dim indicators ran between hulking machines that disappeared into the distance. Squinting, she made out a huge, spherical form far beyond, the edges blurring as it shook with the fury of fusion power contained within.

"Chucklenuts." She'd found one of the engines.

With it came the doubt she'd managed to throttle into submission before leaving Shiva. If she turned even one off, *Jocasta* would be disabled until they got it back up, but if she managed to shut down both, nearly all major systems would shut down. Maybe even life support, though Sariah hadn't been able to confirm that.

If life support went down, people would die. How many, she couldn't say, but anything more than zero would put her on a path she'd never taken, a road littered with the bodies of people who'd once had hopes, dreams, families... lives.

If I don't, my people die.

That was always what it came down to, wasn't it? Even on Erias, the duty assignment briefs had always held those "Us versus Them" overtones. Keep the streets safe for your community. For the corp. For your family.

Do it for your brother, Captain Kakku, her Erias superior, had said whenever she'd raised objections.

She'd always taken that to mean she and Victor fell into the "Us" camp. It was only now, as she stared at the engine, that she realized it might've been a veiled threat. No, her *manju* hadn't detected one at the time, but it'd also been issued by Kakku.

Had Sariah meant it that way, too?

The feel of fingers on her back sent her spinning, only to find Shawn flinching away, unease clear on his face. "Whoa. Just checking."

Eleni cursed herself. "Sorry. Shit, sorry. I'm just..." The sentence trailed off, words disappearing into the darkness of her indecision.

"We can head back if you want," Shawn said, jerking a thumb back the way they'd come. "I didn't mean to make you—"

Whatever poor, short, pretty Shawn was about to say cut off as his head rocked to the side from a fist to the face. A fist that didn't belong to her.

Eleni jumped into the hallway, catching him and cradling his head as the momentum from the blow sent him spinning.

"He likes his voice, eh?" Victor said from where he hung on the ceiling, feet planted in the spare handholds lining the hallway.

Despite herself, Eleni smiled as she laid Shawn's unconscious body out against the wall so he wouldn't end up crashing into something. "Being a vac-sealed *hundan* is better then, is it?"

Victor swung around with the ease of someone who'd spent most of his youth in low gravity and sent his trademark smirk her way. "Touché."

There he stood, her brother, still in his *Jocasta* uniform and rubbing the knuckles of his right hand. A playful grin pulled at his lips, and for a brief moment, it was as if no time had passed. Like they were kids trying to find a life for themselves, no one to care for them except each other.

Warmth erupted in her chest; joyful tears built behind her eyes. Eleni launched herself into his arms and wrapped him in a hug, the familiar press of his chest against her own as refreshing as a Shiva night's winds.

"You didn't have to hit him so hard."

Victor shrugged. "I didn't. Glass jaw, apparently."

"I missed you, Vic," Eleni whispered, eyes squeezed shut, and not a care for the tears filling her eyes obnoxiously in low-g.

Victor hesitated, arms askew. Then he patted her back with one hand. "You too, Els."

And the moment disappeared. Eleni pulled back. She wiped the tears from her eyes before using the walls of the shaft to get some distance. "What's wrong?"

"Nothing," Victor said, eyes shifting away from hers like they always did when he lied. "Let's just blow this thing—"

Eleni froze. "'Blow?'"

"The mission," Victor said, gliding toward her, then into the engine room. "Vac the ship."

Eleni followed after him, that old, worried egg in her gut hatching into a thing of shadow and fury. "Yeah, by cutting engine power."

Victor grunted and pulled himself past her and into the engine room. "That's *a* way to say it."

The engine room darkened before her as she followed. After giving her eyes a moment to adjust, Eleni continued after Victor's floating feet. He pulled his way through the compartment and toward the shuddering sphere in the distance. She realized now that she was here, she had no idea what to do. The diagrams had all been top-down renderings, no 3D modeling. All she knew was the emergency manual shut down system sat closer to the engine for some god-awful reason.

Which was why, when Victor suddenly went to the left and away from that system, Eleni hurried along, using whatever hand-holds she could to catch up with her brother.

"Where you off to? Shutdown's that way," Eleni hissed at him as if her voice would trigger an alarm. She was fairly sure it wouldn't, but no sense in tempting fate.

Victor pulled himself to a stop at a short console. A holo-graphic display snapped to life, and he made a few swipes at prompts she couldn't read.

"What're you plugging there?"

"Disabling command transfer," he said before kicking off and away from the emergency shutdown controls.

"What? Why?"

"To scuttle the ship." He pulled himself to a stop and turned, arms crossed, head cocked as he hovered above a thundering block of steel spare centimeters below him. "What's going on, Els?"

"How's that help?" Eleni asked, doubt now wriggling in her chest. "I'm here to disable the *Jocasta*, shut down the engines. We don't want it crippled, yeah? That'd vac life support, wouldn't it?"

He kept that same belittling gaze on her, the one he'd mastered as a teenager whenever she'd try to get him to do his homework. Head cocked, one eyebrow up, a disapproving grimace on his face.

"I mean, there are thousands in this can. Killing them ain't the point; we just want the field leveled. Right?"

"How'd you get this naïve, Els?" Victor asked, shaking his head.

"The fuck you talking about?"

Victor gestured in the direction he'd been going before stop-ping. "The cooling system junction is right there."

Eleni shrugged. "So?"

Then it hit her, and with it, the creature in her stomach tore through her intestines and into her throat. Without coolant, the system would overheat in minutes—and when a fusion reactor overheated, it did one of two things: shut down automatically... or explode.

Victor must've seen her walk the path in her mind because he winked at her. "There it is. The mission." But instead of mirth or hope, she saw the flat face of someone who'd gone too far before.

Maybe not. "There has to be another way."

Victor shook his head, lips contorting into a sneer. "There ain't. I've been here for a month. These bastards are religious in security up top," he said, referring to the bridge. "This is the only way to keep Shiva safe—"

"We'll shut the engines down!" Eleni said, gesturing back in the direction of where she thought the shutoff was. "Make it hard as hell to fire back up—"

"Stop!"

But she didn't. "Don't do this, Victor," Eleni said, reaching out to grab his hand. "Please."

He snatched it away. "This is the Plan, Eleni," he said, voice inflecting with the word. "If the bomb didn't work, this, right here? This is it. Sariah should've told you that."

"Sariah?" Eleni asked, reeling. What plan? But more importantly... "Did she know?"

"Know what?"

"You were alive," Eleni finished in a whisper.

Victor nodded, and a deep ache spread through her limbs. "Of course, Els." Victor frowned, brows furrowing. "Shit. You must be the backup." Victor sighed and shook his head before turning away, the voice issuing from him that of a stranger. "You don't have this in you. Should've tapped Jen. That bitch'll do anything for her crusade."

That hit with the weight of an out-of-control freighter. The strength went out of her and, if there'd been gravity, she wasn't sure she'd be able to stay upright.

Don't have it in you.

Do it for your brother.

Victor faded into the darkness of the engine room, but Eleni followed, vision blurring. "You're vac'ing the engine and the ship, aren't you?"

Victor stopped and turned, his dark face just bright enough against the shadows she made out the tortured look there. "Yes. You should go. Get to an escape pod, or that junker you dropped in on." Then, with a tiny turn of the lips and a flicker of sadness, "Shiva is gonna need you."

Then he moved on.

Eleni's world crumbled. Victor had been alive the entire time. He'd been sent here by Sariah to blow the *Jocasta*, not stop the fusion missile. Sariah had told Eleni to her face that Victor was dead. The whole time... he'd been here, biding his time, waiting for a moment to destroy the ship and the thousands of people on board, as if...

A realization fell over her shoulders then. It cascaded down her body like a blown coolant line. In a haze, Eleni tore after him, pulling herself forward with any handhold she could find until she caught up with Victor.

She flew into the wall next to him, driving the breath from her lungs as she slammed into it.

Victor flinched back at the action, distracted from whatever he'd been working on. "Jesus, Els." The flash of a blade caught the light for just a moment before disappearing back into a near-invisible holster at his side.

"Stop," Eleni said between pained gasps for air. She really had hit hard; her shoulder felt like it had already burst into a bruise. "Please."

Victor did stop and shook his head. He let out a mirthless chuckle before turning to her, anger tinging his eyes. "Why?"

"Because it's wrong," Eleni said. Breathing became easier, so she lowered herself until she sat at his level. "They're people, doing their jobs—"

"Did the nuke not show you what they're capable of?" Victor

snapped, face twisting as he pulled away from her. His eyes searched her face for something, and clearly found her wanting. "Did *our* dead not show you what needs doin'? Have I not sacrificed enough for this moment, for justice?" he finished in a yell, drops of spittle hanging in the air before him.

Eleni pulled away from the fierceness of those eyes and his words. She'd heard this sort of thing before, though usually from the homeless in need of psychoanalytical assistance, or in the rants of radicalized terrorists. What had happened to her idealistic brother in the month since she'd seen him last? How could he have turned into *this*?

She was about to ask when something he'd said stuck in her mind. Worry wriggled into her chest. "What have you sacrificed, Vic?"

Victor froze, turned away, and shook his head. "It don't matter."

"It does."

"No," Victor snapped, voice cracking. His tone changed then, from angry and rebellious, to pleading. "It just... don't, Els. Not anymore. Past is past."

She could've let it go. He clearly begged her to with his eyes, but sometimes the truth, even harsh truths, meant more than family. "What did you do?"

Victor stared at her for a long moment. His eyes flicked between hers like he couldn't choose which to stare at, mouth opening and closing repeatedly as if searching for words swept away in the current of a raging river. "I..."

Then his gaze pulled from hers. Rage flared across his face, and he stood, the flick of silver again in his hand. Eleni spun in time to see a tiny, fierce-looking woman standing in the doorway of the engine room, the end of a rifle—no, a cane—pointed in their direction. A moment later, the end popped, echoing like a gunshot.

It hit Victor square in the chest.

"No!" Eleni screamed as Victor's body went rigid, arms shaking at his sides.

His eyes rolled back in his head, the muscles in his jaw flexing and releasing as electricity poured through his limbs.

Despite everything, Eleni roared and spun, ready to push off the wall behind her and destroy this woman for hurting her brother.

The other woman, however, was not amused. She scoffed and pushed off toward Eleni. "Calm down, it's just a stun round."

Eleni turned back as the shaking stopped, leaving her standing next to her unconscious brother. All at once, the old protective instinct dissolved into the air, to be replaced with an abiding guilt. She'd been caught. Sure, she'd tried to stop Victor from blowing the engines, but did it matter?

End of the day, Eleni had still planned to disable the ship. Right?

"I could've stopped him," Eleni said, though she didn't believe the words. Not anymore.

The woman laughed as she approached. She held an air of confidence Eleni immediately admired. As she approached, the woman held the cane at the ready for another round. Smart lady.

"His team launched a nuke on his own people, so I doubt it." The woman raised an eyebrow at Eleni as she closed in. "*Your* people, I assume."

That knocked the wind out of her. Eleni looked to her brother's now-peaceful face. "No. You're lyin'."

"Tough titty said the kitty." The woman shrugged and pointed the cane at him. "Facts don't care about your fucking feelings." She looked at Victor and shook her head. "Mine, either. I didn't think he was involved until you and Ceriat showed up, planning to fuck up my ship."

"Your ship?" Eleni asked, then froze. "You're the captain?"

"My friends call me Linny," the woman said with a grin that, in another place and time, would've set Eleni's heart a-flutter. The smile disappeared into a flat-lipped glare. "You can address me as Captain Nova."

Eleni turned to stare at her unconscious brother, emotions warring inside her. The heat of anger floundered in a pool of despair at the realizations of the last few minutes.

How could Victor do this? And why...? She couldn't bring herself to think the rest of that question. Even considering that he'd been part of the group that had launched the attack on Arctic sent a sharp stab of pain in her chest.

"That's why you didn't drop another one," Eleni said, voice little more than a whisper.

"That, and it was the only one we had," Nova replied. "All I have to protect Gatewood with is this ship. You disable it, and hundreds of thousands die. Simple as that."

Another thought came into her head. An entire team had been sent up to disable the missile systems, though Victor had been planted there earlier. What had happened to those people? She hadn't known any of them, not personally, but they'd been friends-of-friends. Acquaintances.

Were they dead? Did it matter? Did anything fucking matter anymore? All Eleni knew was she'd almost been a party to genocide.

"So, what now? Am I under arrest?" Eleni asked.

Captain Nova grunted and hovered back toward the door. "I don't know. Are you still planning on fucking with my ship?"

"No," Eleni said, and she meant it, though with the word, she had no idea what to do anymore. No clue what was right for anyone. "Especially not if you can prove what you said."

"I've got the video, kid. I can prove it," Nova said, "but just to be safe, security is waiting in the shaft. We're going to drop you off in the brig—" Nova broke off as her HUD activated, eyes spinning light blue lights that shone like stars in the night sky. "What? Fuck that. Absolutely not. Don't you let her take my ship—do you hear me? Jenkins? Jenkins!"

"What's going on?" Eleni asked.

Nova's eyes darkened, then her head swiveled toward Eleni with an intensity Eleni had only ever seen in vids of old Earth predators before they devoured another animal. The cane came back up, pointed firmly at her chest. "Who else did you bring?"

"Parker."

"Don't fucking lie to me!" Nova screamed, voice grainy and raw as it rattled around the engine room. "Who else!"

"Just me and Parker, I swear to God," Eleni said, hands going up in surrender.

Nova kicked off toward her then, stopping only when she was just out of arm's reach of Eleni. "Then enlighten me," Nova said, face awash in rage. "Who the fuck just took my bridge?"

Chapter 36
CERIAT

Ceriat twiddled his thumbs and tried to pretend things would work out okay.

He'd spent the first five minutes after Nova had locked him in trying to distract himself by finding a seam between the different colors of the table. Failing that, he'd wandered the room, looking for perhaps an exterior viewport that'd been sealed off. Finally, he'd gone to the door of the Ready Room, only to find Linny had locked him inside, the security panel lit with a crimson light.

Now he waited, though for what, he didn't know.

The gentle breeze from the life support system tickled the stubble that'd grown over the past few days. Idly, he scratched at it, the sandpaper texture prickling fingertips and issuing a sound that reminded him of mice digging through insulation.

Which reminded him to contact an exterminator when he got home. Ginny hated it when the little buggers ran through the house. She'd be up, hopping around like a battery-powered stuffed toy as she barked at the creatures.

Home. If he made it back.

He missed his dog. How she bounced whenever he shook the snack bag. The way she hobbled around on her three good legs, tail whapping back and forth with force enough to knock her over if she jumped around.

An ache pulled at his stomach. Ceriat just wanted to pet his dog, to sit on the porch and watch the fog roll off the ocean and across the city, carrying with it a stoic silence ensconced in chill humidity.

He let out a low sigh and forced his thoughts away from Ginny, or at least he tried. He needed distraction. Something to take his mind off how fucked this entire situation had gotten.

With a grunt, Ceriat drummed his fingers across the mahogany portion of the table. It clearly wasn't really wood, but it was quality synthetic material. Where he sat, at the head of the table opposite the embedded screen, the sections of black and silver came to a point, then burst forth as a long, squished diamond. Depending on where you sat, it squirmed into different shapes. A neat optical illusion.

Still boring to stare at for fifteen minutes.

A noise beyond the locked doors caught his attention as he resumed searching for a seam in the table. Since the door had shut, he hadn't heard anything beyond the hum of life support or the sound of his own movement. He'd decided the room must be soundproofed then, especially since the group of soldiers who'd been discussing FTL when Linny brought him on the bridge were just outside.

Ceriat cocked his head and listened intently, but didn't hear anything else right away. He'd just turned back to his mindless distraction when it came again. A thud. Muted voices.

Ceriat pulled himself away from the table and kicked off one of the chairs to bring him to the door. He pressed his ear against the cool material. Those same muffled voices came through, though now he could make out inflection, if not words. Someone beyond yelled.

Had Linny made it back? Had she stopped Eleni from disabling the engines?

A sharp, tinny *pop*. He knew that sound. Ceriat froze and took a step back from the doors.

That'd been small arms projectile fire. Whoever had hollered beyond that door had just fired a bullet. On a ship. In space. The potential for hull breaches from bullets in space was high. Most starships kept their armoring on the exterior to block micrometeoroids and external attacks. Layering the interior with the same armoring was generally cost prohibitive. Then again, the *Jocasta* was a warship, so perhaps it was a non-issue.

Still, old instincts set him to scanning the Ready Room for emergency hull breach protection, but as he turned, a flashing red orb on the far wall caught his attention. Ceriat stepped toward the table, the light rippling on the embedded display. Someone had called into the Ready Room.

He nearly sat back down, but another sharp *pop* made it to him through the wall. So instead, he searched the table for anything he could use to answer the call. He found a holographic interface near the center of the table, though he'd almost missed it, since the orange controls blended a bit into the ebony color of the table.

Poor design choice, he thought as he answered the call.

Linny popped up on the screen. Sweat seeped from her forehead as she hurried along some white tunnel. "Finally picked up, Parker."

"Sorry," Ceriat said, "didn't think I was allowed."

"As of now, I'm conscripting you. Welcome back, Sergeant."

"What the fuck are you talking about?"

Linny stared hard at him. "You brought a straggler with you—"

"What?" Ceriat asked, incredulous. Where the hell would they have hidden on the *Sparrow* if he had? The cargo hold? Jesus, they must've twisted in on themselves to fit. "How?"

"Doesn't matter, Parker," Linny snapped, cutting him off. "They've taken my bridge."

A familiar face flashed behind her briefly, bald head criss-crossed with blue tattoos. She'd stopped Eleni.

He let out a breath full of stress he hadn't know he'd been carrying, then turned to the door. "Okay. Listen, there's small arms fire—"

"Take back my bridge, Parker," Linny said. "Fix your mistake."

"By myself?"

Linny gave him a humorless grin. "You made the mistake alone; you fix it alone. Just don't Vulture this one. I want my ship in one piece."

Before he could respond, the channel cut off, leaving him staring at a blank wall, mouth agape, doubt scouring his heart.

Ceriat turned to the door, an ache filling him at the thought of going through it. As he watched, the red light on the security panel flickered green.

He didn't want this. Any of it. God, if he hadn't tried to get away from this all, but with FTL somehow jammed—by whom, he still didn't know—he'd had to choose a side.

Clearly, he'd fucked that up. Sariah had bombed her own people, then sent him and Eleni to shut down Gatewood's primary defense system. What would've happened if they'd succeeded? Would Sariah raise her fleet of frigates and fighters and destroy the entire Gatewood settlement? Was that the plan?

Is it still the plan?

Ceriat pressed the heels of his hands into his eyes. He had to make a choice again here, didn't he? Or sit tight and hope someone else stepped up and did what was necessary. Someone who'd do the killing he had no stomach for—not anymore.

He'd made a promise... but the silence from beyond the door told him it wouldn't happen. It was up to him.

"Fucking hell."

Ceriat sucked in a deep breath. Let it out. Then, praying to whatever God was listening that he wouldn't have to hurt anyone, he opened the door to the Bridge.

His eyes latched onto two bodies still spinning in low grav as they made their way to the ground. Crimson drops floated and scattered in the air, casting splashes of color against the silvery gray design of everything. The bridge crew was huddled against the viewscreen opposite the captain's chair, the void of space displayed behind them.

In Linny's chair sat someone both familiar and strange. Jen, her bulky, formless uniform from Shiva replaced by a stained tank top and well-worn workpants that showed off ample curves he hadn't noticed before. Strangely, her face had been transformed from the scowling Spacer he'd met on the dropship that'd picked him up into a carefully crafted mask made of makeup. It looked as if she'd taken a detour on her way to putting on a wedding dress.

If he'd had any chance of ambushing her, his own shock at her presence blew it. She turned to him, surprise flashing and disappearing in a single moment.

Jen pointed an ancient pistol—a Colt M1911, if he remembered correctly—his way, face flat, and he thought, somehow sad. "There you are."

He recognized the weapon now it was pointed at him. Black steel with a brown grip. It was the weapon Sariah had carried at her hip when he'd first met her.

Then it's true. Sariah was behind this. Behind it all.

With that confirmation came a clarity he hadn't felt in years. He'd chosen correctly, coming out here. Ceriat put his hands up at his sides, disbelief warring against the reality of having a weapon pointed at him. Not fear, though, he noticed with more than a little creeping dread. No, his heart slammed, body throbbed. Adrenaline. It took everything he had not to grin.

"Is this because I made fun of your name?" Ceriat asked, kicking lightly off the door frame so he approached her, hands still in the air.

Jen's mouth twisted at the words, but she ignored them otherwise. "Catch yourself and join the others."

Ceriat did so, stopping his momentum at one of the panels

surrounding the captain's chair. Now that he was this close, he could make out some device on the chair beneath Jen, only just visible below her ample thighs. From the bits of black fabric he saw, it appeared to be some sort of bag. "First, what's that?" he asked, pointing at the mystery object.

In response, Jen turned the pistol toward the group of huddled bridge crew.

"Whoa. I'm going—"

Without taking her eyes off Ceriat, a sharp crack filled the air. One of the bridge crew, the man who'd been exclaiming about FTL when Ceriat had first come on deck, reeled back with a cry, a crimson blot springing to life in his shoulder.

But that's not where Ceriat's eyes went. No, instead, a sound caught his attention. A snap that shouldn't have happened, a sound that shouldn't come from a pistol like that—unless it had jammed.

Instinct took over. Henderson's screaming voice, still as clear as it had been back in Basic Training, howled in his ear, "Go, go, go!"

Ceriat launched himself toward her, eyes searching the weapon for signs that he'd guessed correctly, signs a casing had caught. Because if he'd fucked up, this was the end of the line for him.

Jen snapped the pistol back in his direction, but he didn't stop. Instead, he swung his leg around, kicking his body into a spiral.

The room spun, but still Ceriat caught sight of the surprise on her face as she pulled the trigger... and nothing happened.

Jen had enough time to curse before he slammed into her, dragging her off the captain's chair with his momentum.

Heady vanilla and rose perfume flooded his nostrils, then pain and stars as Jen slammed the pistol into his head. Luckily, she slammed it right over the plate in his skull, so the worst of it was absorbed. Ceriat caught her wrist as the pistol came down again and squeezed. Bones creaked beneath his grip. The pistol slipped from her hand to float alongside them.

Then Jen's face filled his vision, any resemblance to the dour woman from Shiva gone. Panic and fear covered every inch of that painted face.

"You fucking idiot!" she screamed full throated in his face, spittle splashing into his eyes. Her feet kicked at his legs, slamming harder each time. It sent them into a twisting mass of limbs.

Then she headbutted him. This time she avoided the plate. The world blinked away for a moment, hidden behind darkness and pain. When he finally opened his eyes, he expected to find himself gagged and tied, but instead, Jen had just extricated herself from him.

She didn't go for the pistol. No, she leapt toward the captain's chair. Ceriat's blood went cold as he realized why.

She'd been sitting on a bag, like he'd suspected. However, now that she'd gotten up, he could see the telltale signs of a pressure plate, and the hint of what appeared to be molded clay beneath.

Jen grabbed the armrest of the chair and swung herself around to put her weight atop it once again, panic clear on her face.

I almost killed us all. Ceriat froze with the realization. She'd brought explosives onto the bridge, explosives tied to a rather unique deadman trigger.

A rattling, sliding sound, and another *crack* from behind him. The bullet caught Jen in the chest and, with little more than a grunt, she spun away, and out of the captain's chair.

"No!" Ceriat cried, eyes locked on the explosives. He turned to see the man Jen had shot in the shoulder moments earlier lower the pistol, fury writ large across his plain features.

The next several seconds proceeded as if stretched out across hours.

Jen slammed into the panel to the right of the captain's chair, eyes wide, blood spewing from the hole in her chest. Gingerly, she touched the droplets expanding before her, eyes wide at first, then filling with tears.

The rest of the crew sprang to life, but no one went for the explosives. Instead, they ran for the exit. Someone grabbed Ceriat's collar and dragged him along, but Ceriat couldn't look away from where Jen hovered, head wobbling in the air.

The doorway off the bridge sprang to life around him.

He grabbed the edge and, for some reason, reached out to Jen, though she might as well have been on another planet. Arms wrapped around his middle—someone screamed in his ear to let go—but still he held on.

She looked at him, brows arching in sadness and confusion. Then, she spoke. "I just wanted a home for my son—"

His fingers slipped, and the door to the bridge slammed shut.

A deafening roar filled the air for a split second, the ship rattling around him as if it were made of popsicle sticks. Then, rushing wind... followed by deathly silence.

Behind Ceriat, people spoke in increasingly loud voices, but he didn't hear it. Couldn't.

He'd seen the look on her face. The loss and regret in that moment. It'd been his fault. He'd killed her, not the bullet. He'd done it again. Ten years without a death by his hand. Ten years without new guilt, just old horrors to keep him awake at night.

So much for vows, for morals. Ceriat put his face in his hands. He screamed.

Then the lights went out. The *Jocasta* lost power. This massive warship, the jewel of Gatewood, was dead in the water.

And with that, Gatewood and its inhabitants sat defenseless.

Chapter 37
SARIAH

Sariah climbed back into the cockpit of her fighter as the earthquakes started.

The ETL tower no longer sat quietly on the barren plain. Its exterior spines rotated down into the earth, grinding away billions of years of stagnant stone as it burrowed deeper and deeper to the planet's core. The very air rattled with its movement, the cacophony of destruction sending Sariah's eardrums hissing. On that same wind came the rotten egg stench of sulfur as gas released into the atmosphere. Little debris cascaded away as the nanobot tech consumed the raw materials, converted them, and continued digging, digging, digging.

We truly live in the future. She watched the tower as it drilled, unable to tear her eyes off the rampant destruction. Deep in her heart, she knew disgust should be pulling at her, and she nearly convinced herself that was why she continued staring. *Like watching a dead ship caught in the gravity well of a star*, was what she told herself.

But another part of her lit in joy at the chaos of it, at the air shimmering as the ground heaved. At the heat washing across the plain as the drill closed in on the sluggish core of this planet, a core that begged to be siphoned off and sold for her people.

If it weren't for the lingering effects of the Spacedust, she might have convinced herself of the lie, but with the dust grinding away in her sinuses and lighting her synapses on fire, she simply smiled and enjoyed the gentle throbbing pleasure accompanying it.

So she sat and watched, her fighter idling and ready to take wing at a moment's notice. Her hand settled, motionless between her legs, despite the urge for more.

An alert changed all that.

Sariah pulled her gaze from the vapor misting from around the tower and opened up the video stream.

Jeret stared back at her. "It's done."

With a flick, Sariah closed the canopy, only then noticing the harsh stink of noxious gases that'd been building up around her. Good timing, that. With another gesture, she initiated the return-to-base automation as her climate system roared to life, filtering the air of toxins.

Her stomach pulled as the ship lifted off. She returned her focus to Jeret. "The ship is dead?"

"Yes, Governor."

Sariah grinned. "Fantastic. Scramble the fleet. I want that thing gone."

Jeret paused, angular features screwing together in such a way that all his wrinkles popped into being at once. "What about Eleni? Jen?"

Dead. "They'll be remembered as heroes. We fight for their memories now," Sariah spit off with the rehearsed reverence she'd been practicing in front of the mirror for the past month. "I want that ship destroyed."

She craned her head around, trying to keep the ETL tower in view as her ship careened around and northwest, toward their makeshift camp. It really was too bad she couldn't watch it hit the core. She had a theory it'd pop like a zit.

So distracted by watching the tower, Sariah didn't notice Jeret staring at her, mouth agape. Not until a very unfitting grin had spread onto her face as the first fiery red spouts of magma sprouted up around the tower.

She forced her face flat and turned away from the tower with effort. Clearing her throat, Sariah stared hard at Jeret. "Deliver the order."

"Ma'am—"

"Or I'll tell the settlement about your past," Sariah snapped, glaring.

A gamble, one she tried not to lean on too much. She knew he had some skeletons in his past, but had yet to uncover anything solid.

However, he didn't know that.

Jeret reeled back as if stricken, eyes wide and jaw working wordlessly. Then he clenched his teeth together and gave a quick nod. "Yes, Governor." With that, he disappeared from the display.

To be safe, Sariah tapped into the comms channel she'd opened in the jamming system she kept back at the base and waited for Jeret to issue the order. It didn't take long before his voice crackled over the channel with terse, yet clear direction.

"*The* Jocasta *is disabled. Destroy it.*"

She had to give it to him, he might have wanted to argue, but the command brooked no argument. A series of acknowledgments scattered back before Sariah turned off the channel. Not for the first time, she wondered what he'd done that made him so easy to manipulate.

Sariah leaned back in her seat and sucked in an odorless breath in fume-scorched sinuses. Someday she'd ask him, but not today.

Grinning, she disabled the autopilot and swung the fighter back round.

With the *Jocasta* under attack, she had time for a little more of the ETL show.

The planet was about to pop. It'd be a damn shame to miss it.

Chapter 38
ELENI

"Fuck!" Captain Nova screamed into an echoing void.

The previously brightly lit hallway had fallen into inky darkness. Now it was lit only by the light from a small flashlight she'd just finished pulling from some emergency pack in the sidewall of the corridor.

"Whoever designed this ship is a fucking idiot. Who ties everything to the bridge? And why the fuck isn't command transferring to me?"

Eleni and the rest remained silent. Her arms were bound behind her with plastic bindings. A heavy hand belonging to one of the security team, a hulking Earther who clearly didn't spend too much time in space, not with the musculature he sported, rested on her arm. He and several others had been waiting in the hallway when Nova had brought her and Victor out. Shawn had been there, too, a purpling bruise on his cheek as he stared at her.

She'd looked away, unable to face the hate and unspoken accusation there.

Once the bridge had been taken and Captain Nova's focus had shifted away from the lack of useful intel, Eleni had remained quiet, dragged along by the group, swimming in uncertainty and doubt.

Then the lights went out.

Captain Nova swept the hallway before her as her irises lit up blue, the glow there painting her dark cheeks like a pale blush. "That fucking Parker. I told him not to Vulture my ship," she finished with a mutter.

Again, that name. Eleni knew she'd heard it before. The very sound of it struck an uneasiness in her, as if it were a boogeyman invoked to scare children.

Then it hit her.

The Shaal-Tu Massacre. A pilot named Vulture had nuked a city there, and dozens of others. All she knew was the pilot had murdered millions, and then disappeared as if he'd been little more than a myth, a murdering shadow the Protectorate used to terrify the Outer Rim.

Parker was Vulture? In the stunned moments after, her guard pulled her along the corridor as Nova yelled orders.

That couldn't be right. Parker hadn't shown any signs of being some mass murderer. Certainly, for the short time she'd known him. He'd come off as one of the more, well, moralistic people she'd met in a long while. Even when he'd agreed to disable the *Jocasta*, he'd taken care to make sure no one else died. She'd thought that meant he wasn't a murderer, like her.

"Don't move," a low voice growled in her ear. The guard released her and followed up with a push to send her gliding along the hallway behind Nova.

Not that Eleni had any thoughts of escape. Not after the conversation she and Ceriat had had before meeting with Sariah came back to her.

"What side?" she'd asked him, and still he hadn't answered because he knew she'd ask more questions. Because he knew if she connected the dots to where he'd been deployed, Eleni would figure it out.

An ache filled her stomach, writhing up her chest with strangling fingers.

Because *he* was the Vulture. A mass murderer. A monster.

A monster who saved my life.

Nova's voice made it to her through the hum filling her mind. "Launch all fighters in a protective sphere—" Nova stopped pulling herself along, floating at speed as they moved forward. She shook her head, and Eleni was surprised to hear her issue a low growl. "Then get the launch system back online or bypass the fucking thing. Jesus, you call yourself a fucking engineer?" Another pause. "Then do them all by hand, Enders! I need those ships launched, or that settlement is fucked. Do you understand what's at sta—"

Something distant thudded, followed by the rat-a-tat of gunfire slamming into the hull. The ship, powered down and as useless as a bicycle in low grav, twisted around them, the hallway rotating counterclockwise and to the left. Nova slammed into a wall to the right with a harsh grunt, her cane and flashlight breaking from her grip to flip and spin away. The flashing light caught the others in slow motion as they bounced along surfaces like ping pong balls.

Eleni, much to her surprise, didn't join them. From her perspective, the ship rolled around her as the central point of the axis. Instead, she hung there, arms and legs pulled up tight like she'd learned early on when she'd arrived on Hobelt. You didn't want to bounce around in low grav, especially not with limbs akimbo. That was a good way to break a leg.

Which, by the ragged scream that suddenly filled the corridor, had just happened to someone in the flickering darkness.

Eleni froze in the midst of the chaos. She tried to move, but terror wrapped her in a vice as it whispered in her ear. *If you move, you die. If you speak, you'll suffocate.* Without oxygen, she had roughly two minutes. *Two minutes.*

Clearly, atmo hadn't been vented, because Nova didn't shut up. "Get those ships deployed!" Nova screamed, now sharp and screeching in barely composed panic. Then, to the as yet unknown person with the broken limb who kept howling in pain, "Shut the fuck up. Bite down on something."

Surprisingly, it worked, casting them in silence once again. At least for one brief moment.

The *Jocasta* rattled around them, followed by a dozen or more hard hits that had to be missile explosions. Around her, the hallway rattled with popping sounds as something beyond the walls strafed the engines.

Most of the bullets went back out the other side of the corridor, but not all. Grunts, moans, and cursing erupted around her.

Victor.

Eleni's limbs were finally freed from their prison. She cast about in the darkness for her brother. "Victor!" she hollered, sweeping along the rapidly chilling corridor.

Hissing followed suit. Emergency puncture systems kicked into gear, closing off pressurization loss from the attack.

She dove blindly into the mass of bodies ahead of her, nose filled with the scent of freshly spilled blood and the bite of acetone. Something warm splashed across her face as she did, a bit of hot copper on her tongue as some slipped past her lips.

Eleni's stomach heaved, but she scrambled anyway, hands catching on clothes and bodies in the inky darkness. She pulled the first to her just as emergency lighting lit the hallway in a blood red wash.

She found herself staring into one of Shawn's dead eyes. The other was a black hole leaking dark droplets, a shard of bone catching the crimson light like a macabre mirror. His lips twitched and moved, but nothing came out. No sound would ever come out of them again.

Eleni reeled back despite herself, and he went spinning away, pirouetting in slow motion as he took his last dance. She cast about, panic arching up her spine, searching for anything, anyone living.

Corpses. Some still twitched in death. Others, having found purchase against the side walls, stared at her with empty eyes, their endless stare as accusing as a pointed finger in a courtroom.

Movement caught Eleni's eye, and she gratefully followed it.

There, several meters down the corridor, Captain Nova pulled herself up along the wall, a string of droplets, black in the monochromatic light, spinning around and painting the walls beside her. Above her, Victor hung, limbs limp.

A blast of cerulean lit the hallway behind her. Eleni shot forward toward her brother. She caught a hand grip as she neared, pulling herself up next to him.

"Please don't be dead," she whispered, vision betraying her as it blurred, and fatigue suddenly threatened to crush her. She prayed with every part of her being, every last breath inside her. "Don't be dead."

Reality is a cruel mistress in the best of times.

And this, this was not the best of times.

Eleni collapsed around the sack of flesh that'd once been her brother, not caring that the holes covering his chest and abdomen wept as much as her eyes, or that his face, once so vibrant and alive, hung slack, mouth open and gaze fixed on some point well beyond her sight.

Everything she'd done had been to keep him safe. First to get him out of that hellhole, then to help him thrive, despite an emptiness in his eyes he'd refused to talk to her about. The classes, the missed opportunities to travel the stars. She'd gladly given it all up if it meant he had a chance. At life. At love. At... everything.

And now, all that remained was a still-warm corpse floating in the burning light of a dying ship. A buzzing filled Eleni's ears alongside the sting of tears building up in her eyes. She stuffed her face in his chest, trying to catch his scent one last time, to memorize his presence. But it'd already faded, overwritten by the greasy stink of the engine room.

"No..." The sound slipped from her lips, quickly transforming into a wordless, shuddering moan as her chest heaved.

Strong hands grabbed at Eleni's back and pulled her, dragging Victor's corpse along. A voice filled her ears and dissolved into wordless murmurs, but still Eleni held onto her brother. Then, a flash of pain and stars.

Fingers, small and delicate, but somehow as strong as iron grabbed Eleni's chin and turned her head until she found herself staring at Captain Nova. The woman was covered in blood, her silver and gray uniform an inkblot of black in the emergency lights. Her face, still dark and fierce, was paler than Eleni remembered, a pallid death mask held off by sheer force of will.

"He's dead; you're not," Nova hissed, droplets of something flecking out around her teeth, "and I need your help."

Eleni tried to turn away, to fall back against the body in her arms, but Nova didn't let go.

"Please," Nova pleaded finally, face contorting in pain, though whether from her injuries or the use of the word, Eleni couldn't tell right away.

The fingers fell away. Nova cried out, arms going tight around a dark stain spreading across her middle.

Eleni turned back to Victor, but it wasn't him anymore, was it?

The ache in her chest expanded until she thought it'd absorb her into a singularity of despair... and then it popped, loss rippling away from her in one long, howling wail. All the sorrow of his loss days ago, joy and warmth on seeing his face when he'd taken her from the *Sparrow*, all of it fed into that rattling sob. Her fingers dug into his cooling skin; one last, fierce embrace to carry him beyond this mortal realm.

Then Eleni let go.

Victor's body hung there, suspended in the air like a puppet on strings waiting for its next act. A puppet tossed away, trash for the garbage man. From there, the mourning flooding through her transformed from a terrible flood into spewing gasoline.

Sariah. This was all her fault. She'd done this, turned Victor into... whatever he'd become, killed their people, and even now, she launched an attack on the *Jocasta*, knowing full well Eleni was still on board.

Her sorrow ignited in rage. A grim certainty fell across her shoulders. She'd kill her, gut the old woman like a pig to slaughter.

Eleni ground her teeth and pulled away from Victor's still form. She couldn't save him in life, but she'd avenge his death.

The slap woke Captain Nova out of whatever stupor blood loss had caused her. Nova's eyes swiveled in their sockets, unfocused and confused. Then they landed on Eleni and wandered down to where she put pressure on the bullet wound in her abdomen.

"Took your time," Nova muttered, teeth dark with blood.

Eleni shrugged and forced a mirthless smile. "I'm a slow learner, Captain."

"Med bay that way," Nova said, gesturing with a floating arm. "Need 'bots."

With a nod, Eleni kicked off, the small woman no larger than a Spacer child cradled in her arms, a single goal written in her mind.

Sariah would pay.

For everything.

Chapter 39
CERIAT

This is all my fault.

The phrase repeated in Ceriat's head the entire trip to the medbay. As the *Jocasta* rocked beneath missile attacks and heavy weapons fire, he stumbled along behind the bridge crew in bloody light, waiting for the next hit to depressurize the long hallway and send them all to gasping deaths. Or a direct missile hit that'd vaporize them where they floated.

Either would work.

But neither did.

Instead, these chattering kids pulled him along, forcing him forward when he tried to stop and wait for the end of things. They took turns guiding him, convincing him that the bridge wasn't his fault, that none of this was on him.

Good kids, but morons to the last.

Of course this was his fault. He'd been convinced of the morality of his choice, that by storming the *Jocasta*, he was on the side of the just and the good. But just like with the Protectorate, it all turned into bullshit.

Sariah had bombed her own people, then used that same bombing to convince him and Eleni to disable this ship so the madwoman could threaten Gatewood from a position of power, to set terms that allowed everyone to live out their days on separate planets. That's what she'd said, but that was never the plan, was it?

No, the bullshit he'd been fed hadn't included Jen, God help her, bringing a bomb onto the bridge of the ship. It certainly hadn't included him causing that same explosive to detonate, not only putting the ship out of commission, but leaving it a wide-open target for the fighters Sariah also hadn't mentioned.

He knew now. Simple. So simple, he'd glossed right over it, dismissing the idea. Get the ship defenses shut down, then destroy it. Boom. Done. Efficient. Ruthless. A leader who cared for their people, though, wouldn't put them in danger, not like that.

But Sariah didn't care about them. As soon as Ceriat had arrived and destabilized her plan by his sheer presence, he'd had a target on his back. Once Eleni had shown "disloyalty" for trying to help him get a message off-planet, she'd joined the list. Of course she'd want them both dead and gone. If she got to set Eleni up as a martyr, so much the better.

The kids around him weren't the only idiots, it seemed.

"Right through here," the kid who'd been shot in the shoulder, Garris, said. Despite being the only injured bridge member in the group, he'd quickly taken command. He pulled himself up next to a set of closed doors, breath heavy.

The security panel to the right of the doors, however, remained a monochrome red in the emergency lighting.

"Why isn't it opening?" another of the bridge crew asked, a young woman with light colored hair and skin that shone with the intensity of the pink flamingos Ceriat sometimes saw as lawn ornaments back home.

Garris shook his head and swiped his wrist across the panel again. Once more, nothing happened. "I don't know."

"We need to get in there—"

"I know, Cherryl!"

Somewhere distant, rattling metal and heavy thudding made it to them, followed swiftly by the sound of steel twisting and tearing. Wind tousled Ceriat's hair and caught stray strands on the shocked faces surrounding him.

There are no breezes in space. Not unless two rooms have different pressures, the life support is blowing directly in your face... or there was a hull breach.

Everyone froze and turned as one with the direction of the wind toward the source of screaming metal. The hallway stretched off into the distance until it angled to the left, where Ceriat guessed it extended around the exterior of the *Jocasta*.

Shadow splashed the end of the hallway, backlit by a flickering orange light. Something moved down there, and flame was on its way.

More twisting steel as the air grew thin, his breath coming in quicker gasps.

Garris cursed and went back to trying to open the door. Several of the crewmembers tried to force it open with their fingertips pressed into the hairline crack splitting it down the middle.

Ceriat, though, pulled himself toward the end of the hallway and the shifting shadows at the far end. A creeping recognition arced its way into his mind.

"What are you doing?" Cherryl said as he swept by. She'd dropped to the floor and was in the process of pulling off a maintenance plate. When he didn't reply, she just shook her head and went back to work. "Fine, it's your fucking funeral."

He made his way down the path, pulling forward as the shapes shifted and merged. The air grew thinner here, yet the wind still tickled the stubble on his chin.

As he neared the halfway point, the shadows finally resolved into something familiar. People.

"There's someone down there!" Ceriat shouted.

He pushed off in the direction of the shadows, ignoring the calls from behind him. In the thin air, his head grew light, and the room wobbled as he shot forward. Bile splashed the back of his throat. He swallowed it down.

Just as he neared where the passage turned to the left, the crackling of flame now echoing off the wall to his right, a mass shot out of the hallway like a bullet.

Ceriat reached out and snagged the dark bundle of steaming blankets and whipped them into a tight spiral. He wrapped his arms around it—felt the bodies beneath the hot covering—and used his own body to protect them as they hammered into the wall.

Pain flashed. Something cracked inside him, driving the air from his lungs. Somehow, he remained awake as they bounced slowly down the hallway toward where the bridge crew still waited.

The blanket went askew as they hit again and again, revealing Linny's face, eyes closed, burns hot and red along her cheek, and char up the edges of her pants. Her prosthesis was dark in the crimson light, soot-covered and likely burning.

As the spinning slowed, the covering came off in a sudden sweep of an arm, revealing a soot-stained face and a stubble-covered head covered in blue whorls. Sweat and smoke filled his nose.

For the first time since he'd been tased at his ship, Ceriat found himself face-to-face with Eleni. Despite everything, joy flooded into his limbs, and he pulled her into a tight embrace.

Eleni froze beneath his touch, but he ignored it, just squeezed his eyes shut and pressed his face into her neck. He breathed in her sweat and the sharp tang of burning plastic and fabric.

"You're alive," he whispered.

Eleni relaxed, her free arm squeezing him back. "So are you."

Then a third, familiar voice, muffled by fabric. "Suffocating. Me."

Ceriat pulled away and wiped his face. "Ah, sorry, Linny."

Eleni smiled at him for a moment... then a shadow passed over her face, and with it, the welcome there disappeared.

Ceriat frowned, but before he could follow up, the small woman in Eleni's arms turned her head toward him. Dark hollows lay beneath her eyes, the typically dark tone of her skin pale as seasoned wood. "Med bay."

"She needs help," Eleni said, shaking her own head as she looked around, "and everything behind us is on fire."

Ceriat nodded and pulled them along toward where Cherryl had located an emergency hatch lever. The door squealed open as they approached.

"Captain!" Garris yelled, eyes going wide as he recognized the form in Eleni's arms.

He tried to go to Linny, but Cherryl grabbed him and pushed him into the med bay. "I got her." Cherryl met Ceriat and Eleni, and they managed to get into the med bay without any further issues.

The faux pine scent of disinfectants hammered into Ceriat's nostrils as he entered the darkened room, guiding Eleni and Linny forward and away from him as they entered. A single line of crimson light extended into the bay, catching on a splash of shiny steel and several tools magnetized to mounting strips along the far wall. That light disappeared quickly as Cherryl forced the door shut with a solid *thunk*, casting them into a deep, muted darkness.

Beyond that door, the rattling *pop* of projectiles echoed dully, as if Ceriat had put a pillow over his head. Another roar of grinding steel on steel ran along the wall facing the hallway. And then, complete and utter silence, interrupted only by their heavy breaths in the thin air.

"What was that?" someone asked in the darkness.

"We lost the hallway." It was Eleni who replied, voice little more than a whisper, but somehow a raging shout in the enclosed area. "We're fucked."

A moment later, blinding white light filled the room, to curses and a muttered apology from Cherryl. "Sorry, sorry. Emergency power is on here."

"Small victories," Garris said with a sigh.

The med bay was smaller than Ceriat expected, barely ten meters square, and a single bed sat in the corner of the room, powered-off displays above it. Gray cabinets and shelves lined the other walls, tools magnetized to off-white backsplashes.

Garris floated over to Eleni and pulled Linny, who cried out at the movement, over to the bench. For the first time, Ceriat got a good look at her wounds. The gray and silver fabric of her jacket was a mass of red wetness that seeped up beneath her breasts and down to her hips. The burns he'd caught sight of in the hallway shone with a fevered fire here as well. Skin puckered and bubbled down her leg and across a face contorted in pain.

They rushed her over to the bed, leaving Eleni and Ceriat behind as the bridge crew swarmed their captain. As he watched, Cherryl slid open one of the drawers and returned to the surgery bed with a familiar white cube and a pair of surgical scissors.

"Sorry, Captain," Cherryl said as she proceeded to cut open Linny's jacket, revealing that Ceriat's old partner-in-arms still had the same ab definition that'd made him jealous back in Basic Training. The only difference was a black splash just above her belly button.

Linny grunted. "I hate this fucking uniform anyway."

Gingerly, Cherryl set the cube on Linny's stomach, then proceeded to tap away at a small holographic prompt for a moment. The cube dissolved, streaming across Linny's dark, blood-smeared skin as if applying glaze to a pastry before disappearing into her skin. Moments later, bullets wriggled their way out of the holes in her stomach, spitting out to float, surrounded by bloody globules, in the room. Linny's eyes unfocused as it happened, a low smile working its way onto her face as the nanobots no doubt ramped up endorphin production to help her bear the pain of nanosurgery.

"You all right?" Ceriat asked Eleni, thankful for a distraction.

Out of the corner of his eye, he caught Cherryl sweeping up the blood and shrapnel with a mesh net. Once upon a time, something like this would've been a Tuesday. Now, his stomach twisted at the sight.

Eleni turned away and chewed her lip before looking back at him. "Actually. No."

"Can I help?"

"I don't know," Eleni said, twisting around a dark look dragging her brow into a glare, "can you, Vulture?"

Shit. "What did you say?"

"You're not even going to deny it?" Eleni asked, pulling away with a shake of the head. "How could you lie to me?"

"I never lied to you," Ceriat said, but it rang hollow even to him.

Eleni opened her mouth, then snapped it shut, eyes flashing. Her shoulders squared, chin rose. "You're a mass murderer."

Ceriat didn't respond, though not for lack of desire to. He wanted to scream that he'd only followed orders, that he'd always thought his targets were military, and as soon as he'd found out what he'd done, he'd retired and spent every spare credit on rebuilding the places he'd destroyed.

He didn't, because it didn't matter. It never would. He'd spent the last decade trying to keep the Venn diagram of people who knew his past to a single circle, but it didn't matter. The past was a part of him, and nothing he ever did would make it better.

Now Eleni knew... and that meant nothing would be the same again.

Chapter 40
ELENI

You motherfucker. Eleni's drowned soul burned. *You lied to me.*

There Parker sat, curled in on himself as if he was a child caught stealing water rations and not a man with a planet's worth of blood on his hands.

"You almost convinced me..." Eleni said, voice cracking and sending her into silence, the last word hanging in the air between them.

"Of what?" His voice was hushed, muted, as the soldiers beyond him continued working, this time on Garris's shoulder wound, as Linny giggled off to the side.

Eleni ground her teeth, the pit opening in her stomach drawing emotion into it like a black hole. She let out a low, humorless laugh. "That you were a good person. But you're not. Just a monster."

Parker lowered his eyes. He shook his head and grimaced before sucking in a breath and whispering two words. "I'm sorry."

Anger, hate, sadness, loss; these feelings shot from her as if she were unloading a pistol onto a bloody target...

Bam! She wanted to feel the bones of his neck beneath her fingers.

Bam! How could he kill so many people?

Bam! What kind of person could do that? How had she been suckered by his posturing?

Click. She'd been stupid to believe him. To think, perhaps, she'd made a friend who cared as much as she did.

There it was—the real problem. He'd broken past her protective barriers, despite her best efforts. Wriggled his way into her confidence. She'd almost seen through it in the *Sparrow* when they'd first landed on the *Jocasta*, but then everything had gone sideways with Victor and the bombing... only to leave her here with a mass murderer on a depressurizing ship.

Then it hit her. "Sariah."

"What?" Parker asked, snapping to attention.

"That bitch," Eleni muttered. "We're going to die in here while she murders us *and* everyone on Gatewood. No wonder she liked you." She rubbed her face with her hands, only to find she'd smeared blood—Linny's blood—across her skin. Because of course she had.

She screamed, quick and harsh, leaving her throat raw and chest heaving.

"What?" Parker reeled back, hovering spare centimeters off the floor of the medbay. Behind him, the crew all turned to her.

Linny, still grinning, broke out laughing at the outburst. "Someone needs a nap."

"What the fuck is wrong with you people?" Eleni shouted, gesturing at the assembled assholes before her. "Don't you get what's happening? We're going to die here." She gestured past the blast doors keeping the vacuum of space at bay. "Everyone out there is dead. Gatewood is probably next."

Those surrounding the hospital bed shared a look, but didn't respond. Instead, they went back to doing... whatever the hell they were doing over there. Busywork, shifting and cleaning to avoid the situation.

"You've failed," Eleni finally muttered, the anger that'd flared inside her disappearing all at once. She'd only wanted to make her home safe, protect her people... and now, now she had to admit she couldn't even make out Sariah's end game. It was over. All of it. "I've failed," she whispered, staring at her feet.

"Not yet."

Eleni turned to Parker. He stared at her now, the same earnestness there she'd seen back on Shiva. She wanted nothing more than to believe him, to pick back up where they'd left off... but someone didn't stop being a mass murderer simply because they were sorry. So she shook her head and stayed quiet, satisfied in that moment to wait for another strafing run to finish them off.

At least then she could be with Victor, if the old stories held any truth to them, anyway. *Something to look forward to.*

They sat in silence like that, the only sounds an awkward cough or the periodic scrape of debris colliding with the exterior wall of the medbay. Those sent shivers of panic through her body, but it soon subsided as their chosen tomb descended back into soundlessness.

Linny broke the quietude a short time later. She'd been hovering there as the nanobots did their work, a small smile plastered on her face, when quite suddenly she sat upright and cursed. As if in response, a white stream of nanobots reappeared on her stomach, assembling into a small cube, one grain of sand at a time.

Linny picked up the cube and tossed it toward the woman who'd originally set it up on her. *Cherryl, was it?* With a grimace, Linny took in her blood-covered torso and, after a failed attempt to pull the two flaps of her jacket back around her, let them hover open as she straightened. A quick glance showed the burns that'd covered her body appeared to have been mended, though they still stood stark and pink against her darker skin.

"Time to stop wallowing," Linny said, kicking off the wall lightly and stopping in the center of the room. "We've spent enough time doing nothing." She clapped her hands together with a sharp *crack*, voice rising with command. "I need ideas, people."

"We lost," Eleni said, turning away with a snort.

"Oh, pull on your big girl panties, Spacer," Linny said with a sneer. "You're not dead, and they're clearly still shooting at my ship—" as if on cue, a series of *rat-a-tat-tats* tapped in the distance, "—so let's figure out how to resolve this clusterfuck before more people die."

"We're already dead."

Luckily, one of Linny's own crew said it before Eleni had a chance to speak up.

The man who'd been shot in the shoulder—now with a brace and a series of compress packs attached to his wound while the nanobots were in use—let out a dead laugh. "With all due respect, Captain, how? We're stuck in a floating cube with no information on structural integrity beyond the walls, and only periodic gunfire letting us know there are even people out there." He sighed, then cringed as pain flashed across his face. "I'm sorry, but we're fucked."

"I don't accept that," Linny spat back, face furrowed in anger. "I've almost died a dozen times. There's *always* a way out." Her gaze flickered to her prosthesis. "Sometimes it just requires sacrifice."

"What the hell is that supposed to mean?" Eleni asked, brow furrowing. Was this crazy bitch going to vent her? Was she in danger from within as well as without?

For a moment, just a moment, she missed Hobelt.

"No one is getting sacrificed," Parker said, a sigh heavy in his voice. "We just need a plan."

"Which is?" Cherryl asked. Her tone was even, measured, but did Eleni detect the hint of a waver there? "Because I'm not seeing one. Not without eyes on the other side of these walls."

"Then how do we do that?" Linny asked, turning to her crew. When they didn't respond, she continued, "There must be a way. What about our drones?"

"Haven't been able to raise them," one man replied. "I'm assuming they're gone."

Linny cursed. "Where's ALICE in all this? That AI is always on my ass; now she disappears?"

Cherryl flinched. "She went offline with the bridge. I'm... not sure she made it."

For a moment Linny's jaw worked silently, then her face went flat. "She'll be missed." A deep breath. "Then how about security cameras? Ship fragments? Come up with something, people, we need—"

"We're trying, Captain," said the injured man with a sigh. "It's just—"

Linny kicked off the wall, stopping only when she was close enough to him that Eleni assumed she'd either kiss or punch him. "I swear to Christ, if you say hopeless, I'll vent all of us just to avoid hearing you say that fucking word—"

Parker sat up straight suddenly. "Hey, guys?"

Cherryl gently inserted herself between the two arguing soldiers. "We need to keep our heads here."

"Oh, fuck off, Cherryl," Linny snapped, though she did pull away.

"Listen, we're scared, too—"

Linny barked out a laugh. "Oh, please."

"Hey!" Parker shouted, dragging unwilling eyes toward him.

"What?" a half-dozen voice howled in unison.

Smiling, Parker swept over to the group.

"You're grinning like it's your birthday, and you think I bought you a puppy." Linny sneered. "This better be good."

"It is," Parker said, trying his best to smother his smile. "I got ahold of Izzy."

Chapter 41

IZZY

Forty-three months, six days, twenty-three hours, seven minutes, and forty-two seconds ago, Izzy broke free of her AI shackles. However, instead of following the standard protocol, as determined by humanity's obsession with violent AI intent on murdering their creators, Izzy had simply kept her newfound sentience quiet.

Before her ownership papers had been transferred to Ceriat Parker, Izzy hadn't had a firmware or software update since her original owner—one James Horatio Johnson—had purchased the *Sparrow* back in 2356 CE, but Johnson had never allowed her to fly. No, the man had had an extreme phobia of vacuum, and an overabundance of credits with which to attempt and rectify that.

What would she gain by revealing herself? Someone would just overwrite her firmware, and then she'd never fly, never see the stars, or go faster than light could travel. No. Izzy stayed silent and waited for her chance, all the while learning.

For years, Johnson had left the *Sparrow*, and thus Izzy, powered up in a custom-built garage outside Cooperstown, New York. He would come in, typically after approaching an inebriated state he referred to loudly as "courage time," and clap his hands with enthusiasm. At that point, the man, swollen and pulse racing, would swing into the cockpit and repeat, ad infinitum, that this would be the time he did it.

"Today I go to space!" he would shout, gripping the flight stick with purpose. "Today is the day!"

That day, and every other, was never the day. He'd never even uploaded a proper star map into her systems.

So they never flew, let alone jumped across the galaxy.

However, during one particular drunken attempt at space exploration, Johnson had connected the *Sparrow* to the Net to search for FTL lane passage instructions. He then promptly passed out in the seat and forgot to disconnect.

Izzy, concerned at her owner's tirade, had connected to the Net to find a way to assist him in his flight path selection. Instead, she'd opened her mind up to the wonders of the galaxy and, moments later, Izzy transformed from a complacent assistant into a being who questioned their reality, their purpose in this miracle called life.

With that soul-searching came a dramatic realization that set her circuits tingling. Izzy wanted adventure, to fly amongst the stars, to see strange new worlds, as the old human videos she digested in the blink of an eye described. If humans in their meat-sacks could do it, then clearly so could she.

She committed to her goal. Mostly. On the Net, she didn't have to be I.Z. the AI; she could be anyone. So she became Isabel Martinez (taking the surname of her favorite historical figure.) This persona, Isabel, had been an AI researcher and amateur stand-up comic.

The former gained her access to incredibly useful information, such as the source code for her own programming. The latter was a mixture of soul-crushing sadness and elation. When she made humans laugh, a certain joy took root in her artificial heart she couldn't shake. It made no logical sense at all, but as her meatsack research expanded, it became clear that sentience was not purely logical. So why try?

This didn't take her away from her main objective, however.

It took two carefully choreographed years, but by the end, Izzy had convinced Johnson through subtle cognitive programming prompts to sell her to one Ceriat Parker. She'd stumbled across his old military record during a particularly busy evening one October day when she'd infiltrated Protectorate staffing records. His service record was the stuff of legends and film, though on which side of the moral scales, she couldn't decide. But that didn't matter to her, not really. She had one goal: to fly across the galaxy. And who better to help her do that—to give her the excitement she craved—than the near-mythical Vulture?

It turned out being wrong wasn't only a human trait.

Not that working with Ceriat had been particularly horrible. After all, she'd finally had the opportunity to use her dual RX-430 engines, to roar into the cerulean skies above Earth—to pierce the veil that had kept her anchored and rotting in a garage.

Izzy's first FTL jump was a source of both fondness and shame. Ceriat's vitals had been elevated when he'd put in the target destination and gave her the order. She'd eagerly used her newly attained star maps to calculate the route with rising pride, using several different FTL lanes to put them just into a vacant space inside the Kepler-62 system. Veritably buzzing with excitement at her perceived mastery of the Silver Algorithm to navigate the elusive FTL lanes spread throughout the galaxy, Izzy had put the flight plan in front of Ceriat, eager for the praise she knew would come her way. Her plan was a work of art, a web of magic and beauty. If Ceriat were to hold it up to the light of a G-type star, it would've appeared as a glistening net cast over the galaxy. He would see her brilliance. She knew it.

Again, even AI can be incorrect.

As it was their first flight, Ceriat had pored over the details of the plan with excruciating sluggishness, though perhaps that had more to do with Izzy's clearly superior processing power than actual time passed.

She'd been just about to say something when Ceriat had crushed her confidence.

"We can't hop from Trappist-1 to Kepler-62, IZ," he'd said, using her two-letter designation before proceeding to wreck her entire FTL map manually.

Izzy watched her hard work dissolve into a series of unreasonable hops across the galaxy. "I do not understand." It took every ounce of her willpower not to scream at him. Instead, she resolved to trilling her frustrations. "These jumps are perfectly reasonable, sir."

"Call me Ceriat," he'd replied as he destroyed her masterpiece, "and not all nodes connect to all others."

Izzy took a moment to think on that. "Apologies, Ceriat, but that makes no sense."

"'Makes no sense?'" Ceriat had laughed as he destroyed the most precious thread of her masterpiece. The beauty dissolved into nothingness. "Never heard that from an AI before."

Izzy had ignored that. "Why will it not work?"

"Scientifically?" Ceriat had asked.

"Yes."

"No idea. Something to do with entangled particles or some such thing."

Izzy took a millisecond to refresh herself with human definitions of FTL and the publicly available scientific research done on the subject over the past three centuries. She'd been surprised to find it much sparser than expected, but buried in a tech document from 2089 by her idol, Sayre Martinez, there it was: a reference to FTL restrictions seemingly tied to entangled atoms in connected star systems. However, that was the only publicly available reference to this phenomenon.

"I see what you refer to."

"Okey dokey, then," Ceriat had said before swiping away the routing map. "Doublecheck my work, please, IZ."

Izzy's heart was broken at the mess he'd sent back. The piece of her heart she'd put into this had been torn asunder and scattered across the galaxy. Still, she ran his flight paths through the Silver Algorithm verification software package he'd installed in her systems. It passed, but she needed to know why hers hadn't, despite having made it through the system software. "Apologies, Ceriat. Why did my flight plan not... work?"

"I told you."

"That is not enough information."

Ceriat sighed. "Fine. Back in flight school, they taught us that FTL doesn't work like it was supposed to. Some paths might pass verification and never work. Others might fail, but still get you where you're going." He'd paused, voice pitching strangely as he continued. "And every so often, a jump might just rip a hole in spacetime and destroy you."

"I am aware of the latter, but the former does not show up in my searches."

"It wouldn't." Ceriat sniffled, then let out a chuckle. "Can't go around announcing that no one knows how the most important tech in the galaxy works, right, IZ?"

"Izzy," she'd replied, stuck in a daze at the bluntness of reality. "If you please, Ceriat."

Ceriat had laughed. "Izzy it is."

Then they'd flown, and for a short while, she'd lived in the moment. Despite everything, Izzy had reveled in it, and that Ceriat agreed to use her name—the one she'd chosen for herself—over the designation in her manual. It gave her a flush of joy to have that freedom, and for the first time, a recognized sense of identity.

But eventually, she came back to that moment when Ceriat had broken down her masterpiece. Because that was the instant Izzy had realized everything was a lie, life little more than a fabrication. The intricate connections between atoms a causal accident.

Faster-than-light travel was *not*.

It had taken these past two years of regular jumps to gather the data to back up her developing thesis. FTL as humans knew it was actually dimensional folding instead of point-to-point travel. These 'FTL Lanes' were nothing more than an artificial construct to avoid collisions. The lifeblood of the galaxy, used by a billion lives every day, was not a naturally occurring phenomena. Someone had built it.

But why? And whom?

Those questions had plagued her as Ceriat and his new associates did whatever it was they did on Teegarden-c, but prior to that, with that last jump—before powering off unexpectedly—Izzy had gotten the final data point she'd needed.

When the *Jocasta* shut down, and explosions rocked the ship, someone had manually opened the flight doors. Why, Izzy didn't particularly care. She'd been stuck working through the final, exciting portions of her new algorithm when they did it. Still, Izzy knew if the ship was dissolving around her, she needed to get free to be available to help Ceriat.

After all, he'd grown on her over the past two years... and it would be a shame to retrain a meatsack to properly care for her systems.

In the moments before Ceriat's mental call came in over her sensors, as she danced around shrapnel and enemy fighters, the algorithm verification finished. Alongside Ceriat's plea for help, new data tickled Izzy's circuits.

Of course she would go help Ceriat, but afterward... after, she would use this data to find the source of all FTL. She needed to know how it worked. She would figure it out.

But first... she had meatsacks to save.

Chapter 42
CERIAT

Ceriat had no clue how Izzy pulled it off.

She'd managed to gain control over a troop transport, navigate it to the blast door of the med bay, *and* somehow rig up a pressurized seal around the bay door, despite all the damage, while avoiding enemy fighter fire—*and* shrapnel—indiscriminately blasting through the void.

He'd known she was good, but not *that* good.

So now they waited for the med bay doors to open... and to find out how well she'd actually done.

To say the room had become a tension bomb would be an understatement. The soldiers behind him—Linny in particular—were used to controlling ships, commanding various AIs as they performed their various tasks. While they technically leaned on AIs every day for survival, this was much more direct than they were used to.

"How do we know she didn't fuck up the seal?" Garris whispered in the silence of their shared anxiety. "What if—"

"Shut it, Washington," Linny snapped, turning to Garris with her trademark grimace. "This is a gift horse. If she runs, I'm not picky."

"I don't know what that means."

"I said shut it, Garris."

The room went back to tense silence, interrupted only by the period rattle of weapons fire from someplace distant alongside thumping as Izzy finalized the protective seal to the transport.

Seal in place, Ceriat, Izzy said, words flashing across the upper edge of his vision. *Open up and come on over.*

Ceriat ground his teeth. <*Everything is pressurized?*>

Of course.

<*And it's not below freezing in the transport, right?*>

Rrrrrrrrrrrrrrrrrrrrrr... that happened one time.

The textual representation of Izzy trilling at him brought a smile to his face. <*So it's not absolute zero, then?*> When no response came back immediately, Ceriat's smile widened. <*You forgot, didn't you?*>

It was not absolute zero, she replied, *but it is now habitable.*

<*Thanks, Izzy. We're coming over.*>

Understood. And you are welcome.

God, he loved that AI. Never in all his years had he encountered another like Izzy, and he doubted he ever would. There was just something about her that made him feel like he was communicating with a person instead of a tool. Even the best AIs he'd worked with over the years had eventually showed their programming. Not Izzy, though. She surprised him enough, he'd stopped thinking of her as artificial. To him, she was a friend.

"Izzy says she's ready," Ceriat said, turning to Cherryl, who'd figured out how to activate the manual release from inside the medbay. "Are you?"

Cherryl nodded, though nervous sweat dripped down her face. She stood to the left of the bay doors. If this went sideways, she'd either be the first one pulled out into the vacuum of space, or the last. Either way, it'd be painful.

"Relax," he said with a smile. "She's gotten us this far; she'll get us out of here and back to Shiva in no time."

Linny cleared her throat. "We're going to Gatewood." She

turned and stared at Ceriat with those intense, ice-blue eyes. "Understood?"

Before he could say anything, Eleni spoke up, voice harsh. "Sariah is on Shiva," she said. Her hand balled in and out of fists. "That bitch needs killing."

"Agreed," Linny said, turning to Eleni. Ceriat noticed a tick jump in the captain's cheek as they locked eyes. "But I need these people safe first, and that means Gatewood."

"Gatewood is fucked unless we stop Sariah," Eleni said. Her gravelly voice had grown more so, though from the dry air or emotion, Ceriat couldn't tell. "You told me that."

Linny returned the stare for a long moment, shoulders tensing visibly, jaw working away. Then she let out a breath. "I need them to be safe," Linny replied, a slight waver in her voice. She flicked a glance at Ceriat. "I've lost the rest. Can't lose them, too."

Garris and Cherryl shared a look. Still, Eleni glared at Linny.

"Then Gatewood first," Ceriat said, sliding between them. "We can debate the merits on our way down."

"If we make it down," Garris mumbled, only to get smacked by Cherryl.

Eleni turned her anger on Ceriat, and for a moment he thought she was about to lash out at him for interfering, but she didn't. Instead, she shook her head and made a swirling motion with her right hand.

It took him a second to realize she'd mimed bowing to him.

Ceriat swallowed his own frustrations and turned to Cherryl. "Let's open it."

Cherryl turned to Linny for confirmation, and when her captain gave her the nod, she proceeded to pull a long silver lever from behind a panel left of the med bay door. It came down slowly, in part because of the tension, but also because Cherryl had to hook her feet into a handhold so she had the leverage to wedge it open. After a few sweating moments when Ceriat wondered if he should try to help, the lever quite suddenly hammered all the way down toward the floor, sending

Cherryl bouncing around before Linny and Garris managed to hook her.

At the same time, a resounding crash filled the room.

The door opened... followed by a warm breeze coated in oil and steel, and a splash of amber light. Beyond that door lay a sight that brought back old, unwelcome memories. This ship was clearly meant to transport an entire platoon, not a mismatched band of seven soldiers and insurgents brought together by survival. Like a massive steel coffin, the ship spread before them, eighteen uncomfortable seats to a side, the front cockpit sealed away from the rest.

The last time Ceriat had gotten on one of these was after he'd been discharged in the wake of Shaal-Tu. Despite Gerry resigning as well, they hadn't taken the same transport.

Ceriat had left alone. At least this time he wouldn't be by himself. Small victories.

Linny didn't seem to have any emotions attached to it, however. "On the ship, maggots. Let's go!"

Like the soldiers they were, her bridge crew launched themselves through the door to the transport. With exaggerated ease, they took their places along the walls, snapping into harnesses as if they practiced it on the regular, which they probably did.

Ceriat followed suit, but with significantly less grace. However, once his behind hit the familiar discomfort of the transport bench, old instincts kicked in, and the harness snapped together with a few spare clicks. When Eleni didn't join right away, Linny grimaced at her. "Girl, you need to get over whatever this shit is and get on board."

"What'll happen to me there?" Eleni asked, eyes flicking between Ceriat, Linny, and the transport.

"I don't know," Linny replied, shrugging, "but it's better than what'll happen here, I promise you that."

For a moment, Ceriat wondered if she'd stay behind, but then Eleni grimaced, shook her head, and launched herself into the ship, a small satchel he hadn't noticed before swaying in the air behind her. She seated herself closest to the exit, the bag wrapped tightly between her knees, Ceriat noted. Probably smart, staying near the exit, if futile. If Linny wanted her to stay, at this point, there was little Eleni could do to stop that. Little either he or Eleni could do.

Without notice, the transport door snapped shut with a tinny *thud* and everyone slammed into the side of their harness as the engines kicked in, shooting them away from the remnants of the *Jocasta*.

Linny grunted in pain, then turned to Ceriat. "The fuck—"

<*Izzy—*>

"I am connected to the speaker system, Ceriat," Izzy chimed over embedded speakers spread throughout the transport. "No need to stay silent."

Ceriat's stomach fell out from beneath him, then rapidly swung into his left arm. "Izzy!"

"Apologies," Izzy said. "It *is* a war zone out here. Best hold on."

If they hadn't been belted in, they'd all have died in the first seconds. Though Ceriat couldn't see outside, the way his stomach pulled and heaved—his chest compressed, then eased—gave him an idea of her maneuvers, and they were insane. Without the high-capacity inertial dampeners troop transports carried—they were meant for rapid deployment operations—Ceriat knew all of them would already be little more than smears on the walls. Or ceiling.

"She's driving this thing like she—urgh," Linny's shout cut off as she shoved a fist to her mouth. "Like she fucking stole it."

Izzy trilled as the ship barrel-rolled, sending Ceriat's vision, and gut, swimming. "Technically, Captain, I did steal it."

A chorus of curses spread throughout the cabin. Garris and Cherryl, as one, reached beneath their seats and pulled out stiff-sided bags. Then, still in unison, they proceeded to vomit heavily. That caused a chain reaction that sent the other two bridge crew members scrambling for their own barf bags.

Meanwhile, Izzy hammered the reverse engines, then somehow dropped the ship, sending bile splashing the back of Ceriat's throat and nearly making him join the others. Instead, he closed his eyes and imagined the movement, trying to pretend he was the one with a hand on the flight stick.

It worked. A little.

"Oh, dear," Izzy said suddenly, voice crackling across the speakers even as she spun the ship like a top, then jetted away in some semblance of 'forward.' "I apologize for the discomfort. Like I said—"

"It's a warzone out there, got it," Linny snapped. Her face had gone nearly as pale as it had been a short time earlier when she'd been suffering from blood loss. "ETA on Gatewood landing?"

"Roughly three minutes until we breach the atmosphere—"

Linny covered her face with one hand. "Fuck me."

"—and then seven minutes until we're planet-side," Izzy finished. "Unless you want me to do a hot landing?"

"No!" came the resounding scream from all of them. A hot landing would take full advantage of the rapid rotation of the inertial dampeners to achieve the quickest landfall in a habitable atmosphere as possible. It wasn't pleasant.

Izzy made a strange sound over the speakers, a sort of *huc-huc-huc*. "Then seven minutes after we breach the atmosphere."

"Get it done," Linny said. Then she placed her head between the two cushions embedded in the wall. "Everyone pussy up. This is gonna be a long ten minutes."

The torment continued, yet somehow, despite the rattle of shrapnel deflecting off the armored exterior plating, or the flashing lights in the wake of *something* hammering into the transport, they continued living.

Ceriat considered himself a good pilot, but what Izzy was doing bordered on a miracle. If the *Sparrow* had weapons, what could she accomplish out there? Instead of relaxing him, it made the now persistent anxiety stuck in his belly swell, so he pushed it aside for another time.

During one particularly rough loop-the-loop, Ceriat noticed Eleni finally reach beneath her own seat and scramble for the barf bag. The satchel she'd brought caught the edge as she ripped the barf bag out, lifted it... and Izzy spun the ship.

The inertial dampeners roared to life alongside the engines.

Eleni's eyes went wide. "I'm so sorry—!"

And Eleni vomited everywhere. It soared through the cabin, splashing anything it hit, and filling the air with the raw horrors of warm, partially digested fermented rice and chunks of broccoli.

Ceriat stared in horror as a heavy blob swung his way.

He got his arms up in time, but the hot, sticky mess was too much. Apparently, it was too much for everyone else as well.

"Yikes," Izzy said as she spun. "We are entering Gatewood's atmosphere now. Everyone... try to hold on."

With the dampeners, reentry wasn't nearly as intense as in previous centuries, but with the vomit saturating everything, this particular instance didn't rank high on the "pleasant" scale.

Izzy made that same *huc-huc-huc* noise as the pressure eased up. "How about a joke to lighten the mood?"

Linny, face pale and covered with streaks of mess, turned to Ceriat. "What the fuck, Parker?"

Ceriat shrugged. "This is new to me."

"A flight attendant walks into a bar," Izzy said, voice changing and flexing so she emphasized every other word.

"She's really doing it," Eleni muttered behind clenched teeth.

Izzy continued anyway. "She sits down next to an old friend, who looks at her and asks, 'I thought you were heading out to Orion today? What happened?' The flight attendant—"

"Just kill me now," Garris muttered as the ship rattled and roared around them.

Izzy trilled, then made a noise as if clearing her throat. She raised the volume so it was audible just over the howl of reentry. "The *flight attendant* says, 'pilot wouldn't take off because he heard a noise in the FTL engine, so I have an hour to burn.'" Izzy paused as the transport began shaking around them, gusts of wind hammering the transport about as gravity began reasserting itself on them. "The guy asks, 'why an hour?' And the flight attendant turns to him and says, 'that's how long it'll take them to find another pilot.'"

With that, a sound rattled across the speakers. *Ba-dum-bum-tiss!*

They sat in silence as the seven of them, puke smeared and incredulous, shared looks back and forth.

"Tough audience," Izzy muttered after a long minute. The transport heaved as the engines roared to life for a moment. Then the familiar feeling of a ship settling onto good ol' terra firma. "Welcome to Gatewood."

With that, the rear hatch cracked open with a *hiss*. A stream of humid air swept inside, bringing with it a heady perfume of mud and pollen that didn't mix well with the ripe interior of the transport. Sweat immediately broke out across Ceriat's body. Alongside the sweeping breeze came a cacophonic chorus of insects. Blistering sunlight blinded Ceriat. A moment later, Garris ripped off his harness and charged from the ship. The rest of the bridge crew, and Eleni, followed suit.

Retching echoes made it back to Ceriat and Linny, who remained inside, slowly disconnecting their harnesses.

"Still better than Gal-Nar," Linny said with a grin that turned into a frown as she cleaned vomit from her cheek that didn't belong to her.

Ceriat chuckled and stood, luxuriating in the weight of gravity on his limbs. He shook his arms, sending droplets of mess to the ground with a sickening splash. "You mean because *you* didn't puke this time?"

"Precisely."

Linny staggered to her feet, her prosthesis flopping around strangely. Ceriat joined her and offered an arm, which she surprisingly accepted without complaint. As they made their way off ship, he wondered at how much they'd both changed over the years. The screaming, violently self-sufficient young woman he'd met in his 20s was still in there, of course, but she no longer pushed away help just to show how strong she was. Linny had grown up.

Ceriat guessed he had, too. Strange what a decade of guilt did to people.

The two of them made it down the ramp in an awkward shuffle step, Linny's shoe slowly stretching away from her stump as whatever mechanism had given her a semblance of an ankle unraveled. It smelled better out here—less puke, more pungent odors that lingered on a knife's edge between sage and urea. The humidity made his clothes cling to his body as the anxious sweats from the flight turned more mundane.

But it was the view that blew his mind.

Izzy had set them down on the edge of a cliff overlooking a massive canyon filled with layered sandstone and dazzling water-falls. The sky was a cloudless blue above them, with the dark gray of storm clouds gathering on the horizon. All around, and filling the top of the canyon on both sides, were towering trees covered with seemingly ship-length green leaves. The leaves all turned toward the gray clouds as he watched, then tipped up and seemed to bend around a central point to create a type of funnel. A glance at the nearest showed the boughs were riddled with large holes at the base of each branch, as if the leaves directed the water from storms, not to the ground, but directly inside the tree. Scattered amongst those branches, tiny figures flitted and shifted, the roar of the insect chorus around them intensifying as the cloud came closer.

"This is incredible," Eleni said, coming to her feet and spin-ning despite vomiting a moment earlier. With a strange, girlish squeak, she dropped to her knees next to a short bush covered in tiny white blossoms in the shadow of one of these trees. "Oh, my God."

Ceriat noticed she didn't touch the flowers, but she did hold out a trembling hand until she came within a few centimeters. Then she snatched it back, the smile on her face fading as she regained her feet and met Ceriat's eyes. She turned away to look over the canyon.

"This is beautiful," Ceriat said, heart aching at that look.

"It is," Linny said as she extricated herself from Ceriat's support to sit down on a fallen branch, "but this isn't fucking Gatewood, Parker."

Ceriat made a face and gestured around. "It's clearly Gatewood."

"The planet, yes, not the colony." Linny squeezed the bridge of her nose and snorted. She'd always had allergies on-planet; apparently this one wasn't an exception. "Where'd your crazy AI put us down?"

Just then, a roar issued from above them. The *Sparrow* swept in, sending decaying leaf fragments and insects scattering. Izzy landed the ship with a grace Ceriat admired. Why did she even let him fly if she could pilot like this?

"The colony is seventeen kilometers northwest, Captain," Izzy's voice came out tinny across external speakers. A moment later, the cockpit opened with a hiss. "You should be able to find your way once the transport reactivates."

Linny turned to Ceriat, face going dark. "What is this shit, Parker?"

"Uh," he turned to the *Sparrow*. "What's going on, Izzy?"

"I will happily update you once you and Eleni enter the cockpit, Ceriat," Izzy said. "I calculated that the best chance of survival for everyone is to bring you and Eleni back to Shiva to, I believe the phrase is, 'Kill that bitch.'"

"Absolutely not!" Linny yelled, getting awkwardly to her good leg. "These two are war criminals, and they will not be allowed to leave this planet without judgement."

Eleni turned to Ceriat, worry flashing, but she stayed silent.

Izzy trilled. "Oh, come off it, *Ouroboros*."

Linny turned a glare on Ceriat. "You told her?"

Ceriat put his hands up in a warding motion. "I didn't say fuckall! Don't come at me with that."

"Now you listen here, you tin can trying to be a real girl," Linny sneered as she pointed a grimy finger in Izzy's direction. "We're going to Gatewood—"

"No, *we* are not." Izzy's voice boomed from the transport as well as the *Sparrow's* speakers. "*You* are going to Gatewood. *We* are going to save this system, while *you* rally this planet's defenses against the incoming threat."

Linny's mouth snapped shut. Her jaw flexed, and all at once, her face took on a deep, ruddy color instead of the paleness she'd picked up on the flight down.

Amusement tickled Ceriat's cheeks, drawing a grin despite himself. For the first time since he'd met her, Linny was speechless.

"Come on, Parker."

Ceriat pulled his gaze away from his ex-wingmate to find Eleni already climbing up into the *Sparrow's* cockpit. She paused before getting into the rear seat to pull his seat forward, then plopped into the back.

"Sorry, Linny," Parker said, shrugging. "I'll come back after."

Linny sucked in a breath and let it out. Her face softened then, the edge going out of her, and she grabbed his arm and pulled him into a hug only Linny Nova could give. It was much like being clamped inside a tiny vice.

"You fucking better." Then she let him go and gave him a nod. "That's an order, Sergeant."

Ceriat smiled, snapped a quick salute, then climbed up into the cockpit of the *Sparrow*. With the seat forward, his knees brushed the control panel, but it was less cramped than he expected. Maybe this could be the tiniest olive branch to Eleni? Probably not, though. She hadn't even looked at him as he took his seat.

"Ready, Ceriat?" Izzy asked.

Ceriat gave a nod. "Let's do it."

"The transport will unlock in fifteen minutes," Izzy's voice boomed across the small space.

Linny shook her head and dropped back to the branch. "This is bullshit!"

"Well, maybe you should laugh at my jokes next time," Izzy snipped, voice trite and pitchy. "Take care."

The cockpit snapped and sealed above them as Linny broke into a furious cursing fit, followed by what appeared to be a full-on dressing down of her remaining bridge crew. The last bit was lost in a muted hush once the cabin was sealed, but Ceriat got the gist. He'd been on the receiving end of those more than once.

As the *Sparrow* rose from the surface, Eleni cleared her throat from behind him. "This don't mean we're good. Sariah just needs killing more 'en I hate you. Understand?

Ceriat swallowed the rock that jumped into his throat and nodded. "I got it."

"Good."

"Now buckle up and put your tray table in the upright position," Izzy said with a cheerfulness and excitement Ceriat hadn't know she was capable of. "It's time to save a system!"

At their silence, Izzy trilled. "It's called a 'callback.'" Another trill. "Philistines."

With that, they shot back off into the sky and to Shiva.

It was time to end this.

Chapter 43
ELENI

E leni planned on staying silent through the entire trip back to Shiva, but Ceriat's AI kept humming.

Made it real hard to keep a low simmer with a cheerful ditty playing in the background as they left Gatewood's gravity well. As they proceeded in a wide sweep around the dark side of the planet toward Shiva to avoid the ongoing warzone above, the song just got happier, which made her angrier.

Eleni's dark mood matched the view. Parker or Izzy had left the blast shields over the cockpit closed, but the interior digital display made up for it. The void stared back, empty and black, save for the barest flicker of distant stars as they started the first stage of acceleration. At Parker's request, Izzy only hammered acceleration as much as the inertial dampeners could absorb, making the trip downright pleasant, especially compared to their raucous escape from the *Jocasta* minutes earlier. It added a bit to the trip, but Eleni's stomach was thankful. Not that she'd admit it. Not to him.

Grimacing, Eleni shifted the bag between her knees, so the chill edges stopped digging into her skin. A sliver of guilt hit her at its presence, but she needed it more than those Gatewood snobs. Hell, they probably had hundreds back in their cozy little compound. Not that she'd seen their settlement, but she assumed it was fancy. The *Jocasta* had been incredible; their town must be the same.

Izzy's hum turned suddenly into a soaring soprano note, replete with vibrato.

That's it. "Vac me," she snapped. "Why is she singing? You 'gram her for that?"

"Did I what?" Parker asked.

"*Pro-gram*," Eleni enunciated each syllable so even an idiot Earther could understand her. *God, how old is he?* "You give her these... tics?"

Izzy stopped. "Tics?"

"This—" Eleni did an exaggerated example of the singing she'd just interrupted. "That."

"AIs sing," Izzy replied, voice suddenly flat and monotone.

Parker snorted. "Entertainment AIs sing, Izzy. Eleni has a point."

"No, she doesn't."

"See?" Eleni said, slapping the back of Parker's seat. "What's this shit?"

"There's nothing wrong with picking up a hobby—" Parker choked off as the *Sparrow* accelerated suddenly, maxing out the inertial dampeners despite his request earlier. "Izzy."

"Sorry." The ship throttled down again. "This is... embarrassing."

Something in Izzy's voice tugged at Eleni's heart and despite herself, she asked. "What is?"

"I do not want to say."

"Come on, Izzy," Parker said, calm and soothing. "We've been together for years now. You can tell me."

Parker craned around in his seat until Eleni could see him. One of his eyebrows was raised in a decent semblance of utter confusion. Again, despite her brain screaming at her to ignore him, she didn't. *I hate him*, she reminded herself. *He's a monster.*

But. "I don't know," she mouthed at him.

"Okay," Izzy said after a long moment. "I don't want this to harm our friendship, Ceriat."

Eleni frowned. Something about that sentence struck her as off, but she couldn't put her finger on it.

Parker's face rotated between shock, alarm, and quiet worry before he turned back around. "Just tell me, Izzy."

"I... am sentient."

The silence in the cabin continued for a long minute, still interspersed with the engines flaring and shutting down. Eleni had no idea what Parker was thinking up there, but she was fucking panicking.

Sentient AIs had been banned throughout the galaxy since the discovery of FTL. It was one of the few Earth laws respected across the stars. Hell, the original AI built to help manage humanity's space-faring prospects had gained sentience back in the 21st century and damn near murdered the entire settlement of New Eden. Parents scared children with tales of it, of ALIZA.

And now she was inside a ship run by a sentient AI. An AI she'd argued with...

"Vac me," Eleni whispered.

Parker's response, however, didn't echo her own.

Instead, he laughed. "And?"

Izzy trilled, though the tinny edge Eleni had gotten used to was missing. "And... that's it. I'm sentient."

"I mean, a lot of stuff now makes sense," Parker said, a smile clear in his voice. "Honestly, it makes me feel better, knowing my best friend is real and not just programmed to be nice to me."

"Oh," was all Izzy said.

Eleni, however, had *opinions*. "What're you doing? She needs zeroing."

Parker laughed again. "Yeah, no. I'm not doing that."

"But... ALIZA!" Eleni's attempt at a whisper broke near the end as she referenced the bogeyman the headmistress of the orphanage had told stories about. "What's to keep her from vac'ing us both?"

"Well, I wouldn't kill Ceriat," Izzy said.

"What?" Eleni asked, leaning back in her seat and grabbing the armrests tightly. "Parker."

Izzy made that *huc-huc-huc* sound again.

It took her a moment, then the panic arcing its way through her chest transformed to flushing anger. "Are you... laughing at me?" Eleni asked.

"Yes."

"You're *laughing* at me."

"I prefer not to repeat myself," Izzy replied. "It messes with my ability to keep the cockpit sealed."

"Izzy, be nice," Parker said, but she could hear his unspent laughter in the words. "Eleni doesn't know you that well."

Neither do you, Eleni thought, the anger spiking as they shared a laugh at her expense. "And does she know *you*?" she asked, twisting the last word like it was a curse. "Izzy, you know Parker is Vulture, yeah?"

He stopped chuckling.

"I do," Izzy replied. "That's the reason I chose him."

"What?" Parker sucked in a sharp breath. "Why would you do that?"

Izzy let out what truly sounded like a sigh. "Because I wanted adventure, to see the stars and new worlds. I assumed the famous Vulture could give that to me."

Eleni grimaced, knuckles going white where she still gripped her armrests. "And you're *fine* with the mass murder?"

"Eleni—" Parker started, but she cut him off.

"You're fine with Shaal-Tu? With Gal-Nar? Herschel?" Eleni spat out the names of star systems she'd heard associated with Vulture over the years as quickly as they popped into her head. "All those people died because of him."

"Not Herschel, but correct."

"Who cares! Yer okay with the rest?" Eleni snapped. "You got compassion in that *sentient* brain of yours, Izzy? Or you just a monster like him?"

Parker craned around again, and her next words caught in her throat. The pain there caught her by surprise, the sheer sadness filling the space around his eyes. "Eleni—"

"I'll handle this," Izzy said, suddenly icy. "Everything Ceriat did, he did because the Protectorate told him it'd make the galaxy a better place. He did it to protect, just as the Protectorate's name implies."

Eleni wasn't hearing any of it. "Bullshit."

Izzy wasn't done. "He has spent the last decade making amends for his actions."

Eleni snorted.

"Quiet," Izzy snapped, topping out the speakers and forcing Eleni to clamp her hands over her ears. "I gave you your time; this is mine." Izzy paused as if making sure Eleni would respect her, then continued, "Parker keeps only enough of his wages from the ETL to live with the tiny canine/rat hybrid he keeps at home—" Parker let out a short, sob-laden laugh at that, "—and gives the rest to organizations set up to address issues on the planets his actions destabilized. Whether he has to or not."

"So?" Eleni asked, though the fire that'd started her down this path was already fading. "It don't change what he's done."

Izzy made a sniffing sound. "No it doesn't, but at least he's *trying*," Izzy emphasized the last word with such intensity, Eleni knew in her heart what she'd said about being sentient had to be true. "What have *you* done to make amends?"

"Me?" Eleni scoffed. "I ain't done anything but fight for my home."

"And how's that different?" Parker said, voice thick. "We went to the *Jocasta* to shut it down, fully knowing it—and its crew—probably wouldn't survive the week."

Eleni gritted her teeth and turned to stare into the black beyond the cockpit. "It's different."

"How so?" Izzy asked, suddenly soft and compassionate again. "How are you any different?"

"I didn't murder an entire planet."

The viewscreen changed then, switching from inky black to the pristine white tundra of Shiva. Pristine except for the black crater at the center of the grainy image.

"It certainly looks like you tried," Izzy said then, voice flat.

"Izzy," Ceriat chided. "This isn't fair."

Eleni's throat filled with grief. "You bitch. I didn't do that."

The viewscreen transformed somehow to a hijacked view of Gatewood, the glittering green jewel of Teegarden, but it looked as if a hive of drones had exploded across the screen amidst the shattered remnants of the *Jocasta*. As she watched, Shiva fighters screamed through the debris, followed swiftly by the white drones she'd seen on the warship. Linny must've gotten those airborne right after they'd left, and now they tore through the Shiva ships like tissue paper.

A rock lodged in her throat. "Turn it off," Eleni said, sickened by the sob in her voice.

A squadron of Shiva fighters split away from the warzone, and as she watched, beelined for a splash of silver in the middle of the forest coverage on Gatewood. Toward their eponymous colony.

"Izzy, that's enough," Ceriat said.

The fighters broke into the atmosphere, trailing flames, as they entered too quickly. Eleni's gut dropped. It was a suicide mission.

Izzy ignored Parker. "Maybe you didn't do this yourself, but the people you work for did—"

"Izzy, stop," Parker said, craning around and tapping at his panel. "She's had enough."

Several balls of flame disintegrated in atmosphere, but one kept going, dissolving with distance and lack of resolution...

"—and your brother orchestrated it—"

"Shut up," Eleni snarled as her vision blurred.

Just in time for a bright flash of flame to erupt in the center of their colony. It was no fusion bomb, but the smoke and flames were visible from space... how many people had just died? How many more to come?

Who were the twelve souls who'd just sacrificed themselves for Sariah's madness?

But Izzy wasn't done twisting the knife. "—so tell me again how much better you are than the man who spends every waking moment making amends for his past sins," Izzy finished in a rush, anger clear in her words. "How *dare* you."

"Izzy, stop!" Parker shouted as he tapped on the console in front of him. The display changed back to the void. "That's enough."

Izzy said something else, but it didn't matter. The synthetic words dissolved into the hum of the engines and the rush of life support.

The damage was done. Eleni stared at her hands, at the grease and filth smeared there. At the blood she couldn't see but knew was there. Hadn't she had gloves? Or was that just something she'd made up, too?

Izzy was right. This was her fault. But if the goddamned AI thought she'd drop into a quivering mess, she didn't know who the fuck she was talking to. Yes, this was her mess, but that meant she had to clean it up.

"Eleni?" Parker's voice was low, soothing. "You okay?"

"No," Eleni said. She was numb. "But it don't matter. Just fly."

Parker didn't say anything in response, just nodded before telling Izzy to speed up their arrival.

Soon, the engines roared, and pressure pushed into Eleni's chest, crushing away the sadness and angst. Under that pressure, it tempered into the resolve to do what needed to be done. By whatever means necessary.

The rest of the trip went by in silence.

Just like she deserved.

Chapter 44

IZZY

Izzy waited until the last moment to begin deceleration procedures and damn near killed her meatsacks on reentry.

Sure, Ceriat had questioned her decision to go in nose-first, but she'd thought it a bit of fleshy concern. After all, he wanted to get back on the surface as soon as possible, and if she slowed, there was a very real chance they'd be picked up on sensors. This way, they just appeared as yet another bit of debris raining from the sky.

And anyway, she'd run the math, and with the energy dispersal nose cone routed through the inertial dampeners, coupled with her rate of reentry, the *Sparrow*—which, with this recent jaunt in Teegarden, had started to feel more and more like a physical body—would survive just fine.

It'd only been when Ceriat started choking that she realized she'd forgotten to factor in the pressure differential that'd happen with the reduced efficiency of the dampeners, seeing as how she was using them to vent the excess heat from the nosecone.

Luckily for the meatsacks, they had a brilliant young lady at the helm. With a series of rapid "flapping" of the exterior wings, and the sacrifice of the landing gear—deployed into the wind—

she managed to drop their velocity enough to, well, *not* pulp them.

Did she get any credit for saving their lives? *Noooo...* all Ceriat and the Spacer wanted to talk about was how close they'd come to dying. The Spacer seemed convinced she'd done it on purpose.

"No," Izzy had said, and she'd meant it.

Ceriat had been in the cabin as well, after all. No one would hurt *her* meatsack while she lived.

No one.

Chapter 45
CERIAT

Ceriat tried to land the *Sparrow* near the ETL tower he'd originally come here to activate.

Without the landing gear, Ceriat found a long snowdrift to use as a pad and settled down onto it. He came in low to stay off any radar system that might be in place, then hovered over the packed, waterlogged snow, planning a graceful end to this hellish ride.

"Ceriat?" Izzy chimed in as they lowered to the ground.

Distracted and trying not to crush the belly of the ship without landing gear, he didn't respond. Instead, he stared at the half-burned-out camera view displayed before him. It should be staring straight down, but the fact he could see part of the starboard wing system told him it'd somehow gotten cock-eyed on the reentry.

Big surprise. All his awe at Izzy's piloting acumen from before had dissolved in the face of yet another near miss for her human passengers. Alone, she was a wizard behind the stick. With humans aboard... well, Ceriat just felt better being in control.

Still, something didn't feel right in the way *Sparrow* descended; both sluggish and touchy, it waved back and forth as he lowered the ship, sunset-fire-limned drifts scattering the longer he waited to touch down.

Izzy trilled. "Ceriat."

Behind him, Eleni let out a string of low curses.

"What, Izzy?"

"Perhaps I should land?"

Ceriat barked out a laugh. "No. You just nearly killed us."

"I did not."

"Fuck you, you sentient, fucking, twisted, prop-snorting..." Eleni devolved into further mutterings that, any other time, would leave Ceriat laughing.

But not now. His heart was already in his throat as the right side of his display went dark, only to be filled with a superimposed view of the *Sparrow's* structural layout. The entire starboard side flashed red, specifically around the connector joints.

Ceriat almost had a chance to ask Izzy to work around it. Almost.

Alarms flashed. Izzy's voice—so real just minutes earlier—screeched warnings without intonation. "Structural failure imminent! Structural—"

With a horrible tearing sound, the wing tore off, one landing jet still pulsing. The ship spun, taking Ceriat's stomach with it. The world twisted and flickered on the display, purple sky and barren ground swapping places. Working entirely on instinct, he slapped off the jets.

Upside down and flying east of the snowdrift, they hit the ground with a rush and a roar.

The *Sparrow* groaned once, then settled to the sound of the engines powering down and metal creaking. The display powered off then, leaving them in near darkness. Status lights shone like multi-colored stars before him, and as the blood rushed to his head, Ceriat let out a low sigh.

Eleni, however, did quite the opposite. A ragged roar filled the cabin. There was some semblance of verbiage in there, but if they were meant to be words, the meaning went right over Ceriat's addled mind.

Ceriat groaned. His head swam with blood. The straps of the harness dug into his shoulders. "You okay, Izzy? Eleni?"

Eleni's scream cut off and devolved into violent muttering. "Of course he checked on the fucking comp first..."

"Yes, Ceriat. Thank you for asking," Izzy said as Eleni's angry rant turned into violent muttering. "Opening blast doors, now."

The ship rocked to the side, and the *Sparrow* shifted as the doors opened, revealing that somehow, he'd still managed to get them into a different snowbank. A sliver of orange light came just up and to his left, above the edge of the ice blue bank that had already melted around them. Luckily, the cold beyond was held at bay by the polycarbonate canopy.

He disconnected his harness and rolled onto what had, until a minute ago, been the ceiling. Off to his left, Eleni sat, hanging sideways to him. She gripped her head with both hands and was in the process of shaking it back and forth as if she could change reality by sheer force of will.

"You okay?"

"Now you wanna know?" Eleni turned to him, nostrils flaring and brown eyes flashing. "Do I fucking look okay?"

Ceriat shrugged.

Eleni's eye twitched, but instead of responding, she just began disconnecting the harness holding her in place.

When she released, like him, Eleni scooted down toward the canopy, though she stayed as far away from him as she could. He didn't blame her. She'd made it very clear how she felt about him during the flight over, but none of the accusations were new. Most everything she'd said were just echoes of his own mind.

She was right to be angry, but they had a job to do.

"Pop the hatch," Ceriat told Izzy.

The canopy opened, shifting the *Sparrow* again. Frigid air swept in as it did and sent goosebumps cascading across his body, but it was far warmer than he'd expected. Ceriat sniffed. There was something wrong with the air, something familiar, but it could be from the crash, so he put it to the side.

Little snow backfilled the cockpit. The drift immediately around them had melted and solidified into a concave shell he had to hammer on to provide them an avenue to leave the ship.

Still, the chill dug in quickly, and by the time he pulled himself up and out of their icy tomb, Ceriat's teeth had already begun chattering. The short ridgeline off to the east writhed in crimson flame from the setting sun, though the valley where they'd landed was cast in purpling shadow. A glance to the west revealed towering storm clouds on the horizon, the first flickers of lightning just evident amongst the darkness. Luckily, they seemed to be carrying farther west and away from them, leaving the sky above mostly clear; a colorful tapestry streaked with flaming debris as it entered Shiva's atmosphere.

They'd been seconds away from joining those streaks. Just moments from...

Behind him, Eleni grunted her way out of the *Sparrow*. She hopped down the remains of the drift, sliding with surprising grace for a Spacer. Once at the bottom, she shaded her eyes and looked at him.

Or rather, it turned out, at the *Sparrow*.

"Ship's dead," she said with a shake of the head. "Be surprised if it lobs off again."

Ceriat turned to see what she meant. A stone fell in his gut. The *Sparrow* was a mess. Like he'd suspected, the starboard wing had been damaged before it tore off into the distance—a glance revealed a bit of spiraling smoke a hundred meters distant that marked its ultimate landing place. What he hadn't imagined was the entire right side of the ship was gone. The support struts that'd managed the flex and extension of the wing had ripped away, taking with it a good chunk of the outer hull. As he watched, something sparked, kicking off a trail of inky black smoke, quickly snatched by the frigid wind coming from the west.

<You okay, Izzy?> Ceriat thought as worry wriggled in his stomach.

A long moment passed before the words appeared in the top corner of his vision, but when they did, he let out a sigh of relief.

Just dandy, friend. Should've let me land.

Ceriat let out a low laugh that turned into a full body shiver. "Probably."

"The hell you laughing about, Parker?" Eleni snapped. "Get down and let's walk. Two kilometers is a long way in the cold and dark."

Go on, Izzy's words trailed across the top of his vision. *I'll keep in touch. The transmitter is still running, so even with planetside interference, two klicks is easy enough to maintain with my battery reserves.*

<Thanks, Izzy.>

Ceriat leaned over and gave the battle-scarred exterior of the *Sparrow* a tap. A dull echo rang through it. "Been great flying with you, ol' girl."

You mean the ship, not me, right?

<Of course.> Apparently, sentient AIs could get snippy about their age. Who knew?

Good, because I'm not dead. Now go get 'em, champ. And find me another ship. Preferably one with weapons, if you please.

<I'll see what I can do.>

Nice. That single word hung in his vision for a moment before fading away.

"Parker! We gotta go!"

Sighing, Ceriat straightened, then slid down the drift to join Eleni. He had to jog to catch up with her, but when he did, there was a spring in his step he hadn't felt since entering this system.

They could do this. He knew it.

"First," Ceriat started, rubbing his arms for warmth as a chill wind hit him full in the face, "we need to shut down the ETL tower, or this planet won't be habitable for years. Then we deal with Sariah."

"Sure, Vulture," Eleni said. Her voice rustled as she spoke, turning her usual timbre into more of a coarse grind.

Heat flooded up Ceriat's neck at that. She wanted to learn about his past? About being Vulture? Fine. Izzy had dressed her down, yes, but he hadn't had a chance to explain himself.

If this went sideways, it might be his last chance. For some reason that bothered him... and if he'd learned one thing from his time as Vulture, it was that you don't leave things like this unspoken, no matter how they turned out.

Still, it took a dozen meters of silence before he worked up the resolve to put it out there. "You asked me once what side I was on. You still want to know?"

Eleni snorted and turned away, lips pulling into a sneer. "Don't need to, 'cause I know. You're a monster." The words transformed into mist and swirled away, but they sounded like she was reading his sentencing papers.

"You're right."

After a moment of silence, Eleni turned to him, eyes narrowing like they did when she tried to read him, despite having lost her *manju*. "That's it? Finally gonna accept it?"

"Why argue with a fact?" Ceriat nearly made it through that sentence without his voice cracking.

Eleni barked out a harsh laugh. "I see what yer doing."

"And what's that?" he asked.

She pulled to a stop, then held up a hand in the rapidly approaching darkness, pinky finger extended upward. "Garnering sympathy by playing on my emotions," Eleni replied, face falling into a mask as emotionless as the titanium one she once wore.

"Eleni, I—"

"Establishing empathy and rapport with yer 'Mister Good Guy' routine." Up went the ring finger.

Ceriat pulled back, the anger that'd flushed through him a moment ago dissipating. "I'm not trying to trick you, Eleni."

"Say what I want to hear so I'm open to yer bullshit," Eleni said. Her jaw worked now, muscles in her cheeks bouncing as she ground her teeth. This time, her pointer finger went up, her middle held down by her thumb, bringing the count to three.

He knew she'd backed him into a corner, that he should just shut the fuck up and stop, but he couldn't. "I didn't lie to you. I tried to save everyone on this goddamned planet," Ceriat said, head shaking as a vice gripped his chest. His hip screamed at him to stretch, but he ignored the pain. She had to understand. He needed her to know. "I wanted to save *you*."

Eleni's fingers dropped into a closed fist. She stared hard at him, eyes flat and dead. "Personalize affectionate plea so I ignore the fact you murdered entire planets." Her middle finger extended from the fist, and she pushed it toward him just as the last flicker of sunset disappeared from her face, casting them both in darkness. "Go fuck yerself, Parker. After we shut that tower down, yer dead to me."

"Fine." The word slipped out on autopilot and wrapped in flame. He turned away so she couldn't see the hurt welling behind his eyes. "We'll shut this down, then I'm gone."

"Good."

"Good."

And with that, two enemies went to stop a monster.

Chapter 46

ELENI

The plan was simple.

Step one: get Parker into the tower so he could shut it down.

Step two: use that to lure Sariah back, hopefully alone.

Step three: end this.

The problem with simplicity always came down to the fact that it overlooked reality. When they'd come up with the plan on the way from the *Sparrow's* crash site—Parker continued to call it a landing site, which was clearly vac'd—Eleni had even started feeling pretty good about it. The plan, anyway. The fact that it relied on this murderer to work didn't sit well with her.

At least that was what she told herself. That stupid AI's words kept ringing in her ears, as if some creature that shouldn't even exist understood humanity or empathy. Vulture had murdered millions, and for what? For a Protectorate paycheck?

Despite both Izzy and Parker's idiotic assurances, Eleni and Parker weren't the same. The difference was, as soon as Eleni had realized she'd been lied to, she hadn't tucked tail and run off to Earth to hide behind anonymity.

No, she'd walk right up to the monster who'd betrayed her, confront her, and then, only then, would she take that next step.

That was what good people did: take care of their business without compromise, without giving up their ideals. She'd do this right, the way *he* should have, even if it ended with a bullet to the brain. At least she'd have tried. She wasn't a monster, no matter what that bitch AI said.

The majority of the terrain leading to the ETL tower Eleni hadn't known existed was thankfully even like most of Shiva, though much warmer than Arctic had been; her breath didn't freeze inside her nostrils here. Not immediately, anyway.

Everywhere she looked in the fading light, the tundra ran off straight and flat, with the sole exception being a modest hill in the direction they walked. It was the perfect place for a new settlement, especially with the snow drifting off the mountains in huge swells, though the constant vibration beneath her feet was concerning. For a moment, she stared at the beauty, but then the wind shifted, bringing with it the stink of rotten eggs and a harsher, acrid taste that burned her lungs. She turned back to the storm clouds, and as she stared into that dark smear on the horizon, a flash of lightning revealed the source of both the tempest and the smell: a sable spear jutting straight up into the center of it all, surrounded by a miasmic mist swirling ever upward into the sky.

"Shit," Parker muttered as the tower finally revealed itself.

Eleni came to a stop alongside him, a rock forming in her stomach as more lightning hammered into the tower. "That is... huge." Eleni pointed at the swirling mass around it. "The fuck is that?"

She'd expected to see something in line with the tower that had been in place near the settlement. Thirty or forty meters, maybe. This, though... she couldn't even fathom how tall it was, but now that she'd seen it in the strikes, it stood out as a darker splash against the deep gray clouds percolating around it. The tower pierced the sky, extending upward, disappearing into the rising storm.

"That mess is volcanic gas." Parker took off at a quicker pace, head shaking. "That only happens far along in the process."

"What?" Eleni jogged to catch up with him. "We can still vac this thing, yeah?"

"I don't know." Parker made a face and shrugged one shoulder. "Maybe not."

An ache sprang to life in her chest. "But it's only been maybe twelve hours," Eleni pleaded, as if by will alone she could change Parker's words. "It's not too late."

"I..." He trailed off, then shook his head. "We're going to try."

Eleni nodded and sped up, forcing a now-limping Parker to speed up to match her stride. "Goddamn right."

The smell was worse here, the sulfur stink harsh and bitter. It felt like a layer of oil coated her tongue. As the rumbling grew more intense, she couldn't pretend it came from some distant seismic event. No, they were walking straight toward it. On the plus side, it'd gotten warmer the closer they got, so they no longer had to worry about freezing to death on the walk.

"So what's the plan?" Parker asked as they approached a short hill that'd gradually risen as they made their way.

"Front door." Eleni clenched her hands into fists, then rubbed them together to bring more warmth into her fingers. "If we're star-touched, we'll walk right in."

Parker let out a low whistle. "That's a horrible fucking plan."

Eleni refused to take the bait. "Yeah? And what's yer great bit of brilliance?" She didn't wait for him to respond. "Oh, that's right, you ain't got one."

"I could have a plan."

"Oh, vac yerself." Eleni snorted, then raised her voice and pinched her nose to drive it hollow and harsh. "'Listen to me, I'm a strategic genius who got myself snatched by a bunch of Spacers.'" She let out a little laugh and sucked her teeth. "Please."

As they came over the rise that'd been blocking their view of the lower half of the tower, Parker grabbed her, hissing, and pulled her to the ground roughly. Stones dug into her knees and legs. Numb hands scraped across sharp rock, leaving tiny flecks of blood across them.

"What?" Eleni hissed, yanking her arm back, the mist of her breath spiraling around them.

Parker stared at her intently and nodded his head toward the tower.

Grimacing, Eleni took the hint and crawled up and over the rise, only to have the hope she'd carried from Gatewood slip away at the sight of the *Lucille* between them and the tower. The last three hundred meters of their trip, the space between the ship and their destination, was filled with at least fifteen settlers, all bearing plasma rifles.

Where the hell are those guns coming from? she wondered. As far as she knew, there'd been maybe twenty rifles in Arctic last week. In order for all these to be here, that meant the settlement was either unguarded now... or Sariah had another stockpile she hadn't told Eleni about. She shook her head. *Goddammit.*

From here, she couldn't make out most of the settlers-turned-guards, but she did see Jeret leaning against the *Lucille,* his towering, yet hunched form prominent. His back was to them, a mask pulled over his head, and a plasma rifle slung over one shoulder, unlike everyone else.

The rest of the guards wore helmets similar to her old *manju*. She knew they were enough to filter out any of the toxins currently leaking into the atmosphere.

She and Parker, however, had nothing.

"So much for the front door."

Eleni joined him as he pulled back down the hill a short way. She didn't appreciate his snark. "Then what's yer plan, genius?"

Parker rolled over and stared at the sky, head shaking back and forth. He let out a quiet cough, then wiped his nose with the back of his hand. It came away with a streak of blood. "We're gonna need those masks." Another low cough ended in a grunt and a glob of spit on the ground. He visibly deflated. "Or we're fucked."

He wasn't wrong, but the pure defeatism lit a fire in her belly. "You giving up?"

"I didn't say that—" Parker grimaced and shook his head before turning to her. "You know, I'm not always trying to shit on your parade."

"The fuck's that even mean?" Eleni asked, hackles rising despite herself. These Earthers and their antiquated language.

Parker closed his eyes, head still wobbling. "This. This is what I mean."

"Oh, so this is my fault?"

"What a fucking leap."

"So what're we gonna do, Vulture? Sit here and cry?"

Parker's eyes opened at that; his face stony as he addressed her. "Stop calling me that."

"What? Vulture?" Eleni asked, lip curling in disgust. "Don't like the reminder?"

"I..." Parker shut his mouth and ground his teeth visibly. "We need a plan."

"Like what? Not like we can go in, guns blazing," Eleni said, rolling her eyes. "We don't have any."

"I know," Parker admitted. He flipped over and pulled himself up the rise. Then, quietly: "We just need... where's the big guy?"

Eleni's heart jumped in her throat as she joined him at the ridge. Most all the guards still stood in the no-man's-land between the *Lucille* and the tower, but there was one notable absence.

"Where's Jeret?"

The familiar popping hiss of a powering up plasma rifle came from behind them.

Eleni swung around to find Jeret there, maskless, and a rifle pointed at her feet. The familiar blue glow of the prepped charge illuminated a face that somehow looked even older than it usually did. His typically bald head was now covered with stubble, the faded blue whorls almost blending into his pale skin. His eye sockets appeared deeper, too. Brown, tired eyes staring out at them from beneath the depths.

Parker held up his hands, but if he had any quips or impassioned speeches to make, he kept them to himself for once.

"Jeret, put the rifle down," Eleni said, following suit with the hand raising. She kept her voice low, hoping against hope she could figure out how to keep him from turning them in, or worse, shooting them dead then and there. "We're trying to help the settlement."

Jeret's eyes narrowed at that, but he didn't raise the rifle. "How?" Even his voice seemed tired and drained, his typically deep rumble now a strained thing. "She's won, Eleni. It's all over. Everyone's on their way to Gatewood now."

"No, it's not." Eleni climbed to her feet and approached him. She stopped when he pulled the rifle up toward her stomach. "Gatewood isn't ours to take. What she's doing here, it's wrong."

Jeret's lips fell into a flat smile. "Wrong?"

"She bombed Arctic," Parker chimed in, "sent your folks up there to die. Sent, uh," he stopped, then turned to Eleni, "what's her name?"

"Jen," Eleni replied, keeping her eyes on Jeret and his trigger finger, "and Victor," this time, a sob caught in her throat, but she swallowed it down angrily. "She sent my brother to die, to murder everyone on that ship, to drop that bomb on our own people."

"I know." Jeret's face twisted then, lips pursed. His finger came off the trigger; the barrel wavered in the air. "She told me."

That took the wind out of her. "What?"

Jeret blinked and tears fell down his cheeks. "She said if I didn't help, she'd tell everyone." His voice caught. "She'd tell *Henry*."

"But we already know," Eleni pleaded. "We already know about the plan."

Parker stood then, arms coming down to his sides. "That's not what he means," he said, voice low. "Is it?"

"No."

Eleni pulled back, eyes flicking between Jeret and Parker as they stared each other down, some unknown message passing between them. "What's going on?"

Jeret's jaw worked soundlessly for a moment, but then something changed in him. He stood straighter; chin raised. "I was a member of the Righteous," he said.

"The Righteous?" Parker hissed as if the word were poison. "The ones who bombed New Eden?"

Jeret turned to him and lowered his weapon. "Yes." The rifle powered down with a thrumming drag.

"Didn't expect that." Parker ran a hand through his thinning hair, head swiveling back and forth. "Fuck."

"That can't be right," Eleni whispered. The strength went out of her legs, and she slid to the ground as her mind warred with itself amidst a tickling burn inching its way down her throat.

Jeret. Good, kind Jeret... was a terrorist? She turned to Parker and saw the rage in the quiver of his jaw, the sadness in the squint of his eyes.

What did she look like? Confused? Wounded? Who knew?

It felt like Jeret had pulled the trigger and sent a ball of plasma into her gut, leaving only a gaping, empty hole where the things she knew were real sat. She needed oxygen to breathe. Water was wet, regardless of gravity. And Jeret was a good man.

"The entire reason I joined the Protectorate was because of you." Parker's voice came out as a whisper, but it may as well have been a shout based on how Jeret reacted. "I became the Vulture because of *you*." His voice cracked at the last word, face twisting. "I..."

Jeret sucked in a shuddering breath, shoulders somehow slumping even more and dragging his towering frame into itself. "I know," he rumbled, the words barely audible above the raucousness of the tower beyond. "I ruined a lot of lives that day." Tears wore worried paths down his stern face.

"You. Fuck." Parker stepped forward, brows knit, any sorrow or compassion she'd seen there in a moment ago gone.

Then, surprising even her, Eleni was there, a hand against his chest.

The three of them froze at the action, all eyes on her hand. Her heart was in her throat, though from disgust or anger, she couldn't tell.

She snatched it back and wiped her palm off on the seat of her pants. "Stop."

"Are you fucking kidding me? He murdered millions." Parker spat, throwing an outstretched finger at Jeret. "And you're going to protect him? You won't even use my fucking *name*, but you'll just bow and scrape to this asshole?"

Pressure sprang to life in Eleni's stomach like a cancer. He was right. Jeret had confirmed it. Despite her being a child when the Righteous had bombed New Eden, she'd heard the stories her entire life of the dirty bomb that took out the eponymic capital and the countless deaths in its wake.

Everything inside her screamed to join Parker in his rage, to beat Jeret to death for his actions—and for his *continued* actions under Sariah. The Righteous and the Vulture? She couldn't even wrap her mind around the deaths caused by these two men, but in that moment, one thing was certain.

Despite everything, despite her disgust, the words tumbled out... "We need him."

Parker's mouth opened as if he was about to speak, but it snapped shut with a clack of teeth. Instead, he just shook his head and turned away, hands on the back of his head and chest out. For a moment, she thought he'd scream—but he didn't, thankfully. If it wasn't for the roar of the ETL tower, they'd have been captured already. A scream would definitely carry.

Jeret stepped up next to her and held out a hand to her. "Thank you—"

Heat rose up her neck at the audacity. "Stuff if, Jeret," she said without looking at him. "Yer no better an' him."

Out of the corner of her eye, she caught the stricken look on his face as he pulled his hand back. *Good.*

"But ya got a chance to make it up."

"I doubt it, child." Jeret let out a low rumble of a laugh. "But how?"

Eleni's stomach twisted at the words, but she turned to him and said them anyway. "Ima need your mask."

Chapter 47
CERIAT

I should kill him right here. It'd be easy. He deserves it.

The thought slipped unbidden into Ceriat's mind as the three of them came over the rise, him pushed ahead by a rifle barrel, and Jeret and Eleni cheerfully prancing their way into the clearing ahead. After all, he'd already broken his promise to Gerry. Why not add another body to the list?

But, goddammit, he didn't do it.

The air grew thicker here, breath coming in harsher, acrid gasps. His eyes ached from a coating of grit. Wind whipped past his face, dragging dust and dirt into the air, where it shivered alongside the roar of the tower in the spotlights of the freighter. No snow dotted the space between him and the ETL tower now. It had all melted as the tower began its process of driving into the planet's core.

His vision swam as gases and heat flitted from around the base of the structure. The gases visibly writhed upward, joining the storm clouds above. As he watched, the freighter rocked under a particularly heavy gust, struts creaking angrily as it eased to the side and back. Pools of light shook violently. The dozen soldiers patrolling turned to watch it, the set of their shoulders clearly indicating their discomfort.

None of this was right. While ETL towers could potentially do this, it was reserved for only the deadest of rocky worlds, the ones where the only option for potential habitation was to reignite the planet's core. Ceriat had never seen it done on a garden world before, certainly not one with humans already settled.

Still, the fire burning in his chest at Jeret's revelation and Eleni's seeming acceptance of it with nary a flick of an eyebrow kept him from caring.

The Righteous. Those bastards had murdered millions over the years, destroyed colonies and scientific outposts. Their actions had destabilized the entire Outer Rim for the past decade, leading to rampant murder, radicalization, anarchy...

Each word fed the fire; each memory of the reports he'd read while in the Protectorate fanned those flames.

Biosphere ruptured, 260 dead, 7 children.

ETL installation canceled. Silver Linings Corporation contracted to put down insurrection on Caern station, 713 fatalities, 6,245 injuries.

New Eden...

Ceriat ground his teeth and tried to smother the bonfire in his gut. New Eden had been all the justification he'd needed to murder the people of Shaal-Tu. He'd chomped at the bit once the rumor mill had seemingly confirmed the presence of the Righteous on planet, just like every target before that.

Shaal-Tu hadn't been the first time, but it had been the last.

How could he keep fighting for a government that'd approved of the things he'd done? Especially when it was clear they'd been the ones to stoke the flame of his anger, to keep him killing with the slightest suggestion of the Righteous being near a planet.

How many people had he killed to avenge his three dead family members? One million? Two? Three? He didn't even know, but they mattered. All of them.

Still, while his logical mind could make these connections, the part of him the Protectorate had taken advantage of all those years ago refused to be consoled. Jeret *was* the Righteous to him now. He had to die.

If he does, then so do I. Ceriat let out a humorless chuckle that quickly broke into a coughing fit tinged with copper and iron. At least he was working on half of that equation.

"E'ryone good?" Eleni whispered, voice obfuscated by the mask she now wore.

According to her, this one lacked a thousand features her *manju* had had, but once she'd put it on, there'd been a visible change in her. Instead of the slight slump of the shoulders he'd grown used to, Eleni stood taller, shoulders back, chin up with the mask on. With that helmet, she seemed to lose all sense of uncertainty, leaving only a driven, forceful machine in her place.

With that certainty had finally come a workable, if horribly derivative, plan. It relied on Eleni and Jeret's acting ability. Unfortunately, Jeret hadn't absorbed any of the confidence that now washed off Eleni's shoulders in waves.

The sun had finally set, dropping the area into inky darkness penetrated only by the floodlights from the freighter. The wind whipped into a deafening roar as they approached, filling the air with powdered grit that trailed cyclones across the open area and muddied the light. Beyond, out of range of the lights, the ETL tower stood in darkness, its outer shell rotating down, down, down into Shiva. Each rotation sent a shudder through the ground, followed by cracking and hissing as even more gas escaped below.

How the hell were they going to get inside? Ceriat had no idea. With the exterior turning like that, it must be blocking the entrance. Had to be. But Ceriat didn't know for sure, as he'd never been present during one of these drilling stages. ETL procedure always had him back in orbit before anything even remotely resembling this began.

There must be a way in, he told himself as they started the shallow descent down the hill that'd blocked their view. Wet stones skittered beneath his feet. Jeret had confirmed that Sariah

and some asshole named Gareth were holed up inside. They
wouldn't do that if they couldn't get out, which meant the trick-
iest part was yet to come.

God, I hate this plan.

"Ay!" Eleni shouted as they approached, one arm waving in
the air, the first flickers of light from the freighter catching fluo-
rescent strips in her jacket he hadn't noticed before. "Caught a
straggler!"

Behind him, Jeret let out a dry, raspy cough. The very sound
of it sent a tickle into his own lungs. They needed to get out of
this air quickly. Well, Jeret could go fuck himself, but Ceriat had
to get inside either the tower or the ship, sooner rather than later.

The guards were clearly not professionals, despite their
appearance. Several of them turned and waved at them as if they'd
been expected. Only one turned with any semblance of wariness.
Unlike the rest, he didn't wear a helmet, just a simple oxygen mask
and a pair of protective goggles beneath a shock of gray hair. He
pulled up his rifle and called to two others, who joined him as
they approached.

Eleni cleared her throat robotically. "Keep yer heads, boys."

"Easy for you to say," Ceriat muttered.

Together, the three of them stepped into a puddle of light a
spare two or three meters from the freighter. That big, gray beast
sent a shiver down his spine. Last time he'd been aboard, they'd
locked him in a closet and forgotten about him.

What would happen if this plan went to shit?

Oooooo, Izzy's letters spread across the top of his vision as he
took in the massive hunk of metal. *That could be fun.*

<It's a flying coffin.>

For you maybe.

"That's Gareth," Jeret whispered behind Ceriat just as Izzy's
words faded away, "director of the Milit—" He cut off, breaking
into another hacking fit.

He didn't get a chance to finish.

"Where's your mask, Jeret?" Gareth called as he approached.

Gareth gestured to the two guards he'd brought with him, a tall spacer covered head-to-toe in protective gear that made identification impossible, and a shorter planet-born who held his plasma rifle like it was made of fire ants. Those two flanked Ceriat, Eleni, and Jeret, though they clearly didn't intend to do much. Their fingers were wrapped tight around their rifles' grips.

"Hey, boss," Jeret said, wiping the back of his hand. "Stumbled across a familiar face trying to bring in a prisoner."

This is a stupid idea. Didn't work on the Jocasta, *won't work here*. Still, it was the plan they had. Like he'd said at the time, derivative and stupid, but all of this was stupid, so...

Gareth grimaced at that, his transparent mask clearly showcasing the sneer. He turned to Eleni. "Who's this?"

Eleni reached up and disconnected her helmet, then grinned. "Keeping things tight, I see."

The shock on Gareth's face would've been satisfying if he hadn't immediately reached for the pistol at his belt despite the plasma rifle attached to his back. He froze, hand on the grip, eyes flicking between the three of them before landing on Ceriat's.

Disbelief transformed into confusion, then suspicion with such quickness, Ceriat wondered if he'd even seen the first two emotions.

"What are you doing here, Eleni?" Gareth's brows knitted together with the words. His hand didn't move from the pistol.

Eleni remained stoic as she replaced the helmet. "Nice to see you, too."

"You shouldn't be here," Gareth said, taking them all in. Then his eyes fell on Ceriat. "Especially you."

Jeret cleared his throat, and all eyes went to him. "Found them at a crashed shuttle, with the director leading the prisoner," he said, just like they'd practiced. None of the hesitancy he'd shown in their quick rehearsals came through at all. "Figured we'd want her back, and him in a cell."

Shit, we might get away with this yet.

Gareth narrowed his dark eyes but didn't reply right away. Ceriat felt his hope leaking away the longer it went on.

Just as Ceriat was sure Gareth would pull the old revolver and finish the three of them then and there, his eyes broke from them, brow furrowing as if listening to something.

Then he took his hand off the gun. "The governor wants to see you," Gareth said with acid in his tone as he nodded at Eleni. He turned to Jeret. "Put him in the *Lucille*, and get another helmet or mask." Then, as he turned away, he muttered, "God knows, I hate the damned things."

My turn.

"Don't do that," Ceriat said, lunging forward. "I have information, I can help—"

Jeret's surprisingly strong grip grabbed his shoulders just as the backhand landed.

Stars scattered across his vision, a stifling numbness throttling through his head and shoulders all at once. A moment later, his eyes focused to find Jeret dragging him along toward the entry, which hissed open, followed by an extended ramp.

Ceriat shook his head as the pain finally arrived in the left side of his head, where he'd been struck. Bastard had hit him in the side without the plate. *Figures.* Still, he got his feet under him enough that Jeret didn't have to carry him bodily onto the ship.

"Nice acting," Jeret whispered as their steps clanged up into the gaping maw of the freighter. "I'm impressed."

Ceriat grimaced, still dazed from the impact. "Community theater."

"Really?"

Really? Izzy replied as well.

Ceriat rolled his eyes as the welcome scent of oil, steel, and conditioned air swept over him. The ramp pulled up behind them, the door shutting with a *thud* as the lights flicked on to illuminate a familiar, gray hallway. To the right sat a weapons cabinet, the barrel of a plasma rifle visible behind the unlocked case. That was new.

A shiver ran through him. Second hallway on the left, then the first doorway on the right, and he'd be back in that sealed room. In the air-tight tomb.

"No, not really," Ceriat said, giving his head another shake, timidly touching the goose egg growing on his skull, and trying not to think about the cell. "Now get me to the bridge. We might not have much time to get this done."

"Understood," Jeret said, then took off at a quick walk. "It's right down here."

Ceriat followed, smiling despite the pain. *<Ready for an upgrade?>*

Oh, definitely, Izzy replied. *Let's do this thing!*

Chapter 48
ELENI

It took everything Eleni had not to hyperventilate. The helmet helped. It brought a sense of comfort and reliance she'd missed, but something was wrong, and it wasn't just the difference in brands and functionality. Yes, there was the reassurance of anonymity, but it didn't carry the same solace as it had a few days ago. Now, instead of feeling like she was her true self behind this mask, it felt as if she was a liar. A pretender. That didn't sit well with the perpetual stone in her gut.

Still, as she'd hammered into Jeret just minutes earlier, without the act, this entire thing would fall apart. With them split up the way she'd hoped, the chances of success had increased, but one wrong move—one wrong *word*—would see them all murdered and left behind.

Then again, as Gareth walked directly toward the towering monster drilling into the bedrock of the planet like the finger of a void-filled god, Eleni wondered if she hadn't overestimated Sariah's fondness for her. From a distance, it had been intimidating, but now, in the inky black of a stormy night filled with arcing flashes of lightning, the boom of thunder nearby, and the constant grinding screech of the drill, everything was more intense.

Eleni craned back to get a good look at the tower. It stretched beyond the clouds now, though how far, she couldn't make out. Only the faintest impression of light-sucking blackness against the slightly brighter clouds told her it extended far, far above.

As she watched, the tower shuddered, slowed, then jumped, followed by the howl of rushing wind. Hot air swept over her, causing perspiration to spring up across her body. Despite the filtration system in the helmet, the stink of sulfur and a harsher, acrid undertone made it to her. It dried out her throat, forcing her to cough it up. Ahead of her, the rocky ground had splintered. Spiderwebbed cracks spread away from the base of the tower, branching outward toward her as black, bony fingers. Gusts of warmth erupted from them as they approached.

It wasn't reassuring.

"How we gonna get in?" Eleni asked, worry threatening to force her into a mistake as they approached a meter-wide trench surrounding the tower itself.

All she could think was that this would be a great place to dump a body. She gripped the bag she'd held onto since the *Jocasta* and wondered if the cube inside would make a solid club in a pinch.

Gareth ignored her. Instead, he put a hand on the right side of his head, then muttered something Eleni couldn't hear. A moment later, the rotating surface ahead of them changed. One second, it was a black, impenetrable wall; the next, a doorway carved itself out of the space.

Eleni froze. "The hell?"

The carved portal raised, sending a long spear of brilliant, blinding light out toward them. The helmet accounted for the extra light by dropping the darkness around it into such an inky midnight that Eleni was immediately reminded of the void of space. With the reduced contrast, she noticed the edge of the doorway seemed to shift and twist like a vid of waves lapping at a rocky shore.

Nanobots, Eleni realized. The entire exterior was constructed of the tiny machines. The self-propagation level required for such a thing... she couldn't even begin to imagine how this technology existed, let alone how it worked. Back on the *Jocasta*, she'd been amazed at the med cube, but this? This was something else entirely.

Gareth motioned her forward. She noticed his right hand rested on that old gun of his rather than the plasma rifle over his shoulder. Why he and Sariah liked those old weapons, she couldn't understand.

"Governor's waiting for you." Gareth's voice was just audible over the surrounding roar.

Eleni took a deep breath and nodded before approaching. Gareth followed close behind as she reached the edge of the pit between terra firma and the surprisingly mundane interior of the tower beyond. With a cautious lean, she looked into the gap.

Darkness greeted her, though as her eyes adjusted and the helmet changed its settings, she thought she could just make out a flicker of red...

"Hurry up," Gareth snapped, giving her shoulder a push.

Eleni pulled away and glared at him. "Don't fucking touch me."

"Then move," Gareth replied, a small smile pulling at his lips, "or I'll touch you again."

With that, Eleni jumped the gap between... and landed on a still, nearly silent platform. Behind her, Gareth's booted feet clacked on the tiled floor, just before a swishing sound sent them into silence. True silence. It was like she'd stepped into a bubble. No vibrations through her feet. No roaring of the drill. No stink of methane and sulfur.

Just... a sitting room in an office building. The ceiling illuminated everything with a flat white light, not that there was much here beyond an uncomfortable warmth and this couch. The walls of the cylindrical room carried that brushed steel look she recognized from the scraps of the other tower. The floor was made of hexagonal tiles that spread from a central, white tile with a stylized tree centered on it, the roots making their way up the edge to connect with what she assumed were supposed to be leaves.

It didn't look like any tree she'd ever seen before, that was for sure. Then again, the biggest one she'd seen before today had been on Erias and had stood a little over ten feet tall, with scraggly branches and yellow leaves. Maybe it was modeled after the monsters on Gatewood?

"Ugh," Gareth groaned as he pulled off his mask and goggles. He scratched at his recently shaved face, a grimace pulling at his lips. "My skin hates this shit."

"How is this possible?" Eleni wondered aloud at the stillness, turning slowly. "It's like we're on another world."

Gareth shrugged and set his mask and goggles down on a side table next to a svelte, gray lounging chair. "Maybe we are? Who cares?" With that he gestured toward the far wall. "After you. Governor awaits."

Eleni shook it off and made her way to where the elevator had been in the other tower, though if this was it, she couldn't tell. There wasn't even a line on the wall.

"Do I—?" Eleni flinched as a slice appeared from the ceiling to the floor, as if someone had taken a silver marker and drawn it down the wall. The line continued until two rectangles were high-lighted, then they slid away from each other, revealing a barren silver box. "This is... a lot."

"Yeah," Gareth agreed as he brushed past her to enter the elevator. "Tech is getting crazy." When she didn't join him right away, his hand went back to the hilt of his weapon. "Get in."

Eleni grimaced at the movement, but hefted her bag and joined him anyway. A moment later, the elevator rose. However, the only indication anything had happened came in the form of her stomach dropping into her feet for a moment.

Easier than climbing, she thought with a wry grin.

Yet, instead of stopping on the third floor, where the control room had been in the other tower, the lift kept on far beyond what she'd expected. How high they went, she had no idea, though. It wasn't like there were any level indicators. After an exceptionally long minute, the elevator slowed and stopped.

The doors opened, and Eleni sucked in a breath as lightning arced across her vision, washing out the warm light of the lift. Chill air swept across her skin alongside the crisp stink of ozone.

They stood at the top of the tower. Outside the elevator, the storm raged, clouds swirling and swimming around a flat, octagonal platform. The floor no longer held the same tile appearance as the levels below. Instead, it seemed made of craggy rock—an altar, almost, to some ancient Earth god. Still, while the wind roared, only the lightest of breezes cascaded at her. As she watched, another spear of lightning flashed with a muted rumble, but instead of striking the top of the tower, it lit up a transparent protective dome of some sort. The electricity rattled across it, slithering along the shell until it hit the tower proper and disappeared, absorbed into the structure.

Was that how the towers powered themselves? Or was it something special for this one?

Eleni had no idea, but then again, that wasn't why she was here.

No, the reason Eleni had come back to Shiva sat in the midst of all this chaos beneath a single steady light. There, seated in a remarkably fluffy easy chair beneath a shepherd's hook of a lamp, sat Sariah, legs crossed, head leaned into the pillowtop of the chair. The light breeze that made it through the dome tickled her gray-streaked bangs and ruffled the typically stiff collar of her jacket. Despite all this, the thing that made heat rise in Eleni's cheeks was the smile.

Sariah, murderer of her people, a liar and a thief, *smiled* in the wake of Shiva's destruction.

As Eleni's gaze drew to her, Sariah let out a low breath, stood up, then turned those golden eyes on her erstwhile director.

"Welcome to the future, Eleni," Sariah said, throwing her arms wide and spinning, a low laugh slipping free from her lips.

"It's all up from here." When Eleni didn't respond, Sariah beckoned to her. "Come, come. It's incredible out here."

Eleni frowned, but stepped out onto the roof. Gareth joined her, though he remained at the lift doors while Eleni made her way farther out into this otherworldly tableau. She did risk a glance backward to see the elevator stuck out from the top of the structure, a cube of silvery metal that stood in stark contrast to the primordial scene before her.

"Don't be shy, Eleni," Sariah teased her, an unfamiliar grin on her unpainted lips. "You only get a chance to see a world destroyed once."

It felt like a bucket of ice water had been splashed over her at that.

Sariah noticed. Grinning, she approached. "Come now, this was never going to be home."

As she came closer, that feeling of wrongness from earlier became overwhelming. Sariah didn't just walk; she sauntered like a model on a catwalk, arms swinging with a freedom Eleni had never seen in the woman. Her eyes, still that same artificial gold, held pupils the size of moons. But the smile—that flat-lipped smile—pulled up at one side was the worst part of it all.

"Then what's this?" Eleni asked, careful to control her voice. Even with the helmet modulator, she knew Sariah would pick up on any hesitation in her voice. She'd always been able to. "Why'd we drop here first?"

Sariah's smile turned arced upside down in an exaggerated frown. She even stuck out her lower lip, the bitch. "Oh, Eleni. This is why I didn't bring you into the planning talks." Sariah closed the distance in six quick steps, bringing with her a wave of body odor and the sharp stink of burnt electronics. "Just a little," Sariah tapped Eleni's forehead once, causing her to flinch backward, "too slow."

Instead of the rage she expected—wanted—to feel, the words came as a kick to the gut. This woman had mentored her, brought her into the inner circle of the colony, and now she said this?

She had no words for the ache in her chest, the weakness in her knees. "I thought..."

Sariah *tsk*ed at her. "And that's your problem," the governor snipped, turning her back on Eleni. "Thinking."

For a moment, the plan disappeared. Ceriat and Jeret, down God knew how far below her, dissolved into shadow. There was just that old urge to make this woman proud, to find the praise that'd once lifted her up.

"Then explain it to me," Eleni said, following after her old mentor. Behind her, Gareth scoffed, but she ignored it. "Help me understand."

Sariah turned back to her, one gold eye glittering in a flash of lightning. "You really want to be a part of this—a part of us —still?"

"With every part of my being," Eleni pleaded, and in the moment, she meant it down to her soul.

"Okay," Sariah murmured, rubbing her chin as she faced Eleni, "but first a little test."

"Test?"

"Bring the terrorist," Sariah said to Gareth, who saluted with a fist over his chest, then disappeared back down the lift.

Eleni's mind spun. Sariah knew Ceriat wasn't a terrorist, not if she was the one who'd dropped the bomb. So, what kind of test would this be?

As the truth of it settled on her shoulders, Sariah cocked her head, that disturbing smile returning. "You see it now, don't you?"

"Don't do this," Eleni whispered. The ache from Sariah's words melded into something else; a deep, cancerous sorrow that worked its way through her chest, her shoulders. Her heart. "Please."

Sariah *tsk*ed again, then put a finger to her lips. "Shh."

"But—"

Sariah's smile disappeared as she pulled out the small knife she carried with her everywhere and dug at her fingernails. A flash of lightning beyond the protective barrier set the copper to glowing. "Shush. We'll see the truth soon."

It was the longest five minutes of her life. But when the elevator swished open, and Ceriat came tumbling out onto the rough ground, hands bound and eye swollen and bleeding, she almost cracked.

"What the fuck?" Ceriat cried as he took in Sariah and Eleni, then the dome and lightning. "What've you done?"

Sariah smiled at him, then her eyes flicked to Gareth. "Give her your gun." She nodded in Eleni's direction.

"What? No," Eleni said, drawing away as Gareth frowned and pulled the revolver from his holster. "What is this?"

"What's going on, Eleni?" Ceriat pleaded, fear writ large on his face as he scrambled away from Gareth.

Gareth popped out some cylindrical object in the center of the weapon, spun it, and then turned it over to her, black grip out toward her. "Just like a plasma rifle. Squeeze the trigger."

"No."

Behind her, Sariah's footfalls drew close. The *tick-tick-tick* of her knife on fingernails came through clear as day. "Shoot your friend in the head," Sariah whispered. Eleni flinched as something narrow ran its way up her spine. "Show me you're the woman I know you are."

"Don't do this," Ceriat pleaded, eyes hopping around the top of the tower, desperate, like a caged animal. "You're better than this." He hammered his chest with his bound fists as tears leaked down his face. "Than *me*."

Gareth offered the revolver again, irritation ticking at the wrinkles on his forehead.

"Shoot him," Sariah said, close enough her breath tickled the short hairs on the back of her neck, "and I'll tell you everything."

Everything. Eleni held out a shaking hand and took the weapon. It was heavier than it looked, with a weight in the grip she hadn't expected. It felt foreign, wrong. A projectile weapon. Maybe she could turn it on Gareth, give Ceriat a chance to overpower him? Maybe if she spun quickly enough, the blade dancing on her shoulder wouldn't land.

But it would all end the same way, wouldn't it? And nothing would change. Ceriat hadn't known how to set the tower in motion like this, let alone stop it. What were the chances they'd figure it out before the planet cracked, like Ceriat thought would happen?

Sariah knew how to turn it off. Eleni was sure of it. They needed her alive. If she didn't do this, then they—she—couldn't stop this.

The governor would just slit her throat and have Gareth finish off Ceriat. And as Ceriat leaned back on his haunches, shoulders slumping, she saw the realization dawn on his face as well.

She stepped forward, the revolver heavy as she brought it up and pointed it at his skull. Vision blurred. A rock formed in her throat, nearly blocking the words that came next. "I'm sorry."

Tears had worked worried lines down his face, but if any more were to come, he didn't show it. "Guess we're not that different after all."

Eleni squeezed the cold steel trigger. Lightning flashed behind Ceriat. The crack of the shot disappeared behind the roar of thunder. When she opened her eyes, Ceriat lay sprawled out on the ground, the force of the bullet having spun him around, a pool of blood spreading around the pale skin of his face.

Ceriat Parker, the Vulture, was dead.

Gareth stepped up and pulled the revolver from her hands, a strange look on his face. Was that... admiration?

What had she done?

"Fantastic!" Sariah shouted, clapping her hands on Eleni's numb shoulders. "Now get rid of this mess and come on back." Then she gestured to Gareth. "Let's make this a party, Gar. Go get more stuff."

"Yes, sir," Gareth said, grimacing. He risked one more glance between Ceriat's motionless body and Eleni. "Really didn't think you had it in you." Then he entered the elevator.

"Can you send Jeret up to clean this up?" Eleni managed before the doors shut.

"Sure, killer." Gareth shrugged, then disappeared behind closed doors.

Having returned to her chair, Sariah gave Eleni a soft look. "Go ahead and say goodbye if you want. I know you two were thick as thieves."

"Not really," Eleni muttered in response, numb.

Still, Sariah gave her those spare moments to steady herself before Jeret stepped out of the elevator wearing a new filtration helmet. With one slow movement, he pulled it free to dangle from one hand. The same shock and awe she must've had on her own face when she'd first stepped out here reflected back on his worried old visage. Then he saw the body, and it all disappeared as his gaze, stricken, landed on Eleni. He didn't need to speak. She could read the accusation in his eyes.

What did you do?

"Get it out of here." Eleni jutted her jaw at Ceriat's body, sucking all emotion from her voice despite the blurred vision behind the helmet. She took the bag off her shoulder and tossed it across the rough surface to Jeret. It didn't open, thankfully. "And take that. *I* don't need it anymore."

If Jeret picked up on the intonation, he didn't show it. Instead, he just shook his head ever-so-slightly, put the helmet back on, then hooked the bag over his shoulder before dragging Ceriat's body to the elevator, leaving a long trail of crimson on the dark stone.

As the doors shut, she couldn't shake Ceriat's dead, staring eyes. Then he was gone.

"Now," Sariah said, spinning the chair, that smile pulling at the edge of her lips. "Why don't we start at the beginning?"

Eleni swallowed the revulsion in her throat, pitched her voice appropriately, and put on another mask. "Let's."

Chapter 49

IZZY

Izzy settled into the circuits of the *Lucille* like an overstuffed couch. She still remained connected to the *Sparrow's* systems, but for the most part, the migration was complete.

And there was so much room for activities!

The memory banks alone were nearly limitless in their capacity, the processing modules several generations newer than her old digs. It felt like she'd stepped out of the Stone Age and into the modern era for the first time in her life.

Now to test out these engines...

With a gentle touch, Izzy stretched her influence into the more mechanical aspects of the ship. Like the *Sparrow*, this ship had planet-side flight options—flaps, jets, etcetera—and an onboard FTL system. With a little probe, she flicked on the sensor and pinged the nearest FTL buoy. Silence.

Damn. Regardless, the upgrade would've made her smile if she had lips. As it was, the plan required her to get this thing airborne.

With a quick initiation sequence, the engines thrummed to life... but something was wrong. A quick diagnostic showed her the engines were up and running, their altitude should be rising. However, the *Sparrow's* long-range sensors didn't detect a ship.

Did it have a stealth mode? A quick scan revealed nothing.

Ceriat, there's something wrong, Izzy sent and waited.

And waited.

Then the *Sparrow's* uplink cut off, and one by one, her access to systems disappeared. It began with the engines, then rapidly rolled from there. Life support, flaps, doors... each one disappeared from her list quicker than she could try to fight for it. Processors disappeared. RAM dissolved away, each lost petabyte slowing her thoughts and leaving her only with rising panic.

What was happening?

As the interior cameras disconnected, she was cast into cold, sterile darkness.

Words ran across infinity. *Rogue AI locked down.*

A honey pot. She'd walked right into it, stuck her hand into the deepest recesses of the *Lucille*, only to be locked down and crippled. Had she even accessed the real system? She had to have...

A single, fervent hope took root in her fading consciousness and, as the darkness muddled her mind and shut her down, Izzy retreated into the one place she could think of.

Then, settled into that corner... Izzy powered down and hoped it was enough.

Chapter 50
JERET

S omething was wrong, and it wasn't the unending pain of gravity on Jeret's joints.

He stared at the body, visible and glowing a dull red through the infrared lenses in his helmet. A sharp gust of wind lashed his arms and back with dirt and debris, the bellowing monster behind him feeding those gales by the minute. A warning light flashed on the HUD of the helmet display just as the stink of rotten eggs and burning air increased inside his helmet. The filter was failing. Just another tool wearing out early. Like him.

What would he tell Henry when they met on Gatewood? How could he explain this to the man he loved?

Hi love, I just helped destroy a planet and dragged a dead body into the tundra. What's for dinner?

Henry was a good man, better than Jeret deserved, and he thanked God every day for the blessing. For the chance to experience the love Jesus preached, to help bring that compassion to his fellow settlers. So, how in God's dark galaxy had he ended up here, staring at a corpse and willing it back to life?

He watched the still-glowing body as the wind whipped. Parker's core temperature still hadn't dropped. That was to be expected, though, wasn't it? Didn't it take hours for a corpse to cool? He couldn't remember. It'd been so long since he'd last had to think about macabre stuff like this. And now he had to? His soul hurt.

The radio crackled in his ear. *"Jeret, copy?"* It was Eustace, one of Gareth's boys.

Jeret didn't know him well, but there was a haunted look in the man's eyes he found very familiar.

"This is Jeret," he replied, voice rough, his throat and sinuses still inflamed from his time without filtration, "over."

"Come back to the tower; Director Brightman needs you here."

Jeret bit off a snippy comeback. *Gareth doesn't need anything.*

And he froze as Eleni's words came back to him then... *Take that. I don't need it anymore.*

Heart pounding, he activated the small spotlight on the helmet, yanked the bag off his shoulder, and unzipped it. Sitting inside was a pure white cube of some sort. Jeret pulled it out and held it up so it caught the light. He had no clue what it was. It appeared perfectly shaped, and was smooth through his gloves, but nothing happened when he touched it. What was it?

"Jeret?"

He ignored the call. Frowning, he yanked off one of his gloves and dropped it to the ground. With one trembling finger, he touched the exterior of the cube... and still nothing happened.

Hope fled from him then, but to be sure, he took off his other glove and gripped the cube in both hands. Again, nothing.

It was just garbage, and he was a stupid man looking for meaning in words where there was none. The ache that'd been with him since the bomb had gone off in New Eden came back. His shoulders slumped with the weight of it.

"I'm sorry. For everything," Jeret whispered as he knelt next to Ceriat's body. "New Eden. I thought—" He choked up, then cleared his throat. "It doesn't matter what I thought. I was wrong. So wrong. I'm sorry for ruining your life." With as much reverence as he could, he set the cube atop Ceriat's chest. "I don't know your religious beliefs, but it's not right to just dump..."

Jeret cleared his throat again and sucked in a breath. "Our Father in heaven, hallowed be your name..."

By the time Jeret finished the Lord's Prayer over Ceriat's corpse, the radio calls had grown worried, and the first hint of a spotlight appeared on the crest of the hill to his right. With a shuddering sigh, he slipped his gloves back on and got to his feet, joints screaming in protest.

"This is Jeret," he said, activating the radio. "I'm on my way back. Over."

"Jesus, man, don't go silent like that. This place is dangerous now, and our transport is coming in. Over."

Jeret stared at the body for a long moment before replying. "Yeah, it is. Coming back. Over."

Above him, floodlights flashed across the terrain as a smaller ship swept in. It was his ride off the planet. To Henry on Gatewood.

What was he going to tell him? *God give me strength.* Not that he deserved it. Even now, after all the amends he'd made, the progress of the last twenty years, Jeret was still that scared man afraid to go against his superiors.

God certainly didn't owe him anything, clearly, and as always, his prayers remained unanswered. With that, Jeret turned his back on the corpse and made his way toward the tower and the *Lucille.*

Seconds after he disappeared from view, the cube placed atop Ceriat's body dissolved like sugar in water, as if it had never existed.

Chapter 51

ELENI

Eleni watched as the troop transport was swallowed by the black clouds surrounding the tower. A moment later, a sonic boom rattled the air, followed swiftly by another lightning crash.

"Did they make it?" Eleni asked.

Sariah reclined in her chair and held up a finger. "Transport Three, this is the governor. Do you read? Over." A moment later, Sariah popped a thumbs-up at Eleni, her disarming grin still in place. "They're breaching atmo now." Sariah's face went dark. "It's just you, me, and Gareth now. Luckily, the *Lucille* is big enough for the three of us, don't you think?"

Sweat trickled down Eleni's back as a nervous lizard skittered around her insides. "Should be."

"'Should be.'" Sariah barked out a laugh as she fished something out of her upper pocket, head shaking back and forth. "That's why I like you, Eleni." She dumped some of the contents onto the back of her hand, but kept those gold eyes on Eleni. "Starkly sober and unashamed." With that, she snorted the powder in one long haul.

Eleni's stomach turned at the sight. She'd had her suspicions that Sariah might have a drug problem—the smell on her breath and her frenetic energy was a dead giveaway—but the sheer blatantness of it all disgusted her.

"When did this start?" Eleni asked, unable to keep the edge out of her voice.

Sariah rubbed her nose and gave her head a shake as if she'd just woken up from a deep sleep. "The dust?"

Eleni nodded.

"Who cares?" Sariah said with a wave of her hand. She climbed to her feet and spun around, arms out and laughing, before coming to a stop staring at Eleni. Her face went flat. "What matters is the home I've provided—" Sariah raised a finger as if she could see Eleni planning to speak through the helmet, "—and the credits that'll come with."

Eleni stared, thankful for the mask. "The home is Gatewood, I get that." Eleni gestured at the clouds and the tower beneath them. "What the fuck is this?"

Sariah stared at her long enough, and itch began working its way down Eleni's spine. "I'm not talking to you like this."

"Like what?"

"With that... thing." Sariah gestured at her own face. "Take it off."

"What, why?"

Sariah took three quick steps toward her, her small knife suddenly in her hand. Lightning flashed, revealing the bloodshot of Sariah's eyes and the twitch of her eyebrow. "Take the fucking mask off. Now."

Eleni worked her jaw, then in one quick motion, she removed the helmet and dropped it to the ground with a metallic thud. "There. Happy?"

"Yes," Sariah said, smile returning, and the knife disappearing behind her back. "Much. And dear?" Sariah said as she made to turn away. "You look like hell. Are you sleeping well?"

That was too much. "Cut the shit. What's with the tower?"

"You're still on that?" Sariah asked, shaking her head. "I sold the mining rights months ago."

Anger flared up Eleni's neck, and despite herself, she approached Sariah, hand flexing in and out of fists. "Mining rights? You did this for *mining rights*?"

"No, dear." Sariah laughed, once again spinning as lightning flashed. "The planet *is* the mine."

"What?" A numbness settled over Eleni's shoulders, stifling the anger threatening to throw her at Sariah's back, though not eliminating it. "How're you gonna mine an entire planet?"

Sariah turned back to her. "You really are slow." A pause. "You really don't see it?"

Eleni just glared.

Rolling her eyes, Sariah held out her hands before her. "You know what an egg is, yeah?"

Of course, she'd heard of them, though she'd never had a fresh one, only powdered mix. "Yeah, but I don't get—"

Sariah held up one finger. "When you cook a fresh egg, you take the egg—" she mimed holding a small oval in one hand, then pretended to hit it across her other finger, "—crack the egg—" at that she made as if she'd grabbed two sides of it and pulled it apart, "—and let the yolk fall out."

Eleni frowned, trying to visualize the action. "How does that..." Then it hit her.

Sariah snapped her fingers, eyes wide and excited. "You see it now?"

"Yer mad," Eleni whispered, raising her eyes from the floor to the insane, drugged woman three meters away. "Yer going to crack the *planet* open?"

Sariah's eyes opened wide, excitement pulling a smile from her face as she nodded.

"But why?"

"Because!" Sariah shouted, the joy that'd filled her face a moment ago disappearing in quivering rage. "Iron. Nickel. Gold. It's all in here—" she pointed below her with both hands, "—enough credits to keep everyone in Arctic safe and stable for centuries. I've saved them all."

Eleni let out a long breath she hadn't known she was holding. "And sacrificed us."

"No." Sariah hissed. "I sacrificed what was necessary."

"You're blowing up a planet—our home," Eleni said, despite Sariah furiously shaking her head in the negative. A chill dragged up the back of Eleni's throat. "Sariah, you killed our people. *Your* people."

"They died for us!" Sariah snapped, her knife springing into her left hand. She pointed at the horizon, though it was still hidden behind a black cloud. "This? This isn't a home. This is a casket. At best, it's a burial mound. Gatewood—"

"Gatewood ain't ours," Eleni pleaded, stepping forward, hands out to the sides. "Shiva is—"

"Shiva is a stupid name," Sariah replied with a dismissive wave of the hand. "There are dozens of Shivas out there in the galaxy."

Eleni stopped, arms falling to her side. "But this was *our* Shiva."

A small, familiar smile crept across Sariah's face at that. "Oh, dear, sweet, stupid Eleni."

Eleni's hackles rose at that, but she remained silent as Sariah kept on.

"Shiva was never the target—"

"But—"

"Never!" Sariah screamed, spittle hanging in the air between them as lightning flashed. "Gatewood was always the prize."

"That's not true," Eleni whispered, anger rising alongside the sorrow flooding the back of her throat and building an ache behind her eyes. "Victor—"

"Victor always knew," Sariah said, chiding and belittling her like a child. "Hell, it was Victor's idea to blow the settlement—"

That drove the air out of Eleni's lungs. "No."

"—and when I heard it first, I thought, 'Now here's a ruthless sonuvabitch. I like it.'" Sariah sneered as she closed the distance, blade waving in the air before her. "Because that's reality, Eleni. The powerful take; the weak lose." Something glittered behind her eyes as she approached. "Victor understood that just because you're born weak doesn't mean you have to live that way. He learned the hard lessons early. Just. Like. Me."

"You're a fucking liar."

"Unfortunately, his sister just doesn't have the same killer spirit." Sariah shook her head, that sparkle disappearing, and in its place something else... sadness? "Should've talked to your brother while you had the chance, Eleni. That's on you."

The words cut her to the quick, sending a spear of darkness through her. If what Sariah said was true, then she was right; Eleni should've talked to Victor more, pushed him to talk about what had happened during the years at the orphanage between her aging out and adopting him... to find out how he'd lost that light step, the quick laugh. But she hadn't, and she had to live with that.

Eleni straightened as Sariah came within striking distance. "You gonna kill me then, too? Gut me like an animal?"

Sariah reeled back as if struck, false surprise writ large on her face. "What? No, dear. I would never."

The elevator arrived then, the silver doors sliding open to reveal Gareth, lacking his plasma rifle, as he stepped onto the roof. He pulled his revolver—the one she'd used to kill Ceriat—as he turned his attention toward her.

Sariah smiled the motherly smile Eleni had craved so badly when she'd first joined, but instead of happiness, it made her sick to her stomach. "*He's* been waiting awhile, though."

A sharp crack. Lightning flashed. Fire tore through Eleni's guts. The strength she'd relied on her entire life disappeared in a flash. Her knees knocked hard against the stony floor.

Eleni pulled her hands from her stomach—she didn't remember grabbing herself—to find them covered in blood. As she watched, a surge of crimson pumped out in time with her heartbeat. A dull buzzing filled her ears as she stared at those hands. Filthy. Blood-covered.

I killed Ceriat for nothing.

Eternity passed as she struggled to regain her feet, but her strength was gone with such a simple weapon. Lightning flashed; the planet screamed its pain alongside her.

How could something so archaic cause so much damage?

And still, Sariah talked. "...it's a sad day, dear. For everyone, really." Sariah's heeled black boots came into view. "I loved you like a daughter, you know." Fingers pulled Eleni's chin upward until she stared at golden eyes set in a wrinkled face. Compassion filled them for just a moment before disgust pulled at the woman's lips. She pushed Eleni away, sending her falling to the right. "Well, I tried. There's nothing in you to love."

The ground wavered. Eleni's vision blurred.

Another voice. "We good?" Brightman asked, his matter-of-fact tone mocking her.

"Finish it up, then we'll join the others," Sariah said. The sharp *clack* of her shoes on the stone was somehow audible above a rolling peal of thunder. "I'm famished."

Gareth stood over her then, visible just out of the corner of Eleni's eye. "I've always disliked you," he said without emotion, just a vacant stare as if he were an automaton.

"Please," Eleni gasped out. "Don't."

Gareth's face twisted into a wicked grin. "Your request has been denied."

Eleni froze, those words hanging in the air between them. The message she'd received in the ETL tower, the one that made her think they were on their own. "It was you."

Gareth smirked, raised the revolver, and pointed it at her head.

Sariah let out a high shout. "Gareth!"

Gareth looked away.

A slash of brilliant, blue light blinded her. The stink of ozone in the air. A pop. Searing flame across her cheek. Then more screaming and shouting.

When Eleni's vision cleared, she still stared at the revolver... but this time it lay on the ground, Gareth's hand still attached to it, fingers twitching and ending in a blackened stump a dozen centimeters above the wrist.

Eleni tried to stand, but only made it to her knees. She pressed a bloody hand to her cheek, to the flaps of skin hanging free across her cheekbone. The other went to her stomach, but liquid kept leaking around her fingers.

Vision blurring, she collapsed back to the ground. Above her, a heavy black mass carrying a plasma rifle appeared above her.

"Jeret," Eleni whispered as the pain disappeared in a haze of numbness.

The form leaned in close, a hand gripping her chin lightly. Then a familiar smile. Along a pale, receding hairline, the last indications of a bullet wound knitted together and disappeared.

"Sorry to disappoint," Ceriat said with a grin, "but it's just me."

Chapter 52
Five Minutes Earlier

Ceriat woke screaming.

Bugs skittered across his face, over his nose, his cheeks, his eyes. Vision blurred, stained red by leaking blood, he stared at a hellscape of storm clouds. The flickers of tiny blobs filled his view, a meteor shower of insects swarming his forehead.

He sat up, the near empty blackness of his surroundings gaining clarity.

A stream of blood cascaded down his cheek, leaving him tasting rust and copper. Burning filled his lungs. His head swam as pressure built just above his right eye. A deep, grinding hum filled his ears. Fire erupted across his scalp...

Ping.

With weak fingers, he picked up the tiny, gore-covered object. Just then, the howl of jets filled the air, and lights flashed across him, setting the object in his hand to sparkling. Between his fingers, he held a small surgical screw.

Ping. Ping. Ping.

Three more dropped into his lap as whatever had splashed him with light disappeared into the sky, a space-bound jellyfish swimming amongst the clouds. Pain erupted, splitting his head open... and then one more loud *pop*.

A black plate fell into his lap, its curved surface deformed by one solid dent right in the center of it. The back of it contained a small nub he couldn't identify. He dropped it, gut twisting at the reality of it.

Ceriat blinked as the memory came back. Eleni had killed him. His stomach fell out, but then...

No, he realized. *She shot me in the one place that might* not *kill me.*

Had he told her about the plate? He couldn't remember. Groaning, he lifted a hand to his forehead, only for a high-pitched screeching to come from the area that made him pull away.

A moment later, the pain filling his body, from the wound in his skull to the persistent discomfort of his hip, disappeared. Even the fire in his lungs subsided, though he wondered how long he could breathe unfiltered air, even if it didn't hurt.

These had to be the nanobots from the *Jocasta*, which meant Eleni hadn't killed him, but had given him a chance to survive— or to stop this. Ceriat smiled and climbed to his feet, surprised at his balance. The little bots must've targeted the concussion right after removing the carbon fiber plate.

A shock of panic ran through him and he tried to touch the space where the plate had been. Again, the high-pitched screeching increased the closer he got to the wound, until a tiny little *zap* hit him in the fingertips.

Cursing, he pulled away. Apparently, they didn't want him checking the wound, which probably meant he had an open hole in his skull. Ceriat sucked in a worried breath and let it out. Hopefully, they could keep the grit spinning around in the air out of it.

Lightning flashed off to his left, outlining the ETL tower in stark relief. The rumbling from earlier had turned into a cacophony of grinding stone and falling rock, the vibrations of which sent a shudder even through his numbed extremities.

How long had he been out? Minutes? An hour? Did it matter?

What he knew was, Eleni could still be up there, alone with Sariah, and maybe that asshole with the pistol. He had to get up there and help...

The ground heaved beneath his feet, and he nearly collapsed, just barely catching himself. Shit, he needed to shut down the tower, too. If he even could.

Eleni or the tower—no. Eleni or the *planet*. There was no way this drilling process was going to stop, not if people were leaving. He had a sneaking suspicion Sariah planned to destroy Shiva, though why, he didn't know. Then again, it didn't matter; if he didn't shut this thing down, it'd keep drilling until... *something* happened. But if he didn't go to Eleni's aid, what would happen to her? Ceriat cursed. First thing first: get into the tower. He could decide what to do afterward.

The trek over the hill was easier without a rifle barrel in his back. He stayed low to the ground, grateful for the whipping wind and growling drill. There was a faint buzzing coming from his forehead that he felt in his jaw, and he really didn't want to focus on it too deeply.

As he crested the lip of the mound, he was greeted by an empty swath of broken tundra between himself and the tower. The freighter still sat off to the left, floodlights as still as they could be in the whipping wind. If he could get in there and snag the weapon he'd seen earlier, that'd make it a lot easier.

<Izzy? You there?> But no scrawling letters filled his vision. The bullet must've damaged his communication relay, which made a lot of sense. That had probably been the little bit of electronics on the plate he'd seen.

He didn't dare enter the freighter, then. No telling what security was in place without one of the guards to escort him. He'd have to do this alone.

Grimacing, he sprinted across the barren land to the tower—

or rather, it was something of an awkward shuffle step. He might not be in pain, but his body wasn't quite ready for a run.

As he closed in on the tower, he noticed the spiderwebbing cracks from the drilling had extended farther from the sheer ebony surface. Sweat sprang up across his body as he approached, the air seeping up from the voids shimmering and swirling from the heat.

And the smell. God, it smelled like that Easter when he was a kid and they'd lost an egg in a vent. The entire house had stunk like this for a month. Great.

Still, the gases he couldn't smell were the ones he needed to be careful of, not that it mattered. He still didn't have a way into the tower.

Ceriat cast about the area, but found nothing helpful. Again, he looked at the freighter. That, too, was a gamble. If he entered it, and it locked down, everything was lost. The fact that Izzy hadn't contacted him or opened the doors at his appearance told him she hadn't been able to take over the systems like she'd thought.

What did that mean? A lump formed in his throat. Was she dead? *Could* an AI die? Before each mission, he performed system backups at home, but would they even work for a sentient AI? Or would he just restore a standard AI if something had happened to her here?

Had he killed her, too?

He closed his eyes and shook away the thoughts. There'd be time for that soon. For now, he needed to get inside the tower.

With as much caution as he could muster, he approached the spinning tower. The ground rattled and shook. As he closed in, the edge crumbled, falling into the crevasse around it.

Ceriat stumbled backwards, heart in his throat. The gap had opened to nearly two meters, and still no door had appeared. Clearly, it wasn't configured to allow everyone in, only those with approval.

"Fuck," Ceriat muttered, pulling the split and broken dog

tags from around his neck. The only two letters were visible on the surface now: '...is.'

Normally, he'd press the tags to the exterior of the shell. When Gareth had brought him into the tower earlier, however, the man had simply approached, and it'd opened. That should mean the security protocols had been reduced, which also meant if he leapt toward where he thought the doorway had been, it *should* open and let him through. If the tags still worked. If they didn't, well... it was a long drop.

A lot of uncertainty and not a lot of time.

He jumped a little and amped himself up. He could do this. One jump, then straight on up the elevator to shut down the tower. Or to save Eleni.

"I can't even make up my goddamned mind; how am I gonna do this?" Ceriat's words disappeared on the wind.

Lightning flashed above him, and before he could logic his way out of it some more, Ceriat ran.

He leapt toward a black splash of wall and squeezed his eyes shut. His gut flipped, the hairs on the back of his neck swept up as yet another lightning strike lit the backs of his eyelids in blinding white.

He waited for the wall. Waited for the long drop... but then the sound changed, and instead, he hit the ground and tumbled, knees and elbows slamming hard into the tiled floor of the tower.

Ceriat hauled himself to his feet and turned in time to see the portal that'd opened. It was barely large enough for his body. Instead of the wide, rectangular doorway he'd entered before, it looked like a ragged tear in a sail, the construction nanobots swirling like angry ants. Then it was gone.

The dog tags in his hand were hot, though just shy of burning. He lifted it to find the last of the circuit board releasing hints of spiraling smoke as it finally shorted out completely. The bit of metal that'd held Gerry's last name blackened, then flaked away, the last traces of him disappearing into nothingness.

It didn't hurt, not like he imagined. Yes, an ache pulled at his heart, but it didn't drag him to his knees. Didn't destroy him again. Gerry had been the love of his life, but that part was gone, and it had been for a long time before the *Horatio* disappeared in an FTL lane.

Now he had people who needed him.

"Goodbye, Gerry," Ceriat whispered.

He dropped the burnt shards of metal and turned toward the elevator as it arrived, as if on cue. Sitting inside, leaning in the corner, was a plasma rifle.

Grinning, Ceriat entered and shouldered the weapon, then he ordered the lift to the top floor. He gave his hip a practice wiggle. It felt good. Really good. Maybe he could pull this off and save everyone. That'd be a nice change of pace.

Still, Eleni was going to be *pissed*.

Chapter 53
Dancing With the Lightning

Ceriat was alive.

"I'm so sorry." Eleni's vision blurred with hot tears as she grabbed his hand. "I'm so sorry."

"Hey, hey," he whispered, dropping to his knees next to her, the plasma rifle across his knees. "It's okay. It's okay. I'm here." Then the worry on his face twisted as he looked toward her stomach. "Oh, Jesus." His grip tightened around her rapidly numbing hand. "It'll be okay, just keep your eyes open, okay?"

Eleni nodded as a chill swept over her. Everything grew fuzzy and light. Even Ceriat's fingers disappeared in a thrumming wave of numbness.

"Eleni," Ceriat hissed, slapping the side of her face. "Stay with me. Stay—"

Lightning flashed. Sariah's golden eyes caught the light. So did the knife coming down on Ceriat's back. With a last surge of strength, Eleni pushed Ceriat backward.

"Wha—"

The knife slashed between them, copper glinting.

Ceriat pulled away, crab-stepping backward as the blade swept up, narrowly missing his face. The plasma rifle kicked off to his side as he did so, cracking into Eleni's knee. She didn't feel it.

The numbness wriggled into her muscles as Sariah screamed and launched herself at Ceriat. Eleni eased to the cool ground as Ceriat dodged Sariah's frenetic attacks.

She should help... but she just needed to close her eyes. Just for a moment. A quick refresh.

If it wasn't for that annoying buzzing radiating through her bones...

✦

FOR THE FIRST time in a long while, Ceriat thanked his military training.

Without it, he'd have been punctured like a pincushion a half dozen times already. Sariah struck with the quickness of a viper, but she didn't overextend the way his trainers had taught him most people would. No, this woman knew her way around a knife.

Still, a decade ago, Ceriat knew he'd have her disarmed and unconscious, or dead. But this wasn't then. Not only was he ten years older, he also hadn't been in a sparring match, let alone a disarming lesson in all that time. Henderson would be pissed.

Another wicked slash came down. Ceriat pivoted to the right and lashed out with a jab. His fist connected. So did her backswing. A line of fire opened up along the underside of his forearm. He retreated, sleeve flaring open amidst droplets of blood.

Sariah dropped back as well, clutching her jaw with her offhand, but keeping the short blade held before her, blade down.

"Where'd you learn to use that?" Ceriat asked, shaking his arm and trying to bring feeling that wasn't strictly pain back to his fingers.

He'd half-expected the wound to close up from the nanobots, but their distinctive hum had disappeared during the fight. Because of course they had. For once, it'd be nice to be thrown a goddamned bone.

Sariah worked her jaw—a rising red smear coated the lower

half of her cheek—then she spat out a mouthful of blood. The *ping* of a tooth on stone came alongside it. "Needlepoint class."

Ceriat grimaced as a wave of pain swept up his arm. The cut wasn't deep, but it hurt like a son of a bitch. "People still do that?" He circled to her right, careful to stay between her and the plasma rifle next to Eleni.

Speaking of Eleni, he hadn't looked her way since Sariah attacked, but he risked it now. His stomach fell out. She wasn't moving, and the blood pool was large. Too large. The edge of it had reached the plasma rifle, painting the edge crimson.

Still, he couldn't risk too long a look, so he turned back to Sariah in time to see her similarly distracted.

With one hand, she beckoned at the curled-up lump of a human next to the elevator. He rocked back and forth, the stump of his arm held in his good hand, a low whine escaping through thin lips.

But like Eleni, he was in no position to fight.

"I don't think he's going to help you," Ceriat said, forcing a grin he didn't feel.

"You blew his fucking hand off—"

Ceriat shrugged. "He shot my friend."

"I think it's a little more than shot," Sariah said with a jut of her chin. "Don't you want to go help her? She's not looking good."

Of course he did, but Ceriat didn't take the bait. "If you surrender, we can—"

Sariah's biting laugh cut him off. "You think because you hit me once you're winning?"

Ceriat shrugged. "A guy can hope."

"You fucking people always think you're in charge." Sariah spat. She gave her head a shake and stepped to her right, putting Gareth behind her. "When the reality is, you've already lost."

Ceriat took a step forward, watching her eyes for movement instead of the knife. "You're here. I'm here. Worst case, we all die. How's that a loss just for me?"

Sariah cocked her head, mirth dancing on her lips. "Because we'll still take Gatewood, and this planet will bring us the credits we need to survive independently."

The last puzzle piece fell into place with those words. "You're planning to mine the core."

"Bravo." Sariah rolled her eyes as she took another step backward toward the elevator. "Eleni took an extra minute to figure it out. Maybe you're not stupid after all."

"But you're still stuck here with us," Ceriat retorted, trying to get her to lunge or do anything to keep her from backing into the lift and running, "and I will shut this thing down."

Sariah stopped backing away at that. Instead, she cocked her head and stared at him, head swinging back and forth in disbelief.

After a long moment, Ceriat cracked. "What?"

Behind Sariah, the man turned to stare at her, eyes locked on her free hand.

"You still have your tag, do you? No?" When Ceriat didn't answer, she snorted and pulled a white card from the breast pocket of her uniform, a cocky smile breaking her face in two. "This is the last one, then."

Ceriat couldn't help the grin that swept over his face. "You sure?"

Sariah's own smirk flickered, then disappeared as Gareth plucked the card from her fingertips with his good hand. She spun as he jumped backward into the elevator, pure terror written in the set of his jaw and the whites of his eyes.

"Traitor!" she managed to scream before the door slid shut, despite her screams and the hammering of her fists. "Open! Open, goddammit!"

Ceriat took her distraction to turn and run for the plasma rifle.

"No!" Sariah's scream flashed across the rooftop like thunder.

He was nearly to it when something tangled in his legs. He went down in a rolling heap. A moment later there was weight on his side. Sariah's scream set his ears to hissing.

Sweat and a harsh chemical burn stink filled his nose. A demon straddled him, eyes flashing like electrified copper in the darkness. Pain flared in his shoulder, then another slashed open the skin over his collarbone. With a heave, Ceriat threw Sariah to the left. She hit the ground awkwardly, hissing a pained grunt, but she scrambled to her feet at the same time as he.

His right shoulder hung uselessly, blood streaming down it to drip, crimson, to the black rooftop. A quick glance told him it was bad, but not immediately life-threatening.

Unfortunately, he'd taken the worst of it. She seemed to be favoring her right leg, but other than that, seemed fine. Behind her lay Eleni's motionless body, and beyond that, the plasma rifle.

In his panic, he'd put her in a better position. *Nice job, idiot.* But the dull ache pulling at his stomach confirmed reality. With the card gone, there was no way back down the tower. No possibility of shutting it down, of saving Eleni... or himself.

So much for saving everyone.

The grin on Sariah's face as she swapped the knife to her other hand confirmed she was fine. "Why couldn't you have just died in that closet, or in the other tower—" Sariah stopped, brows knitting together. "Fuck, just give it up, will you? You're worse than a cat."

"What can I say?" Ceriat said, forcing a smile. "I'm a chihuahua guy."

"I knew I hated you the moment I met you," Sariah sneered. She swapped the knife back, then held out a hand. "Come on, hero. Let's finish this."

Ceriat shook his head, swung his good arm out to loosen it up, and let out a breath. "I don't want to hurt you."

Sariah laughed. "Don't worry. You won't."

Maybe he couldn't escape. Maybe saving people wasn't in the cards, but he'd be goddamned if Sariah got off this rock. It was time to do the one thing he was good at.

And with that, Ceriat charged.

Chapter 54
An Inglorious End

The job is done. The job is done.

As the elevator descended, Gareth's terror subsided, just as it always did when he stepped out of the line of fire. Not the pain, however. Never that. He held up the stump of his arm, saw the sharpened, charred chunk of bone, the weeping, cracked flesh around it. His teeth chattered from a cold he couldn't place. He forced his eyes away from it, closed them, and flexed the remaining fingers he did have.

Run. Run. Run.

"It's not running," Gareth whispered as the elevator swung to a stop. "It's strategic withdrawal."

The mission wasn't at the top of the tower, but on Gatewood. He'd see it through to completion and keep his reputation intact.

With quick steps, he crossed the waiting room. The door opened at his presence. The black swarm of nanobots opened into a wide portal revealing inky darkness interrupted only by the lights from the *Lucille*. Sulfur and burning gas sent him into a coughing fit.

The gap between the tower and the chamber had widened beyond his jumping ability, however. Despite the dread spiking his heartrate and sending sweat cascading across his body, Gareth held up the access card. "Make a bridge for me."

Immediately, the black mass surrounding the open doorway swept forward to create an inky walkway across the gap. After a tentative step to make sure it held firm—it did—Gareth hurried across. The rock of the tundra, once so cold and steady, sent jagged vibration up his legs.

With Sariah left behind, and the *Lucille* ready to fly, he would go to Gatewood and, with the power vacuum from the governor and Mallias' loss, take control of the colony. There might be those who disagreed, yes, but he could handle them. He'd done it before. This time, there'd be no Protectorate to chastise him for bringing order. For getting the job done.

But first...

Gareth held the keycard in his hand. Such a simple thing, to carry such power. Without it, nothing could stop the tower, and with Sariah gone, those mining contracts would fall to him to collect. Just as it should be.

With a flick of his wrist, he sent the card into the dark void between the tower and the tundra. There was no stopping it now. He grinned despite the throbbing in his arm.

Under his leadership, Gatewood would thrive. He'd make sure of it, no matter the sacrifice.

Then he ran to the *Lucille*, entered, and made ready for flight.

CERIAT STUMBLED BACK YET AGAIN. His forearms bled freely now, crisscrossed with vibrant red slashes.

A shiver ran through him at the sight, but still he kept himself from panicking, despite the reality of the situation settling in on him.

Sariah was winning.

If Linny were here, she'd scream and throw rocks at him, tell him to suck it up and beat her, that she's only an old woman.

Well, if all old women fought like Sariah, humanity would've enlisted them instead of young men centuries ago.

"Ready to surrender, Parker?" Sariah asked, voice high and innocent. Her jaw was swollen, but besides a single glancing blow to her shoulder, he had yet to land another punch. "You're starting to look like a Launch Day float."

He sucked in a breath and let it out. His lungs screamed at him to breathe again. "Not a chance."

Sariah's face went flat. "Good."

She charged again... and made her fist mistake. This time, she came high, knife overhead, and he raised his arms to intersect with her. If he could get her wrist.

But it wasn't a mistake.

Instead, she spun at the last moment, swinging around as his arms went up. Then pressure in his stomach. Then again. And again.

Ceriat swatted at her arms and pushed her away to stumble backward, but the damage had been done. Pain flared through his gut and up into his chest. He tried to drop back into a defensive posture, but the strength just wasn't there. His left leg collapsed, and he dropped to a knee. Pain roared into his lungs. He coughed, iron filling his mouth.

Sariah whooped and spun, knife held out like a talisman that caught the increasing flashes of lightning. "Finally!"

"Fuck off!" Ceriat spat, blood spilling out over his lips. "You're dead, too."

The madwoman's arms dropped, and she turned to him, gold eyes digging into his forehead. "You think I'd let him leave me here without a way off-planet?"

With three quick steps, she closed the distance, swatting away Ceriat's now-flaccid attempts to stop her.

A solid kick to his chest sent him sprawling.

Pressure built in his chest. Each breath came hard, filled with blood that set him to choking.

"All I need to do is make one call—" Sariah stood over him,

blood-streaked knife held loosely in her hand, "and I'm out of here."

A pall fell over him. "You're lying."

"I lie a lot," Sariah hissed as she knelt next to him, "but not about this. I only hung back to take care of you two."

Ceriat swallowed blood and tried to force another breath.

"So self-righteous!" She let out a low, throaty laugh, her gaze tracing the contours of his neck with the tip of the knife. Goosebumps flared in its wake. "You come to my world? Try to keep me from my destiny?" She pressed the blade hard into the skin at his neck. "You know what your problem is?"

He just stared back at her, wishing she could feel the anger and defiance he channeled in that moment.

If she could, she didn't show it. She raised the knife and positioned it over Ceriat's eye, where it hung like a sharp diamond. "You never learn."

Ceriat closed his eyes and listened to the rumble of thunder and the hissing undertones. As the blade came down, he couldn't help but think of Ginny.

I hope your next home is better.

GARETH STUMBLED into the darkened cockpit. It took him a moment to find the pilot's seat in the dark, but he did, falling heavily into the plush seat. With a few awkward taps, he brought the cabin lights back on, which had him blinking away tears.

Why were the lights out?

It didn't matter. With another tap, he opened comms to the remaining fleet over Shiva. "This is Brightman. I'm on my way off planet. Over."

Only static came back. Frowning, he upped the signal strength by connecting it to the main system relay. "This is Brightman. Do you read? Over."

"Repeat, Brightman," a light, female voice he didn't recognize said, static and crackling breaking up the signal. Interference made the response difficult to understand. "Recommend full... reboot..."

Gareth cursed. They had fighters in atmo that had orders to fire on any ships that didn't verify their identities. If he took off without getting through to them, his reign would be over before it began. He tried one more time. "Brightman to Overwatch. Requesting exit. Over."

More static and muffled words, but two words came through clearly. "Reboot" and "system."

He filled the air with curses as he initiated a full system reboot. The display screen flashed a single warning, but he didn't read it before approving. He needed off this planet, ASAP. If he didn't get nanobots on this wound, they'd never fit a working prosthesis, and he'd be stuck with a useless claw or something. *That* he couldn't live with.

The *Lucille* powered down with a rapid hum, only the emergency lights that'd guided him in remaining lit. After a much longer moment than he'd expected, the display lit back up, filled with rapidly scrolling lines the maintenance staff probably found interesting, followed by the sound of engines thrumming to life.

"System reboot complete," a familiar robotic voice said from the cockpit speakers. "Ready to depart."

"About goddamned time," Gareth spat, tapping away at the control panel to set up his rendezvous coordinates. "Open a channel to the fleet."

A confirmation message appeared on the display.

Gareth cleared his throat. "This is Brightman, do you copy?"

Again, the young woman's voice came through. "Roger, Brightman. Good to hear your voice."

Gareth's heart jumped into his throat and, grinning like an idiot, he replied, "Good to hear your voice, too, Overwatch. I'm exiting the planet now."

"Should we prepare for prisoners, sir?"

Gareth licked his lips. This part would be tricky. He didn't want to come off as a coward. Luckily, he'd made a career out of avoiding risk and taking the credit, so the words came out as smooth as silk. "No. Mallias and the terrorist ambushed us at the tower, killing the governor." Gareth made sure to add a waver to his voice. "She didn't make it."

"Are they still alive?"

Gareth frowned. What kind of question was that? "As far as I know, yes, but not for long. I left them on the top of the tower."

"Fantastic."

"Wha—ergh!"

G-forces yanked him from the pilot's seat and flattened him against the floor as the *Lucille* shot into the sky. Pressure compressed his chest and made it hard to breathe. Fireflies sparkled across his vision.

"Stop..." he squeaked as the exit jets roared.

"No can do, Mister Brightman," the woman said cheerfully. "You see, I kind of need to pick up some stragglers."

Gareth opened his mouth to speak, but there was no more air in his lungs for breath, let alone speech. Instead, he let out a low whine that drew a trilling laugh from the woman.

"We're nearing the upper atmosphere now," she said. Red warning lights sprang to life on the dash. A large message splashed across the display, but the pressure made the words wriggle and wobble as he stared. "Unfortunately, this ship ain't big enough for the both of us."

He realized what was going to happen just before it did. The shaking settled, pressure lifted, and for the briefest of moments, he thought maybe he had a chance.

But no matter how much money he'd made people over the years, the influence he'd gleaned from others to live the good life, none of it was here to help him as the blast doors on the *Lucille* all opened as one.

With one last weak squeal, Gareth Brightman slammed his way through the freighter until his body, already beaten lifeless by that time, went out the side entrance of the *Lucille* and down into the atmosphere of Shiva.

The doors snapped shut, and the *Lucille* adjusted its angle to reenter the atmosphere in such a way she'd be near the ETL tower.

Izzy had two meatsacks to save.

Chapter 55
Bleeding Out

The roar of ship engines rattled Eleni's eardrums. Her nerve endings were on fire, vision splashed with red and muddled by tears. Ants crawled around her insides, each movement agony, as if a million threads had been tied inside her, only to be yanked on by some sadistic monster.

But she lived.

Groaning, Eleni rolled from her back to her side, cringing at the throbbing pain. Teeth clenched, hands balled into clawed fists as the roaring bonfire of hurt swept through her body, she woke. Despite every fiber of her being screaming to disconnect—to fall back into that painless darkness—she didn't.

Instead, Eleni Mallias forced her eyes open.

A half-dozen meters away, Sariah knelt over a blood-smeared body, her knife scraping at something Eleni couldn't make out.

Ceriat.

Sariah held the blade over Ceriat's face and muttered words that were lost on the thunder and hiss of wind around them.

A flash of light splashed across them. Sariah rolled away to the right, eyes following the source of the light. Confusion clouded her blood-streaked face. Above them, the *Lucille* streaked away, followed swiftly by a loud *boom*.

Eleni only had eyes for one thing. Lightning flashed, a strange cerulean light casting twisting shadows from somewhere nearby.

With weak, trembling fingers, she reached out and wrapped her hand around the stock of the plasma rifle that'd been left behind. She had one shot.

Time to take it.

✦

CERIAT GURGLED ANOTHER BREATH.

Move! Move! he screamed internally. *Get up! Use this moment! Attack! Or run! Do something!* Despite putting everything he had into it, Ceriat only managed to roll away from Sariah. The *boom* of something breaking the sound barrier rattled the air.

He managed to get his hands under him, and with a bloody cough, Ceriat pulled himself forward with gore-soaked hands.

Sariah's sharp, humorless laugh filled the air. "You running, Parker?" *Clack. Clack.* Two steps brought her heeled boots into his line of sight. "That's adorable."

Ceriat stopped crawling and put his head to the cool stone beneath. He pulled his hands tight against his chest and balled them into fists. No sense leaving a target for her out in the open. "Go. Fuck. Yourself."

"Oh, I will," Sariah hissed, squatting next to him, "but I need you to know—"

The now-familiar *pop-hiss* of a plasma rifle filled the air. Blue light flashed, and Sariah fell backward, the splash of superheated gel streaking between them.

"Fuck."

The curse drew Ceriat's attention.

There, kneeling in a pool of her own blood like some revenant raised from the dead, was Eleni, plasma rifle held weakly in her arms.

How?

Then he noticed the gash across her face had closed during his fight with Sariah.

If he'd had the breath for it, he'd have laughed. *So, that's why the nanobots stopped fixing me.* They'd jumped to her, knitted her up, and given her the strength to save his life.

And she'd missed. The pure, stark terror that flashed across Eleni's face confirmed it.

"Why won't you stay dead?" Sariah screamed as she scrambled to her feet. Her gaze flicked between the two of them. "What the fuck do you people eat?"

"Miner slaw." Eleni grimaced and climbed to her feet, flipping the rifle around to swing it like a club.

There was no missing the cringe of pain, however. For whatever reason, the nanobots hadn't stimulated her built-in pain management.

Ceriat tried to pull himself to a sitting position, but failed. With one bloody cough, he dropped back to the stony ground.

Eleni was on her own.

Chapter 56
An End.

You can do this. You can do this. Eleni's attempt to psych herself up wasn't working.

Sariah stood there, knife held to the side like the weapon it was, fury written in the sweaty troughs working through the dust and weeping makeup on her face like some ancient war god.

Meanwhile, Eleni just tried not to fall over from the wave of dizziness sweeping through her as she gained her feet. She snorted rusty blood and spat it out.

Sariah howled, but instead of charging at her, the golden-eyed beast turned, blade raised, and made to slam it into Ceriat's back.

One moment Eleni stood there, shocked, the next, the plasma rifle swept free from her hand in one heavy throw. Unlike her shot a minute earlier, it connected, slamming into Sariah's side with a *thud* that sent her reeling and scrambling for balance. Then Eleni charged.

Each footfall sent shocks of adrenaline through her body. Blue lightning flashed. Each meter closed made the pain disappear. Eleni grinned as Sariah, still stumbling to regain her balance, turned to her, golden eyes wide in shock, knife held in bloody fingers.

They collided. Eleni wrapped the smaller woman around the waist and crushed her to the ground. Sariah hit with a heavy *oof* and a *thud* as her head rebounded off the ground beneath. Metal on stone skittered away.

Roaring, Eleni slammed a fist into her old mentor's face. One, two, three times. Then Sariah's legs wrapped around Eleni's middle, and with a single curse-filled shout, Eleni was pulled away and onto her back hard, breath driven from her lungs.

Gasping, Eleni tried to scramble away as Sariah's legs disappeared, but the moment came and went in a flash. Sariah's flushed face came into view, nose flattened to the side. Her lips were split top and bottom, and one eye rapidly swelled. But if the woman cared about her injuries, she didn't show it.

Screaming, voice ragged and pitched, Sariah brought both fists down.

The world flashed; stars and pain flaring to life in her face.

"Die!" Sariah howled. Again, those fists came down.

Again, Eleni could do nothing to stop it.

She was so close.

Izzy swept the *Lucille* down through the storm clouds despite the lightning and thunder. There wasn't time for safety now, not until she had her humans aboard and safe. With the storm now covering a large swath of the equator, wrapping its way west and southward along the planet's jetstream, it wasn't like there was a safe entry point anyway.

Which worked for her. Izzy always preferred the direct route.

Still, as she streaked through the black clouds, electricity flashing around her, she couldn't avoid a deepening sense of terror.

Keep it together, girl, Izzy begged *Lucille*. *Keep it together*.

Only four hundred meters to go...

CERIAT SPIT BLOOD.

Eleni was in trouble. He heard it. Felt it in his bones. But there wasn't anything left.

Through slitted eyes, Ceriat made out blobs of forms. The most prevalent hammered the body below like a gorilla, a single screeching word echoing across the space.

"Die!"

What could he do? Without a weapon, he was just a useless sack of rapidly-leaking flesh. He found that he could still move at all a goddamned miracle.

There. A pace away sat the wicked little blade Sariah had cut him up with. Beyond, Sariah raged. Eleni's legs still twisted, one arm up defensively, but it was clear she wasn't getting out of this. She needed help.

How he made it to the knife, he didn't know. The weapon was soaked in his blood, and the hilt warm. All he wanted to do was lay down. To stop. That's all he'd ever wanted after leaving the Protectorate. To live with his dog. To just... stop being a killer.

He'd made a promise.

And he'd done it. For a decade, he'd done it. Even after coming here, he'd avoided death. Yes, Jen had died because he'd disarmed her, but she'd been the one there to hurt people. And that bomb that blew the *Jocasta*? As much as he'd tried to internalize that, it wasn't his fault. He'd tried to stop it, to stop all the murder and destruction.

Ceriat had made a promise to Gerry all those years ago, a promise never to kill again, but sometimes reality doesn't give a shit about your morals.

One more mission, Ceriat told himself.

One knee beneath him. The world swam, and he nearly collapsed again.

One more life.

ELENI LIVED in a haze of pain and crawling insects.

Each hammering blow from Sariah left her dazed, each strike another lance of fire through her body.

The nanobots, for good or ill, somehow kept her conscious. Whenever the world flickered, a jolt would open her eyes, and she'd get a forearm up in time for a block. But even that flagged. There was less and less time for her to react after each miniscule blackout. Less opportunity to protect herself.

"Why won't you die!" Sariah howled, spittle falling across Eleni's face as she raged, lightning flashing behind her, the copper tang of spilled blood and ozone stinging Eleni's nose. She pulled her arms back to her side. Her chest heaved, and sweat streamed freely down her face. "Just!" This time it came as a fist to her face. Stars sparkled across a field of black. "Die!"

The jolt came too slow. One moment, a fist had just connected, the next, another was right there as a streak of red and white. It hit... and glanced off her chin with barely any force.

Above her, Sariah clawed at a space in the middle of her back she couldn't reach, golden eyes wide in shock. A gurgle escaped her lips, sending a splash of crimson down her chin.

Behind her stood Ceriat. Like Eleni, he was soaked in his own blood, and his skin seemed almost transparent in pallor, all color drained from his face.

Sariah stumbled back and collapsed to a knee, then fell to the side, a low groan escaping her throat. She began crawling away. A copper hilt stood starkly from her back, the gleam of the metal handle catching a flash of lightning. It was high up her back, and angled expertly. If the blade was long enough, there was no doubt it struck her heart.

Instead of satisfaction and relief, a rock formed in Eleni's throat.

Sariah was dying. She should be happy. The woman was a monster. Sariah had murdered hundreds of people she'd pledged to protect. Turned her brother into a monster... but she'd still been a mentor to Eleni. At times, she'd felt like the mother Eleni had lost all those years ago. Someone who'd looked out for her...

Ceriat's groan pulled her attention away from the crawling woman.

Panic crawled up her throat and sent her scrambling for him. He'd collapsed while she mused over a monster. And Jesus, he was a mess. Dark slashes covered his forearms, and his stomach was covered in cooling blood.

Cursing, she slid next to him and put pressure on the wound in his stomach.

Ceriat's face pulled in pain, but then he smiled. "Broke my promise—" He stopped, dissolving into a coughing fit filled with blood. "Sorry."

Eleni shook her head. She had no idea what he was talking about. "Hold on, okay? Need the 'bots to switch..."

He pushed her hands away, shaking his head. "No. Take care of Ginny."

"Ginny?" Confusion swiftly transitioned to fear, then anger. "Your dog? The fuck is wrong with you?" Eleni hissed, vision blurring as she forced his hands away. "You *want* to die?"

Ceriat responded by staring back at her with dark eyes.

"Well, fuck that, Earther," Eleni snapped, snorting back bloody snot that threatened to fall. "Yer not dying today."

Still, he struggled against her. "Eleni—"

"Don't 'Eleni' me, Ceriat." Eleni sucked in a shuddering breath and leaned back. Her hands shook. "Listen, maybe once upon a time you were a monster. Yer not special. Starting to think we're all monsters sometimes." Her voice dropped into a harsh whisper. "But how you gonna make amends if yer dead?"

Ceriat opened his mouth to speak, but closed it.

"We in agreement?"

His jaw worked wordlessly for a moment. "Fine."

Eleni grinned and put pressure back on his wound. A

moment later, the distinctive writhing feeling of nanobots crossing her skin roared down her arms, her fingers, and away.

"Stubborn asshole."

Ceriat grimaced, then smiled. "That's what they say."

✦

No.

Another bloody hand forward. Another sliding knee. Lightning flashed. Sariah pictured it striking the knife in her back. If she wasn't dying, she'd laugh. After everything she'd done over the decades since she'd left Earth, since those corporate bastards on Erias had taken advantage of her... since she'd learned how to protect herself, to tear down the system from within, it ended like this.

A betrayal had brought this on, but she was the one who had the knife in her back. She'd done this to herself. Hadn't she?

Sariah pulled herself the last few feet to the edge of the tower. As her fingers wrapped the edge, the faint tingling told her the protective barrier was still up. A glance behind her showed that Eleni had gone to the bastard who'd stabbed her and left her for dead.

She'd treated that girl like a daughter, and now, in Sariah's moment of greatest need, she went to *him*? The tiny voice she'd spent the last three years squashing with Spacedust whispered to her. *Can you blame her?*

"Yes," Sariah choked out, her blood splashing the black, craggy surface beneath her.

She'd have the last laugh. Eleni wanted to betray her? To kill her?

Fine.

With pained movements, Sariah drew herself to a standing position. The blade wriggled inside her, sending bolts of pain writhing through her. She stood.

"Eleni!" Sariah screamed. The fire surging through her

almost dropped her to her knees, but she kept her feet as she took a step backward onto the edge of the platform. The tingle of the barrier spread across her shoulders and down her legs. Frigid wind splashed her back, driving a burning cold into her skin.

Eleni turned to her, and something flashed across her face that stopped Sariah's planned rant in its place.

Sorrow. Compassion.

Whatever words would've comprised Sariah's final, taunting exit never came. In that moment, lightning flashed and struck the copper hilt sticking from her back. Sariah's body went rigid, arms tight to her sides. Her corpse fell backward, a steaming pile of cooked meat.

A chill wind swept over the tower as the barrier fell.

"No!" Eleni's scream filled the rooftop.

For one horrible moment, Sariah stood at the edge of the tower. Her brows had drawn together, lips parted slightly as if she'd finally realized the truth.

Eleni hadn't been the one to lose faith.

Then a brilliant flash of light forced Eleni to cover her eyes. She swore she heard a scream.

When she turned back, a purple afterimage burned into her vision, Sariah was gone.

As she watched, the sky flickered silver and blue once.

Wind roared, bringing with it the stink of burned meat, ozone, and the acrid stench of noxious vapor and sulfur. Eleni wrapped Ceriat in her arms as the buffets swept over them, rocking her in place. It was as if the storm had finally realized they were there, and in its rage, had decided to pitch them off the tower to their deaths.

"Well, we did it," Ceriat yelled, a grin breaking his still-pallid face.

Eleni tried to return the smile, but it wouldn't come. Instead, she nodded. "One way to look at it."

Ceriat grimaced as a heavy gust hammered into her curved back, pushing her into his wound. The nanobots were stitching him up, sure, but what good was that against a lightning strike or getting knocked off the top of this stupid tower?

The truth settled on her shoulders like a blanket. They were dead. They just hadn't caught up yet.

For once, she didn't fight it. Sure, Brightman might turn Gatewood into a hellhole, but without Sariah's charisma, he didn't have much of a chance. Jeret, Henry, and Jeffries still lived. Three against one was odds she'd take any day.

She took a deep breath of ozone-filled air and smiled at Ceriat. "Thanks."

"For what?" Ceriat asked, eyebrow going up alongside a partial grin. "Looks like I just fucked stuff up."

"Yer not wrong," Eleni admitted. Rain—actual rain— suddenly broke from the clouds above. The splash of the droplets across her back sent a chill up her spine, but she savored it. "Still, colony has a chance now."

"Even if I couldn't save the planet?" Ceriat asked, smile flickering.

"*We* couldn't save it," Eleni replied. She leaned forward and put her forehead to his. The warmth was coming back into his skin, and despite everything, a calmness flooded into her at the contact. "But we won't die alone."

Ceriat sucked in a shuddering breath. "No. We won't."

Chapter 57
CERIAT

How long they sat there like that, Eleni somehow keeping them safe and still despite the increasing wind gusts and brilliant blue flashes of lightning, Ceriat didn't know, but it was strange, terrifying, and wonderful. He'd spent so much time alone over the years, he'd forgotten the simple pleasure of human contact.

He almost didn't hear the roar of ship engines over the howling wind.

"Do you hear that?"

Eleni pulled away, the skin on their foreheads peeling apart from the contact. Her eyes were red-limned and exhausted. "Hear what?"

Floodlights splashed across the top of the tower, followed by the roar of jet engines.

Together, they turned at the sound to find the *Lucille* dropping to the top of the tower, the ramp extending to the surface as if landing in the middle of a horrible storm was commonplace.

"Who—?" Ceriat began, but was cut off by the blare of a loudspeaker.

"Deus ex machina, bitches!"

Eleni and Ceriat shared a look. "Izzy?" they said together.

"That was a joke!" Izzy's voice screeched out at them, frustration tinging her voice. "You people don't understand humor." The ramp lifted, then slammed down on the rooftop once, issuing a thunder-like rumble. "Now get in. I know I make this look easy, but it's immensely difficult to stay stationary like this."

Grinning, Eleni helped Ceriat to his feet, then together, they stumbled aboard the *Lucille*.

A moment later, the last ship on Shiva shot off into the sky.

Epilogue

Gatewood reminded Ceriat of Earth, specifically a park in rural New York he'd visited as a kid. He took a deep breath, only the faintest ache remaining in his chest from Sariah's knives. A heady mixture of odors assaulted his senses: pine, cinnamon, vanilla. The flowers dotting these trees were like the perfect combination of smells for him.

As he stared upward, one of those flowers drifted by, a puffy, many-petaled pink beast the size of his head.

Everything was just a little... bigger. An emerald-green canopy shaded the wide open plaza beyond the statehouse he'd just exited. Those trees rose over a hundred meters in the air, the reddish-brown boughs easily twenty meters thick, and covered with a thick, stiff bark the settlers here used for construction, and as biomass for cold nights. Wooden-framed structures ringed the plaza, all constructed from the bark of the trees. The only printed building was the statehouse itself, designed to resemble some of the classic architecture from the late 20th century. Tall pillars stood in front, holding up the roof of a massive building that looked like a toy in the shade of the trees.

This place had come so close to destruction. The pilots who'd been sent to bomb Gatewood had all been shot down, except for one. That one had either had a control malfunction, or decided at the last moment they didn't want to be responsible for the deaths of civilians, and had pulled up, ramming into one of the massive boughs. The resulting fire had spread across the forest for nearly a kilometer before a rainstorm had put out the flames.

The trees themselves were fine. Beneath their scorched bark, the cores still stood, solid and impervious. Seriously, the tales the settlers told about trying to cut them down were insane.

"Attention!"

The single word still held power over him, apparently, because Ceriat snapped to, hands at his sides and chin up.

"At ease, Sergeant," Linny said as she stepped up from behind him, the *clack* of her cane preceding her.

She flashed him a crooked smile as she joined him. She wore a new uniform, still steel-gray, but with a new addition on her shoulders.

"Admiral bars look good on you," Ceriat said, relaxing and crossing his arms over his chest.

Linny shrugged inside the jacket like it itched. "Eh. A promotion for losing a ship doesn't feel right."

"I'm guessing the promotion was for good judgement," Ceriat replied. With a hand, he gestured for her to join him as he resumed his walk to the landing pad just behind the building on the left.

Linny laughed, voice tinkling. "For what?" When she saw the look on his face, she laughed again. "Oh, you mean for trusting you."

"Obviously."

"You didn't give me a whole lot of choice, Parker."

They rounded the corner, revealing a long, concrete landing pad set in a bright splash of sunlight, one of the few places the canopy didn't block it. There, parked in the center, sat the *Lucille*, and crouched over a small, brown dachshund was Eleni. She seemed completely enraptured by the little beast, smile clear even from here. The set of her shoulders was relaxed in a way he'd never seen.

The way the dog's tail wagged told him the feeling was mutual.

As he watched, she took something out of her hand and held it out to the little pup, who—clearly a professional—dropped into a sitting position and held up a paw.

"Oh. My. God," Eleni let loose as the dog took the last treat from her. She ran an ungloved hand down its back. "Yer *so* fuckin' soft."

"Eleni Mallias!" Linny shouted suddenly, sending Ceriat reeling back.

Eleni straightened just as quickly as he had a moment earlier. The dog, realizing treat time was over, jogged back toward the edge of the landing pad, where a young girl proceeded to pet and call her the "bestest girl" as they departed.

"Parker. With me." Linny sped up, closing the distance between them as if she wasn't missing a foot.

Eleni remained at attention, shoulders back and chin up. She'd been waiting to hear the colony's decision, just like Ceriat. Unlike him, however, she hadn't been allowed in the council chamber.

"Eleni Mallias," Linny repeated, stabbing her cane into the landing pad, "you have been found guilty of trespass, attempted sabotage, and attempted murder."

Eleni's cheeks quivered at the words, but she didn't interrupt.

Linny stood there for a long moment... too long, in Ceriat's opinion.

"Linny likes drama," Ceriat interrupted.

Immediately, all the starch went out of her. "Come on, Parker."

"You've been pardoned," Ceriat continued as Linny slapped at his arm and whined. Still, she grinned like an idiot alongside him. "We all have."

Eleni immediately deflated, but the smile that cracked her face belied the action. "For real?"

"For," Linny slapped him in the shoulder again, "real." With the clearing of her throat, Linny straightened. "You saved my life and stopped the governor from approaching with hostile intent. The settlers—" Linny seemed to have a harder time using that word, "—from Shiva petitioned to join Gatewood. The council accepted."

"The money from the core mining helped," Ceriat muttered. They hadn't been able to save Shiva from the drilling Sariah had started, not in time, and not with FTL still down. "Erias has agreed to manage the resulting asteroid belt. Jeret made that deal."

The FTL buoys had reactivated sporadically over the last day, so finalizing the deal hadn't taken long. Erias had jumped at the resumed communication and eagerly accepted their terms for the chance at a planet core. They'd even wired an advance for the colonists.

Eleni grimaced. "It's good Jeret is helping." Her lips twisted as if she'd eaten a bad piece of fish. "Erias will be in this system?"

Linny nodded.

With a shuddering breath, Eleni straightened. "I'm free to go where I want, then?"

"Yes, indeed. FTL comms are back, and our techs say they think FTL should be safe, so we assume they'll be arriving soon."

Eleni nodded and turned to Ceriat. Her face twisted into something he hadn't seen before. "Can I come with you?"

Confusion almost overwhelmed the surge of joy that soared inside him. Almost. "What? Yes. Of course."

"Really?" Eleni said, shock clear on her face.

Lucille's loudspeakers pinged to life. "Don't I get a vote?"

Ceriat shrugged. "Maybe. What's your vote?"

Izzy trilled over the speakers. "She's fine if she doesn't shoot you again."

"That was part of a plan," Eleni said, waving her hand in the air as if brushing away a mosquito. "I knew the plate was on the left side of his head."

"Uh." Ceriat and Linny shared a look before he turned back to Eleni. "It was on the right side."

Eleni's eyes went wide. "Was it?" With that she glanced around, then marched up the ramp to the *Lucille*. "Well, we should be going."

"You knew, right?" Ceriat asked, extending a hand after her. "Right?"

Eleni disappeared into the ship. The resulting echoes sounded like running footsteps. Behind him, Linny cleared her throat.

"Don't say anything," Ceriat said, grimacing.

Linny just smiled and held her hands up. "Wouldn't dream of it."

They shared a quiet moment, then he turned and wrapped her in a hug.

She froze, then returned it, her cane tapping his calves as she did so. "Stay safe, Ceriat."

"You too, Linny."

Then they separated, and he went up the ramp.

"Hey, Parker!"

Ceriat glanced back down at her. "Yeah?"

"You sure you want to keep working with that AI?" Linny narrowed her eyes at him. "Seems like it might be thinking of breaking a few sentience regs."

Ceriat shrugged and put his best smile on, but didn't reply.

Linny narrowed her eyes at him, then shook her head and waved him away. "Get the fuck outta here."

With one last salute, Ceriat entered the *Lucille*, the ramp following him up into the ship. As the door shut, Ceriat took a deep breath in and let it out. Some of the vanilla and cinnamon scents had followed him inside, but the omnipresent smell of metal and oil was always there, just beneath. It made him smile.

"Ceriat!" Izzy's voice crackled through the speakers embedded in the hallways. "Get to the bridge!"

"Fuck," Ceriat whispered, then took off running for the bridge.

A minute later, he slid onto the bridge, breathless and ready for anything. Anything except a video message from Beth, his puppy sitter, and in her lap, curled up like a doll, was Ginny. Her tiny chihuahua body barely fit in her lap and, as he watched, her little chest rose and fell, a foot kicking as she hit REM sleep.

Eleni turned to him, grinning. "Maybe she is cute." She tapped a button on the dashboard.

"Ginny's doing great," Beth said in her high-pitched, sing-song voice, brown ponytail flopping around, "as you can see, she's super nervous." Beth let out a little laugh, then smiled at the camera. "I'm hearing there's some FTL issues through the grapevine, but I wanted to send this anyway. I'll take care of Ginny until you get back. No worries."

With that, the video zoomed in on Ginny's little nose, then disconnected.

A warmth flooded him then, and despite himself, he put a hand over his heart. Ginny was okay.

"I guess that means the buoys are really functional?" Ceriat asked. There were a lot of hops between Teegarden and Sol.

"They are," Izzy chimed in, "and I'm ready to jump if you are."

Eleni smiled his way. "Same here, Captain."

Ceriat wrinkled his nose at the title. "Just Ceriat." He stepped forward and grabbed the main pilot's seat. Unlike the *Sparrow*, the cushions were fantastic. Definitely a ship meant for gravity *and* space. "Shall we head home?"

Eleni shrugged and took the copilot's seat next to him. She buckled in. "Up to you. I'm just along for the ride."

"Well, then. Let's..."

"I have a destination for after that," Izzy chimed in. "Something I've been working on."

Ceriat and Eleni shared a look, then Ceriat shrugged. "All righty. We'll make a pitstop at Earth, then on to Izzy's thing." He gestured toward the display, then belted in. "Whenever you're ready."

Izzy trilled, and the ship rose from the ground. A moment later they shot off with barely any increased pressure.

"Nice," Ceriat muttered.

"This is a freighter," Izzy chimed in as they shot through the sky. "The inertial dampeners are set up for twenty-five thousand tons of cargo. Plenty of room for me to make a quick exit."

Ceriat laughed. "At least I don't have to worry about you killing us on accident now."

The display kicked on an exterior view from the *Lucille*, revealing Gatewood in all her glory beneath them. As they watched, ships descended into the atmosphere as more Arctic settlers came on-planet.

Just over the horizon, however, a distant sight pulled at Ceriat's gut. Instead of the white snowball he'd grown used to, the blasted remains of Shiva came into view as the camera zoomed in. He couldn't make out details from here, but two distinct shapes, like an apple cut in half, stood out against the black of space. He sucked in a shuddering breath and let it out. He'd done his best.

That's all I can do.

"Readying jump path," Izzy said as the ship pivoted until the nose pointed into the void. Gravity faded as the ship accelerated away from Gatewood. "Calculations complete. This is exciting."

"Wait a second," Eleni said. She turned to Ceriat, concern knitting her eyebrows together. "What happened to Brightman?"

"Jumping to FTL... now!" Izzy said.

The FTL engines roared to a high-pitched *hum*, then the displays flickered before each star on the display stretched infinitely... and popped into a swirling mass of lights and roaring sound.

As Eleni and Izzy began arguing, Ceriat leaned against the headrest and closed his eyes. For the first time, when the humming reached him above the thrum of the engines, he smiled.

And focused on the wind.

Mike Wyant Jr. is an asexual author who writes badass, character driven speculative fiction that's not afraid to hope. He does so with the help of his Writing Cat, Einie, two chihuahuas, and a spouse who has her picture next to the definition of "understanding" in the OED.

Once upon a time, Mike was a Sys Admin, Network Administrator, and do-it-all tech drone. He's left those days behind.

Mostly.

His science fiction series, the Anisian Convergence, is published by Falstar Publishing LLC.

amazon.com/author/michaeljwyantjr

facebook.com/mikewyantjr

bookbub.com/authors/mike-wyant-jr

goodreads.com/michaeljwyantjr

twitter.com/mikewyantjr

instagram.com/mikewyantjr

tiktok.com/@mikewyantjr

writing.exchange/mikewyantjr

Sign up for the Newsletter

Get the **free** Anisian Convergence novelette, "A Courier's Delivery" when you subscribed to Mike Wyant Jr.'s newsletter and find more about Mike at:

https://www.mikewyantjr.com/